Second Thunder

Second Thunder
Seeking the Black Ishayas

BY
MAHARISHI SADASIVA ISHAM
MSI

THE Ishaya FOUNDATION
Publishing Company

1-888-474-2921
www.theishayafoundationpublishing.org

ISBN #978-0-9843233-2-6

Dedicated to all the forms of Almira walking the Earth
Vitam impendere vero
— Juvenal

"Maitreya sheathed Nuriel and stood grinning widely at him."

CONTENTS

ILLUSTRATIONS

FOREWORD
Vision and Life

"Whenever the poetry of myth is interpreted as biography, history or science, it is killed. It is never difficult to demonstrate that as science and history, mythology is absurd. When a civilization begins to reinterpret its mythology in this way, the life goes out of it... Mythology is the song of the universe, the music we dance to even when we cannot name the tune."

— Joseph Campbell

Civilizations die when they lose their founding visions. Why should anyone work to be great if there is no potential to be great? If the visible is all there is, why not dedicate life to wealth or possessions? What matter who is harmed in the process? Everyone involved will be dead within a century anyway. Who cares what happens on this strange little planet circling an average sun out of two hundred billion suns, lost near a remote spiral arm of an average-sized galaxy out of a thousand billion galaxies? Surely we are much too small to be significant in any Cosmic sense. Is not life itself merely an aberration, an accident of fate, an inevitable consequence of random gatherings of molecules in a nearly infinite Universe?

Without the supporting infrastructure of visionary Truth, the meaning of life collapses toward the meaningless. Visions are not false, they are not fiction or fantasy. True visions express the highest aspirations of our souls — aspirations impossible to express in any other form. This kind of understanding of vision is vital in today's world. The invaluable contribution of modern visionary work is to give form to the ideas that no longer conveniently fit into our accepted patterns of belief.

Our reliance on scientific dogma has divested us of our old world-views, profaned our gods, slain our heroes, voided our magic and shrunken to pathetic size all the larger-than-life men and women that freely walked the planet of our ancestors. This has created a life for the average human that is often boring, pointless, dull, frightening or extremely painful.

But every buried Truth will in time grow again through the dark soil of doubt and fear. For there are still (and always will be) true Heroes on this planet, just as there are still (and always will be) true gods as well as their Eternal Source — the One that is the inner life of all the gods, the One that is the root of the Hero's strength, the Magician's magic, the Healer's power to heal, the creative genius of the Artist, the supernal wisdom of the enlightened. It does not matter if everyone (or even anyone) remembers this fact. Reality is not democratic.

Who creates visions? No one — visions are an expression of Truth, are therefore never invented, not created in the usual sense of the word. The visionary opens to the underlying continuum of Reality and formulates in language what is discovered there. The spirit of the One enters into the visionary (the visionary breathes the breath of life known as Inspiration); the result is a new expression born from the underlying field of the never-changing archetype.

This and the subsequent volumes of the Thunder series are visionary works. They are expressions of where we've come from and where we're going; they are a report on the human condition; they are statements of Universal Consciousness. As such, their usefulness lies in example rather than in specific instructions for living on this Earth. Practical guidance of the Ishayas' Ascension is available through personal instruction, but the Ascension techniques themselves are not now and never will be recorded in any book.

These texts make no attempt to be scientifically rigorous. For example, it does not matter if Martanda was once a planet in our solar system between Mars and Jupiter — where now are only found the lifeless rocks known as the asteroids — or whether Martanda circled a different sun, or was even quite far removed in our galaxy. Our expanding scientific knowledge may one day answer this question; but for now the exact location of this once lovely and populous world is not important.

What *is* important is the unending existence of humanity. Humankind is vastly older than our histories have recorded, vastly older than our archaeologists or anthropologists have even begun to dream. Since the dawn of creation, there have been individuals throughout the Universe who have been capable of Self-knowledge. This is the only definition of humanity that is consistent or meaningful. There never was a time when human beings did not inhabit this Universe. Nor will there ever be a time when Self-conscious races are absent from created space-time. The form of the bodies, the specific details of anatomies, the size and shape and number of heads or limbs — these are not important. The essential underlying truth — that every human contains within his/her heart a spark of the Divine Fire — is the only important fact.

We are gods in mortal flesh, but by our choices and actions do not live so. There are no boundaries in us but those we artificially create and maintain by our beliefs in limitation and judgments of good and evil. This need no longer be so! Not for even one more instant. Freedom is available for anyone who seeks it, for *we* are the Myth-makers. *We* are the Dreamers of dreams. The power of the mind can be forgotten or denied, but its rich brilliance will remain, scintillating like a perfect jewel, just beneath the murky waters of our denial and despair. And the fortunate truth is that any one — any child, any adult burdened by the cares of life, any aged one, all but broken by the struggles of this harsh, cruel world — any one at any time may suddenly without warning awaken to the underlying Truth of life. And the really good news is that even one is quite enough to transform the world. People are a great deal more like popcorn than they have realized or yet begun to remember. When any one slips through the illusory boundaries of limitation and fear, all will follow.

Dance with me, children of this latter age.
Dance with me as I sing of the One.

The Diamond Staff

Shall I sing of my garden,
many green and growing,
Of Para, her streams,
forests and hills,
Of my sphere of silver and blue,
O wanderer from a far land?

INTRODUCTION
The Vision of the Source Universe

Dance with me, children of this latter age.
Dance with me as I sing of the One.

This is an invitation to share my vision.

Other worlds lie just beneath the surface of our rational minds.

In one, infinite yet unconscious forces interact mindlessly in chaotic patterns, creating and destroying as if randomly, by accident.

In another, gods and heroes struggle against manifest evil in the all but hopeless quest to save their worlds from destruction.

In yet another, every moment without exception unfolds in perfect harmony with the will of the Creator-Of-All-That-Is.

The experience of alternate universes is more often than not repressed in our modern age. This is tragic, for repression leads to confusion, to distorted perception, to fear.

There is nothing in life to fear. Para, the Source Universe which has given rise to all others, floats throughout Eternity as a radiant golden sphere, bathed in the azure flames of the infinite Light and unending love of the omnipotent One. That Universe is perfect. And since it is the Source of all other created universes, all must also be perfect. Apple trees create only apples. Love creates only love. Perfection creates only perfection. It is only identification with the projected dream-worlds that leads to suffering.

Even then, it is dream-suffering. Only our age-old yet moment-by-moment decision keeps us bound to our individual dream-creations.

This can end at any moment: Para surrounds, underlies and permeates every particle of the dream worlds. Because this is true, anyone anywhere at any time can experience the One Ascendant Reality. It can be found anywhere, but is most easily discovered inside your heart. It is the essence of every good thing: life, consciousness, joy, love.

The experience of Para results in a state of consciousness named by various Earth traditions: *salvation, nirvana, enlightenment, infinite awareness, satori, Cosmic Consciousness, Eternal Freedom, praying without ceasing, the peace which passes all understanding, Perpetual Consciousness.* The name is supremely unimportant; the content of this experience is everything.

Whatever we choose to call it, no suffering of any kind is possible in this state. Life is lived in permanent joy, in infinite love, in unbroken contact with the Source.

In an instant of frozen time, no longer than the gap between two heartbeats, a being fully and permanently in contact with the Source Universe shared his vision with me. This was a free gift, a wordless joining of his infinite mind with mine.

In the years that have passed since that magical, suspended instant, I have only begun to appreciate what this means to my life, to remember that which I long ago knew fully well but then forgot. I am an Unbounded Being. Living in a human body, I experience the infinite Ascendant continually. The Thunder books are an attempt to explain this state of consciousness, to describe the Reality of the wonder of this experience.

Words are finite, limited tools, most loved by longing minds. They will forever fall short of the experience of Truth. Truth is lived and can be shared; the best words can do is point the finger of understanding at it. Words can say, "The Moon is there." They do not and cannot give the experience of the Moon. At their best, they will inspire one to seek the experience they describe.

~~~

Seeking the Black Ishayas records a series of visions and experiences I had while studying with the Ishayas. The total elapsed time was only several days, but the total vision time was of many years.

The experiences flowing through me were far removed in space and time from the reality of this world. They were of a series of other lifetimes that uncannily paralleled the outer occurrences among my friends, particularly Edg and Sharon, at and around the Ishayas' monastery.

During this period, I fought a life and death struggle with my ego. It nearly mastered me on four separate occasions — not coincidentally, after the instruction in the Second Sphere Solar Technique, the Lunar Technique, the Earth Technique and the Second Cognition. The visions inspired by learning each of these techniques coincided exactly with changes in my personal life that were intense and, in one case, as terrible as I could have ever dreamed possible: the loss of Sharon.

If I had known from the beginning how much I would give up to gain enlightenment would I have continued on? Probably not. Only in hindsight do I see the beauty inherent in my personal tragedy.

Everyone's path is different. The incredible ease with which some grow under the Ishayas' care never ceases to amaze me. I look at my life and it seems I have always chosen the hardest possible path — and yet I know there was no other choice for me. And there are others who have suffered much more greatly.

Whatever it takes. That is the only attitude that is real, the only attitude that works, the only attitude that assists one to reach the goal. *Whatever I have to do in order to realize enlightenment, that I will do.* This was the viewpoint I adopted in the Himalayas, and the only one that could have carried me through my trials to the end.

For those who seek enlightenment, no other frame of mind can be substituted for this one. No other frame of mind will succeed. One must be willing to give up *everything* — every belief, every judgment, every attachment — then only can there be progress. For it is exactly where one digs in one's heels and says, "So far and no further" that the ego draws the battle line.

It is not possessions; it is attachments which cause trouble. What must be given up? Nothing. What must one be willing to give up? Everything. When one is ready to be free from everything, life begins in earnest. The dawning of the True Light is never far behind.

The Thunder series describes the opening of the consciousness of the human race to ever deeper and subtler experiences of enlightenment. There exists a collective consciousness of humanity that underlies and permeates all of our beliefs and experiences. This collective identity is responsible for most of our world-views and individual experiences of reality. To change this collective belief system is typically quite slow, as it takes continual effort on the part of many over a long period of time.

In this and the subsequent books, the collective consciousness of humanity is personified and individualized as Lord Gana, a semi-divine prince who lived far before recorded history. Since Gana is the representative of all humanity, his struggles to master his own beliefs and judgments have the effect of transforming everyone else. At times aware of his universal status, at times ignorant of it, Gana moves through various life-experiences in the attempt to master the lower aspects of his nature and rise to complete consciousness. This continues with ever-greater complexity as his understanding of the connection of the individual to the Universe unfolds.

Gana does not work alone. He is never long without divine inspiration — which most often takes the form of an unusual master of form transmutation, the Vidyadhara Airavata, also known as Heramann. Airavata is quite old and quite wise, the last of the ancient Vidyadharas, an intelligent race that was prevalent before the descent of our current human species. Usually unaware of his subtle and Eternal connection to the underlying essence of the incarnations of Gana, Heramann is nevertheless often drawn to assist him in his growth.

The omnipotent Power of the upward current of the Laws of Nature is also always present to support Gana; but he is not often aware of this. This force is personified as his feminine aspect, Almira. Almira is the second half of Gana's soul, ever conscious; she is the Goddess, always in divine communion with the One; she is the Earth Mother, the Source of all Good for humanity, the personified Holy Spirit.

Gana is also ever watched, protected and guided by the incarnate wisdom of higher consciousness, portrayed in the Thunder books as his seven Teachers Vasuki, Mordom, Rodavi, who was later reborn as Joab, Vaga, Atri, Brihas, and Matri. Their relationship to Gana is one of gentle guidance and discipline.

All the other characters in this History are either manifestations of partial aspects of Gana's infinite mind or else are his creations. Some of these creations are positive and represent the creative forces of nature: his children and the peoples he attempts to save from destruction and guide to higher levels of understanding. And some of these creations are negative, the destructive forces of nature personified and given form by Gana's incomplete understanding of life: the Emperor Valin and Valin's agents and minions, the Asurs and Rakshasas. In both cases, although having independent form and life, all his creations remain rooted in Gana's mind.

Thus the rest of the Thunder series is a history of humanity's age-old attempts to achieve a stable and upwardly directed civilization. They stand also as a description of an individual's journey to enlightenment through numerous births.

Either reading is correct, for we are continually creating our own world. We project our beliefs and judgments outward; these return to us as our experiences of others, of history, of life, of matter. Each of us dreams our own world — this means that each of us is ultimately responsible for our own creation. And therefore, each of us can change any of the rules governing our world at any time, resulting in a completely different world-view and a completely different world. Full realization of this simple fact is an acceptable definition of enlightenment. It is the Ishayas' hope that learning of the different levels of reality woven into this work will assist others to rise more quickly to the recognition of their primary authority in their own worlds. Then the healing of this Earth will be the sooner accomplished.

— MSI,
dedicated on Diwali, 1995

Come!
Listen!
Hear first my song of Gana,
Immortal father of our race!
Gana the shara, Gana the one true adan!
Gana the damned!
Murdered by his sister's son
Before the World Tree's seed was lost
Or the Sundered Gems stolen
From the Living Statue's hands!

— The Rajanya Mordom,
Last Oathmaster of Emura

Gana

1
The Solar Technique

I wonder, by my troth, what you and I did, till we loved?
If any beauty I did see, 'twas but a dream of thee.
— *John Donne*

Sharon and I received the Solar Technique — the First Technique of the Second Sphere — from Nanda Ishaya one beautiful June afternoon high in the Himalayan forest.

We were Ascending in our favorite grove. That magical place was about half a mile up the trail from where I first met Boanerge. The stream divided there into seven shallow falls; the moss draped over the multi-colored mountain stones in verdant beauty; countless lush and fragrant wildflowers grew there, transforming this lovely site into a sylvan paradise. This small grove was the favorite haunt of many small forest creatures; for some reason, it was more filled than anywhere else with enormous butterflies and brilliantly colored birds. All-in-all, this one spot was to us the most heavenly of the extraordinary gardens of the Ishayas' forests.

We often sat there, staring into each other's eyes, feeling our love expanding beyond all previous limits. The outer beauty of the cloud forest was as nothing compared to the wonder of Sharon's deep blue eyes, flawless face and luxurious golden hair, and yet the magnificence of her soul was greater far than her physical form. She could have been maimed or born deformed; yet still would I have loved her for her radiant internal glory. I had never felt this strongly about anyone before and doubted I ever could about anyone else again: she was immaculate, a perfect jewel in feminine form. She was life, she was joy, she was the incarnation of spiritual power, she was beauty and the good fortune of a life lived to the highest standards of perfection. That she loved me was highly improbable, given my pointless past, and yet every day she demonstrated in every conceivable way she not only loved but adored me. Why?

Nanda found us in our favorite grove, sat beside us that lovely June day, Ascended with us for half an hour, then gently said, "Jai Isham."

We slowly opened our eyes and responded, "Jai Isham Ishvaram, Nanda-ji. Thank you for coming to see us."

He laughed, his gentle brown eyes as ever brimming with unlimited joy, and lovingly continued, "You two are progressing well! Durga and I are extremely pleased with your growth. We've decided to begin you on the Second Sphere techniques today."

Sharon gave a little laugh of delight and replied, "Nanda-ji! The First Sphere fills me with such bliss, how can I possibly contain more?"

He chuckled and answered, "The container will continue to expand, dear heart. Your experiences, they are stable?"

"Oh, yes!" she exclaimed. "We're Ascending about ten hours a day now; every day I'm floating inward more deeply and clearly. All of life dances in joy for me. Here in the forest, I feel so connected with everything, I feel the life threads intimately intertwining: the plants and animals and birds are all connected to each other and to me. I feel at one with all of life, all the time. Is this a taste of Unified Perpetual Consciousness? Will this increase until I see the One Ascendant Reality in everything, always?"

"With Ascension, Unity grows from the very beginning, Sharon. All that is required is sufficient time." Suddenly a cloud passed over Nanda's face as he looked at her. He scowled briefly, then shrugged slightly, and continued to me, "Your Ascension remains unchanged? Still seeing fire everywhere always?"

"It never changes," I answered, despondent. I had grown accustomed to it, but still didn't like it at all. "Light fills everything, burns through everything. Even my dreams at night are nothing other than fire — it feels as though flames are engulfing me always. And yet it's not painful — they're not hot, not cruel, just constant, very bright and underlying everything. Every thought, every dream, every perception is filled with celestial fire. Light, burning light, always and forever brilliantly burning light. Will it ever end?"

"Oh, you'll break through in time. Exactly when is hard to predict. Has Boanerge returned to you again?" Nanda's tone was hopeful.

I did not like the position the Founder had put me in. Why had he appeared to me alone? And why only in vision? I had faithfully reported his messages to Alan and the Ishayas, but I knew they felt — as did I! — there was a great deal more he had left unsaid. His instructions to me on the two occasions he appeared were incomplete, insufficient to direct me or anyone else confidently ahead. I had written of my experiences as he had instructed me and was thinking of calling the book, *First Thunder*, but this seemed a rather poor beginning and not much of an answer to the need of the time. How was Ascension to be taught to humanity? How was this precious Teaching supposed to leave this secluded valley and enter the world? And why now? The Ishayas believed Ascension had been founded nineteen centuries ago by the Apostle John and faultlessly preserved in isolation by his successors ever since. Why suddenly change such a long history of secrecy? And why was I the seer and the messenger for Boanerge? I had little knowledge and, other than this continual experience of light, little significant experience. If he wanted an innocent newcomer, why not pick on Sharon? Her experiences of Unity were as constant as mine were of celestial fire; there was no question she understood volumes more than I. Or would not one of the original Ishayas, Durga or Nanda, have been a much more logical choice?

I sighed and answered, "No, Nanda, he has not. Maybe he expects me to establish Perpetual Consciousness first; I don't know. I can't understand why he came to me in the first place! I know nothing. I'm an amateur at Ascending."

Nanda chuckled again and said, "Perhaps it's safe to assume the Son of Anger sees more deeply than we do. Or perhaps there is a great deal more about you than you have begun to remember. Or perhaps there is subtlety within subtlety here — surely John and Isha have a master plan — I don't know why we feel we should necessarily understand it!

"At any rate, Durga and I have decided further instruction for the two of you now is appropriate. I'll give you the First Technique of the Second Sphere today. Then tomorrow, we may give you the Second Technique on the trek up to St. John's Cave. Or maybe when we arrive there. We'll see...

"This technique is called the Solar Technique because it opens the connection inside you to the Sun. This exists inside everyone as the upper part of the sushumna, the subtle energy channel in the spine. This connection begins at the heart and passes through the seventh chakra, the seventh seal at the top of the head. By mastering this technique, you open your awareness to the higher dimensional worlds. This is known as the Path of the Sages: it is said the fully enlightened leave the body at the moment of death along this route."

"What are 'the higher dimensional worlds'?" I asked, intrigued in spite of myself.

Nanda smiled and replied, "There are Seven Regions of Light that surround and permeate our three-dimensional Universe of name and form. The Solar Technique opens you to direct cognition of these."

"Our Sun is a gateway or vortex to elsewhere," commented Sharon, apparently understanding him perfectly. I wondered sadly if I would always feel as if I were in kindergarten around her. Whatever I slowly and painfully learned, she already knew fully and with complete fluidity of grace. How could I not adore her? The love between us had only grown more and more full and rich in the past two months. Whenever I was apart from her, her face often floated before me in vision. I did not know how I could possibly love anyone more, and yet every day I found I was loving her more, in every conceivable way. What great good had I done in the past to deserve the love of such a one? Her beauty of heart, mind, soul and body were unmatched by anyone I had ever met — and yet she loved me! How could I be so fortunate?

As I was thus drifting, the Ishaya was answering her, "Exactly so, yes. We think our Sun a thermonuclear furnace, some 96 million miles away that brings us warmth and light and life. And it certainly is that! But it is also much, much more. And there is that in each of us which resonates perfectly with the Sun. We have the Solar Path built into us; by opening to that, we discover our oneness with the Sun."

"What does that mean?" I asked, returning temporarily from my rapturous thoughts of Sharon. "How can we be one with our neighbor star?"

"We are all made of the same material," answered Sharon. "We are all stardust. I think that one of the greatest delusions of the waking state is the belief in our separation. We feel separate from each other, from all of life, from our own Self."

"There is no separation in Unity Consciousness," agreed Nanda. He picked up his rudraksha necklace with one hand and said, "We are all connected, just as are the seeds on this gold thread. This reality of Unity is called the *Sutra Atman* in Sanskrit — the *Thread of Souls* in English. Each of us is connected to everyone else, to everything else. I to you, you to me, you to the plants and animals, we and the plants and animals to our Mother, the Earth, all of us to the Sun. None of us could live in isolation — all of creation is woven together in a tapestry of joy and love and wonder. The Second Sphere is called the Universe Sphere because it opens us to the Reality of this connection. We begin with the Sun because it is after all the prime giver of light and life in this corner of the Universe. And because the Solar Path is within each of us."

Nanda explained the exact structure of the First Technique of the Second Sphere to us, then sat and Ascended with us through the long afternoon. I felt intimately connected to the Sun while using the new technique, but there were no extraordinary experiences, just a deep and abiding peace.

~~~

Nanda said he wanted to continue Ascending in our grove a while longer when we finished; Sharon and I walked back to the monastery to clean up before dinner.

As we strolled back, arm-in-arm, Sharon commented that the new technique was causing her to feel more centered or grounded than she ever had. Her experiences in general were usually deep and still: she hadn't had any more intense revelations since Delphi, but was always stable and clear. I asked her why she thought the intensity had declined for her; she replied she'd desired a smooth and comfortable growth.

"Does this mean I asked for speed?" I asked, confused. "I don't remember that. A little simplicity would feel pretty good about now."

"Maybe you did desire the fastest possible growth once," she replied, a hint of concern playing through her azure eyes. "And that set your course. Is it so hard for you?"

"Yes, no, I don't know. I guess I can handle it OK. I wonder if I could change my mind and request a slower path?"

"Well, I'm sure you could, but would you really want to? You complain often, but would you really want to slow down? That doesn't sound like you."

I was about to say I thought I probably would, but just then Mark Edg rounded a corner of the trail in front of us. Seeing us, he stopped and waited for us to walk down to him.

Edg was, as usual, wearing expensive black silk. I had never seen him in anything other than dark blue or black. He appeared as intense as ever. I had never exactly been able to bring myself to like him, but I had to admit he seemed to possess a peculiar power and authority greater than most of the others — greater in some ways, perhaps, than even Durga and Nanda. I did not understand him, nor did I feel I ever would, but something about him always fascinated me. I felt a little like a mouse must feel when it is being eye-frozen by the snake about to devour it. Edg's riveting gaze burned through my soul. Part of me was terrified of him, part of me was fascinated by him, part of me was attracted, part of me was repulsed.

He waited for us under a luxuriant overhanging vine that could have been a rare kind of wisteria — scarlet blossoms showered in fragrant profusion overhead and on both sides of the path. Two hummingbirds busily darted among the blossoms, seeking nectar. A trio of black and white monkeys scuttled by on urgent business of their own, disdaining even to look at or speak to us.

"Edg!" I exclaimed. "Nanda just started us on the Second Sphere."

"Ah, good," he replied without warmth. "That's nice." He spoke mechanically, apparently lost in his own world.

That was fine with me, but Sharon felt drawn to ask him, "Edg! Are you all right?"

"Hmm? Yes — and no. Have either of you ever heard of the Black Ishayas?"

"The Black Ishayas?" I answered, frowning. "Black Ishayas? How could that be? The Ishayas wear white to honor their vow of purity, except Nanda of course, because he was born a Brahman."

"Of course they do now," he replied impatiently. "But Durga told me there was once another Order — the Black Ishayas — also founded by the Son of Thunder, the Apostle John. Durga told me they were as different from the Whites as night is from day. They took no vows, for example. Some of them were said to have married — not from attachment but to fulfill the need of the Universe. But they didn't enter the world either — John created their Order as a safeguard for these Ishayas here — to keep them on a straight path, to oversee them and remind them if they ever strayed from the Apostle's intent."

"Another hidden monastery of Ishayas!" Sharon exclaimed joyfully. "What a wonderful concept!"

"I don't think they ever set up a monastery," Edg answered earnestly. "I think the Blacks drift in and out of the Earth plane — like celestial beings, only human. Fully realized souls, checking in from time-to-time to make sure the Ishayas keep moving ahead according to Isha's desire. Like Boanerge himself. Only different somehow."

"Why should the Ishayas need another rudder other than Boanerge?" I asked, slightly disdainful. "Surely he is competent to fulfill their need. I can't conceive they could ever run aground under his guidance."

"I'm sure I don't know! But the thought is thrilling to me. Maybe there are more than two kinds of people. Some people become Novitiates; they follow the White Ishaya path — they take vows to guide them to enlightenment. And then there are the householder types like you two and Steve and 'Dite — I suppose we could call such as you potential Red Ishayas — red for love and passion. But I've never felt comfortable with either role. What if there is a third type? Similarly focusing on enlightenment as do the Whites and the Reds, but different somehow? Maybe I'm a Black Ishaya myself! I never seem to fit in very well in either the White or the Red Universe. So, what if? I would like to know more about them. Wouldn't you?"

"If they exist, I certainly would like to learn more about them," Sharon agreed enthusiastically.

I echoed her words, but my heart was elsewhere. What did I care if there were two or three or one hundred and eight different kinds of Ishayas? I had all I could handle right here and right now.

I did not realize then how vitally important Edg's quest was going to prove to me in just two days.

~~~

We retired early that night. Durga and Nanda gave a remarkable lecture about the three-fold nature of Creation, but my heart was not in it. I just wanted to return to my room and Ascend with my new technique.

But before I began that evening, I sat on my narrow charpoy and wrote a letter to my kids, telling them I missed them. I didn't know when (or ever) I'd leave the Himalayas and return to the States, but I did want them to know I loved them.

Some kind of love, I berated myself. *Leaving them for some fool's quest.*

This was not the first time I'd been divided against myself, but this time it had strange and completely unforeseen consequences.

I reached up toward the light to turn it off, but my hand never reached it. Space and time tunneled around me as the energy of life burst up through me and out, carrying me with it.

I suppose the weeks of celestial experiences combined with the power of the new technique to crack the veil of my former world-view. Like an egg on the edge of an iron skillet, the old boundaries were crushed and would never be fully restored.

My body froze as my mind was freed from the confines of all previous experience.

2
Can a God Die?

Seventeen starships fled the ruin of Kanaan-dora
One only was destined to survive Martanda
How much more tragic a fate that the shara Gana never ascended
The gold and emerald lion throne of the Solar Kings of Emura.
                                   — Joab

I found myself walking through a misty forest of virgin fir,
hemlock and cedar. The trees were ancient, venerable, wise in
ways we humans but imperfectly understand. Seabirds' calls
echoed dreamily through the twilight forest corridors. Softer still,
almost beyond hearing, pulsed the surging rhythm of a distant
ocean.

This forest was like a park — the trees were so large and tall
there was almost no undergrowth. Suddenly a doe looked up at me,
startled by my presence. She did not flee — humans had never
given her cause to fear them.

A small stream wound through the wood, chuckling merrily
over its stony bed. Nestled away, all but invisible in a cathedral-
like grove of hemlocks, stood a small wooden cabin. Its one
chimney's smoke curled lazily toward heaven, mingling gently with
the soft gray-red haze of day's end.

Thus it began.

~~~

My body had no substance. I floated through the cabin's walls
as if they were of fog. The inside of the cabin, sharply in contrast
with its simple exterior, revealed vast wealth. The fireplace was of
ornately carved marble; rich tapestries of gold and silver weave
hung on every wall; huge precious stones — rubies, diamonds,
emeralds, sapphires, pearls — were inlaid in complicated patterns

between the lapis lazuli and flags of pure gold on the floor. The only mark of technology was the holographic model of a starship, floating silently behind the maroon velvet armchair in which despondently lounged Gana, the last and greatest shara of the previous home-world of humanity, Kanaan-dora. I floated toward him and into him, remembering at once everything that he knew, learning in an instant all that he was even as I forgot everything of my Earth life.

Shara is an ancient word, persisting still through the changing ages from the language of the progenitor of humanity, Swayam. Like many such words, this sequence of sounds contains within its vibratory matrix a nearly infinite expansion of meaning and power. From meditation on this word alone, every secret of time and space could be discovered. For simplicity, "Sun Prince" will make a useful translation of shara, as will "Sun Princess" for the feminine form, sharan.

Long before our world was populated, the sharas and sharans guided humanity. Their Starlord and Gemstone Council was the sole governing body of this galaxy while our Earth was still mostly the property of over-sized lizards.

Collectively, the sharas and sharans were known as the Solar Race. They were the younger offspring of the immortals, direct-line descendants of the first and mightiest of the Lords of Etan, Swayam. As such, they were as much above the common peoples of the galaxy as the modern human is above the animals.

The primary task of the Solar Race is to guide humanity toward higher levels of understanding. In ages when the sharas and sharans are known and honored, our Earth prospers. In ages when the Solar Race is forgotten or ignored, our world suffers from bizarre perversions of self-defeating forms of government. One feature of Earth in the next millennium will almost certainly be a rediscovery of the undying existence of the Solar Race.

~~~

The Sun Prince Gana was never surpassed by any other shara. His wisdom, compassion, strength, mastery of every branch of knowledge, generosity, humility, and nobility were never equaled and are not likely ever to be. But at this point when I joined his personal history, even though he was unexcelled in knowledge and power by any among his peers, his growth was incomplete. His mind had not yet remembered that it encompassed everything of creation, that it was a part of the perfection of the Source Universe Para, the One, the Ascendant, the root of all that is. Therefore, Gana did not understand that his life was necessarily flawless, composed of unending joy. And therefore, this Sun Prince was not free from the potential for doubt and fear. Today, for example, a series of unfortunate discoveries about the trustworthiness of his nephew Irnga had propelled him into a thoroughly dark mood.

The boy can't be a traitor! Why would he betray me? How could he hope to gain from this?

The shara's shimmering silver robe, created and sustained by his mind, hung limply around his shoulders this evening, its ethereal beauty dimmed by his depressed thoughts. With his left hand, he idly fingered the two gems, Starbha and Kaysta, hanging from his neck on separate golden chains. Kaysta had the color of an orange-red ruby, but burned with its own internal radiance. It was brilliant, glorious, wonderful. Starbha, equally perfect, equally bright, resembled a self-luminous yellow sapphire.

Kaysta and Starbha had once been one, but were torn apart by the Asur Emperor Valin in his attempt to destroy our human race. In his effort to repair them, Gana had filled them with the essence of his life, pouring so much of his spirit into the gems that Kaysta and Starbha almost became two extensions of his nearly omnipotent mind. For the shara knew that if he could but reunite the jewels, he would gain sufficient power to restore his damaged world and heal his people. If he could simply rejoin the Sundered Gems, his civilization would be unending, his past failures corrected, his terrible mistakes forgiven. The Sun Prince *knew* this beyond the slightest doubt. But Gana also knew beyond the slightest doubt that he lacked the skill.

As he mindlessly fingered the gems, the shara stared sadly at the slowly swirling iridescent liquid in the crystal chalice in his right hand. He both longed and feared his intuitive knowledge of this draught would prove true.

To be free from this curse of immortality! Thus Irnga's treachery might yet serve me well. Why should I not drink it? Let its fire course through my veins, end this mockery of a life! What use my existence without Almira? I died with her on Martanda! Let this body find its way to the earth and the destiny of worms.

The only other occupant of the cabin was Airavata, the Vidyadhara Heramann. Heramann was ancient and emerald and golden and scaly, a reptilian creature that stood just slightly taller than Gana's knees.

Masters of form transmutation, the Vidyadharas usually kept their native shape, similar to that of lizards or dragons. They were our greatest allies in the Rakshasa wars with the Asur Emperor Valin on Martanda: without their assistance and guidance, it is doubtful any humans at all would have reached the new world. The Vidyadharas were an ancient race, proud and wise. As a general rule, they have had little intercourse with humanity, for they find our highly changeable passions too difficult to understand or to trust. But this particular Vidyadhara was always finding himself to be an exception.

Airavata paced nervously back and forth before the Sun Prince, deeply troubled in empathy with him. He glanced at the shara with his emerald-green eyes from time to time, trying to decide how best to help him. So far, for more than an hour, he had not spoken: he simply could not understand what was so troubling his friend. Had not they done well during these two years, founding this new world? Perhaps the recent trouble with his son Kartika and Kartika's wife Ila was still bothering him? But that was after all a small thing, a family issue, not a sundering that could possibly last long or so affect Gana. Surely the young people should be permitted to start having families. Gana could not oppose them forever; obviously he recognized that full well, and was simply testing the depth of their desire. Or was there more here than it appeared? Were there other reasons Gana so adamantly refused their repeated entreaties? What could they be? Humanity needed to begin again! The loss of Kanaan-dora and Martanda must not be the end of this promising young species.

Heramann, reaching his decision, abruptly stopped his pacing in front of the Sun Prince and said, "I don't understand this melancholy, my Lord! Valin and his armies are defeated; the Asurs and their servants, the demonic Rakshasas, are exterminated from this part of the Universe! Why this untimely despair?" Concern for his friend was causing his voice, normally soothing, gentle, very like a cat's purr, to be tautly strained, harsh, one step removed from a feral growl.

Gana, staring still only at the chalice, replied softly, "At what cost, Airavata? Your race is ruined; the ten thousand of Emura are all that remain of the billions of Kanaan-dora. Not only our home-world but also the lovely Martanda has been destroyed: there remains but the smallest flicker of humanity left. The peoples of the galaxy have been shrouded in mist; the Solar Race has been eclipsed.

"And truly! how can Valin ever be defeated? The Lord of Darkness lives in everyone's heart now. We have only exchanged one enemy for another — and a worse. I feel no joy in our victory." Reaching his own decision, Gana raised the chalice to his lips, drained it and let it fall onto his lap. He more than half hoped it would roll off and break. It did not; he scowled at it savagely.

What cost my trust, Irnga? If this be poison, you will live with this knowledge forever. I do not envy you your choice. Do you envy me mine? Will Valin enter oblivion with me? Or will he remain imprisoned in my heart, a victim of this dead body forever? A curious fate for one so evil. Just, at least. Perhaps this is why the Etan Lords thus changed me.

"How can you so speak, my Lord? Emura is glorious! You founded it wisely; it will endure for countless ages: it rests firmly on the broad shoulders of Truth and Beauty!"

"What truth, Heramann? What beauty? The equator burns with demonic fire! Unquenchable, unpassable, a sundering wall that will in time divide Emura from Calantha and destroy us! We possess but scant resources; our technology fails more rapidly daily! One starship, Airavata! Only one escaped Martanda. And even that is rusting, sliding into uselessness. How long can Emura endure? How long will my impoverished people meet the harsh challenges of this new Earth?"

Of what value this world without my beloved? Better far to leave here, now, then struggle longer against such vain odds. I cherish no life without Almira's love.

"Nothing can stand against your will, my Lord! What can you not accomplish? Even death has fallen before you!"

"The cruelest betrayal of all! Of what use this boon? All I loved has been destroyed, torn from me, slain! Four only of the Solar Race survived the Martanda landing: myself, my son Kartika, his wife Ila, my nephew Irnga. I was mad to accept the Etan's gift! What future have I without my beloved Almira? Nothing save despair — despair and loneliness." Gana longed for an answer from his closest friend, but expected none. He raised his eyes slowly to stare at the Vidyadhara. They were on fire from the intensity of his need.

If only she had lived! If only she were with me now! Almira, Almira! Why? Why did you come to me, why did I lose you? How could I have deserved you, even conceived of you? No. All unexpected, you came to me and swept me helplessly away with you, just as the dying leaf of fall is taken by the swift river: now it rushes ahead; now it turns in quiet eddies, now, if not destroyed by the raging water or captured by some submerged limb or unknown shore, it reaches its final home — the boundless expanse. That is the whole of my destiny now, my beloved Almira — death and oblivion.

Heramann, correctly reading Gana's desire but entirely missing the mark, replied, "You know how Rodavi would answer these impoverished words, shara."

"Speak not of the Oathmaster! All his good will did not save Kanaan-dora! His was a life of failure."

He could have saved her, had he truly loved me. He betrayed me! He betrayed us all! Fool that I was to listen to him!

"Your master planned for thousands of generations!"

"And failed! His foolish mysticism alone destroyed us! No, I am more — much more! — concerned with feeding my ten thousand than in following Rodavi's obscure prophecies about an ideal future. I no longer cherish his memory." The longing vanished from Gana's heart and was replaced by a thicker cloud of gray sadness.

There is no hope now. None. If I live or die is meaningless, as is this life. Life! What a despicable mockery. Kanaan-dora! That was life. Or even if we had succeeded on Martanda. There were seven million of us there! That was a sufficient seed for a new world. But now? Ten thousand only! What vanity. And most of those ancient, decrepit. What hope is there here? Kartika was right to oppose me. Without children, we will all wither and die. I have been and am a fool. They will be better served by my son as their guide. There is no reason for my life to continue. I am useless, outmoded baggage from an earlier age, worthless without Almira and Rodavi. Why did I think I could so tempt fate? Madness! It was insanity to destroy Martanda! I should never have listened to Rodavi and that Etan Krishanu! There must have been another way!

Heramann, hoping to recover the lost moment, grasped the hands of the Sun Prince and searched long in his eyes. They were haunted, almost fearful, yet smoldering murkily within their depths were an almost infinite knowledge and an almost omnipotent power. The Vidyadhara could see no means to reach him.

Discovering no common ground, he said sadly, "My Lord. I cannot help you. You must tread that path alone. I dare not follow your soul that far. Your son...Kartika has requested my presence in the southern hemisphere, in Calantha. I was unsure about the journey. But now... I see I must leave you alone with this. I will return... I will return to your Emura in the spring."

Gana gazed at him with an unreadable expression, at last nodded curtly and replied, "May we one day share ice again, old friend. Tell Kartika... tell my son I forgive him. May he one day learn to forgive me! And tell Ila I was wrong to oppose her desire. They have my permission to have children. And they have my permission to come back to Emura. So do the five hundred that followed them to Calantha. Tell them, `With the spring, Gana will return to guide you again.´ Go from me now, dearest friend, before I change my mind."

Alone I will face this final challenge. Face it and live or face it and die. But alone. So much is certainly owed the Vidyadhara.

Heramann wished to argue further, but could think of no appropriate words. Instead, he shimmered once like a rainbow seen through a vial of green and gold and then, transmuting into his second favorite form, that of the falcon, flew to the open window. He perched for several moments on the sill, looking thoughtfully through his gentle emerald eyes back over his shoulder at Gana. His beak opened as if he were going to speak; instead, he closed it with a snap. Shaking his head, he flew swiftly away. One brilliant green feather floated slowly to the floor as witness to his flight. It looked very lonely on the hard cold gold.

The Sun Prince gazed at it sadly, saying softly with a deep and increasing melancholy, "Kanaan-dora. Martanda. Rodavi. Almira. My dearest, dearest Almira. What a price. What a terrible price!

"Why, my Lord? Why do you permit these great evils? Why do you allow such as the Asurs and Rakshasas to exist in your garden? Why were Martanda and Kanaan-dora destroyed? Were all the eleven billions of my world so meaningless before your eyes? And what of our seven million on Martanda? Do you so lack compassion? How could you have permitted such meaningless tragedies? Why, my Lord? If you are truly Eternal Love, why? If ever I have served you well, surely I deserve an answer. Tell me!

If ever once you have loved me, favor me with but a single glimpse of your omniscient brain!"

People are rarely upset for the reason they think. Consequently, that which they think they desire is not often even vaguely what they long for, deep in their innermost hearts. This may be an obvious truth for the most part of humanity, but even a nearly perfected being such as Gana was not altogether immune from such self-deception.

The distance between surface desire and the fulfillment of inner motivating desire had worn exceedingly thin for the Sun Prince and was disguised by the most gossamer of silks. The force of his passion could not be denied: a bolt like lightning erupted from the center of his chest; every cell in his body screamed in agony and fear as he was thrown backward into his chair.

What was left of independence writhed helplessly in fear.

I am poisoned! Dying! Irnga! You have *betrayed me! Why?*

Rodavi's voice echoed through his mind, *"Shara, shara! never fear;"* the golden peace radiating from the authority of his master's calmness created a single fragile moment of silence.

But an instant later, Gana's unanswered longing pushed him through the final barrier: a thousand-thousand suns exploded to life inside him, forcing him up, out. Every cell in his body burned with glorious fire, so brilliant as to be far beyond pain. The beginning of the infinite Cosmos could not have been more intense! He was the Universe being now created! He was the light! He could not move, but his body contained everything within its unimaginable fire.

An enormous pressure forced the breath from him; his heart stopped. A voice (not Rodavi's, but eerily familiar nonetheless) called in triumph, "My Lord Valin shall again be free!"

Irnga? Mocking me in the end?

Seven rings of fire exploded to life before the shara, each a distinct color of the rainbow but brighter than our sun. They were spinning at high speed and throwing off sparks of color. A thin golden thread connected them like so many brilliantly colored beads on a necklace.

At that moment, Gana almost understood everything of space and time. Almost the wounds that plagued his mind and heart were healed. Almost his peoples were restored, his answers received, his planets recreated. Almost the seven rainbow wheels burned perfectly clear. Almost... But not quite.

Gana's unfulfilled longing pulled him back from the threshold of omniscience.

A single thought, *Death,* resonated through him; the fiery wheels vanished. And then nothing remained but silence. There was no longer a body to feel, no longer senses to experience, no longer a mind to think. Nothing was left but this vast silent radiance, consuming him utterly as it expanded and brightened without limit.

~~~

The soul of Gana, caught by the impossibility of death in an immortal body, desperately seeking alternatives, spiraled first into memory.

The Sun Prince stood again on the bridge of Dalmara's Pride, the only starship to escape Martanda. A single one of the seventy decks below was filled: a mere ten thousand were aboard, the ragged remnant of the seven million who had fled Kanaan-dora six months earlier.

Beside him on the bridge stood the last three of the Solar Race: his nephew Irnga, his son Kartika, Kartika's wife Ila. Irnga was still largely maddened from his recent encounter with Valin: he stared ahead blankly as he wrestled with the Asur Emperor within. Whether he had heard any of the conversation was not apparent. Ila was sobbing quietly: she had just realized the Etan's horrible request meant she would never see any others of her family or friends again. She was leaning into her husband, seeking solace if not understanding. Kartika was holding her tightly and staring grimly at the two holographic images facing them. A vast quantity of words waited to pour in wild protest from his mouth, but his adamant will kept them restrained in deference to his father.

Gana, seeking confirmation in their faces, read their emotions with a glance then answered the projected images, "You can't be serious! I won't do it. The idea is absurd! There has to be another solution. You know that is unacceptable."

The hologram of his hoary master, Rodavi, showed that he was, as ever, experiencing nothing but calmness in the face of this latest adversity. Or was that concern lurking within those ancient gray eyes? *There should be,* the Sun Prince thought savagely. *We have lost so much.*

Gana decided the Oathmaster was experiencing nothing other than his unchanging peace; almost viciously, he turned his defiance toward the other image being projected onto his bridge. That was of the Etan Krishanu.

The Etans were the immortal forebears not only of the Solar Race but of humanity in general. The later volumes of this series will deal mostly with the Lords of Etan; in this work (with some notable exceptions) they appear mostly in memory.

Krishanu was as handsome as any of the Lords of Etan: his was a beauty as impossible to state in words as is the scent of a perfect rose, a beauty that resoundingly defeats the power of any language to express. His magnificent azure face also appeared completely calm, but Gana could sense from the tightness of his stance that the Etan Lord was not altogether free from anguish over this decision.

The Serpent King Sesha was, as always, coiling loosely on Krishanu's right shoulder. Its fiery eyes were half-closed; the temporal problems of governing the Universe never seemed worth more than the most casual interest. What difference if Valin won or lost? Life was the one constant; it would continue forever. Imperfection was impossible in Narain's Garden. Why did the children forget that so often?

Heramann, in his falcon form, was perched atop the Etan's other shoulder. He was much less calm than the Serpent King about what he had just heard. He was, in fact, highly incensed and complained bitterly, "Gana is right, Krishanu! No Etan has ever so toyed with death! Not Orah, not 'Sravasa, not 'Ishtar, not even your father Swayam! I tell you, this is utterly mad! I will not participate in your idiotic scheme! There must be another way!"

Krishanu gently stroked the Vidyadhara under his beak, trying without much success to soothe his ruffled feathers. "If I knew another road I would certainly walk down it, old friend. But I have been given a map for no other. And we must wait no longer, lest this stolen moment flees from us and Valin discovers this trap. His armies revel in their victory; the Asur Emperor thinks he has wholly won. We must be swift, lest he discover Gana's escape."

"But Martanda, Krishanu! You can't destroy an entire world! It is too beautiful! Too precious, too — "

"Airavata! This issue is *not* open to debate! You don't understand how small a price this is to defeat Valin. I command you, Heramann! By your unending loyalty and service to Etan, I command you! Carry Sesha to Gana. Now! or our time will be lost, our secret discovered."

Airavata was wild with agony, but could not deny the force of the Etan's final order. With a barely audible cry, "Hrai!" he leaped upward and, doubling in size with each turn, flew thrice around Krishanu. Diving swiftly, he clutched the Serpent King in his talons and was at once gone beyond the range of the projected image. His voice came echoing back, "I promise you, Lord of Etan! One day, we shall share ice again!"

Krishanu stared at Gana, his eyes only imperfectly masking his grief, and said, "As soon as Heramann and Sesha reach you, shara. Not a second longer." His voice was gravelly with his pain. Was it truly to be Martanda now? Would any payment ever stop this evil?

"I understand," Gana answered dully. "Forgive us, if you can."

"Shara!" exclaimed Rodavi. "The Etan Lord has nothing to forgive. Do not blame yourself. The fault belongs to no one. Or else to all. I too have a parting gift for you. Remember it well, for it is both a blessing and a warning. And a protection, if you so deem it. *Never in pride rely solely on your own strength. Help will come when you need it, even when least deserved, if you but allow it. Be receptive to the good flowing to you always.*

"Never fear, shara. As I have preceded you from age to age, so will I forever. Doubt not, you are never alone: my love is with you always. Trust in the order of life: I promise you, we will rejoice together again beneath a new sun."

Gana stared at him with despair as his mouth said the only thing that came to mind, "Thank you, my father. I will remember." It sounded hopelessly inadequate; he cursed his voice its penury.

~~~

The dream-memory ended, Gana was left with his current present: a poisoned body, a soul captured by silent nothingness of infinite light.

A final thought floated through him, *I have died.* There was no longer fear nor the slightest regret, just certainty of the fact, marked by a quiet acceptance. Memory of his new civilization Emura came once only: an image of a sad, dark place, a powerless wraith that vanished as quickly as does the shallow dream of a summer afternoon's dozing half-sleep.

Gana found he could open an analog of his eyes in this analog of space and time. The seven fiery wheels were still burning before him. For a moment, he thought he saw a nearly infinite series of worlds in each of the seven. There was a subtle, instantaneous decision; the unchosen worlds vanished as if they had never been.

Seven worlds alone remained. Seven tasks were left to perfect his omniscient mind. Seven lives more were to be lived to complete the training the Oathmaster Rodavi had so painstakingly begun.

Again I ask you, gentle readers, a question that means more than you have perhaps yet begun to dream:

Can a god die?

3
Almira's World

Our Universe contains worlds within worlds,
Each more glorious, wonderful and perfect than the last.
— Rodavi
True enough, but every world is within the mind.
— Mordom

Suddenly the emerald wheel, the fourth of the seven, expanded around Gana. For a timeless instant he was confused as infinite verdant emotion engulfed him in light and sound. In another moment, the light divided and multiplied; Gana found he was alone, on his knees in a vast forest. Had he wandered out of his cabin? No, he remembered dying; further, this was no forest of Emura, nor like any other of his experience.

The smallest tree was six paces across; the largest spanned at least a league. They seemed a kind of cedar; but if he looked closely at the needles, they became less tangible, more abstract in shape and texture so that positive identification was impossible. There were neither animals nor insects, no underbrush, not the tiniest decaying twig or bough. Did the trees never drop a needle? Were they alive? It was as if the forest were a sculpture. Was it newly created for his arrival? Or did it eternally exist, never-changing? And was he only an accidental visitor? Perhaps he was here for a reason he did not understand. Could he ever understand? Perhaps logic and reasoning meant nothing in this world.

The shara wandered aimlessly, having no desire but to experience the wonder of this beautiful, silent forest. If he had stood still and his thought had ended, might he have become

another tree? In spirit at least, if not in form? There could be worse
fates than being a tree in such a forest.

But Gana continued to walk and think; eventually a strong
certainty there was nothing else in the world swept through him.
For the first time, he felt his aloneness.

So instantly as if to answer his feeling, he realized he was
hearing a great river or fall and behind (or within) it, the rising and
falling of a distant ocean and behind (or within) that, a beautiful
voice singing.

With increasing melancholy, he assumed his mind must have
invented these sounds, must have rejected the unchanging
sameness of this perfect, park-like world. The heaviness of his
thought introduced sadness. The spirit of the land did not favor
such emotions — the first faint breeze stirred the air, carrying
distinct words,

> *"When shall you awaken to our garden,*
> *To our streams, forests, and hills,*
> *To our sphere of silver and blue,*
> *To this Para our home,*
> *Lost wanderer from a far world?"*

To Gana, the voice expressed the essence of womankind:
nurturing warmth, unquestioning love, divine joy. His response
was instant and certain: he ran forward, crying, "I come! I come!"

~~~

The shara ran through the forest for a long time, yet did not
grow tired. Food and drink were no longer necessary to sustain his
body made of light, but he was not yet aware of this. After running
for so long, he thought he must surely be thirsty; abruptly the
cedars ended. He leapt, then slid, then fell headlong down a nearly
vertical bank of black slate. Such a fall would have been terrifying
in his former life, but here he experienced only joy: he began to
laugh. As he plunged faster and faster, he chuckled, chortled,

guffawed, whooped, roared with mirth as he had not since he was a young shara with the Oathmaster Rodavi — before the twin vultures Power and Authority gradually enslaved him to their dark necessities.

The slope decreased; his fall ended gently on the grassy banks of a huge lake. His exuberant laughter continued giddily as he sat looking around. The air was dancing in life: it moved, played, sparkled in infinite points of light, constantly altering its color, ceaselessly humming its silence.

If I were not here, would the air still sing? The thought drifted gently through him then merged into the faint sound of the ocean far off to his right. He looked that way, but could see nothing other than this lake, stretching to the horizon. The farther shore was also invisible; this caused a wrenching throb in his chest. He did not then realize why.

To his left, a large river joined the lake; far away yet perfectly clear was a high waterfall. Its sound was also distinct, subtle yet definitely there behind the rushing power of the mighty river. Above the fall was a magnificent range of mountains, snow-capped, flanked by evergreen forests. He wondered what kind of trees they were; at once his eyes learned to make the distant close.

Long he played with his new-found power, telescoping the mountains and their robes of trees: virgin forests of fir, hemlock, cedar, spruce, pine. Finally he remembered his thirst and knelt to drink. The water was cool and very sweet. A stream of living hue entered him, enlivening every cell with multi-colored light.

His desire to find the singer arose again; all other thoughts were overshadowed by his problem: his path led across the lake! Even his new vision could reveal no further shore, nor anything but water and sky.

As he stood there perplexed, a tiny white speck appeared in the furthest distance. It moved at an incredible speed: as soon as he thought of telescoping it, it was at his side. "It" was a beautiful swan, not larger than those of Emura, but unflawed, without the slightest blemish. The bird bowed, bending its graceful neck; the request to mount it entered Gana's mind.

As he responded to the impossible without doubt, once again his desire knew no limit: the shara Gana sat comfortably between the wings of the fleckless swan.

~~~

The steady motion of the bird floating over the water produced an overwhelming desire to rest. The shara's eyes drifted closed, at once he dreamed. He was floating over a valley of flowers: red roses and blue and yellow irises. All were content in the bright sunlight and knew nothing of fear until one tragic day when space for further growth proved limited...

The single thought, *No,* melted the flowers into two human nations on a small island. Both peoples dressed in medieval style: one, mostly red; the other, blue and yellow. The reds were farmers: the coasts of the island were beautifully terraced with every kind of garden. The blue and yellows were technological: the highlands were filled with large collectors that resembled nothing so much as huge hand mirrors. The two races lived together peacefully, benefiting from a mutually profitable trade: energy for food. But today on the common lands there was a rare assembly inside a canopied ivory pavilion, built for the occasion: a blue technological girl had committed the unthinkable by loving a red agrarian boy; all were gathered to review the terrible problem...

Again the single thought, *No,* melted the two nations into bands of striated color, his wings: he was a gaudily iridescent butterfly. Higher and higher he flew over a saffron field, trying to reach the sun: he knew if he could but reach it, he would enter a new and vastly superior world. But suddenly the azure sky darkened; a dark wind smote him; he fell, broken, ruined...

The shara awoke to the touch of a cool rain on his face. The drops, coming from a flock of golden cumulus, were radiant silver. Although the clouds were thick, the sky lost no color because of their presence: both existed simultaneously in the same place. A faint desire moved in him; he opened his mouth. Every drop was different! Mango, tangerine, peach, apple, pear, cherry and other more exotic flavors raced through him, rippling shivers of ecstasy along his spine. Responding to the joy, his eyes developed one step further: he learned that he could at will see at any speed. The shower became a slow-motion dance of ethereal beauty.

As he was thus playing, the thought moved through him, *We are here.* Simultaneously, they reached land.

~~~

There were no forests on this new shore, but the air was redolent with fragrant gardens and orchards. Intuition made the direction crystal clear, but awe slowed his eagerness: he knew his goal was near. And he knew his goal was the master of this extraordinary world of Para. What knowledge, what power might she possess?

As he slowly made his way through the rocks, his mind created ever more wonderful appearances for her, envisioning absolute beauty in human form.

Even so, he was unprepared. At first he could not look at her, she was so bright: all the unlimited brilliance of this perfect world came from her alone. She was golden, silver, all colors, but her loosely flowing robe was most frequently white. The word "beautiful" has been too much used and abused to be a fit raiment for her: all streams of individual beauty found their fulfillment and fullest expression in the ocean of her radiance. Unrivalled love, compassion and wisdom flowed from her in visible beams. She was like the cedars: she could have been created a moment before, or she could have stood at the center of this small stony amphitheater forever, constantly growing in understanding, expanding in power, maturing in transcendental wisdom.

She smiled at him gently and said softly, "Almira."

This was her only word, but contained within its simplicity was a nearly infinite expansion of meaning which exploded in his mind: *I am Mother, every mother you have had, or could have had, or wished to have. I am Sister, all the sisters of your past and future. I am Daughter, Dependent, Devotion, Joy. I am Wife, Abundance, Harmony, Completion, Salvation, Glory. I am Beauty. I am Grace. I am Prosperity. I am the total of all the Love you have ever created or ever might create. I am your Receptive Self. I am your Life. I am the Dynamic Power by which you act, think, exist. Never have I been away from you; never shall I leave you.*

Her arms opened, beckoning. He walked forward slowly, divided between the glory of her presence and the perplexing question how his dead wife, the sharan Almira of Kanaan-dora, could not only have preceded him to this wondrous place but have been transformed into this extraordinarily beautiful goddess. When he reached her, she cried, "My shara!" and knelt before him. Again came a flood of meaning, *My Father, Brother, Son, Husband, Compassion, Acceptance, Understanding, Freedom, Inspiration, Honor, my All, my Consciousness, my Creative Source. As I have ever been, ever shall I be: yours.*

The dual realities of his past memories and his present experience continued to divide the shara's mind: how could this perfect being be his wife? Ever more puzzled, he lifted and embraced her.

Touching her for the moment ended his confusion: Gana's doubt subsided as he melted into her, river into ocean. As the flowing current of his individuality merged back into its Source — the infinite Silence of the One — the full range of his Universe was transformed into pure light, into pure love. For an instant, Gana regained his status as one of the four primary beings of creation. Gana was again the Deathless Dancer, the Master of Time and Bliss, Lord Isha himself. The shara was no longer merely *of* the Universe but *was* the Universe. Gana knew everything there was to know and could do anything there was to do simply because he had remembered that he was everything there was and there was nothing anywhere that he was not.

But permanent perfection was not yet his: Almira pulled away, saying, "No, my Lord. The Grandfather's curse is far from ended."

A lost and forgotten door burst open in the shara's mind: with dark terror, Gana remembered the omnipotent Creator and his wrath, *"To the furthest limit of Non-entity do I therefore send thee!"*

But Almira banished his fear with the peaceful majesty of her words, "Good, you begin anew." *I have been with you always: in you, outside you, for I knew the Grandfather's curse could never be eternal. Not even Narain's Firstborn can destroy a soul. The light of the One shines in every particle of existence always.*

Throughout your fall, through every cycle of time I accompanied you. Even when you forgot me completely, I never left you: wherever you are, there am I always, even as is light with the sun. For I am yours forever, even as you are mine.

~~~

They began to walk slowly inland. This new shore was cultivated with countless beautiful gardens and orchards. Each tree was covered not only with blossoms but also with green and ripe fruit. Every type of plant he had ever seen grew there in abundance, together with numberless unknown varieties, of all conceivable hues. The scents were delightful, a symphony of fragrance; each occupied a vital part in the whole; none worked against any other, none overshadowed any other. But there were no insects, no creatures, no animate life in Para.

"There are no animals here, Almira? Except for the swan on the lake, I have seen no others."

There are no others here because you have not yet re-created them. You have not yet mastered your connection to your source; hence you cannot yet manifest life at will.

"Why the swan then?"

Narashamsa came here when you did. 'Hamsa is the last helper to everyone. Men sometimes call him luck, sometimes fate, sometimes God's will. Yet is Narashamsa more than this: he is all that is good for you, a ray of your own infinite consciousness, the connecting link between you and your master form, sleeping now until you re-awaken fully.

Narashamsa

Leaving that to be understood later, Gana picked a particularly appealing fruit. It was golden yellow, looked vaguely like a mango, and smelled delicious. Suddenly he saw that although he had picked it, it was still on the tree! He took another; the obliging fruit instantly replicated itself, remaining exactly where it had been, continuing to grow at its own pace toward perfection.

"This is most peculiar, Almira!" he exclaimed with wonder. "Is death unknown, even impossible here? With the question, he discovered he could stretch his mind to *feel* the land: he learned that the beauty of the surface was only the covering of a much fuller and richer beauty — a beauty that lies forever beyond the ability of words to express — a beauty that is as fundamental as the concept of perfect order in the created Universe.

Almost Gana understood omniscience then, but the limits of habitual thought caused his mind to stir, shattering unrestricted Unity of knowing into finite boundaries of questioning. What was this place, this world Para?

~~~

With no obvious transition, they stood in a small verdant meadow, high in the snow fields on a mountain far above the waterfall, river and lake he first discovered in Para. In the center of the emerald grass was the source of the warmth in the ice: a steaming spring and a perfectly round, boiling pond. Gana stared for a long time at the water, entranced by its simplicity and beauty.

Almira's fingers lightly caressed his hand, then motioned for him to look up. He followed her lead and turned to gaze over the world.

The sky! It was magnificent! None of his experience could match it, not even those of the Victory of Death, when the air was filling with the smoke and ash of the ruin of Kanaan-dora. The vibrant golds, oranges, blues, silvers, reds changed, shifted; long bands of striated cirrus came and went, now quickly, now slowly, alternating with tiny, fluffy cumulus and massive nimbus banks;

long fingers of tinted stratus reached out toward them and receded. Was the sun dancing just below the horizon, never rising?

Almira looked at him with deep love as her thoughts flowed through him, *Often we came here, before...* Suddenly she cut off the memory-vision with what almost seemed anger, instead raised her hand and said, "Watch!" A golden beam streamed from her palm. She moved her hand; the clouds moved with it. She re-arranged them, changed their hues, painted unlikely yet exquisite sunrises, simply, gracefully.

She motioned for him to try. The shara held his hand similarly and willed; the energy passed forth! Gana became the world's sculptor: creating, changing, destroying.

She began again; together they melded their thoughts of beauty in the sky, creating a whole greater and grander than either could have achieved separately.

Ecstatic, he cried, "The sun! I want the sun to rise!"

Almira lowered her hand and stared at him. He was certain the thoughts entering him were not all she was thinking; he could not identify the expression in her eyes. *You must not, shara. This is Dawn Mountain. Were Orah to rise, this would cease to be what you created it to be. Would you steal the glory of the Cathedral of the Sun? Better far to let everything follow its own nature.*

Gana, feeling stubborn, insisted, "I tell you, I want to see the sun!" The peculiarity of this new world was beginning to take a toll.

At that instant, a rainbow bridge appeared in the far distance and rapidly approached them. Its crimson side was the brightest; a tall man in a full flowing scarlet robe led the arc toward them. Soon he stood before them, an ancient but highly dignified sage with wise gray eyes and full flowing gray beard and hair.

Almira bowed to him and said, "Welcome, my Lord Vasuki, First of the Seven. May your charges ever prosper! Will you stay long?"

"I come to honor you, Daughter of the Sun. Later perhaps, if your returning man continues to reintegrate. A simple gift, a warning, then return where I am more needed." Vasuki smiled broadly at Gana and continued, "Well done, shara. Your success in imprisoning the Asur Emperor Valin and defeating the Rakshasas has justified the long patience of your people and the longer faith of your wife."

A second man, identical to him in every way, emerged from and then knelt before him. Vasuki dropped his eyes to him and said, "Yes, go to him in grace with the Power of Life."

The double rose and walked to Gana. Taking a large ruby ring in the shape of a serpent from the index finger of his right hand, he gave it to the shara, saying, "Wear this as token of the Perfection of the First of the Seven." As Gana slipped on the ring, the double stepped forward and merged into him.

As soon as Vasuki's ring was on his finger, Gana's mind advanced one step further: even as he stood with Almira and Vasuki in this small meadow on Dawn Mountain, the shara stood also at the ocean.

A man with the cerulean skin of an Etan was lying on a huge serpent floating on the water. With a deep intuitive knowledge, Gana realized that he was in the presence of Narain, most powerful of the Four.

Narain was staring intently at a small white torch on his hand. Glancing at it, the shara discovered it was no flame but was Almira! rapidly gesturing as she expressed her thought.

As soon as the shara recognized her, Narain smiled; the golden sphere that is our Universe materialized in his other hand. Taking it from him eagerly, Almira bowed to him and vanished.

The shara glanced back at Narain's face and was shocked to discover he now looked at him! At him, but at the same time, *beyond* him, *through* him: at his past, his present, his future. That one glance read Gana completely, knowing all there was to know. If Almira was comprehensible to him (at least in part), this one experience proved Narain was not. Her love and wisdom were unmoved by specifics: it was a Mother's love that cherished and protected because of her nature. But he was more, was Father: infinite wisdom and transcendental love were there, but so was a strength greater than Almira's, an authority so vast as to defy all limitation. One might run from the omniscient eyes and omnipotent hands of Narain in terror; one might fall before him in surrender. A single thing only one who had seen him could never do: forget him.

Narain looked through Gana and knew him utterly; the shara's eyes dropped in confusion...

~~~

On Dawn Mountain, a painful throbbing at the base of the shara's spine spoiled his newly created reality, turned his mind and senses back toward their accustomed usage. The vision of Narain at the ocean disappeared. Had it only been his imagination? How could Narain have instantly appeared only instantly to vanish?

"Curious," murmured Vasuki, "I had not anticipated..." Shrugging slightly, he added, "Each of your seven tasks will grow progressively harder, my Lord Gana. This promise I give: when you most need me (and when I am permitted), I will lend you my direct aid. This warning I will also speak; remember it well: *Never in pride rely solely on your own strength. Help will come when you need it, even when least deserved, if you but allow it... Be receptive to the good flowing to you always.*" So saying, the Oathmaster stepped off the cliff and withdrew toward the dawn.

"There is a cave. Nearby." Almira said slowly, staring after the slowly disintegrating bridge. She must have been deep in memory, for she continued to speak, "There you and I are eternally united in perfect peace. But considering your present level of understanding, we cannot even visit there yet."

Almira sighed.

The world paused: the colors dulled, the light decreased, all motions of water and wind were stilled. Even the pool behind them stopped boiling.

The shara, his body on the verge of death, his mind on the verge of despair, his heart on the verge of chaos, stared at her with a terrible awe and learned in that instant of silence that any sadness, even the faintest, could ruin this world.

This taught him he had infinite choice. He could choose Emptiness, which would mean the immediate destruction of Almira's Para. Or he could choose the perfection of the One, which would mean the immediate fulfillment of every world. Or he could choose any reality between Emptiness and the perfection of the One, which would mean the Universe would continue more or less as before.

Gana chose.

Almira smiled; light and sound and hope were everywhere reborn. And the rebirth was glorious: everything was as bright and clear and freshly alive as if newly created.

Again without an obvious transition, Gana and Almira stood once more in the orchards; they began walking swiftly inland. A deep intuition drove the shara on: he led Almira unerringly toward a small hill in the center of the cultivated lands. On the hill was a grove of vine maples, flowing from early spring to late fall in rapid cycles. Following their autumnal display of versicolored beauty, the trees drew in their leaves, rested momentarily, budded, then attempted again and yet again to attain arboreal perfection.

In the heart of this sacred grove was a circle of viridian hemlocks; in their exact center was a marble fountain. Its statue, an angel with four arms, showered aureate drops which turned to azure then argent as they fell, so that the pond was a lambent silver. Gana was charmed by this fountain; he felt a fundamental secret was hiding there, a greater and higher knowledge than he had ever known. He knelt and stared at the water.

Almira said, "Beloved," *I must leave you for a moment.* Gana did not answer her and hardly noticed as she walked away. He was too busy playing with the moving beauty of the fountain: slowing-stopping-starting its dance with his wonderful new eyes.

But after she had been gone a *very* long time, he felt a slight motion deep in his heart. It was from far away, some other place, some other world! Before he could understand it, the branches of the hemlocks stirred: out of the trees stepped a beautiful doe. She came to him and knelt gracefully before him, placing her tender muzzle in his hand.

He raised her head and looked into her eyes. Their depths revealed more than gentleness: there was an intelligence that was at least equal to the human. And yet there was something more — something that, again! aroused that feeling, that temporary impulse of — ?

Once more the hemlocks moved; a magnificent buck came through the trees. He also bowed, but did not touch the shara. The doe rose; together they bounded off, leaving Gana alone with this impossible problem.

The first creatures in a world otherwise without animate life! Almira must have known of these two, but would she not have told me? Therefore, she must not have known. But how could she not? Where lies meaning in this? What other powers are there, lurking beneath the benign surface of this paradise?

For days of hours, Gana sat staring at the fountain, thinking, yet came no closer to understanding. Finally he grew tired of so using his mind and stood to seek Almira. At that instant, his heart again moved. But this time, the faint inner disharmony was accompanied by memory: the death on Martanda of his wife Almira flashed through his mind. The shara had loved no other in life; it was the deep loneliness of her loss that was moving his heart even here, in Para.

Now, this is utter foolishness! he thought. *How can I miss her when she is here?* The memory and simultaneous judgment flashed through his mind in an instant. Marking that moment, the air around him burst into life with myriads of butterflies of all possible tints and shapes. They flew chaotically off in every direction; again Gana was left alone with the fountain.

Never before animate life! Who is playing with me? Almira? Why? Why did she leave me? Where did she go? Or is some unknown other attempting to confuse me? Why? Or was it the feeling of loneliness that was responsible? How?

Gana tried by will to create more beings but could not. He quickly learned to mold the light of the One into forms; soon he could approximate color, textures, smells. But he could not create life! *Is this surprising? How can life ever be formed? Life is of itself, complete unto itself. Every impulse of being evolves in gradual stages. How long does it take inanimate matter to create the first cell? If those deer and those butterflies just now appeared in Para, they must have come from elsewhere, even as did I.*

Sitting before the fountain, surrounded by many poorly and well made but lifeless animals and birds, Gana could find no answer at all.

~~~

The strangeness of Almira's absence inspired the shara to question his Universe again, *How can such a world exist? Or such a being as Almira? For how much of Eternity has she maintained her vigil? And for what?* His life in Kanaan-dora flickered briefly before his eyes. Nothing of much importance there...

"The Dome of the Spheres!" Almira's words abruptly pulled the wandering part of his mind back from its reverie. Or did it? The doubts and memories had changed his reality again: he was now sitting beside her, gliding over a small circular lake, riding on the swan. On the far shore was a large golden dome, supported by twenty-seven tall columns of ornately carved marble. Seven huge weeping willows lowered their ancient arms with grand sweeping gestures toward the dome; the trees' reflections in the lake formed an emerald pathway leading to it.

"Where did those deer come from? Or the butterflies?" Gana asked, more intrigued by these odd experiences than by the approaching dome.

Almira smiled at him and said, "Loneliness." *It was your longing that connected you to your power. Full mastery will come later, after your seventh triumph.*

Almira's thought seemed subtly colored by an emotion Gana did not recognize. Was she concerned about him? Shouldn't she be? He did not seem to be integrating with Para very well.

They stepped off the swan and walked into the Dome of the Spheres. In the exact center was an ivory pedestal, sculpted with serpents; on it slowly revolved a golden sphere, bathed in a cool copen fire. This golden sphere was inexpressibly lovely; it shone with an internal radiance greater than anything else he had seen in this world.

They stopped before the golden sphere; Almira looked at him as if she expected him to speak.

It was lovely, but not of much greater interest than anything else. In fact, the obvious wisdom of the seven ancient willows just outside was more fascinating — it seemed so intense as to be almost human. Or more than human. And the carvings on the twenty-seven marble columns were also mysteriously profound — they felt intimately connected to his body. The dome above was a hemisphere of purest gold; the floor was a highly polished silver that reflected perfectly.

Too perfectly! Neither the twenty-seven columns nor the serpent pedestal appeared in the floor! As far as its flawless silver polish was concerned, there was nothing above but the dome! Was its image painted there? No, the floor mirrored Almira's presence perfectly. With a prickly sensation along his back, Gana looked down and discovered he was right: the floor ignored him! Where his reflection should have been, there was nothing, nothing at all!

"I'm not here!" he exclaimed. Fear abruptly rose in him and grew stronger, twisting his mind. It could not be resisted, could not be stopped: it inexorably increased in force, leaving him helpless before its onslaught. His mind began to buckle from its terrible might: visions of other worlds and lives burst through him, their unfulfilled needs and unanswered demands thrusting impossible memories upon him.

Gana screamed in terror. Who was he? Naisan? Mars? Balzor? Barlrin? Alazar? Gana? A thousand memories of a thousand lives forced themselves into him, claiming their reality, asserting their dominance. Who was he? What was this place? What was happening to him?

Almira's thoughts had their own imperative and forced his to submission, *Shara! My time fails. Concentrate all your powers now. And remember.*

"Open." *This golden sphere is your Universe, bathed now in the azure fire of your Evolving Imagination.*

They floated into the sphere, which rapidly expanded around them. Thoughts from Almira continued, explaining his perceptions, *We pass through the Seven Regions of Light. One day, I will re-introduce you to them and to their ruling beings. Inside them, here, this small dark area the astronomers of Kanaan-dora knew as the Universe... Here is your galaxy, the Milky Way... Here, your Sun... Here your Earth. How gray she is! Surely the Asur Emperor Valin is not so well chained as you and the Lords of Etan believe. Alas if it be so! If we do not succeed in your present body, I fear you will be forever lost to me; Navril Hagar will again wander the Universe unfettered... Here is the Northern continent you named Emura... Here your cabin... Here your physical body, made of food.*

Gana's mind reeled. The chain of cognition was too fast, too intense: each level of body or reality or size or time competed for dominance. When they passed through the Regions of Light, he not only saw and heard but became a part of them all, briefly, yet long enough to gain distinct impressions of the all-powerful beings dwelling there in unrivalled splendor.

As they reached the Universe, he experienced the whole of its infinite complexity, one thousand billion galaxies bursting forth before him and within him. It was glorious but terrifying.

The last reality was the worst: as he confronted his physical body, he realized with a violent jolt that awareness of it had never left the deep recesses of his mind. Until now, he had been convinced of his death and had therefore accepted everything with near perfect innocence, feeling the many mysteries of this new world Para would in time become clear. But the easy crossing of the plain had ended; the steep journey into the mountains had begun: as Almira brought him as witness to his body, he was pulled into it.

He resisted, struggling with all his will. He shouted to her, "Illusion or reality?" but there was no answer. He felt she was still there — watching, waiting — but he could not drag his eyes from the body in the chair.

At the same time, a curiously uninvolved part of him was observing that the body was decidedly real, not illusion. It was not dead: it was as if frozen, as if the movie of its experiencing had stopped on a single frame. The body — his body — *it!* — *him!* — was sitting as he remembered, but the eyes were half open and drawn upward, the mouth was agape, the back arched. No, it was not dead, but then it was not quite alive either.

He was ensnared by a repulsive mass of immobile flesh!

No, this was the body Almira had loved!

No, what had she cared for the surface? It was the inner being she had married, which part was now present, brought here by the new, transcendent Almira, to witness this revolting corporeal protoplasm!

Rodavi! Rodavi, help me!

The thought of the Oathmaster calmed him; he wrenched his eyes from the body and looked around the cabin. Everything was as he had left it, except the crystal chalice lay broken on the floor, the fire was long dead, dawn was showing an early rosy brume. Had it really been only a few hours?

A wave of tranquility came from Almira with the thought, *You don't have to struggle* — when suddenly there was an explosion and a tearing pain in his lower back. Again the shara was drawn toward his body. But this time, space and time distended around him so that his forward fall became a slow-motion dive.

Falling down — down into his — his physical body... falling down into his body... his body... falling down into his physical body... his physical body... Civil War in Emura... Barlrin, last Sun King... The Rain of Fire... When will Lord Gana come again...

Almira's thoughts floated after him, from a great and increasing distance, *My Lord! You have been enslaved for too long! I am losing you! You, a god by nature, have believed in limitation and death, bestowing thereby false form on Chaos. By your forgetfulness, you have created enemies throughout the Universe!*

Even now they work to end you, for then would they truly live. In your stead! They were created by you, are nothing other than illusions born from your omnipotent mind, but you have given each of your seven great enemies enough energy to ruin you!

You have only one choice: you must re-learn the right use of each of the seven centers in your body. Each of the false dreams of your immortal mind must be unmade, must return to its Source. Only then, when you have finished each of these seven tasks, will you fully remember your godhood. Do you understand, my beloved?

He tried to shout, "No, of course not!" but he could not stop his fall, could not speak a reply, could hardly think at all.

A sanguine flame enveloped the body in the chair. As he continued to fall toward it, Gana stared at it with a peculiar dread that seemed almost like longing.

Almira's thoughts continued ever more slowly, ever more distantly, *I am permitted to aid you directly in your first four tasks, in the fifth and sixth only indirectly, in the seventh, you will have to aid me.*

But you must begin now: my stolen moment flies from me. You do understand?

As he was drawn completely into the raging blood-red fire, he again tried to scream, "No!" but his tongue remained frozen.

One final thought chain from Almira floated after him, *Sleep; awaken whole. Ever will I love you; ever will I believe in you. Remember me!* And then the flames surrounded him, devoured him, consumed everything that had been the Sun Prince Gana, founder of Earth's first civilization Emura, greatest shara in the history of Kanaan-dora.

4
The Lunar Technique

Though I speak with the tongues of men and angels, and have not
love, I am become as sounding brass or a tinkling cymbal.
And though I have the gift of prophecy,
and understand all mysteries
and all knowledge; and though I have all faith, so that I could
remove mountains, and have not love, I am nothing.
— I Corinthians XIII

I returned to awareness of my body in the Ishaya Monastery in the Himalayas. My body was exactly as I had left it: I was standing, my hand was still reaching up for the light, but now it was dawn — I could see the early light coloring the forest mist on the hillside through my narrow window.

I sat on the charpoy with a large, "Whuff!" and wondered what in the world (or out of it) had just happened to me. The experiences I'd just had were as real or more than anything else of my life on Earth. Was this a clear memory of a former existence? Or was this a taste of the higher dimensional planes Nanda mentioned yesterday? I had not the slightest idea, but I did notice the extremely peculiar fact that Gana and Airavata and Almira were still inside me — not as memories merely but as vibrantly alive realities, as real or more so than anyone else I knew.

I felt more split than I ever had. I attempted to formulate the vision of Para in words to Alan and Sharon that morning at breakfast, but found little understanding in either. I felt Nanda and Durga would not be a whole lot of assistance either. Who could help me now? Only Boanerge came to mind, but he was most notable for the inconsistency of his presence.

Now the trek to St. John's cave began to appear more interesting. Until now, I had felt it would prove a distraction from the real business of long hours spent Ascending, but now I was so torn between wildly divergent realities that any hope at all seemed vastly preferable to none. I didn't know if there was any way to inspire the Apostle to return and explain what was happening to me, but perhaps traveling up into the mountains to his cave might at least demonstrate a willingness on my part to be open to his guidance.

My responses to his two previous visions had not exactly been positive. Perhaps he had grown weary with a soul as stubborn as mine and had decided to blast me with the million volt experience I'd just had. Or maybe he'd decided to choose another to fulfill his plan to bring Ascension into the world. I could hardly blame him if he had — I was about as unresponsive as anyone could be. I had no special gifts or talents — why would he want me to carry this priceless Teaching out of the monastery? It made little or no sense.

And yet the life I had been privileged to view — the life of unlimited power and wisdom of the shara Gana — was so extraordinary, so far beyond anything of even idle dreams of my previous life. Could that somehow have been my past? Or did I have some other kind of connection with that remarkable Sun Prince, whose life was so removed in time or space that no one else on Earth even knew of his existence? Or was it all allegorical, created for my education by Boanerge or my own subconscious? If so, what was I supposed to learn from it?

I had no answer to any of my questions, but my curiosity was growing larger and larger whenever I touched upon the vibrantly clear vision, burning ever more clearly through my soul.

~~~

There was not much time for dwelling on my experiences that morning, however: we were busy preparing to trek up the mountain to St. John's cave. The Ishayas were sincerely hoping the Apostle would appear to them and give them clear guidance.

The day began early with four of the local Himalayan natives guiding sixteen mules into our courtyard. We quickly gathered our gear in the courtyard after breakfast — it was an eight hour hike up the mountain; we were planning on staying there for at least a week.

All twenty-one of us from the monastery were trekking today: no one wanted to miss the adventure. I doubt anyone really thought Boanerge would appear to us, but the thought of hiking farther up into the Himalayas appealed to everyone.

Edg walked next to Sharon and me and continued being rarely talkative. He was extremely enthusiastic about last night's lecture and was quite intent on my listening to him about it. I much preferred to focus on my Vision of Para and Gana and Almira, but something about the forcefulness of his presence pulled me into his words. As we slowly wound our way higher and farther into the Himalayas, Mark Edg waxed profound to us about the nature of the Universe.

"Did you hear what they said last night?" he asked us with great excitement. "I was right about the three kinds of Ishayas!"

"I didn't follow the talk, in all honesty," I replied, already a little bored. "Nanda had just given us the Solar Technique, I'm afraid I was more engrossed in it than in the Ishayas' words."

"They were talking about the three-in-one structure of creation," said Sharon, squeezing my hand and smiling at us both. "They described how all of life can be divided into three: subjective, objective and the link between the subjective and objective."

"Oh, that's right," I said, vaguely remembering. "Or, in other words, the knower (me on the inside) and the known (everything on the outside, my body, my world, my Universe) and the connection between the knower and known, the process of knowing and doing — my sensual organs and organs of action. But how does this relate to the Black and White and Red Ishayas you were theorizing about yesterday?"

"Think how these three manifest in creation," said Edg, becoming even more intense now that he had involved us. "Remember how Durga explained last night that the interplay of these three Universal Principles creates the three fundamental tendencies of all Natural Law: creation, destruction and energy?"

"Well, no, not exactly," I answered, not understanding why he cared about this.

"I'm a little hazy on that point too," said Aphrodite, joining our conversation. The gorgeous Greek was as ever at the side of her lover, Steve Young; when she stopped focusing on him to join our discussion, the handsome young American started paying attention to us as well.

"I think it's like this," said Steve. "Does not the same force that creates the subjective also cause the expansive nature of life? Is not the same creative energy in our souls the same as the creative energy in the Universe? Does not the force of evolution manifest throughout creation?"

"That makes sense to me," agreed Sharon. "One force of evolution must be at the root of all that is everywhere — in the human and in the world. That force is known as *sattva* in Sanskrit, I think. Embodied, it is the aspect of God known as Vishnu — or, I would assume, the Holy Spirit in the West."

"Yes!" exclaimed Edg. I had never seen him so excited. Why was this so vital to him?" And that force is represented by the White Ishayas — those Ishayas that follow the white path of purity, those who take vows, those that uphold the simplest and most direct path to enlightenment."

"If there are three fundamental tendencies throughout creation, there must also be three separate paths," I said, beginning to see his logic. "Although Nanda has not spoken of it, or at least not to me, you must be right. And he must represent the Red Path — he wears saffron robes. What does the Red entail?"

"The tension between the Black and the White, I imagine," answered Sharon. "Infinite expansion pulls against infinite contraction. Matter vs. anti-matter. Creation and destruction eternally co-exist, else nothing could be. So red represents the energy or passion that exists between them. That force is known as *rajas* in Sanskrit. Rajas actually means red, I think. It is represented by Brahma, the Creator, God the Father in the West."

"This all reminds me of the yin-yang symbol," said Steve. "That also represents the three, does it not? The one part is male, white, yang, creative; the other is female, dark, yin, receptive. The one creates Heaven; the other, the Earth. One the Sun; the other, the Moon. One the light; the other the dark. Both always co-exist, which is why they are pictured flowing into each other, in a constant state of movement, of change — thus the third force is represented by their flowing transformation."

"That was beautifully said," I commented with absolute sincerity. The young American seemed to be growing faster than anyone else. The depth of his expanding mind often impressed me.

"Well thanks," he replied, blushing, then added, "but it only makes sense. Infinite creativity and infinite destructivity must co-exist always. So there is no true evil as such in the Universe, there is only the flowing interplay of the three. What appears bad from a human perspective must simply be a case of inadequate information. Only when the bud is destroyed does the flower bloom."

"My point exactly!" exclaimed Edg. "Where is the destructive power hiding among the Ishayas? Ignorance must be destroyed for full consciousness to dawn. It has to be!"

"Perhaps Boanerge embodies that principle," said Sharon. "He only checks in periodically to move the White Ishayas when they get stuck. That strikes me as being the energy known as *tamas*. Shiva in this part of the world, or God the Son in the West — the aspect of God that has the power to destroy."

"But Christ embodies pure love!" exclaimed Aphrodite, confused. "Where is the destructive power in love?"

"Oh, I think I know that," said Edg grimly. He grinned mirthlessly at us all and added, "Pure love will always destroy anything that stands in its path. Ruthlessly."

I did not like that at all. Somehow Edg's words intensified the continuing vision of Gana and Almira; I staggered slightly and felt dizzy. For a brief moment, I felt as if I were there again, in Para, sharing in the transcendental light and joy of Almira's presence.

"Honey, are you all right?" asked Sharon with concern.

"It's been an interesting few hours," I commented. "Edg. You talk about three powers in creation. But what about the Fourth? The Ascendant itself? Are there not four fundamental realities? Where does your neat theory of Black, White and Red fit with that?"

"Four?" he scowled at me. "If we want to count the Ascendant, perhaps Nature itself represents the fourth or colorless kind of Ishaya. Or the Goddess. God the Mother. I don't know."

I had little interest in Edg or his theories; fortunately the trail narrowed and steepened as we climbed along a rocky ledge with enormous cliffs on both sides. Single file and close attention to foot placement became imperative; all conversation stilled. I was pleased that further speech with Edg was difficult: there had never been a time his presence did not make me uncomfortable. This had only increased since he started focusing on the Black Ishayas. What difference if they existed or not? Boanerge and the White Ishayas seemed sufficient to bring Ascension into the world. What if Boanerge was a Black Ishaya? Well, so what? What difference what any of them were called? My path ahead was mine, regardless of anyone else's labels.

I didn't care to understand the three-in-one nature of the Universe. I didn't much care if the Ascendant manifested three characteristics or hundreds — and yet I couldn't stop thinking about it. I remembered Nanda had once described the Ascendant as Infinite Consciousness, Eternal Existence and Absolute Bliss. Subjectivity, the knower, that was obviously Consciousness;

objectivity, the known, that must be Existence; the connection between them, was that Bliss? What then was the fourth? The Infinite, Absolute, Eternal part? Did any of this relate to my visions of Para?

The trail we were following from the monastery presented us incredible views of the eternally snow-clad Himalayan peaks, and yet less and less of my attention went to them. Ever since awakening from my trance-vision that morning, the scenes and individuals of that world were growing stronger and clearer in me. It was as if the celestial light that had been burning through everything of my external world for the past two months was now taking on definite form.

When the trail widened out, I tried again to relay my experiences to Sharon. She listened to me with compassion but I could tell she followed little or nothing of my visions. Could I blame her? I hardly understood them myself.

Was I a piece of the soul of the shara Gana? Was that a memory? Where had that life of power played out? In our solar system, on our Earth, only far removed in time? Or had it been in a distant star system? I had no idea and wondered if I ever would. Was it even relevant? Was the whole experience designed to further my growth, or was it simply an unstressing dream, created by the unfulfilled parts of my psyche, with no particular reason? I had never had a dream so real. No — that was no dream, that much was certain, else its images would not still be flowing so powerfully through me here. What then?

I longed to share my new world with Sharon and felt deeply frustrated that she could not join me there. And yet, was she not there? Was she not Almira? Or at least a part of Almira. And yet she had no knowledge of Almira, nor of Para. What was the last thought Almira shared with me? *I am permitted to aid you directly in your first four tasks, in the fifth and sixth only indirectly, in the seventh, you will have to aid me.* Was my present lifetime in some way related to those later tasks? How? I had no memory of earlier triumphs.

~~~

My frustration continued to increase during the long trek up into the heart of the mountains. The beauty of the journey grew continually as we traveled farther up and further in, but it was mostly lost on me.

The wonder of the valley of our destination reached even me, however: there were twenty-seven caves there of varying sizes, most possessing steam vents or hot spring pools. Natives brought some of their hardy herds to graze the surrounding slopes in late summer, but now in June, the receding snows were only beginning to allow the ground cover to flourish. Alpine flowers of all sizes, shapes and colors were profusely blooming; if my senses had not been so over-shadowed by supermundane visions, I would have been entranced by St. John's Valley.

A few hermits lived in the valley year round. How they survived there through the winter months was inconceivable to me. They were quite friendly to the Ishayas and helped us settle into the caves. Edg, Steve and I shared a small cavern with a hot spring that protected us from the cold of the high Himalayan night. We laid out our bedrolls, placed out a few prized possessions and joined the others to Ascend before dinner.

~~~

Ascension Cave was directly connected to St. John's Cave; the histories said that exactly here the Apostle had appeared on two separate occasions. It was large enough for a hundred or more; there was a steaming pond in its center that kept it warm and humid.

Before we Ascended, Nanda took Sharon and me aside and said, "Durga and I have reached our decision: we want you to move through the Second Sphere as quickly as possible. I'm going to give you the Lunar Technique now, the Earth tomorrow and the Second Cognition the day after."

"Why so fast?" I asked, startled. "I thought it better to spread instructions out by several days or weeks."

"Ordinarily, yes. But these are special times. John has come to you twice. You are, it seems to Durga and me, the key to our next step, the missing understanding for our expansion into the world. If that is truly meant to be. We want you two to learn the Twenty-Seven Ascension Techniques in record time. The Son of Thunder has marked you — it is his example we are following here."

"Whatever you think is best, of course," said Sharon eagerly. She seemed exhilarated by this fast progress. My misgivings did not seem to deter her in the least.

"Before you do this," I said, hoping to dissuade him, "I should tell you about a vision I had last night, after you gave us the Solar Technique. It was unlike anything I've ever experienced before." I briefly outlined my memories of Para, Gana, Airavata and Almira.

Far from changing his mind, my story inspired Nanda to respond with, "Wonderful! Wonderful! This is all so wonderful!"

"What?" I asked, thinking I must have misunderstood him. "How so?"

"Don't you know? Have you in the West forgotten everything? No, I see you don't. Amazing. Before he was Christ, who was Isha?"

"Well, Jesus of Nazareth."

"Yes, yes, of course, but before that birth?" Nanda sounded a little impatient.

"I remember reading once that Christ was the prophet Elisha and John the Baptist was Elijah in a previous birth," said Sharon thoughtfully. "And I suppose there must have been other births before those. Moses, perhaps? or Jacob? I don't know."

"The Ishayas have always maintained that long before any of those births, Isha was known as Ganapati — Lord Gana, or literally, the Lord of Souls. Ganapati is said to be the founder of our present human race!"

"My vision was real then?" As I asked, I felt the world again fade as Para and the experiences of Gana returned and intensified.

"All true visions come from the Ascendant. About the details? I have no idea. I have heard echoes from the past that we are not native to Earth. I don't know! I suppose Boanerge would. But I have heard of the Vidyadharas before — and of the Solar Race. You may know as much as any one now living about these subjects. Write down your vision, will you? In as much detail as you can remember. This could be critically important."

"If you wish," I sighed, frustrated and again despondent. Why was I always the one to be afflicted by these things? "So there's no choice here? I have to learn the next technique now?"

"You don't have to do anything, ever. I'm simply saying that is our choice for you." Nanda was not offended, but I could tell he was a little amused by my attitude. It was easy to see why: everyone else eagerly sought instruction. I was always the problem child, resisting what everyone else desired with all their hearts.

Sighing again, I resolved to try harder in the future. "Nanda-ji, I'm sorry. I seem to make life harder on myself than is necessary."

"That is a common mistake in the waking state," he responded warmly. "So, with your permission, then? I will proceed. Good. The Lunar Technique has several important functions. The first is to open what is traditionally known as `the Path of the Gods.´ If someone dies after the first stage of enlightenment, Perpetual Consciousness, is gained but before the highest degree of Unity is established, the soul leaves the body along this path. Becoming an angel, a god, the soul goes to a world of the angels, of the gods. This is a much slower path of evolution through the celestial regions. The goal eventually reached is the same as that attained by the soul traversing the Solar Path, the Path of the Sages, but it takes much, much longer.

"Opening this channel now will increase your celestial perception; it will open your sixth chakra, ajña, commonly known as `the third eye.´ By mastery of this technique, you will gain complete and perfect ability to see and hear the celestials — the devas, angels, elementals, nature spirits and others that live in subtler dimensional reality than we humans."

"So this technique develops Exalted Consciousness," said Sharon, engrossed.

"Exactly. The Second Technique of the Second Sphere hastens the development of the second stage of enlightenment."

"Why here?" I asked, a trifle grumpily. My resolve was cracking already. "Wouldn't it make much better sense to stabilize Perpetual Consciousness first, then develop Exalted Consciousness?" I was incorrigible. I often shocked myself by my crudity. Here I was, about to be instructed in this two thousand year old technique and I had the effrontery to question the aged Custodian of this wonderful Teaching.

Sharon frowned at me but Nanda smiled as warmly as ever and replied affectionately, "If our purpose was simply Perpetual Consciousness, you would undoubtedly be correct. But Ascension's goal is the permanent experience of the highest degree of enlightenment, Unity. We don't want anyone to remain stuck in a lower level of consciousness. So even before the experience of the Ascendant is stabilized, we start laying the groundwork for the rapid growth of consciousness in enlightenment. Do you understand?"

I really had no idea what he was talking about, but I was sure the Lunar Technique would be as simple and powerful as the other five I'd learned; I resolved again at least to attempt to be outwardly grateful to Nanda and to practice Ascension to the best of my ability.

~~~

Nanda, Sharon and I were the last to enter Ascension Cave. As I sat beside her on a stone outcropping near the cave's mouth and held her hand, the declining sun, not yet quite moved past the Himalayan peaks, caressed her golden hair, lighting brilliant ringlets of glory around her radiant face. *You are She,* I thought, then closed my eyes to Ascend.

I began with the Lunar Technique as Nanda had suggested. After a single repetition, everything of Earth was forgotten as I entered a new world, completely unlike Para and yet oddly connected to Gana and Almira...

5
Nativity

Change is the essence of the world:
Static existence is impossible.
Life not consecrated to Evolution
Degenerates into a race with Death;
A people not committed to growth will be no more.
Yea, the very rocks will curse then forget them.
— Rodavi

Gana will return in the spring of Julius Adan.
— The Rajanya Mordom

Born unknown yet born to rule,
Mars will purge my Tala with fire and sword.
— Joab

The winter was famous for its length. Even the eldest said they could not remember its like. Some who planned poorly had to borrow at interest from their neighbors; a few more than usual died from the long cold. But the miracle of spring began at last; the fragrant narcissus and golden daffodils carpeted the valleys as the sapphire snow flowers and saffron and indigo crocuses chased the ice back into the mountains. There was some flooding as heavy spring rains added to the melt; nevertheless, it promised to be a peaceful and productive year for all the land of Tala.

The capital of Tala was known as Sulara, the Golden City of the Adanai. Sulara was a magnificent city, filled with gold and jewels and prosperity. It was built far to the south, in the same region where legend held that the Founder Gana was long ago poisoned. Stretching away in the ocean in those days was a crescent chain of islands, each warmer than the last, source of much of Tala's produce. Beyond the furthest and the hottest, the air grew so searing none could pass southward and live. Thus no seamen had ever reached the Uttermost South; no one knew whether the ocean beyond the Burning Sea cooled again and there was more land, or whether the temperature kept rising, inexorably rising until the water boiled and the world ended in the flames of hell.

One of the last of the Sun Kings of Emura, the Adan Marcellus the Lesser, once decided to see if any of the stories of fabulous treasure lost beyond the Burning Sea were true. He manned seventeen ships with his bravest soldiers and most loyal mariners and set sail southward with great pomp and ceremony on mid-winter's day.

This journey was strongly opposed by Oathmaster Vasuki, the Sun King's chief Counselor. But Marcellus was adamant and refused to listen. Angered by the adan's stubborn will, the Oathmaster refused to accompany him and cursed the journey, saying no one who dared venture past the southern islands would ever see Emura again.

From respect for the Oathmaster's wisdom (or from fear of his prodigious prophetic skill), the Sun King decided at the last moment of choice to leave his youngest son behind. Over-ruling the shara's loud protests, Marcellus with his other six sons and only daughter anchored him in the smallest ship just off the coast of the southernmost island, leaving a trusted old friend in charge.

For eleven days, the shara bitterly bewailed his fate. He paced, he screamed, he swore, he cursed, he bribed, but nothing he did succeeded in convincing the ship's old captain to violate Marcellus' orders and follow the fleet southward.

Finally the shara conceived of drugging the captain's ale; this obstacle removed, the seventeenth ship set sail southward at dawn of the twelfth day.

The shara's jubilant exultation was short-lived: just after noon, the lookout espied a lone rowboat, drifting northward. Aboard were six mariners, dead, and the shara's only sister, alive, but severely burned over her entire body.

The rajanya Mordom, last Oathmaster of Emura, recorded no one could pass living to the South. But as none of the Oathmasters had ever said what, if anything, lay beyond the Burning Sea, greed and curiosity never wholly abated; many strange stories were bandied by drunk old men and purblind fools of their perilous journey to the Uttermost South.

But the truth was that the sharan's dying words, "The fleet is burned! All! All have died! Father has murdered us all!" served to deter others of Marcellus' mind: no sane man dared brave the Burning Sea again. And the few mad souls who did attempt to seek their fortunes by sailing through the demonic fire that encircled the globe did not live to tell of it.

~~~

In the adan's palace Zephyra in Sulara, the Sun King Julius sat stooped behind his polished ebony desk, idly running his fingers over the seventeen starships inlaid in silver on the desk's top. Julius did not know that the symmetrical designs represented starships. No one in Tala knew that. But this harmonious ordering of the patterns was a time-honored symbol of the adan's authority: it had been faithfully and painstakingly duplicated for eighty-two thousand years.

The adan liked to stare at the unbroken flow of the designs; for some reason, he usually felt quite soothed whenever he looked at them. But at other times, something about their shape, balance and congruity inspired such a deep longing in his heart that his eyes filled with tears.

This evening, Julius' mind was only superficially attentive to the inlaid silver: the Sun King was sadly reviewing his life, looking within, seeking wisdom. Just today he had learned some of his subjects were whispering darkly about him: they were concerned their adan was going to live no longer than any ordinary mortal.

What bothered him most was that he had thought this was his private secret. For he knew they were right: he was far older than should be a Sun King of a mere eighty autumns. His was a life of failure! He was certainly as mediocre and just possibly the worst of the long line of degenerating Adanai.

The glory of the Solar Dynasty had been diminished by his birth! It was not that he had ever wished to be a daystar like Gana, the god-like creator of Emura; nor had he even wished to be a glorious comet like the mighty Balzor, founder of Tala from the ruin of Emura; no, he had longed merely to be a fixed star of the firmament: an unerring guide by which his people might avert some of the shoals, reefs and pounding surfs of life.

But he could deny the obvious no longer — it was not to be. He had never been and was certainly not now of even the slightest assistance in saving Tala from itself. No, he was nothing but the dimmest of the heavens — a distant, dying star. Useless to himself and incompetent for his people! An aged, decrepit fool! All his efforts to check the failing of Tala were for nothing! The Talans' addictions — chemical, physical, emotional, criminal, spiritual — continued to grow larger, more varied and more intense. Like a wildly multiplying cancer, the death of civilization loomed ever more certain daily.

The Sun King straightened suddenly, ran his powerful hand through his graying hair to help order his mind, then glanced a final time over the Senate bill on his desk. Half laughing, half crying, he muttered, "We must never fail to try," then swiftly signed, *Julius Adan, XXXI, Tala*.

He dropped the pen onto the bill and began running his fingers over the inlaid silver designs on his desk top again as he thought, *Thirty-first adan since Balzor! If I could only have been as wise! Could forging Tala from the ashes of Emura have been any harder than saving Tala from itself? Perhaps I have been too gentle: perhaps my father Yamaya was wiser when he assassinated the eighty-nine sharas at the feast on Mordom's Day. Perhaps — but what can fear accomplish? Tala was no better after his reign of terror than before. And possibly it was a great deal worse.*

Why has God abandoned us? Why did Joab desert Tala after helping found it? Why did he train no Oathmaster to succeed him? We have been without visionary interpretation of Rodavi's mysteries of the One since Tala began! How can I lead my people when I am as blind as they! They need so much more than I can give them. By the Sacred Myth of Kanaan-dora! We are lost! Doomed! We need hope, we need inspiration, we need—-

Julius' melancholia was rudely interrupted by the bursting open of his study's door. In rushed Teva, the chief physician, crying with joy, "It's a shara, sire! A shara!"

The adan leaped up, wildly scattering the two hundred sheets of the Senate bill all over the seventeen inlaid silver starships on his ebony desk. "At last! By Gana's grace! A boy! The fulfillment of my desire! Thirty-second from Balzor is he! *Mars,* I name him, for the Planet of War shines before the constellation of Desire in the Sign of the Lion this night; my son will need to be no less to deal with this damaged world." Julius believed this child was surely the fulfillment of the Oathmaster's prophecy, "Seek Gana in the spring of Julius Adan." *Did not Mordom foretell his birth in this century? Why, then, must this not be he?* Julius' mind shied away from Joab's commentary, "Born unknown, yet born to rule." *Ancient prophecies certainly distort with time...*

For the first time in long years of men, Julius, thirty-first adan of Tala, walked alone to the Temple of Kanaan-dora, knelt before the Living Statue of Gana and intoned a simple and humble prayer of thanksgiving.

~~~

Perhaps it is not altogether out of the bounds of convention to emphasize this passage. That was no ordinary statue Julius honored with his gratitude: the immortal shara Gana, poisoned by his sister's son Irnga, was sitting still, alive-dead-frozen, in the temple named in memory of Kanaan-dora. Long ago, all those that

Gana had loved lived full lives, aged and died; their children assumed their positions and prospered in the new world.

Eighty-two thousand years might appear a rather long time to be in a coma. But what is the passing of years to an immortal? If Gana cannot age and cannot die, why would it feel any different than a single night's rest?

Yet if this were truly the whole of his experience, what is to be made of the Oathmasters' prophecies of his imminent return? Perhaps it has not yet been made sufficiently clear that the Guardians of the One, the Oathmasters, lived such an exalted state of consciousness that the future was as an open scroll to them. No secrets of space or time were hidden from their eager, numinous minds. If they had unequivocally declared Gana was returning this very spring, you may be sure that it was so. What then of this Living Statue of Gana?

To solve this seemingly complex riddle, it might be worthwhile to consider this question: If an immortal sleeps, of what does he dream?

There is a great deal more to every Universe than most commonly understand. This will become more clear as this history unfolds. Our world is built of magic, not rocks.

Shouts of triumph and the pealing of bells were heard throughout Sulara as fleet messengers and swift ships were dispatched to all parts of the realm with the glad news. The messengers changed their mounts often and the sailors had bold winds, yet it was many weeks before all heard: even though slowly and painfully dying, Tala remained a vast and glorious nation.

It was a peculiarity of the age that the citizens of the furthest provinces rejoiced most in the birth of the Sun Prince. One reason for this was that the rumor of war was growing (no one knew why) in the border villages: small, nearly abandoned towns, once prosperous cities built close to the Burned Lands. Though the adan's men never entered the poisonous black desolation, the peasants whispered of a defeated tribe (no one knew which) growing stronger in a hidden fortress (no one knew where), vowing vengeance for their forefathers' defeat by the Reviver Balzor.

These rumors rarely reached the grandeur of the Golden City Sulara; no one there lay awake fearing the strange winds blowing across the barren ruin of Emura. Yet even so, there were in fact many throughout Tala who did not rejoice in the birth of an heir to Gana's line.

~~~

Such was the troubled world of the infant shara. But for many years, he enjoyed the best of Tala: Julius provided him with the most advanced instructors in every branch of knowledge and warfare. The Sun Prince showed a profound ability in all things, but especially in the martial arts. Even while still a boy, veteran soldiers could not stand against him with bow or sword. His strength drew from the deepest of wells: many were the bruised wrestlers of thrice his weight.

The people deified him: "Mars is without doubt the God of War! This shara is the Purifier foretold by the Oathmasters Mordom and Joab; he will carry us to the fulfillment of Rodavi's Vision, to the Golden Age of Peace. He alone will save us from the evil ones of our civilization." Most usually added after this a long list of all those who would surely be purged by Mars when he grew to manhood. It should not be particularly surprising to anyone of our modern world that the aggregate of the various lists condemned everyone of Tala to death and/or eternal damnation. Judgment is a bitterly sharp two-edged sword, is it not?

The Sun Prince waxed in power and lacked no thing, save the nearness of his parents: vital matters of state forever occupied his father; his mother had spent so much of her life's essence adorning the multitude of magnificent court functions that she died soon after the birth.

~~~

Now the dream becomes slightly more complex. A mere quarter hour before the shara Mars was born, there was another birth not far east of Sulara, that of a cowherd. The small hut of his parents was as modest as the palace Zephyra of the Adanai was ornate. Yet perhaps because of this very simplicity, none of the Golden City's problems visited there; no ashen cloud of troubles obscured the pure fire of love in his parents' uncomplicated hearts. Although no ringing of bells and cries of exultation proclaimed this, the birth of their only child, their joy was no less real; gratefully they thanked Almira for Her Divine Mercy.

As the baby lay in his mother's arms sleeping his first sleep, his father Sanel returned from proclaiming his gratitude to the stars. Kneeling beside the straw mat, he whispered, *"Naisan-auta.* This is your name, noble one, for you are a miracle of spring, a fresh breeze to our old age."

Sanel spoke the literal truth: this birth was highly unusual. Leora had many years before experienced her change: their last sad hopes for a child had long been dust.

But a year ago to the day, as they walked their high meadow, heard the rush of freshly reborn springs and rejoiced in the bursting forth of re-awakening life, once again the old longing welled up within her breast. As they sat among the tiny white star flowers and looked with love and sorrow over the re-beginning world, her tears flowed freely, marking her prayer for understanding.

Suddenly beside them appeared an old, gray-robed hermit, holding a small cloth-covered black parcel. His face and hands were deeply lined; what was left of his hair was completely colorless. But his eyes were saturated with joy; something about their depths expressed an almost superhuman wisdom. Leora looked up at him with shy curiosity but said nothing. Sanel, however, remembered him: he had seen him many years before, climbing through the high alpine meadows. It was rumored that this hermit lived alone in a cave farther up the mountain; perhaps the snow had only just melted enough so he could return to the world? Few in recent years had seen him; even fewer cared whether he lived still or had long ago died. Most said he was mad; some odd ones named him an Oathmaster like Mordom or Joab. No one knew where he had come from or why he lived where he did; one story was that he had always lived on the mountain and always would. He certainly looked no older today than he had those many years before...

As these thoughts raced through Sanel's mind, he stood rather clumsily, gave a half-bow and said, "`Welcome, descendant of the Sun! May the self-luminous peace of Rodavi's Way shine forever upon you and lead you in joy to Almira's World.`"

In a voice filled with life, quite surprising from his aged frame, the hermit answered, "`I honor the Sun in you! May the light and truth of Para dawn even here on Earth to guide us until Gana's return.`" It has been many years since last I heard that greeting, Sanel! I thank you for knowing it. But then, you remember much of Emura's knowledge, don't you? More, perhaps, than any other of Tala. A curious occupation for a cowherd, is it not?"

"Is it not?" echoed Sanel, somewhat confused. "I suppose it is. I have always been drawn to Joab's writings, as was my father before me and his father before him. I don't know why: I have never used anything I have learned. And I don't know why I spoke that to you now; it seemed somehow appropriate."

"It was. More than appropriate. It was, in fact, the third sign I have been seeking. I *know* now what must be."

The hermit unwrapped the black cloth he was carrying. In it lay the gem Starbha, as brilliant, glorious and wonderful now as it was on that long-ago day when Gana was poisoned. Leora and Sanel stared at the jewel in wonder. They could think of no suitable words, but both were asking themselves how the world could have been instantly transformed to become as they had long hoped and dreamed and prayed but never before dared believe.

Glad to see his assessment of the chosen pair was correct, the hermit chuckled softly and continued, "Before you have seen the moon reborn thirteen times, you will parent a boy child. He will be well marked in the eyes of God and of man: he will heal my Tala with his love and his sword. As symbol of the truth of my words, I have brought this gift to you. My requirements are four: Tell no one of Gana's Starbha, not even your closest friends. Leora, place the gem on your womb every evening until the baby is born. After the birth, hang Starbha around his neck on this golden chain. And Sanel, most important of all: *never* let him remove it for any reason whatsoever."

~~~

Sanel and Leora's son Naisan grew without the aid of formal education; the closest he came to entering Sulara was when he climbed the mountain to watch the final moments of the sun's ride and saw the many golden reflections from the spires and turrets of the capital in the far distance. Although he thought the City of the Adanai beautiful, he felt its evil and did not wish to go there. Thus whenever his father journeyed to the Golden City, Naisan refused to accompany him. Sanel wondered, but respected his son's desire.

Neither was the boy in the slightest fond of humanity: he told Sanel once, "They are not different from Sulara: outside, they are fair to look upon; inside, they are corrupt with decay." But Naisan loved the trees and flowers and laughing streams, and spent his days playing with the beasts and birds. No animal existed that did not love him, nor was there one that would refuse any of his commands. He was riding the elephants and lions before he could walk; even the giant eagles came to earth at his bidding and carried him wherever he willed.

All of this at first alarmed and then astounded his parents. "Who is this child of ours," they said to each other when he was still little more than a baby, "that the most vicious of the brute-folk pay him homage?"

Thus the boy matured in the wisdom that far transcends books; always was he watched and subtly instructed in the ways of the world. But his teacher did not show himself; Naisan did not know or even suspect the vigilant gray eyes that followed him everywhere.

6
The Lion's Wounds

Whosoever attempts the jungle
Without an experienced guide
Is apt to end his life in the belly of a tiger.
— Rodavi

Mars will be no stranger to pain.
— Mordom

Mars shall thrice die before leaving Tala to Peace.
— Joab

On a mild azure day, sixteen years after his birth, the shara Mars led a score of his closest friends from the city of his fathers. It was the last of a fortnight of sunny days: the lingering snow was gone, the sod again firm. A legion of scuttling fluffy clouds painted that a spring storm might soon descend with passion; but for now the young world was emerald, azure, dappled, beautiful.

The Sun Prince was mounted on a superb ivory mare named Victory after the stallion Balzor had ridden to the final battle of his Revival. A second reason for the name was a prophecy of Mordom's successor, the Oathmaster Joab: "Seated upon the broad back of Victory, Mars and Venus will enter Sulara to claim their ancient throne. Know then that the Four Years of Trial are upon you. Thus only will my Tala rise to the wisdom of Rodavi's Way, to the Golden Age of Peace."

This naming was not strictly vanity: in speed and endurance, Victory *was* very like the horses Gana had rescued from Martanda: none alive could outdistance her. Julius had felt her a suitable gift for his son's birthday — Mars was now a man! The sharas of Tala had bowed to their coming adan, the prophesied Purifier; Mars had felt the authority that was his and rejoiced.

Immediately outside the seventh gate, the shara dug his spurs into the mare's flanks. She burst forward with grace and power, quickly outdistancing the others. His ebony hair streaming behind him, Mars thought, *What pleasure, this spring wind! Someday, I will thus ride my Victory to battle, even as the Founder Balzor rode his Victory. What an unsurpassed joy that would be! To use my sword for something more valorous than humbling inept gladiators!*

He was deep in the forest and far ahead of his friends when his desire was answered: a massive force struck him from the mare. Bleeding from half a dozen claw wounds, the Sun Prince struggled to be free from the mauling lion. Victory, barely mastering her own terror, attacked the beast with her swift, sharp hooves. But it was the most unequal of matches: the lion stopped ruining Mars only long enough to destroy her.

For the first time in his life, Mars tasted doubt. Victory's sacrifice allowed him to stagger to his feet and draw his sword. But both arms were badly torn: like a kitten batting a ball, the lion ripped the blade from him, slashing him deeply across the chest.

Helpless now, with awareness rapidly fading, the shara knelt as the beast crouched for the final attack.

~~~

A low call rang through the air; the lion paused, then leaped over the Sun Prince and bounded off.

Through a blood-red fog, Mars saw a young cowherd approach Victory, lying motionless in a rapidly expanding sanguine pool.

The peasant touched her wounds tenderly, took a brilliant golden gem from inside his tunic and held it over her heart. Victory whinnied in surprise, then stood slowly on wobbly legs. She kicked once, amazed to be well, then knelt before the cowherd, placing her soft muzzle in his strong hands. He gazed long into her warm brown eyes and spoke to her in a sweet tonal tongue that deeply moved Mars' heart in spite of his raging pain.

"Who are you?" he whispered; the cowherd stood and walked over to stare down at him.

Mars' friends were nearby now, searching for him. Their shouts echoed gaily through the forest, "Mars? Where are you? Shara? What game is this? Mars! Show yourself!"

The peasant leaned over the Sun Prince and hissed, "If you hurt the mare again, I will send my lion back to finish his work on you. Fool! She deserves only love, never punishment. Don't you see she nearly died for you today, in spite of your cruelty? How can you be so blind?"

Three of the shara's friends came through the trees; the cowherd at once ran off, crying, "Your friend and a lion did not meet well! If you hurry, you may yet save his life. The mare, at least, is well." Then he was gone.

~~~

Fever racked Mars' body for days as he danced with death. Once, the physicians were sure he had died: his breath and heart stopped for a full hour. His spirit was for a time freed from its chains of clay: the shara had strange visions of a fantastic world of perfection where he possessed superhuman powers, a world from which he was violently thrown after failing to complete seven impossible tasks.

The Talans rejoiced when their Sun Prince returned to himself. But their exultation was premature: that particular lion was not so easily defeated, its claws had more deeply torn Mars' spirit than his flesh. The shara's pride, born of his effortless chain of victories and nourished by the masses' unthinking adulation, could remain dominant no longer. He had been defeated! Defeated! He, heir apparent of all Tala, descendant of the half-divine Solar Race of Gana, owed his life to another! To a cowherd at that, by the unlikely Myth of Kanaan-dora! A peasant! How could he have fallen so low?

As Mars' ego now lacked a supreme cohesive emotion, other, base desires began growing and ever more forcefully asserting their authority. He resisted at first, but the opportunities were endless. Within a year, his friends were numbered among the most vicious and destructive in Sulara.

Helplessly ensnared by the strangling coils of Tala's decline, Mars squandered his life in poisonous delight. Even so, he fought against himself: although he fell far, the light in him was not — could never be — utterly destroyed; at irregular intervals, it regained dominance. But such times came less and less often; the depths were ever more diabolical, ever more perverse.

Thus did five years pass. The good of Tala now feared his ascension to the throne, fast impending: Julius aged rapidly, witnessing his only son's sybaritic decay.

~~~

On his twenty-first birthday, the shara walked alone near Naisan's meadows. The day of the lion, Victory had discovered a different Lord: she no longer permitted anyone of Sulara to mount her. Disdaining to ride an inferior horse, the Sun Prince waited for her to mend. As she did not, Mars walked.

Today the light strove mightily in him. He dismissed his retinue and wandered far over the verdant spring earth. Kneeling beside a still pool, he stared into the clear water, warring inside.

What was the use of his gold, his palace, his servants? What difference that he could break a man's back with his bare arms? No one in Sulara could best him in battle. But what of that? For seven years he had seen no equal, no competition, no need to improve his skill. He was the greatest warrior since Balzor and he was bored! No, worse than bored, disgusted with life. The puny Talans worshipped him as if he truly were the God of War. Once that had seemed glorious, but now he hated the awe in their weak little eyes. There was no one worthy of his skill, no one to challenge, nothing to do! Why had he been born at such a preposterous time? Tala had seen only one minor insurrection in its fifteen centuries. He was a granite rock in a sea of mud! No wonder he drank too much, no wonder he found the soft thighs of women more appealing than affairs of state! Why was he here? Better far to have been the compeer of Balzor! Then there were at least real enemies, deeds to be done, a realm to conquer!

The Oathmasters had predicted he would purge Tala by fire and sword. But how? Must he invade every hearth and insist upon single combat? And why bother? What improvement if he murdered half the Talans? The survivors would be just as frivolous, just as disgustingly weak, just as useless. Would any of them be the least bit closer to understanding Rodavi's visions of the One?

Desperately frustrated, Mars struck hard at the water: the rainbow-colored fish swimming there were all too satisfied with their foolish fishy freedom. By the Myth of Gana, did none of the insipid Talans ever question *why?*

There was a sudden motion across the pond; Mars looked up, startled. An exceedingly lovely girl with long raven hair, dressed in the simple whites common among the peasants, stared at him; tears were flowing from her bright azure eyes.

Desire inflamed him; he leaped up. Too late! She ran away through the dark forest before he could splash through the pond and reach her.

Her track, at first easy to follow, vanished suddenly, leaving the Sun Prince perplexed and angry. He searched in widening circles, cursing, but found nothing.

The day was rapidly ending; the shara turned homeward, devising a particularly evil series of horrors for the arena as consolation. In the fading light, he failed to see the hidden root until he had tripped over it and fallen forward onto his hands. Before he could rise, something that felt like a mailed fist struck him from behind; his mind exploded in cascading spirals of sanguine and ebony.

The light of the setting sun playing through the spring-green leaves revealed the prophesied Purifier, the Undefeated Sun Prince Mars, lying senseless on the ground.

~~~

When the shara awoke, the sun was long gone. Thick clouds covered the waning moon and the stars; it was completely dark.

Mars sat up slowly, trying to collect his thoughts. It was difficult because of the raging pain in his back and head. He had known headaches before, more and more severely in his degenerating life, but this was something more — a wholly new kind of misery. His entire spine and skull were burning, screaming in unbearable agony. Holding his head, he sat unmoving for a long time.

Eventually the pain diminished slightly; he looked around and saw, higher yet not far off, the dance of firelight. He rose slowly and cautiously approached it.

Someone was sitting there, staring at the flames. He wore a plain gray woolen robe; the gentle saffron light revealed an ancient face. A faint memory stirred in the shara, *Help will come when you need it, even when least deserved, if you but allow it.* From where was that? He searched his mind.

It eluded him for a long moment, then came in a rush: after the lion, when he had those fantastic visions, one was very strong and remained long afterward. A gray-eyed sage (vaguely like this old hermit!) had ordered him to complete seven tasks and had warned him of — ? Of strength, that was it. No, it couldn't be strength. Why fear strength? That surely wasn't right. What, then? Although Mars looked deep in memory, the thread was lost.

"Are you going to stand there all night, or come warm yourself?"

The shara leaped backward, reaching for his sword, but it was gone! Never before had it been away from him! As his thoughts bent again toward violence, the old hermit chuckled, "I have waited long for you, my young shara. You can't be surprised?

Surely you realize everyone for leagues heard you coming. But I suppose the lions were not hungry enough to consider you worth their time; I am quite alone. Are you going to join me or not?"

The Sun Prince strode forward, saying imperiously, "I am Mars." It fell flat, however, even to his own ears. Had his approach to the fire really been so poor?

"Perhaps you are; perhaps you are indeed. Though in earlier times, titles were earned before they were bestowed. Well, our venial world changes. Sit, drink; this will remake you." He held up a wooden mug containing what looked like ale.

The shara was hardly familiar with commands from others. Yet after only a few minutes of strained silence, he really could see no other logical act. "Mars will sit," he said, taking the draught. Its sweetness surprised him, filled him with an unaccustomed feeling of wholesomeness. The pain drained from his head and back and did not return. "Tell me of yourself," he ordered the old man: the hermit's strangeness was arousing deep stirrings of a spurned past — ancient yearnings, lost memories, forgotten dreams.

The response was a full, rich laugh, almost incongruous with the time-withered body. "What is to tell? I was, I am, I will be. *You* are my present concern. Look here!" An image slowly formed in the fire. A gathering of — mourners! And on the deathbed —

"Father! How is it — What sorcery has — ?"

"Not sorcery: direct manipulation of natural law. Kanaandora's impeccable science has not yet altogether vanished from the world, you see. What is before you is real and current. An immeasurable pity! Your debased life finally breaks him. Sad thus to lose Julius Adan before his time: even though a mediocre Sun King, he was a good man."

A violent whirlpool sucked at Mars, not for the first time in many years of struggle and failure, but now by far with the most force: the hermit's ale was not without its subtle power. "Father... I never thought..."

The shara stared at the ground, journeying far into his mind. Then another impulse moved in him, not created or strengthened by the old man's drink. He straightened, a rather different light in his eyes. "So. The shara Mars is now to be Mars Adan — Sun King of all Tala!"

"Not so! Look again!" More images in the flames.

"Why, there I am, and — by the all-conscious sun! On Victory again at last! With that accursed beautiful sharan I saw today before me! Where — ?"

"Not so, not so again! Study yourself." The old man wiped his mouth to cover his smile. When had this Mars ever called one dressed as a peasant a sharan?

"It is certainly me! My cloth, my sword, my visage — but no! *No!* I see! Not me! What! Who! No, I remember! That cowherd of the lion! I did not remember how very alike... Where does he go! If he thinks —"

"He does not *think,* he *knows.* Naisan-auta will be crowned in your stead. As the Oathmaster said, `Seated upon the broad back of Victory, Mars and Venus will enter Sulara to claim their ancient throne.´ You haven't forgotten?"

The shara leaped up, clutching again for the missing sword, roaring, "Traitor! I forbid this! You! I!"

"Hrai! Down child! Silence!" Mars was pushed backward by an invisible hand. He struggled until his knees bent against his will. Then he collapsed, looking like a rag doll shara. Defiance raging in him, he tried to shout but found he could no longer even do that.

The hermit's voice was calmness incarnate. "Do you, Sun Prince? Do you, indeed? Can you see the alternative?"

As his anger gradually melted into despair, Mars watched war descend on Tala from the Burned Lands, his unprepared army defeated, himself tortured and perversely slain, his people brutally demeaned and enslaved.

"So. *She* told me truly, there is faint hope: you can still use those large brown eyes for something more important than undressing beautiful women. Destruction is the predestined future if this Mars reigns, shara. Does your vanity thus command you to be the last adan of a free Tala?"

Mars discovered he again had control of his tongue and said tiredly, "Why should I believe you?" He could not remember ever feeling more weak. This improbable evening had more than succeeded in its attempt to outdo this improbable day.

"There shall be no *proof.* You alone must decide. As must every human. All Truth comes from within, from the heart. But this much more I can tell you: when I saw Emura was doomed, I — "

"What? Are you insane? Emura fell *nineteen centuries* ago! If it ever existed at all. Yet you pretend — "

"Oh, Emura existed. And it was a brilliant, even a sublime civilization. Tala's histories are true: for more than eighty thousand years, the Burned Lands thrived with an industrious people, descended from Gana and Kartika and the ten thousand refugees from Kanaan-dora and Martanda. But the same demonic degeneration now destroying Tala eventually triumphed there." The hermit paused for a long moment, sighing, eyes half closed, floating in memory.

Mars was thoroughly lost. This hermit's words were impossible, mad, and yet — and yet, there was *something* remarkable about this self-styled relic of a bygone age; the Sun Prince was surprised to find he almost believed him. His escalating conflict began to affect his sense of balance: the ground began rolling under him in oceanic swells. Instantly, he felt seasick.

The old man continued at last, "When I learned beloved Emura was doomed, I, though a young man at the time, concluded we must ensure Gana's line. So I kidnapped Aharon — "

"Insanity! He thinks he's Joab!" But this protest was far weaker. The hermit's second mention of Gana abruptly transformed the shara's conflict: his awareness violently seethed as dark doubt warred with golden but tenuous belief. Terror thrust jagged spires through his wildly struggling mind; his only refuge was the old man's soft voice. But to believe him would give the victory to impossibility! His tale was absurd! Mad! And yet, and yet... *If only the ground would hold still...*

The hermit continued, ignoring the shara's complaint, "I kidnapped Aharon Hanif, the heir of the Solar Dynasty, your distant forebear. For seventeen generations I protected his line, until it regained the strength of its founder, Gana: Balzor was born.

"What you could not know were the facts left unrecorded: Balzor was but the cousin of the true heir. When his mother fled for her life across the Burned Lands, Alazar was crippled by radiation in the womb. But his twisted body was balanced by a profound clarity of mind: realizing fortune had favored us through the power of his cousin, he abdicated his right. Thus I announced Balzor as the Founder; Tala was born.

"The fortunate truth is this: Nagid Alazar's line has not failed either. I never again told them who they were, but I have held them to Rodavi's Way: generation after generation, I have kept them close to me, following the simple life of shepherds and cowherds in this small valley. They have therefore not become corrupt and weak as has your family."

Mars flushed under the hermit's steady gaze and hard words and looked down, but answered with contempt, "My people will never accept a cowherd as Sun King, even if this impossible insanity were true and he were descended from the rightful heir." The last defense of royalty had never before failed him.

The hermit sighed again and answered, "Probably true, shara, for they are grown dull of mind and cold of heart. But, we are not offering them a choice: you two were created identical. Further, I have long instructed him in your knowledge. No, Naisan-auta *will* be accepted. In *your* name."

Mars felt his wrath engulfing him again. But suddenly it broke and drained away, leaving him alone and afraid, a hurt child. Instead of further protest, he covered his face with his hands and moaned, "For so many years have I been divided, for so many years have I failed. Who can help me now?" His mind, molded by the years of absolute power, had rebelled; but his heart had gone out to the hermit: he knew him to be a man of knowledge and power, a living example of everything the Sun Prince had lost, demeaned or destroyed. He longed to accept him as teacher and friend, for he really had grown to believe this was in fact the Oathmaster Joab, miraculously preserved unchanged through the long centuries.

The hermit smiled warmly at him and answered gently, "It is not my task, Sun Prince. But you may one day rediscover your past, if your desire for truth is allowed to grow. You may not find it particularly easy. But what other challenge in your life has meaning? I have this important advice for you, remember it well: Be receptive to the good flowing to you always; never in pride rely solely on your own strength. If you but allow it, help will come when you need it, even when least deserved."

Mars jerked upright, gasping, as his recent life was thrown screaming into the void. One thought repeated, thundering over and over until it became a flood of absolute acceptance: *The words of the Oathmaster Rodavi in my visions. The exact words. The exact words!*

Standing slowly, the shara bowed stiffly, then knelt before Joab. Taking his aged hand, he looked up boldly into his gray eyes and said evenly, "Sir. What must I do?"

7
The Birthright

For those who know the One Immutable,
There are no doors closed in this world or the next.
— Rodavi

When Mars mounts Victory
Venus shall leave the heavens to praise him.
— Mordom

When Venus openly walks this earth again,
The One shall shine forth clearly through human hearts.
— Joab

A week before Mars came into the forest, Naisan sat at the same pool as would the Sun Prince and watched the rainbow-colored fish dance to please him.

The bushes across the water rustled; he looked up, startled: no animal had approached him unknown for many years. Standing there was a young woman, so sublime, so beautiful he could only stare at her like a helpless child, enraptured. Her royal azure eyes revealed depths of love he had never before encountered, nor had even believed existed. He could neither speak nor even think of any suitable words; but she laughed pleasantly and, walking around the pond, said in a low, sweet voice, "You may call me Venus." He threw himself at her feet, but she lifted him and said, "No! My Lord, as it is in our shining world, so for a season is it to be even here. Never have I been away from you: never shall I leave you."

As Naisan fell into her, he felt the world transforming in the brilliant spirals radiating from her heart, becoming a world of light, of love, of Truth, a world that reflected more and ever more of her native splendor, less and ever less of the mundane life of his past. Never had he dreamed such perfection could exist; never had he known such ecstasy; never had he experienced such a flawless union of joy and peace...

But that evening, he stood before Joab at his fire, protesting, "Why did you not warn me? And how has she come? And why? And why to me, ignorant child that I am? And how has she come? And what is this that she speaks of, dealings with humankind? Would she have me leave Alazar's forest? And what is that world visible around her? It is terrifying in its absolute glory! She is too far beyond the human for my soul to withstand! She will destroy me by her love! Save me, father! My heart bursts!"

The Oathmaster smiled up at him and answered, "Peace, my son. Your scattered thoughts are like the crimson and burnished leaves in the first gale of autumn. Sit, calm yourself."

Naisan quieted only slightly within his master's silence: his heart was painfully expanding from the pressure of Venus' presence; every premise structuring his mind was under assault. "Father, explain to me why she is here," he said as calmly as he could, then sat beside him.

"I called her here. There are several ceremonies in the tongue of Kanaan-dora —"

"You never taught me such!"

"Can a pond become an ocean in a decade? Can the sun be contained in the torch? You have learned everything needed for your reign; still more shall be given you. But everything, only after your victory in war. Doubt not, you are never alone: my love is with you always. And never fear; as I have preceded you from age to age, so will I forever. Trust in the order of life: I promise you, we shall rejoice together again beneath a new sun."

At the word, "reign," Naisan started; when the Oathmaster said, "war," he opened his mouth to protest. Finding no break, he instead dropped his eyes. Now he looked up sharply, ignoring the impossible memories his master's words were threatening to reveal and said, "Then explain to me sir! who Venus is. Or at least, who I am. Why should she come to one such as I?"

Joab laughed merrily, "To explain either of you properly would take so long Sulara would be ashes, Tala, a wasteland. But I will speak the needful.

"Because I have well taught, you have well learned of Tala's founder, Balzor. But what I have not told you is of his cousin, Alazar.

"Alazar was the true shara, the rightful heir of Gana's line. But while he was still in the womb, his mother Lenila was forced to flee the Asur Overlords across the Burned Lands. Alazar was born poisoned from radiation: deformed, crippled, hardly capable of speech. Even so, his mind was powerful and clear: his brilliant strategic skill was the immediate cause of Balzor's success in the rebellion that ended the slavery of the Fallen Years."

"The First Minister of Tala!" exclaimed Naisan, fascinated. Joab's tales were always full of the unexpected. The hunchbacked servant of Balzor was the true adan? What a novel twist to history!

"Alazar was. The point of the lesson is this: his line has not failed either. The true heirs to the throne have never again been told their heritage, but I have closely guided them through the centuries."

"I don't think I like where this is leading," said Naisan heavily, no longer fascinated.

"Nevertheless, I never speak untruth, as you know. *You,* Naisan-auta, are the heir to the throne of Tala. To answer your question more fully, I shall now describe each of your forebears, the descendants of the shara Alazar."

Naisan sat quietly through that long night, staring unseeing at his powerful hands as the Oathmaster slowly, thoroughly, majestically unfolded the shimmering tapestry of Tala's history. Each member of the Unknown Race of the Adanai (each of his own ancestors!) was placed as one more rock in a fieldstone wall, sealing him further and further away from the pastoral innocence of his childhood. And yet the firelight reflecting from the rapid flickering of his eyes within his half-opened eyelids showed his deathless master that the histories were opening him to ever larger and deeper passageways in his mind.

As the night gradually stilled into the expectant silence of the early pre-dawn, Naisan found himself trapped in the ordained role, trapped and yet almost content with his fate. A calm certainty swept through him; he looked up firmly into Joab's ancient eyes as the final words fell from the Oathmaster's lips, "You, being the only child of Sanel and Leora, are therefore the last of the descendants of Nagid Alazar, and are furthermore the embodiment of both branches of your grandsire's grandsire's line. Can there be a doubt that you are thus the true adan of Tala?"

Naisan did not hurry to break his silence: he wanted the quietness of the night and the darkness to speak for him. When he did begin, his words were well spaced, his emotions tightly controlled. "You know I have no choice but to accept this genealogy. Your memory is complete; I have no doubt you have personally watched over and subtly guided each one of my one hundred and seven ancestors. Therefore, I must accept your assertion that my birth is royal. But Joab! Father! I have no desire to reign! I am content — no, more than content — I am supremely happy to live in these cultivated fields and sylvan meadows and care for the creatures of the wild, the domesticated beasts, the joyous free ones of the air!"

"Nonetheless, child, you are the Purifier, the Complete Shara long ago foretold: `In spring, Gana will come again as Mars the Purifier, come again with Venus to re-establish Rodavi's Way.´ Spoken before the fall of Emura that was by my master, the unsurpassed rajanya Mordom."

"But *you* prophesied Mars and Venus would reign a scant five years before leaving this world! Are you cursing me to that short life? And what of the real Mars, already shara of Sulara? What will he care for my lineage? You surely don't expect him to stand aside and offer me the throne of his fathers? I don't even want it!" Was there no way to reason with him?

"Nonetheless, Naisan, you are going to be the next adan of Tala. Did you think I have so painstakingly instructed you of the court of Sulara for your idle pleasure? Why? Further, deep in your heart, you *know* this is what you wish! How many times have I seen you staring at the moonlight shining on the City of Gold? Did you think I would overlook your longing? No, my son, your half-known, half-denied prayer will soon be answered, and in a way that will fulfill the Oathmasters' words."

"But father, why? Can't you tell me? This is worse than a sentence of death to me! Humanity? They are so impure, so evil, so despicable!" Would no words touch Joab's heart?

"Naisan, Naisan! So much of your mind remains closed to you. You are at once more and less than you now think: life is both much simpler and infinitely more complex than you have yet experienced. The full range of the Universe is not just outside you, it is also inside you! And yet you are not even as permanent as any of the numberless grains of sand on the ocean's shore! You are one of the Four, the Deathless Dancer Gana himself, and yet your prized body is as ephemeral as a mirage! You are infinite, immortal, and yet your warm flesh is far more dead than alive. You are born in a night, breathe a handful of meaningless breaths and die with the dawn, yet your activity alone projects this complex Universe; your thought alone maintains it; your wish alone at the end of time will destroy it; your memory alone will re-begin it! Do you not find this incredible?"

Naisan, not wanting to understand him, gave up with a sigh and a question, "Venus?" If Joab insisted he was to be the adan of Tala, that was the end of it. He might as well try to change the moon into the sun as argue with him, once his mind was set.

"How can she be described? She is like you in that she is another of the Four, different from you in that she fully retains knowledge of this. She feels strongly for our small world: she witnessed its founding with Gana and will come again after the Downfall of Para to destroy it. She was together with you in the beginning and will be with you always. Love her and protect her well: your success is impossible apart from hers."

Joab chuckled quietly and added softly, mostly to himself, "So, for that matter, is your life."

~~~

As Naisan and Venus rode Victory through the silver-steel gates of Sulara, the heralds cried, "Mars returns! The Sun Prince is alive! The shara Mars! The shara returns!"

Forgetting for a time their sorrow for Julius, the people rejoiced: Mars had been missing for the better part of a fortnight. Those who saw him come were amazed: the golden jewel on his chest flashed brilliant aureate light that spoke more to the mind than the eye; the fragrance of the multi-hued garland around his neck was so sweet and penetrating that people two leagues away threw open their windows to fill their lungs greedily. But most wonderful of all was the young woman seated before him: although dressed in simple peasant white, she possessed a beauty that was absolute. Like perfectly coherent laser light, her glory was so unblemished as to make the mind attempt to see her imperfectly.

In less time than it took Victory to carry them to the palace, swift Rumor spread her wings over Sulara and sang that an immortal had come to Earth to save the shara from himself.

Naisan looked around with awe. *The golden avenues of Sulara, wider than any river! The ornately carved buildings of marble, studded throughout with priceless diamonds, emeralds and rubies! The fragrant orchards! The magnificent hanging gardens, luxurious with every kind of flower! The flawless statues, seeming almost to live! The showering fountains of gold and silver!*

Naisan did not permit himself to stare as much as he would have liked at the glorious complexity of the City of the Adanai.

But what he saw of its wondrous beauty convinced him the old tales spoke truly: Sulara was built for Balzor by the Lord of Etan, 'Ishtar.

The City of Gold was huge, but Joab's training was complete: there was nothing in Sulara Naisan could not name.

~~~

Dismounting before the seven-tiered palace Zephyra, Naisan said to Victory, "Go with our servant Alexander. He is stalwart and good, the best groom in my father's service. I will visit you when I can. Come, Venus, the adan needs us."

Because some nearby heard his words, the tale spread that the Oathmasters' prophecies were fulfilled: the goddess had come. This same fact caused measureless love in some, dark hatred in others. Thus the irreversible division began, the division predicted two thousand years before by Mordom, the division planned and encouraged by Joab since the founding of Tala.

Tears of joy ran unnoticed down the groom Alexander's face as he thought, *I did not know he even knew my name!* But as Naisan and Venus wound deeply into the heart of Zephyra, they left behind a long trail of ignored and highly insulted courtiers. Naisan's standards were not particularly similar to Mars'.

~~~

Only once were they forced to halt in their approach to the Sun King. A tall, middle-aged man, elegantly dressed in ebony satins, stepped from a dark passageway just outside Julius' bed-chamber. "So, Mars! You are to be adan at last." His subtly impassioned tone and the depths of self-centered pride shining in his eyes rippled a shudder of horror up Naisan's back.

"So it appears, Firad. Venus, you must now meet father's sister's husband, the shara of Urlad. An intimate companion for many years." Naisan could not match the intensity of Firad's gaze, instead let his eyes explore the magnificent statuary of the hall. Tala had had no shortage of extraordinary sculptors, that was clear.

Firad noticed the drift of Naisan's words but chose to make light of it. Pulling on the point of his neatly trimmed beard, he replied, "And to continue so, I trust. Charmed, my sharan. A more lovely one it is impossible to imagine. Will you grace the palace long?"

Venus neither looked at him nor made the slightest response. Deciding he could no longer avoid the moment, Naisan glanced in the general direction of Firad and filled the silence before it became quite unbearable, "Venus and I shall marry before our solar sphere Orah returns to his southern march, my — uncle."

"This spring? Then I salute my coming Sun Queen." His full bow was precise, impeccable in its sophistication. Others might be angered by strange silent insults, but he at least was sure of himself. He would charm his way into this rustic female heart.

But the female heart was unmoved: Venus continued to gaze only at Naisan. She might have been as much a statue as the others in the hall for all the movement she had made since Firad first appeared. Was she even breathing?

The shara of Urlad's bow was forced to continue well beyond his habit. What was wrong with the girl? Was she so thoroughly uncultured? He straightened slowly, stiffly, trying to control his anger. It would not do to be seen upset with Mars: far too much was at stake to fall out over a foolish maid. "Ah, my shara. Are you quite recovered? Join me tonight for the boar fight?"

"When has Mars appeared in better health, uncle? But those make cruel sport; I will no longer attend such. Indeed, many of this shara's habits may have changed since last you knew me. Much of my past seems nothing but the perversions of a cruel and deceitful child."

"Who could rejoice in this? Can the heir of Balzor be ruined so quickly by a mere woman?"

"You perceive Venus as human? I pray your perception will improve, Firad! A terrible fire comes to Tala; a relative of the Sun

Kings, nay! a descendant of the adan Falazan himself, should purify his innermost heart."

"The child instructs! If you no longer desire *me* for the sake of this, this — *peasant,* so be it. But never lecture me! Such talk is for simpletons only: there is no meaning here beyond what man creates." Calmly, Firad, calmly. Let the light of pure reason defeat this foolish infatuated boy.

"You consider the order of this world, the profound and beautiful harmony everywhere obvious, an accident of fate?"

"Only fools think it more! Man's will is the only truth I have seen in my fifty years. By force did Balzor create Tala! By force did Falazan crush the Solphglen Rebellion! This is the wisdom raising my people to their present unrivalled heights. You think your Zephyra ornate, your Sulara beautiful? Who could compare it to my pleasure gardens in Ixtor, my palace of Barafel! No, this childish fantasy aroused by your passionate devotion to this peasant maid is but another rendition of the illness crippling your father. Imagine! A Sun King dying at one hundred and one! The tombs of our forebears are troubled by the anguish of their rotting bones! Look to your grandsire Yamaya, boy! There was a true adan. Not a man in the whole of Tala dared speak evil of him from terror of his long hands. Is it not said, `From fear of Yamaya Adan, the sun did not scorch the Earth, the rivers did not flood the Earth, the rain fell on time, the people prospered?´ Study him well, you will succeed in life." Firad stopped, panting a little. Such logic could never be countered.

But Naisan did not share the initial beliefs and responded with deep-voiced power, "I have learned of the ways of Yamaya, Firad! I do not agree that his terrible acts inspired nature to be orderly, rather the decent and pure lives of the majority of his subjects. Is it not also said that Yamaya never studied Rodavi's Prophecies and did not know Joab's History itself predicted his death by the boar ten years into his second century? In his hundred and ten years, it is clear Yamaya never sought the root of the Seven and the Four: the One immutable beyond all creation."

"Do not speak such absurd mysticism! Not before me, Mars! Many have spoken of the One, many have wasted their lives seeking it, no one ever found it! It doesn't exist! It is as meaningless as the question, `What lies beyond the Burning Sea?´ And just as useful. How can that chimera compare with the practical wisdom of your grandsire?"

"You are wrong, uncle! The One is the root of every life, even yours! Only those addicted to power for the ego's sake alone cherish the memory of Yamaya!"

No longer capable of concealing his wrath, Firad gave a perfunctory half-bow and strode away. His hard metallic heels pounded a harsh staccato onto the marble flags of the corridor, matching the intensity of his thoughts, *So be it, my dear nephew Mars. So be it! Since you thus turn to weakness, I alone will save Tala! A scant half dozen stand between me and the throne of the Adanai. There is no significance in so few deaths. Fool! Within the week, you will be a tragic memory; within the year, I shall ascend your throne. But cautiously, Firad, cautiously: the name of the shara of Urlad must never be associated with the letting of royal blood...*

~~~

"On him, you waste your breath," said Venus softly, squeezing Naisan's hand. "He leaves now to plot your death."

"What!" exclaimed Naisan. "One argument unmakes his long friendship with Mars?"

"No, that emotion is not in Firad Dalgazor's galaxy, beloved. He is incurable. You needn't try to help those who refuse to change."

"But how can I so judge? The shara of Urlad seems not so different from any other here. Should I not offer myself to assist all equally?"

"Only those who come to you, Naisan. They will decide of their own free will. You need only be yourself. And be patient."

Naisan did not answer her. He was staring after Firad, thinking, *Does not everyone deserve life? What right have I to decide whom to help?*

~~~

Julius' bed-chamber was empty save for his seven physicians and the adan on his deathbed. The physicians were earnestly discussing whether to increase the medication or bleed him again. They started when they saw Naisan, then hastily bowed to him.

He ordered them away with a simple wave of his hand. But Teva, the chief physician, protested, "Your father has but moments left. You will drink the dregs of his life." Was not this dissolute shara the primary cause of the adan's premature death?

Venus laughed kindly and soothed his belabored heart, "Do not fear, beloved physician! Believe me: the presence of this Mars will only succor your friend and Lord Julius." For a long moment, Teva stared at her: he had heard fathomless depths of peace in the soft melody of her voice. Bowing again, he hastily left, fearful of causing her the slightest displeasure.

The Sun King looked very small and wan in his enormous indigo bed. The sparse light filtering through the heavily curtained windows could not disguise the fact that the radiant fire of his life had been all but extinguished.

Naisan and Venus walked softly toward him over the deep lambs wool rug, then leaned over him from opposite sides of the bed.

Naisan looked up at Venus suddenly, seeking strength. Smiling gently, she shook her sable hair at him, then brushed her fingers over Julius' lips.

The adan's eyes fluttered open; recognition formed slowly in their murky depths. "Ah... my Mars. The brave Sun Prince dawns. . . again. At day's end."

Taking a deep breath for courage, Naisan answered him, "Neither am I your son, nor is this the end of this song. Not now. Not, indeed, for a very long time." He held forth Starbha from his chest and moved his awareness into it; golden light beamed from the jewel to the adan's heart. Julius started violently; his eyes flew open; color raced back into his face.

"Why! I feel — I feel *alive!* How — ?"

"That can wait. You suffer now only from care for your Mars; of that disease, my words alone can heal you." Naisan, finding that his actions naturally reinforced each other so that they became progressively easier, told of the shara's vow to recover his meaning, of his quest, of the Oathmaster's sage counsel.

As he spoke, a soft light that had failed years before was reborn in the adan's eyes. When he heard of Joab, alive, he even laughed joyously and exclaimed, "Long have I prayed this was so! Did he not say, `Tala shall not fail to see me until my words are fulfilled?´ And if he could live through the fallen four centuries, why then not through the fifteen of Tala's glory?"

~~~

When the account of Mars ended, Julius said with strength and vibrant life, "Now, tell me of yourself! With face and voice so like my son's! And yet so much wiser. And tell me of this sharan, so like a goddess in radiance."

"Adan, this is Venus! The immortal evenstar herself, here to succor us in the hour of our vital need. And I... I am Naisan-auta, who is — who is naught but a cowherd." His eyes dropped, he paused, reddening, unable to continue.

But Venus laughed gaily and spoke in his stead, "Do not believe him, my adan! Naisan is his name and a peasant he was born, but he is in truth Mars, here to purge Tala by his love and by his sword. He does not fully understand this yet; nevertheless, it is his fate.

"There is more. Even the physical frame of this Naisan has a lineage. From modesty alone he fails to reveal it to you." She recounted the history of the crippled Alazar, of Joab's patient watch through the centuries, of Naisan's heritage and birthright.

A long and increasingly uncomfortable silence ensued.

Finally Julius, having realized his health was not exactly a free gift, pyramided his hands in his lap and said slowly, "I am much amazed by your words, fair sharan... His appearance, Gana's fabled gem Starbha on his breast... that garland of celestial flowers he wears... my recovery... your wondrous presence here... All these declare the truth of your tale. But... but I cannot in good faith to the Talans cede my throne without larger proofs than these."

Naisan, discovering a previously unknown but violent fire raging in his breast, asked harshly, "What, Adan?"

Julius, smiling widely and rubbing his hands together as eagerly as if he were a *very* hungry child with a *very* large hot fudge sundae within easy reach, answered, "Rodavi's prophetic works repeatedly mention `the One´ that lies beyond space and time. The One was the Oathmasters' greatest secret, the source of their wisdom and miraculous powers. Throughout history, they but rarely shared this mystery, never with the Solar Dynasty. If you are truly who you say, you should be able to teach me of this."

"Why should we do anything more?" asked Naisan curiously, his anger instantly transformed into surprise. Who else of Tala could have asked this question? "Was not healing your body more than enough?"

"Of what use health without knowledge! Of all the boons in creation, this alone I require to renounce my sovereignty."

"Very well," answered Naisan, shrugging slightly. "Beneath the ever-changing phenomena of existence lies the never-changing One. This Ascendant, this Absolute, this One immutable is the root of the power of the Seven, the seven deathless Oathmasters. It is the glory of the immortals, the Lords of Etan and the celestials. It is the essential reality of the Four, the four primary beings in creation: the Creator, the Grandfather; the Maintainer, the Dreamer

Narain; the Destroyer, the Dancer Gana; and the Mother of all, Almira.

"We revere the shara Gana of Kanaan-dora, founder of our Solar Race, as being an incarnation of the Cosmic Dancer Gana; we also believe his wife, the sharan Almira, was in truth a full incarnation of the Mother, Almira. But if they were or were not does not really matter; the point is that the One, the Ascendant, is the Source Universe from which everything and everyone springs. That is all."

"That is not all! So much was written by Rodavi! And Mordom! And Joab! And many other Oathmasters of Emura. It is not enough, it is not nearly enough — I want more! I want to see the One; I want to touch the One; I want to smell the One; I want to taste the One! I want to *know* the One, Naisan!"

"Such understanding has never been gained by the Solar Dynasty, Julius! Never in Emura, let alone Tala. Choose another boon, something more suitable to your life and times. If you wish, I could give you Joab's staff, cut by Solon himself from a single diamond before Kanaan-dora was founded. The diamond staff of the Oathmasters, Julius! Then you would possess true power. Or, I could discover for you the lost Crown of Emura, set with sixteen flawless rubies and formed of the serpent and lizard aegis of the house of Gana. What matchless wealth that is! I might even be able to produce the mate of Starbha: Kaysta, lost now for eighty-two thousand years. What greater treasure could there be in this world? But do not ask me to teach you of the One Unchanging. That may not be."

"Nothing, Naisan! Not power, not wealth, not precious treasures! Nothing else will satisfy me! If you desire me to call you Mars and give you my throne, this alone *must* be. I would not be the first: the Oathmaster Mordom, for example, was a shara."

"He was not! Mordom was a rajanya: his mother was a sharan, but his father a merchant. No purebred descendant of Gana has ever had the knowledge of the Ascendant."

"*You* do! Again I say, I will have no other payment! Deny me this and I will expose you!"

"This is blackmail! Choose another boon, adan! I will give you this garland I wear, made of the Everlast flowers of Venus' home world. You and those who love you will never grow older or even be sick as long as you wear it. Perfect health for you and yours for as long as you wish, adan! Think of that! What value the experience you seek compared to this?"

"You cannot dissuade me! Of what use immortality without knowledge of the One? I shall know this secret!"

"Choose again, adan! If it is knowledge you seek, ask me what lies beyond the Burning Sea, I will tell you. Ask me of any star in our galaxy, I will show you. Ask me to recount the entire history of man to you, I will do so gladly. Ask me any secret of time or space, I will reveal it to you. But do not ask me to teach you of the One. Don't you understand? It has never been given to the Solar Dynasty. Can't you see? Tala will be destroyed if you do not crown me!"

"Be that as it may, I don't care! I have waited all my life for this opportunity. If ever I have been just or kind or good, I now claim my reward! Teach me of the One immutable, the only quest of my father's that had any meaning. And then I shall joyously pass you my crown and throne that you may grapple with this sad world, if that is what you truly want."

Naisan looked up, deeply frustrated, and said, "Venus, what should I do? He is adamant."

She smiled gently at him and replied in singing tones, "The adan chooses as is his right, dearest love. Write history as you will! That is *your* birthright."

8
The Burned Lands

The one duty of man is to defeat the demon within.
— Rodavi

The path to Mars' second death will be razor thin,
Narrow cut between fathomless fear and endless terror.
— Mordom

Yet it will not be without joy.
— Joab

When the shara left Joab, he did not hurry: he was confused in mind and sore of heart. The Oathmaster had ordered him to pass through the Black Mountains west of the province of Urlad, cross the Burned Lands and seek the Ebony City Zared.

"And then?" Mars had asked, incredulous.

"Then, you will be told what to do. No more need now be said."

The Sun Prince thought this all odd in the extreme; nevertheless, he had agreed to try. But he had not realized how difficult it would be even to cross Tala. The loneliness was intense: never before had he traveled far without scores of retainers. But what made it unbearable was a simple thing, wholly predictable, yet wholly unexpected: no one bowed to him! Each time it did not happen it was a shock, an untenable insult.

Even though he *knew* in his heart of hearts he could not endure even one more look of disrespect, yet still, hour after hour, day after day, he proceeded doggedly westward. And as the days slowly grew into weeks and the weeks into months, a certain humility also slowly began growing in him. It was not a large advance, but the contrast the shara felt was certainly real.

Sometimes he was almost cheerful: this adventure was without doubt the noblest undertaking of any heir of the Solar Dynasty. Even if it were also the strangest...

~~~

It took the Sun Prince three full months to cross Tala, three months of wide detours around villages, three months of doubting his sanity for undertaking such a bizarre mission, three months of intense despair and loneliness.

Once, as he lay in a field of new wheat and stared sadly at the small white clouds racing overhead, a messenger from Sulara thundered by, the hooves of his ivory mare raising a large cloud of dust in witness to his passing. From the gold trappings on the horse and the messenger's sable satin sash, the shara learned the regal power had been transferred: a new adan now ruled in Sulara.

Clamping his jaw tightly on the blade of straw he was worrying, the Sun Prince rose with grim determination, dusted himself off, and continued on.

~~~

As soon as he left the fertile lands behind and started into the Black Mountains west of the province of Urlad, the shara felt invisible eyes watching his every move. He imagined challenges behind every boulder, unseen adversaries menacing him from every ravine. But he never saw anyone. Was it all only imagination? He found the pass where Joab had told him it would be; the shara Mars entered the Burned Lands.

The slag from the death of Emura was no longer as devoid of life as it had for centuries been: a low heath of sticker-bushes and hardy succulents was growing in many places. There was occasional water, not pleasant to taste, but adequate for life. Save for its unhindered vistas of nothing, it was not yet again a beautiful land. But the day was approaching when it would once more be fair and productive. When the Etan Lord Orah loosed his solar fires onto Emura, he had been quite specific: "For twenty-two centuries will you be desolate. Then again will my children enter and enjoy you; you will be greater than before." Of the entire northern world, only the small island of Tala had been spared the Etan's wrath, mostly because of Joab and the half-dozen treasures from Kanaan-dora he protected. Not the least of which, of course, was the statue-frozen body of Lord Gana.

What might lie beyond the pass? The Oathmaster's instructions were simple but vague. "Follow the setting sun," he had said, for "somewhere far away" lay Zared. But how far? Was it a week? A month?

It was by no accident that the Sun Prince had not been told his goal was quite close to Tala's eastern border, all but impossible to reach by traveling west. Since he did not know, Mars continued onward in that forbidding land, thinking, *What foolishness. Am I quite mad?*

~~~

Before three more days had passed, Mars *was* nearly insane. The feeling of being constantly watched had steadily increased; his days were tormented by doubt, his nights, sleepless from fear.

Shortly after dawn of the fourth day, Mars, finally convinced all was a plot to destroy him, turned back toward the east. That moment of defeat was exactly what had been long awaited: suddenly a wild-looking, black-dressed, raven-haired and carmine-skinned man appeared from nowhere and exclaimed, "Welcome, shara! You have been long expected."

"What! Are you really there!" shouted Mars, terrified.

"I am. Most assuredly. But I must confess to wondering if you are quite all here," the newcomer replied, a hint of a smile playing over his dark lips.

"Not here? Not here? Then where? But wherefore are you here, you ebony-robed barbarian? Are you aught but a bestial apparition in my madness?" Now how could he flee this demonic nightmare?

"Are you indeed aware you are mad? Then have you at long last begun to be sane; Joab's faith in you may be justified after all. Yes, I know the Oathmaster; I know you also, my dear Mars: this humble rajanya is today to serve as your guide. Once I was commonly known as Maitreya. But you could call me of late, `Delusion,´ particularly for the Lost. Or perhaps, `Damnation,´ for the Dead."

Chills of fear shivered along the shara's back. But his firm belief was that the best strategy in doubtful situations was to attack. "Whatever be your name, self-styled rajanya, stand off my path! Else you will join your forebears!" He drew his sword to underscore his words, but his heart whispered it was an empty threat: this infernal vision filled him with a dread that drained the strength from his arms, left him weak as a terrified child.

"Violence as always, eh, Sun Prince? Must you attempt to scorch all of creation? Well, be it as you desire. Let's see if you are better against my Nuriel than were your forebears." With a flourish of his velvety black robe, the rajanya Maitreya produced a huge sword. It reflected the early light with such brilliance that Mars wondered in a strange moment of pre-battle silence if its entire length were coated with diamond dust.

The shara swung powerfully, but Maitreya parried the stroke with ease, twisting his own blade enough to cause Mars' sword to fly ringing into the air.

As the Sun Prince ran after it, the rajanya leaned on Nuriel and roared with laughter. "Are they grown so puny in Sulara? To think the descendants of Lord Gana once stood against me for hours! I fear Joab may be in error after all."

Mars approached him more cautiously this time, regretting he had let the cowherd take his sword. Although this substitute had cost him two of his five rings, its balance was poor, its steel inferior. The Oathmaster had said it would make no difference if he carried a weapon, but he must not have known of this barbarian.

But then, how could this rajanya have learned of his journey? Well, no matter: no one had dared insult Mars' prowess before; let this fool learn the hard way who the Sun Prince was.

Mars' thrust was wide, Maitreya broke the skin on the shara's chest as response. Mars feinted forward, parried the counter, then spun quickly and thrust upward. His sword passed through the space where the rajanya's chest should have been, but encountered no resistance. The Sun Prince stopped in confusion, but Nuriel struck again, questing his heart. It took all Mars' agility to keep from being killed. As he stumbled backward, Maitreya pressed after him, swinging his long blade in mighty arcs that bent and battered Mars' sword as if tin were one of its principal alloys.

"Who — are — you!" The shara gasped, his vast strength barely saving his life.

"Not content with the last answer? Maybe you're asking that backwards: are you sure you know who you are?" One more swing at Mars and the shara's blade was again torn from his grip, taking with it much skin from both hands. Acknowledging the futility of this approach, Mars did not go after it. Maitreya sheathed Nuriel and grinned widely at him.

"What is that supposed to mean? I am Mars of the Solar Race of the Adanai, son of Julius of Gana's line of Emura and Kanaan-dora. That is who I am, you barbaric Rakshasa of the night."

Maitreya laughed uproariously, "You mouth words you do not believe or even begin to understand! What do you know of Emura or Kanaan-dora? Let alone the noblest shara Gana? What progress have you made in knowing Truth? Or understanding yourself? No, Sun Prince, the only important fact is this: you have been so slow in coming, our journey will be hard even by my standards. You must enter Zared by next summer's solstice." The rajanya immediately started westward, taking huge strides.

The shara stood sucking his knuckles and blinking after him. Short on other ideas, he retrieved his sword and ran to catch up.

~~~

Mars soon confirmed he was no longer the strongest man in his universe: the endurance of his guide made him seem a weakling by comparison.

The rajanya felt the best way to effect the cure was to beat the disease from him: he drove the Sun Prince mercilessly. They rested three or four hours at night, often only one or two, frequently not at all. Food and water were taken rarely, at dawn or when Maitreya decided to stop for the day. There were no respites, no conveniences, no comforts of any kind on this journey.

For the first week, the shara, loudly complaining, refused to cooperate. But the rajanya's stinging words never missed their mark; Mars continued on.

~~~

Throughout their months together, the Sun Prince longed to return to his people, his friends, his country. But only one of them knew where there was water in that wasteland: Mars realized after the first fortnight such wishes were futile dreams. His only hope for survival was to follow, trusting that his rough guide was indeed sane.

~~~

As soon as the shara stopped protesting, Maitreya began what soon proved to be a constant river of discourse about the lost civilization Emura. As the days stretched into weeks, Maitreya's words became more and more magical, more and more alive with power: Mars not only heard but experienced the magnificent splendor of Emura, her millennia-long decline, her terrible burning death from Orah's wrathful fire.

Over and over through the web of Emura's history the rajanya wove two recurring themes: the Solar Dynasty of the Adanai and the Oathmasters.

The Sun Kings of Emura were descendants of Gana and therefore maintained in their flesh direct contact with the original Solar Race — the sharas and sharans of Kanaan-dora. Their task was to wield the temporal power, which they did with greater and lesser skill throughout eighty thousand years.

The Oathmasters were masters of the One, the non-changing Ascendant Reality that underlies all of creation. Their task was to use their power and knowledge to guide the people into Rodavi's vision of a perfect future. The Adanai and the Oathmasters. The Oathmasters and the Adanai. Over and over and over again. Day after day, week after week, month after month. Would it never end?

Of the Sun Kings, the one mentioned most frequently was the last and most evil: Barlrin. No vice was too extreme for the last adan of Emura; no crime of injustice intolerable if even the faintest diversion for his jaded tastes could be mined from it. Compared to his life, Mars' dissolute past was as the frustrated petulance of a lonely child, crying for attention.

Of the Oathmasters, the one mentioned most frequently was the last and greatest: Mordom, a man like Maitreya in that he was a rajanya, the unusual product of a marriage between a sharan and a merchant, a man unlike Maitreya in that Mordom was the last and greatest of the Oathmasters of Emura. If ever an individual could possess enough personal power to deflect a degenerating civilization from its mad rush towards self-destruction, such a man was the rajanya Mordom. Or so Maitreya portrayed him, making the Oathmaster appear as superhuman as did the myths of the Talans. It was the nearly infinite tension between Barlrin and Mordom that choreographed the final dance in the ruin of Gana's high civilization.

"Better to die in truth than live in compromise," exclaimed Mordom as he was sent to his death in the Burning Sea. So all Tala's histories read. But when Maitreya repeated the words, there was a peculiar tone in his voice that made Mars almost believe the rajanya had actually been there, had actually watched the last Oathmaster laughing merrily at his impending death and defying the adan: "'Reveal where your son Aharon Hanif lies hidden? Is that the price of my life, Barlrin? Then again I answer you, mighty Sun King, I shall die before I oppose Joab's act.'"

The painfully blue sky! The deep clear turquoise of Emura's southern sea! The creaking of the unmanned rigging, set with full sail! The agonized wailing of the assembled thousands! The grim ebony-robed warriors and the grieving scarlet-robed Novitiate Oathmasters! The pompous pageantry of Emura's largest and most opposed state execution! The unconcerned smile of Mordom, chained alone to the ship carrying him to his death! His joyful laugh as the mooring ropes were axed! Smaller and smaller the golden sails as the last Oathmaster was carried southward to his doom...

Mars shook his head to regain the present: how could Maitreya's descriptions have such power? Mars *had* been there, he was certain of it. He had seen the execution of Mordom! Seen it as if he had been sitting in the chair of supreme authority, as if he had been the Sun King Barlrin!

Mars looked hard at Maitreya through narrowed eyelids. Who was this rajanya, really?

~~~

After nearly four months, as they struggled through deep sand and had been without water for three days, Maitreya abruptly stopped his histories of Emura and talked of the Fallen Years, of the founding of Tala, of the coming war. "I have become the Prophet of Zared, the Ebony City. It was not an enjoyable task, but it was my last but one in this world. The Zaredians are the descendants of the Asur Overlords of the Fallen Years. They are beyond all hope of repair, incapable of experiencing the One with their degenerated bodies. They must be destroyed, lest they further damage our world.

"For years, I have prophesied that an immortal will descend to them in human flesh, a god who will be their Sun King and lead them in war to conquer Tala. Next summer's solstice is the moment of my Incarnation Prophecy's fulfillment, therefore must witness you coming to Zared from the east. You must be a god by then, shara."

"Me? A god? Are you serious? How in the name of the seven planets of man — "

Maitreya roared his deep, rich laugh and replied, "I admit it very unlikely! But their prejudice will blind them. They know only of Talans who are farmers or fat merchants. You are a rather different breed of animal. And we may yet provide you with one or two improvements to speak eloquently of your divine status." He smiled broadly at the Sun Prince.

Mars stared back at him in disbelief: for a brief moment the rajanya separated into seven distinct individuals, each wearing a robe a different color of the rainbow, each handing him a gift of awesome power. *Rodavi!* thought the shara with great confusion. *Rodavi, can it be you?*

Mars stared at him in awe and asked, "What's going on, Maitreya? Am I dreaming all of this?"

Maitreya laughed again and answered, "What kind of a dream follows predictable and consistent laws, shara? The dreams we humans normally experience do not seem particularly consistent or predictable. Perhaps this is because we do not understand space on a large enough scale. Or perhaps it is because our view of time is too small. And yet the dream appears real, sometimes frightfully real, to the dreamer. Only by altering our definition of reality can we hope to escape from our self-created illusions.

"See the point? I have often told you this entire Universe is a cunning fantasy, a particularly involved dream. Why do you suppose you never asked me who is doing the dreaming?"

"I never thought it worth asking, I imagine."

"You never dared ask!" exclaimed Maitreya, grinning at him.

"All right!" scowled Mars. "I'm asking now. Who creates the illusion? Let me think. For such a universal dream to be, there must be two requirements: an immortal dreamer and a mind that understands everything of creation. So is it created by the Seven, the seven deathless Oathmasters? Or by the Four primary beings in the Universe, Narain, the Grandfather, Almira and Gana? Or, since the essential reality of the Seven and the Four is the One, could I not as easily say the creation is of one only? This is why we sometimes call our Universe, `Narain's Dream,´ I suppose. How am I doing?" He asked rather sheepishly, as Maitreya had practically doubled over with laughter.

When the rajanya could talk again, he exclaimed, "Words! You think they are so important! And yet you have not the faintest idea what they mean. Listen, shara: the ultimate truth of everyone is the One. Don't you see that every single human being is the dreamer! Even you, shara. We all create the Universe, everywhere, all the time, at each and every moment of the space-time continuum. You are surprised by this only because you think of yourself as limited by natural law and causation rather than as you truly are: one with the One, the Deathless Dancer himself. You are made of magic, yet believe you are made of dust. As you believe, so you are. Because this is true for everyone everywhere at all times, our world is always perfect."

"How can you so describe the world?" asked Mars, perplexed. "What of evil? Why do I go to Zared if not to foster the good and eliminate those who would destroy Tala?"

Maitreya replied sternly, "Don't confuse levels of Reality, shara! Evil is a creation of your present level of thinking, your current state of consciousness; it is one inevitable result of your beliefs in sin, error, problems, weakness, death. The simple and fortunate truth is that evil is a dream, simply an illusion: it does not exist except in the minds of those who believe in it. Because you don't yet understand this, you have no choice but to live this life.

"As long as you believe in the possibility of suffering, you will weep for the awful agony of this world. But as you evolve, as you consciously dis-create more and more of your false conclusions about life, you will learn more and more thoroughly it is your beliefs that are making your Universe so. *Your* judgments of good and evil, *your* acceptance of pain, *your* belief in suffering is creating your Universe as it is.

"*You* are the dreamer, shara! Wake up!"

Mars stared at him open-mouthed: for a brief moment the rajanya separated into seven distinct individuals, each wearing a robe a different color of the rainbow, each handing him a gift of awesome power. *Rodavi!* thought the shara with great confusion. *Rodavi, can it be you?*

Mars shook his head to clear it; the vision passed. Was it simply hallucination? Too little water for too long? No, they had just drunk, hadn't they? A sweet spring, before they were talking about — what were they just talking about? About dreaming, right? Dreaming? Why bother to talk about dreaming? That couldn't be it. No, the rajanya had just been telling him about his prophecies to Zared, right? Wasn't he?

Mars certainly wasn't thirsty now. His lips were moist, his throat quite comfortable, his body rapidly rehydrating, his skin pouch full. Shrugging, he ran to catch Maitreya, now far ahead.

~~~

As they climbed a steep ridge the next day, the snow-covered peaks of an extensive mountain range gradually became visible. The shara was surprised to hear an uncharacteristic concern in his guide's tone.

"Those are the Guardian Mountains, a southern extension of the range known as the Backbone of the World," said the rajanya slowly, weighing Mars with his glance.

"Due to their formidable height and the difficulty of crossing them," concluded the shara, mystified by Maitreya's subtle change in character. Was the desert journey beginning to wear on him? Never before had the rajanya evidenced the slightest fatigue, nothing other than superhuman strength and wisdom.

"No, although this is true." Maitreya sighed a little to see that Mars was still adamantly refusing to awaken. He concluded again there was no way to continue the cure without assistance and added, "There are only two passes. One is out of the question at this season; the other can be used for only six months. But it is an early winter, that route is treacherous at best."

"Why cross them? Don't they shrink to foothills farther to the south?"

"They do. But humans should never go that way: that is the land of the Danavas and the Asurs, the first step on the road to the Rakshasas."

"How evil can it be that you fear to go there?"

"It is not evil, not in the sense you mean it. Yet is its power such I doubt anyone could rescue you if ever you ventured there. Many have been the good lost there forever."

"Can there be another living area in this desolation other than Zared? How could it have survived Orah's wrath?"

"It did not. But its life is quite other than that gifted by the Etan Lord; it quickly regained its former existence. No, I do not relish talking of Danavas and Asurs, Sun Prince: that will only bend your path; our time is too short already. Were they to reach out for you, our hopes might crumble, even though Venus and Brihas are in conjunction before the Constellation of Life in the sign of the Crab these nights."

Maitreya stroked his extravagant beard for a few moments, re-analyzing. Not discovering another solution, he added, "We may rue the time, but there is one you should meet — if he approves of it. Uchai-sravasa lived here long before men first came from Kanaan-dora; I do hope he will meet you! He is the last of the true Singers, the final Etan but one in this world."

"An Etan Lord? Here? How can he survive in this waste? How does he eat? Who cares for him?"

The full laugh of his guide was his first answer, an answer that continued for a very long time. Wiping the tears from his eyes, the rajanya continued at last, "You may yet again become the innocent child, shara! 'Sravasa lost the need for bodily nourishment while others of his family were still children, long before Martanda was lost to Valin, long before Swayam's paradise Etan was destroyed. As for caring for, that is a field of knowledge quite beyond your current capabilities. If you even succeed in seeing him, I would feel satisfied. If he likes you, that would be a good sign. But if he sings to you or tells you a tale, that would make the most outstanding good fortune imaginable. There could be no more significant event in a human life."

"But! How will he know if he likes me? Will he question me at length?" Mars had changed in these months. Perhaps it was because of Maitreya's living histories, perhaps simply because of the forcefulness of the rajanya's presence. Whatever the cause, the shara had grown extremely embarrassed about his past. He did not want it observed by anyone, no, not even with compassion.

"Ha! Such would hardly be necessary for Uchai-sravasa. At most, one word from you will suffice."

~~~

By mid-afternoon of the second day following, they reached a cleft in the igneous rocks which opened into a small cave. The floor was smooth, a kind of clear mica set in hexagons of basalt. On a ruby quartz platform near the far end of the cave was a full-sized sculpture of a man, apparently carved from pegmatite. Several large crystals sparkled in it oddly; for an instant, Mars thought it was alive.

The Sun Prince studied the cave carefully, but discovered nothing else. Disappointed, he looked at Maitreya and found he was staring at the statue. With a motion of his beard, the rajanya indicated he should do the same.

Mars stared until his eyes blurred, but could see nothing unusual about the sculpture other than the particularly wonderful art that had created it. Whose skill had formed it from the volcanic rock? What age had owned such craftsmen? Such a perfect representation of a young, muscular and beautiful body! The shara glanced again at Maitreya and found he had not moved at all. For a thoroughly strange moment, Mars thought he also had become a statue.

When Mars looked back at the pegmatite sculpture, he almost screamed: a man was there, staring at him. With judgment? Or simply curiosity? His body was that of a powerfully built twenty-five year old human, but the skin was faintly cerulean. His head was so magnificent as to beggar description: every perfect face the Sun Prince had ever seen would pale to a grotesque parody of life in this one's shadow. His luxurious golden curls swirled gently from side to side as he slowly moved his head to study the shara. His golden robe was luminous with its own self-contained radiance; it also almost seemed to have entered into life. After what seemed hours, the Etan said in the richest baritone Mars had ever heard, "Speak, young one."

"This is the greatest honor of my life, most excellent Lord. I am the Sun Prince Mars, the shara son of Julius, descendant of Gana's Solar Dynasty of Emura and Tala. Maitreya brought me here to meet the Etan Lord known as 'Sravasa. Might you be he?"

Deafening vibrations rumbled and rolled in waves. It took the shara some moments to realize it was laughter, coming this time from two sources. "You have fallen far, offspring of my adopted brother Gana. Yet are his virtues with you. A few unavoidable experiences more, they will manifest. You are a good human, no longer so very far from Rodavi's Way."

The rajanya sighed and sat down. Mars followed his example. Gathering his courage, he asked, "'Sravasa, what is your history? I have heard of the race of Etan only in myth and history before; Maitreya tells me you are a singer."

The Etan said nothing; Mars felt his cheeks reddening.

Several hours passed in silence as the sun set outside and the cave became completely dark. The rajanya and the Etan sat as if they were both made from stone, neither one making the slightest motion all evening. Mars tried to copy them, but found it impossible not to change position now and again. He dozed around midnight, but awoke when the crescent moon cleared the horizon. Again the Etan began to speak, this time in an extremely peculiar sing-song. Was it meant to be music? If so, it was so bizarre the Sun Prince could make nothing of it. Glancing at the rajanya, he found Maitreya was sitting even more erect, his full attention still on 'Sravasa.

The shara felt increasingly frustrated for several minutes. Suddenly the Etan raised his right hand; there was a cracking sound deep inside Mars' skull. His mind began drifting with 'Sravasa's vibrations, floating or expanding through space, carried by the long vowels and many soft consonants. Gradually the music became visual: nebulas and galaxies were created before his eyes. Titanic struggles erupted between nearly infinite forces; innumerable suns were destroyed in battles more vast than his strangest dreams. Enormously powerful beings cried for the deaths of their sons and daughters, the stars themselves. Evil forces were loosed then chained then freed again as the Universe expanded before him.

The pulsating rhythm of the Etan's song coalesced again and again into the extraordinary visions. Then the whole moving cosmos melted into a glorious golden radiance, extending to infinity in every direction. One step further Mars expanded, beyond the infinite light into the One, a formlessness that was the source and goal of both all light and all darkness. The shara at that moment knew he was everything; he knew he was everywhere; he understood everything; there was nothing, nothing! he could not do if he could only remember to desire it.

This too passed; only the One light that was more than light was left: limitless, unchanging, eternal, formless...

~~~

Beginning as a faint but distinct vibration, the Etan's voice broke the Ascendant into individual perceptions — the Universe as before. The words became more and more distinct until Mars perfectly understood their meaning. The tale became less rhythmical, less musical as 'Sravasa gradually recreated the shara's familiar world.

"The spheres were new and golden then, when Father Swayam walked alone. The mountains had not lost their wings, nor had the

World Tree grown. The waters were not flowing, nor had the oceans formed.

"Alone he walked, alone he sang, for thrice ten thousand years; in every world he wandered, the silver rains began, the rivers carved their channels, the fragrant grass danced the hills and plains in verdant life.

"Yet in the end, when all was done, he was still alone.

"Swayam-bhuva looked with loneliness through our now vibrantly living Universe and cried, `Mother! You bade me build this home! This garden have I made! Sculpted well, painted beautiful, created as you told me! Where then lies hidden the completion of my soul?´

"His desire slipped backward in his heart, turned his body to death and his mind to the silence of the One.

"An inverted impulse in the unformed pre-thought, and then! Before Swayam stood the Three: Almira, Narain and the Grandfather.

"Almira gave him a golden sphere; the Grandfather, the seed of the World Tree; Narain, the jewel Kaystarbha. Gazing at these for twenty-six years, Swayam did not breathe. The first instant of the twenty-seventh year, Shatarupa came from the sphere, cracking it in half; the upper part became the birds and insects, the lower, the beasts and fish.

"Thus having completed the task given him at his creation, Swayam built his paradise Etan on Martanda for Shatarupa; together they gave birth to a thousand and eleven sons and a thousand and ten daughters.

"The younger thousand and four sons married one thousand and four of their sisters; they have spread from the ruin of Etan throughout the galaxy.

"Older than the thousand and four was Bhishaj, the Physician. He married Althea, the Healer; together they roam the whole of creation, aiding all life.

"Orah, the Dancer, sixth eldest of the sons, married two of his sisters, Chavva, Life, and Leor, Light. Surrounded by countless thousands of their descendants, they rule still on our sun. The present human race is numbered among their children; the Solar Race of Kanaan-dora and the Adanai of Emura are among their most recent offspring.

"Krishanu, the Archer, Orah's twin, was killed eighty-two millennia ago when the planet-prison Martanda he guarded exploded. When Martanda was destroyed, sixteen of your starships fleeing the death of your home-world Kanaan-dora were incinerated along with seven millions of your people. Only one starship with ten thousand aboard survived to reach this new world. It was, however, a partially successful sacrifice: the Asur Emperor Valin has been imprisoned since that day. Without their Lord, the Asurs and Rakshasas are not so powerful as they once were. Considering the deplorable condition of your Solar Race, this is a rather fortunate fact, is it not?

"The three eldest daughters, Malinda, Mirabeth and Mirabel, the Weavers, devoted their lives to the service of the Grandfather and have remained single. These three spend their years weaving space and time into patterns of Ascension and Forgiveness. This is hard to put into your words, but their work is responsible for the feelings of creativity, inspiration, joy, praise, gratitude and love you humans experience.

"Three of the eldest sons, Saranyu-vanya, the Scientist, Lemuel-tamara, the Artist, and Yehokhanan-Ishtar, the Architect, helped humanity more directly until one-by-one they grew tired of your strange temporal whims. 'Vanya and 'Tamara live now on the single planet of the double sun today serving as our pole star. 'Ishtar remained here the longest; it was not until Tala's founder Balzor aged and died that he abandoned this world to wander the Universe alone.

"The eldest of the thousand and eleven, Uchai-sravasa, the Singer, is here before you. To fulfill Almira's request, he has promised to remain in these Guardian Mountains until the Downfall of Para.

"Thus have I answered your query, shara.

"Now you two children should be going: a blizzard is coming; you will be hard pressed to cross the pass before it is upon you. If you require further assistance, Maitreya, the Vidyadhara Airavata is only a few hundred leagues farther north." So saying, the Etan's living form gradually stilled; soon the shara's eyes could again see nothing but stone.

Maitreya, standing in one fluid motion as if he were a puppet whose string had just been pulled, said cheerfully, "Coming?"

The storm broke on them with its full fury in mid-afternoon, well before they could reach the summit. They huddled together in a cave for two days while the blizzard raged. When it ended, the shara saw it would be difficult if not impossible to journey on: the snow was well over their heads; the rough trail was invisible.

The rajanya stretched his hands toward the north and called in a low voice, "Heramann! Airavata!" His resonating echo continued away and ever away, far beyond any logical physical limits.

Mars looked at him curiously but said, "Maitreya, why have you stopped talking to me? Every time I have spoken to you since the Etan's cave you have answered in monosyllables at best. Are you angry with me? Have I failed you in some way? If so, please tell me; I cannot progress without your assistance."

"What do you remember of your experience with the Etan?" asked Maitreya quietly, staring still out over the blindingly white world.

"Funny you should ask. I have been trying to understand exactly what 'Sravasa said to me. I remember almost nothing. He told me of some of his brothers and sisters, that much I know. The ruler of our sun, Orah; Krishanu, the Etan Lord who died on Martanda to free Gana and the ten thousand of Kanaan-dora; 'Ishtar; some others. Oh, and he sang about the first Lords of Etan,

Swayam and Shatarupa, the deathless mother and father of all the rest. That's all I remember."

"You recall nothing of wordless experience, light without form, infinite space?" Maitreya turned to stare at him. There was a strange, almost insane look in the rajanya's eyes.

Mars shuddered and answered, "Nothing. Was it important?"

"Important?" laughed Maitreya wildly. "Important? Far beyond important, shara. That was the only significant event in your short life! You will never again be the same, having once experienced the absolute One. It is the fundamental truth hidden behind the surface of everyone's mind, including yours. Beneath all the moving waves of thoughts, judgments and perceptions lies the eternally still Ascendant, the One. That is the root of your being, Sun Prince, even if now you refuse to remember."

"I don't understand you!" cried Mars, incensed. "What do you mean, I `refuse to remember?´ I told you everything I recall. Why do you torment me?"

"Who could forget the One without conscious choice? Your mind is so filled with useless dreams and false beliefs you cannot remember even the simplest reality." Maitreya grinned widely at him, thoroughly enjoying the shara's mounting wrath.

"You utter fool!" screamed Mars. "What right have you — "

The rajanya suddenly leapt across the four strides that separated them and, striking the shara with full force on his chest, shouted, "Hrai!"

Mars' protest abruptly ended as his mind re-opened to itself. He floated again inside the formless infinity the Etan had revealed to him. Only this time, his eyes were still open, reporting to him Maitreya's hirsute smiling face, not a hand's breadth from his own. How could his mind be experiencing two things at once? It made no sense.

There was a strange background noise that seemed to be coming from very far away and yet was in some way related to Maitreya's highly amused face; in another moment, Mars realized it was the rajanya's wildly guffawing laughter. "I don't understand — " he began, but then stopped in confusion, for his own voice sounded equally distant, as if his words were coming from the other side of the valley.

"Of course you do," retorted Maitreya. "But you don't want to believe it. Now we begin your real training. This world you see with your eyes is a dream, shara, nothing more. The only truth is that which you are now experiencing: infinite, always the same, never-changing formlessness beyond all light and all darkness. That is your one true Self. The other self, the one in which you so adamantly believe, is nothing but a particularly cunning lie, created by your dreaming ego."

"I don't understand!" exclaimed Mars, frightened by the hugeness filling his mind. "What do you mean? The world is real. I am real. You are real. What are you saying?"

"There can be only one ultimate Truth, shara. One or the other *must* be a lie. Either the infinite never-changing One or the finite ever-changing world is false.

"You think you understand your Universe. You think you are the heir-apparent of Tala, son of Julius, descendant of Gana. And you think you know exactly what that means. But you have already met several who do not fit into your neat little highly-structured world. Joab. Myself. 'Sravasa. Think, Mars! How could Joab have lived for nearly two thousand years? Even the most cautious of your forebears never saw their fourth century. How could a few words from the Etan have given you this experience? How could I have re-begun it by simply striking your breastbone? Can't you accept, even for an instant, that your world of space and time is only an illusion? A particularly odd dream? You have created it by your beliefs; you maintain it by your continual judgments; you will end it when you no longer accept its reality! Wake up, Mars! The Universe will be yours to do with as you wish if you but understand this for an instant. There are no boundaries for you except those you have created in your past insanity and are fighting madly to maintain."

"I don't understand you!" cried Mars in rising fear. "What have you done to my mind? I don't like this!"

At that moment, the Vidyadhara Heramann in his emerald and gold lizard-like form hopped into the cave; Mars shouted in terror, "What! Who! Maitreya!"

The rajanya laughed uproariously and said, "Airavata! What took you so long? You are most welcome." He embraced the Vidyadhara, lifting him fully off the ground. Heramann's tail thrashed viciously from side to side in angry protest; Maitreya chuckled and let him down. The Vidyadhara responded with a curt nod as the rajanya continued, "Airavata, I want you to meet a descendant of Gana. He is the most unusual Sun Prince I have ever known: Uchai-sravasa gifted him a tale of the Lords of Etan *and* a song of the One."

"Hrai? Most extraordinary. Greetings, human. In honor of your forebear, my murdered friend, you may also call me Heramann."

The Vidyadhara's voice was soothing, gentle, very like a cat's purr. Mars, mostly still experiencing the infinite One, had ended his fear by concluding he was asleep and dreaming; he answered lightly, "I am honored, ah, Heramann. I am the shara Mars, son of Julius and Ambarina, thirty-second in descent from Balzor, the Founder of Tala. Would you be offended if I asked you of yourself? Never have I even heard of such as you. These Burned Lands are indeed filled with marvels." What a perfect dream. It seemed so real.

Heramann chuckled, "There is little to say. I am as you see me. I am a — perhaps the last in this world — Vidyadhara. Originally we were as the stars in the heavens, many millions enjoying love and laughter along the Watery Way. There was no aging for us, no sickness, no death. It seemed then we would live forever and spread to all worlds; in time we did create a wondrous civilization on fifteen planets of eleven suns.

"But Almira did not gift the Vidyadharas the ability to create more of our kind; as the millennia have passed, we have decreased in numbers. Many abandoned this world when the oceans began burning with the Rakshasas' fire; many entered the Long Ice and breathe no more, hoping to awaken at the End of Time, when all beings of our Universe are restored to knowledge of the One.

"We had dwindled to a few thousand when Gana and your other forebears came to Martanda. But we assisted them in the final war with Valin; after the Asur Emperor was defeated, we helped 'Ishtar build Gana the City of Coral, Emura's glorious Phedra, and Kartika the City of Silver, Calantha's lovely Galatea.

"A few of my kind may live still in this world, but I have not seen any in many centuries. If we remain on the others of our ancient worlds, I know not. Hrai! Perhaps the desire to share ice will come again; I will seek them out. But for now, I am content with my solitude."

"You can really travel to the stars?" asked Mars curiously. The Vidyadhara's words had quite thoroughly captivated him; he had forgotten his conclusion he was dreaming; he had forgotten the One; he had forgotten everything but his astonishment at this incredibly ancient being. Was every one of the old tales going to be proven understated? How could reality be so different than he had long believed?

"Hrai, he is a clever child, Maitreya. Many things I can do, descendant of my poisoned friend Gana. Tomorrow, for example, I shall help you around the land of the Danavas and the Asurs."

"What? How could you help us through this deep snow?" What a curious thought! He was so very small!

"Such puny drifts are no barrier to those with knowledge of the One, Sun Prince. Which fact does make the rajanya calling me here seem rather ludicrous. Well, his true purpose will doubtless become clear in time.

"Maitreya, you woke me at a most inconvenient moment. And this conversation has dragged on too long. I will say good night now. Good night." The Vidyadhara hopped out of the cave and dove into a snow bank, from where a soft snoring was immediately heard.

"Well," said Mars. "Well."

"Well, you were saying?" asked the rajanya, grinning widely at him.

Mars looked at him blankly, as usual remembering nothing.

Heramann, shaking the snow off his scales, greeted them cheerfully at dawn, then laughingly asked, "Ready, young one?"

"Ready for what?" responded the shara with rancor. "If we two cannot leave here, I fail to see how one of your size can do us much good."

"Hrai! Perhaps so for you, never for the other! If Maitreya has waited, it can only be because he desires my slight company. Is this not your mysterious intent, wielder of Nuriel?"

"Your intellect is as ever, Airavata," chuckled the rajanya as his large smile burst through his enormous beard. "I felt three might stand a better chance with the Danavas and the other delightful denizens of this part of the Burned Lands."

"That makes a most unusual way to approach the Ebony City Zared!" exclaimed Heramann, giving him a long and intense stare out of the corner of one of his emerald eyes.

"Without question! Yet it must be so: he chooses this path." Maitreya glanced at Mars to see how this assertion would affect him. The Sun Prince was staring at them vacantly: as always, he was doing his best not to understand. Shrugging, the rajanya continued, "Shall we go?"

"Which way?" asked Heramann, hoping for a less embarrassing alternative. "Yours or mine?"

"Mine, if you can bear it. Our shara still knows nothing of life. Although he of course believes quite firmly that he does."

"Be it so, Oathmaster. I honor your wisdom by reserving judgment. Climb aboard!" Suddenly, the Vidyadhara expanded enormously. As Mars looked up at him in awe, Heramann raised him gently and placed him on his right shoulder. The rajanya had already somehow scrambled onto his left.

"Now, Maitreya. You are sure about the direction, the necessity of this charade?" Heramann's voice was huge, rumbling like approaching thunder.

"Our Sun Prince is not whole, Airavata. Let us proceed; may Venus and Lord Brihas shine graciously on us all!"

Without further protest, the Vidyadhara carried them with huge strides over the pass into the Burned Lands on the western side of the Guardian Mountains.

~~~

After the shara talked himself out of his surprise, he began thoroughly enjoying this swinging ride. Feeling quite light-hearted, he sang a song from his childhood, centered on dragons.

Heramann guffawed and said icily, "So! The Vidyadharas *are* remembered by you newcomers. Though not very favorably! Devouring maidens, indeed! None of us ever took to animal slaughter, what to say of masticating our allies and sometime friends!"

"Oh! I am sorry; it is the only song I know about anyone like you. But Heramann, tell me — how was it you survived when Orah burned Emura?"

"I was not here! The forgetful nature of the human race had long bored me; I was at the time sleeping on the Polar Ice. The heat of the Etan Lord's wrath caused me to awaken, thinking it surely must be time's end. I have since roamed the world again, helping your folk on occasion, more often spending my days alone, singing the wonder of Almira, contemplating the glory of the One."

~~~

That night, Maitreya walked slowly in a wide circle around them, dragging the point of Nuriel through the dust. Mars thought this a most peculiar use for so magnificent a sword, but as the rajanya finished, a ring of fire shot up around them, so high it seemed to join together overhead. Mars felt oddly chilly in the sudden heat, but Heramann was not at all pleased: he shrank down to the size of the shara's boot. Mars stared at Maitreya with wonder, but received as response only an enigmatic reflection in the rajanya's dark eyes. Did that look mean these matters were too great for Mars to understand? Or did it mean he should know exactly what the rajanya was doing and was fooling himself by pretending that he didn't? Or something else entirely? Shaking his head to end the endless internal dialogue, the shara lay down and was quickly asleep. His body at least was grateful for another opportunity for a long rest.

~~~

A deafening roar awoke the Sun Prince in a cold sweat sometime after midnight — he had been dreaming of the lion's attack five and a half years before. An icy fear gripped him so powerfully he was afraid even to move, but the rajanya pulled him up and had him sit back-to-back with the Vidyadhara. Heramann was now as tall as Maitreya and looking very wary.

There was no further sound. Mars slowly calmed his heart and eventually drifted to sleep again. As soon as his mind stilled, the roar came again — from all sides as well as above and (he swore) below. It was not like the scream of an enraged lion, but was somehow more than sound: terror tore at all his senses; there was a responding violent pain in his lower abdomen. He clutched at his body and would have fallen forward, but Maitreya and Heramann held him in place.

There was a gigantic — *something* — visible behind the ring of fire. Again came the more-than-sound roar; the firelight flickered and died. In the abrupt darkness, all was chaos. Mars felt an utterly cold and slimy hand grasping his leg, pulling him from his companions. He tried to shout but had lost all control of his voice. *Help me!* he cried in his mind. *Help me, Maitreya!*

The rajanya leaped up, swinging Nuriel in a wide circle over their heads. Brilliant light sparked from its blade; Maitreya said in a stern but strangely muffled voice, "You cannot have him! Not now, never again! He has been touched by Uchai-sravasa!" In the sword's other-worldly light, Mars could see a gigantic but formless blackness leaning over them.

A huge, deeply carmine slit that might have served the monster for its mouth opened, revealing an intense infernal glare that subdued Nuriel's light. A ghastly cachinnation came bellowing from it and gradually transformed into words, "We shall see, Maitreya! Oh, how well we shall see!"

The formless presence vanished; Mars fell forward, holding his burning abdomen as the sanguine agony engulfed him. All was cold nothingness for a long time.

Once more that night, a deep pain wrenched through his body; the shara swam again to wakefulness.

Heramann and Maitreya were talking quietly in the soft moonlight as calmly as if nothing at all had happened. There were no fires anywhere; the disk of the galaxy shone clearly overhead in all its blazing majesty. Two planets, Venus and Brihas, were closely conjunct near the horizon. Everything was the representation of perfect peace. Had it all been a dream?

As the flow reversed and the dark oblivion claimed the Sun Prince once more, he heard the Vidyadhara ask, "Why do you think he's going to such bizarre lengths to stay so deeply asleep?"

"The larger the task, the larger the dream," Maitreya answered simply.

~~~

The three walked abreast the next day: Mars in the middle, Heramann (about as tall as the shara's knees) on his right, Maitreya on his left. The Sun Prince felt too dull to talk for many hours; the pain in his viscera remained severe. About noon, it began to lessen; he asked, "What was that?" Even the question caused the world to gray.

"It will be best not to discuss the Rakshasa, shara," responded the rajanya curtly, then launched a long lecture on Emura which could have been entitled, "Helpful Insights derived from the Life and Times of the Twenty-Second Sun King after Gana." Mars usually enjoyed such histories; today he heard none of it.

In mid-afternoon, the shara tried again, "Maitreya! What is the source of the Rakshasas? Where do they come from, what is their history? Are they related to the Lords of Etan, the Vidyadharas, or men? And I want to know more about the Danavas and the Asurs. I cannot resist these terrible dangers without knowledge."

The rajanya stopped walking to stare at him. Reaching the only available conclusion, he chuckled kindly, "You *are* stubborn, aren't you? Very well; if you insist. But not here." He led them up a small hill into the full sunlight, then told Mars to sit facing the west. Maitreya stared at the sun for a few minutes, sighed and said, "Mars, I want you to listen carefully to this history of Rakshasas, created especially for you. Now, Airavata."

The Vidyadhara swung his head sharply around and stared up at him. Why was this tale his? Seeing no obvious answer in those ebony eyes, he began slowly, "Hrai, shara. Listen well, as Maitreya bids you. There is a connection between Rakshasas and everyone. All beings have behind them a shadow, a sometimes formless and sometimes formed nothingness, visible whenever they face the light. But when there is darkness, this formless shadow expands and takes its larger shape as fear or despair or dark, glittering cruelty.

"This nothingness was long ago captured by Navril Hagar, the Asur Emperor Valin. He fed it into his infernal fires of Emptiness and created Salash and Pacshash and their common wife, Yakshin. From the eugenically engineered three of them have descended the entire Rakshasa race. The Rakshasas of this world live in the Burning Sea, which is certain death to all other living creatures, but journey forth at will to feed upon human energies. From the Day of Despair when Lord Gana was poisoned, their numbers have increased and are found everywhere in today's world. They remain still and forever humanity's worst enemies. As they are masters of travel through parallel dimensions, few even know of their ways. You have long tasted the gall of their perverse evil; Maitreya is not convinced you have yet conquered the Rakshasa who has had the strongest hold on you. Thus is he reluctant to talk about their race. He would prefer you not to move your attention that way, it will only serve to increase their power over you.

"The Asurs and the Danavas were descended from the Solar Race of Kanaan-dora. The Asurs fell the furthest — lusting power, they studied Valin's Emptiness and degenerated into a form and existence similar to the Rakshasas'. Extraordinary length of life and many remarkable powers are theirs, but the price they paid is horrible.

"The Danavas attempted to master the forces of nature, but never sought knowledge of the One; therefore their relative perfections only heralded their ruin. They live in a dream world now, in which there is no longer change or progress. Very rarely, one of the Seven enters there, but never much succeeds in touching them: their blindness chains them to a static, meaningless existence. They are contented but deeply asleep: all but dead in their artificial paradise."

The shara asked for a deeper understanding of the Seven, but the rajanya abruptly jumped up and hurried away. "Swiftly!" he called back to them. "You have filled this place with evil. We must be far from here by day's ending."

Maitreya had them begin the night back-to-back. He created the circle of fire as before, then sat and placed Nuriel across his knees. Heramann looked perfectly miserable but said nothing.

Mars wondered why the rajanya was so taciturn, almost sullen. *Why is Maitreya afraid to speak of our enemies? Don't I have the right to know what terrors I am facing? What other dark secrets is he withholding? Who is he really? The Vidyadhara called him,*

"Oathmaster." Was Heramann simply complimenting him, or has Maitreya concealed most of his past? Why? Yet how else could he so intimately know of Emura and my own forebears?

A strange and wonderful thought suddenly occurred to Mars. 'Sravasa had confirmed what Tala's histories recorded: the Founder Balzor was aided by a Lord of Etan, 'Ishtar. They were supposed to have been the closest of friends for many years. 'Ishtar not only taught Balzor enough of Etan's science to defeat the Asur Overlords, he built the Golden City Sulara for him. The histories said 'Ishtar's love was so great for Balzor he promised to grant him any knowledge save the secret of immortality itself. It was only when Balzor, growing feeble with age, at last requested this ultimate boon that the Etan abandoned his friend and Tala, or so the stories went. But no history recorded what happened to him after that! And even Uchai-sravasa had said nothing specific of his brother's current whereabouts. No, it was perfectly logical: Maitreya must be none other than 'Ishtar, from love returning to redeem a shara of Balzor's line!

"Maitreya!" Mars exclaimed with great excitement. "You told me before we met 'Sravasa that he was the last Etan but one in this world. Who is the other? Is it you?"

The rajanya stared at him with surprise. This was not a simple perversion caused by the Rakshasas! Who else was daring challenge Almira's will? Was it the Danavas? Or the Asurs? Mars was withdrawing from him! He was hardly still here at all! And yet — and yet, it was just possible this knowledge could be powerful enough to hold him. Or, failing that, at least angle his departure so they might — in time — rediscover him. It was a gamble, but there no longer appeared to be another choice.

"I am certainly not an Etan, shara. The simple truth is that you already know all about the other Etan Lord I mentioned, if you would but choose to remember.

"Do you recall a certain ancient building in Sulara, I think it is still called the Temple of Kanaan-dora?"

"I have visited there," answered Mars, disappointed. It had seemed such a splendid idea. "Why?" What possible relevance, this?

"What do you remember of it?"

"Not much. It is quite old, hemispherical, hollow, a virtually empty amphitheater made of gold. Inside, there is nothing but a large seed, said to have come from Kanaan-dora, and three statues: a white snake, a black lizard — no! A Vidyadhara! — and, holding them, a well-wrought sculpture of Gana, created by the Last Oathmaster of Emura, Mordom. That is all I can recall. Why?"

"You have listed all that is important, Sun Prince," answered Maitreya with a slightly crooked smile. "But I know for a fact Mordom was never a sculptor. In truth, that last is no statue — that magnificent statue is not stone; it is Gana himself!"

"What? That is impossible!" Instantly the vertigo Mars had experienced before Joab's fire returned, more intense than before. The world began wildly spinning around him in spirals of light, his last (and only) anchor, the rajanya's voice.

"The oldest stories are the truest, shara. Humankind is not native to this world. We settled here when our last home, the planet Kanaan-dora, was destroyed by the Seven.

"Unfortunately, before coming here, the seven million refugees from Kanaan-dora landed first on Martanda. Their large array of orbiting telescopes had discovered six temperate, water-based planets in nearby star systems; the Starlord and Gemstone Council voted for the fairest and closest, Martanda, not knowing who was chained there or understanding anything of the earlier history of humanity.

"The Oathmaster Rodavi and the shara Gana alone attempted to dissuade them, but they had no reasons other than the cryptic prophecies of the first Oathmaster, the founder of Kanaan-dora, the shara Solon. They were unanimously outvoted.

"But Rodavi and Gana were right, of course: the fair appearance of Martanda was a superb lie, created by the Asur

Emperor Valin. The landing of the refugees freed him from the prison the Lords of Etan had forged at the cost of their paradise Etan. Gana's wife Almira and almost all others of the Solar Race were captured, tortured and eventually murdered by Valin; only ten thousand of the refugees of Kanaan-dora escaped when Martanda exploded.

"Before their starship fled Martanda, Gana's nephew Irnga led his battalion across the Formless Sea of Emptiness and attacked Valin's Fortress. He was a rash youth, brilliant, but not subtle enough to war with the Asur Emperor. Valin permitted him the taste of victory: Irnga recaptured the two halves of the priceless Kaystarbha gem, Kaysta and Starbha, thereby giving Gana and his ten thousand the power to escape Martanda.

"But there was subtlety within subtlety. Valin knew Swayam and the Lords of Etan would destroy Martanda rather than let him remain free: he penetrated Irnga's heart and escaped the ruin of Martanda as his passenger.

"As soon as Martanda exploded, Valin emerged from Irnga and, gathering what was left of his Rakshasa armies to him, attacked the last starship. The Lords of Etan and the Vidyadharas joined with Gana in that interstellar battle for the fate of humanity.

"Lighting the Rakshasas' fire that girths this world was Valin's final act before his defeat: he hoped to escape the victorious forces of the One in the Burning Sea. But Airavata carried Gana after him into his lair; together they chained him again.

"The last battle forced the ten thousand to this Earth; they had no choice but to remain here. Thus Emura was founded in the northern hemisphere of this world simply because there was no longer an alternative. This is why they so named their civilization: `Emura´ means `Marooned´ in the tongue of Kanaan-dora.

"After Valin was defeated, Swayam and the Lords of Etan deemed the shara Gana worthy of immortality. In this way, they hoped to provide what was left of humanity with permanent stability in the form of an undying Sun Prince.

"But everyone made a crucial error: Valin had not entirely abandoned the shara Irnga. The portion of the Asur Emperor's spirit in Irnga's heart gradually took control of him. Within three years of Emura's founding, Irnga had fallen far enough to attempt the murder of his uncle.

"Gana had tasted Swayam's amrita and could not die. But neither could he anymore live: Irnga's poison of Emptiness wound itself into the genetic material of every cell in his body. Gana has remained in the heart of Sulara for all these millennia, statue-like, forgetful, dreaming long and strangely involved dreams of new worlds and lives."

~~~

Mars could hardly see through the jumbled confusion of colors and sounds engulfing him. What was happening to him? Why had Maitreya stopped talking? Where had they gone?

A little iridescent caterpillar with brilliant crimson eyes was crawling toward him through this miasmic fog of chaos. It reared up toward him as it came, offering stability as counterpoint to the world's violent insanity. Mars held out a finger toward it; the caterpillar grabbed him with its forelegs.

"No, shara!" shouted Maitreya and Airavata together, but too late: the caterpillar's jaws closed on the finger. Mars vanished with a small explosion.

The rajanya and the Vidyadhara stood blinking at the place where the Sun Prince had been sitting.

"Hrai," said Heramann.

"Damn," said Maitreya.

9
The Heart of Compassion

A simple task for one man
Can prove a living hell for another.
— Rodavi

It will not seem the same world
When Mars and Venus rule in Sulara.
— Mordom

By which he means:
Many time-honored beliefs will change.
— Joab

Three days after Naisan and Venus entered Sulara, the watch on the outer wall of the city detected a large and unexpected cavalry coming from the north. A message was at once sent to the palace Zephyra; the guard was called.

"Strange," commented the gatekeeper Aldis as he lowered the portcullis. "My desire opposes this act my duty demands. There must be three hundreds of them! Who are they? From where do they come?" His heart pounded an answer, but his mind refused to accept it. His pulse throbbing, he clutched the stone of the colonnade and stared over the approaching cavalry. His aged eyes misted with his dream.

"What must we do?" asked Kabil, captain of the archers gathering on the walls. His hair and temperament were fiery; the sight of the approaching cavalry filled him with rage. This challenge demanded immediate action! "Who are they?"

Aldis answered quietly, "Surely, Kabil, it is the Annunciation. In Emura, on the third day prior to the coronation, the Adanai returned to our world to honor the Sun Prince."

"You absurd dotard!" cried the captain, his anger intensifying. "Never in the history of Tala has there been such a miracle! You are impossibly senile. Why hasn't Julius' reply come?"

"I don't know," answered the old gatekeeper, abashed. Why had he uttered such foolishness to the captain? He didn't believe it himself. There must surely be a more reasonable explanation for this cavalry's unexpected appearance. "Let us hail them." He lifted the Horn of Emura. One of the few operable relics of the lost civilization, it made the voice sound harsh, but also many times louder. "Who are you? What is your purpose? Halt, identify!"

The response was immediate, thunderous, perfectly clear and yet not speech: even the deaf reported full comprehension of the words. "The Sun Kings of Emura! Open your Sulara!"

Some on the walls were struck dumb by these words; letting their bows fall, they stared vacantly into space. Others were infuriated; their eyes burning with rage, they twanged their bowstrings again and again. A few cried uncontrollably; two or three laughed hysterically; seven fainted. A quarter of the Talans were not in the least affected and stared with wide eyes at their fellow soldiers.

Aldis, cursing himself for doubting his heart, moved to open his portcullis. But Kabil, seeing treason, ordered his men to hold the gatekeeper.

Thirty seconds, a minute, again came the resonating command, "Open, open your city! We are the Adanai and Oathmasters of Emura, here for the Annunciation of the shara!"

Half the archers threw down their weapons; a few babbled in absolute terror; some knelt and prayed. A wrestling battle raged around Aldis and a few others desperately trying to open the gate.

A third time came the command, "Open! Open to the Sun Kings of Emura!" and Aldis' portcullis *melted* and collapsed. The cavalry entered.

A fifth of Kabil's men loosed their arrows upon his command. The points were vaporized; the shafts passed through the cavalry, doing no harm, and clattered onto the ground.

Again they fired, but these multiplied into wisps of vapor that the rising sun refracted into rainbow patterns of subtle-hued beauty.

The archers drew their arrows a third time, but just then Firad's son, the shara Dagora, raced to them from Zephyra on Victory, crying, "Stop! In the name of Julius, stop this madness! You fight a dream! They are the collective memory of the Sun Kings and Oathmasters of Emura!"

The first horseman, smiling with good humor, leaned toward him and said, "You alone lead us to the palace, child."

Every one of the hundred thousand of the Golden City gathered to watch this procession. First came Dagora on Victory, then in single file the cavalry. The few unmounted men and women who had also come from the north walked beside the horsemen on their left side.

Goddess Rumor raced among the crowds, speaking visions, truths, and lies, "Tala comes of age today. Thus begins the End of the World, the Downfall foretold by the greatest Oathmaster Rodavi. All the prophecies now come true. They will murder Julius. There will be a true adan again. They are here to bless the shara. Gana returns to claim his throne. Today re-begins Rodavi's Way. They will destroy us all."

Some felt fear, some anger, but most love for these invaders, especially for their leader. His deep azure eyes and shimmering silver robe gathered all eyes as witness to his extraordinary beauty. The magnificent opalescent gem on his chest, the un-hooded emerald and golden falcon on his left shoulder, the ivory snake coiling on his right, seemed the perfect complements to his authority: clarity, power, wisdom. His flowing dark hair was uncrowned, but every other rider wore a duplicate of the Crown of

Emura — sixteen flawless rubies set in the golden filigree of the crossed serpent and lizard aegis of the House of Gana. Each also bore a brilliant golden gem identical to Naisan's Starbha.

The cavalry halted before the Solar Palace Zephyra. The enormous oak doors engraved with the image of the seven-masted ship that carried Mordom to his death opened ponderously inward.

Julius came through them first. His gait was not merely sound but positively youthful: freedom from the responsibility of Tala together with his expanding experience of the One was acting on him like the nectar of immortality, Swayam's amrita. Sweet life was coursing through his veins like a young man's blood; more than half the lines had already vanished from his face. Concern for Mars was far from healed, but was no longer a raw open wound — it had become an occasionally throbbing scar. Even though his own son was being dispossessed for a peasant, this vision below was proving the correctness of his decision: this was the first Annunciation since the Fall of Emura! The cowherd must be what Venus claimed he was: true heir to the throne.

Julius stopped on the top stair, raised both arms in blessing to the Talans, then stepped aside to let all below see Naisan.

In deference to his successor, the adan was wearing a full length robe of deep royal purple. But Naisan was dressed in a brilliant golden mesh that reflected the sunlight with glittering glory. The Talans gasped to behold him; not a few believed then Mordom's prophecy, "In the spring of Julius Adan, Gana will return to you as Mars the Purifier."

Naisan was not as sure as his subjects. The past three days had been a torture as he had attempted to master his new world. The complex demands of being Mars were bad enough, but to be a newly reformed Mars! Meeting so many! Breaking old relationships while cultivating new without arousing suspicion! And yet — and yet, Naisan was exhilarated by his new life; something inside was telling him with great satisfaction he was no stranger to regal power. And those coming below were proving beyond question he was to be Sun King of all Tala, the first rightful adan since Joab kidnapped Barlrin's eldest son, Aharon Hanif. An Annunciation! Shivering with the raw excitement of youth and hope, Naisan stepped to the opposite side of the stair.

And now the Talans could see Venus, coming last through the palace doorway. Every eye was immediately enraptured by her beauty. She wore (as always) the simple white of the peasants, but it was infinitely complex: her white was composed of iridescence; she radiated her own subtle multi-hued light, resonating more to the deep inner knowing inside their hearts than to their physical eyes.

Venus was Light, was Truth, was Beauty, an immortal incarnated for a brief time on the stage of the human. Unlike the many who forget life is a drama, penned by mutual consent and acted for reasons usually not remembered nor even understood, Venus retained full knowledge of the reality of the One Unchanging beyond space and time. In every situation she was in perfect and complete control.

She took her position between Julius and Naisan and smiled peacefully at the assembled thousands. Raising a single graceful hand slowly, she beckoned the Annunciation forward.

The first horseman dismounted and climbed the stairs. Taking the opalescent jewel from his chest, he knelt before Venus and presented it to her with both hands. The falcon on his left shoulder stretched upward and, raising its wings, beat the air in salute to her. The serpent on his right shoulder gathered itself into a pyramided coil and bowed its head to her.

Smiling gently at them, Venus took the gem in her left hand and raised it aloft. Brilliant iridescent light radiated from it in discrete rays to every one of the Adanai. In an instant, the entire cavalry melted into light and flowed back into the jewel.

Again the gem flashed, this time in a single beam that penetrated Naisan's heart. He staggered backward, then fell to one knee. As his mind raced to understand the visions of the gem's power, he stood again slowly, almost clumsily, and said to no one in particular, "I *see!* I *remember !* "

Meanwhile, the jewel was rapidly fading, becoming as transparent as a thinning soap bubble on the verge of death. One final time it flashed, now to the twenty-seven unmounted men and women who had come from the North. Almost before the witnessing eyes had recovered from this final burst of light, the twenty-seven merged into one — into the living embodiment of Rodavi's tradition, into Joab.

The Oathmaster cried, "Thus your shara absorbs the virtues of the Solar Dynasty! Now re-begins the tradition of the Annunciation! Know this to be Mars incarnate, first true adan of Tala! No one who values life may oppose his will!" The diamond staff of the Oathmasters was suddenly in his hand, blazing with fierce radiance. Thirty-two of the assembled thousands screamed and clutched at their eyes: by their hard and unrelenting thoughts, they had been discovered no longer worthy of beholding Sulara.

~~~

Perhaps you can stretch your mind with me and remember watching this Annunciation in Sulara. The twenty-seven Oathmasters and the three hundred and seven Adanai of Emura were larger than life, glorious in their manifest wisdom and power. To see them passing by was as wonderful as if the world had suddenly become perfect. As the Sun Kings of Emura rode through Sulara, not a few of the witnessing thousands found their lives permanently transformed. Perhaps you were there? Perhaps you remember?

This vision of the Annunciation contains many clues to the nature of reality. Which was the illusion? The cavalry? Or the witnessing Talans? Or both? Is this book the record of a dream, created by a seeking mind, struggling to discover Truth in a Himalayan cave? Or is it the recording of an exact history?

The Oathmasters were united in their assertion that this Universe we believe real is a particularly involved illusion. But this does not change the fact dreams can seem quite frightening to the dreamer. Therefore, the only significant question in human life is, "How can I wake up?"

Life is a race between the knowledge of Truth and death. Dying while remaining asleep and dreaming loses. Only awakening while still alive makes human life worthwhile. To assist in this process is a noble task; it is the sole purpose of the Ishayas' Ascension; it is the sole purpose of this book.

But knowing this and doing this are two very different things, as Naisan is about to discover.

~~~

The day before the coronation, Naisan walked with Venus and Firad's son Dagora through the labyrinthine complexity of Zephyra's Enclosed Garden. During the Annunciation, Naisan had felt himself irreversibly opened to a different life, a different world. Always in Venus' presence, he felt something of the ideal Reality of the One, the essence of her spirit; but when the Adanai of Emura had joined with him, he had felt that he was actually there, in Para, in her supernal world of absolute light, in the heightened awareness of continual perception of the One. Part of that consummate reality was still with him now, two days later: his intuitive ability with humans was now as complete as it had been with the animals since his birth.

This made dealing with the Talans at once easier and greatly harder. Easier, because now he knew immediately what anyone around him was thinking and feeling. Harder, because he was not experienced enough to keep negative emotions in others from affecting him deeply. Thus yesterday, when his new friend began to be deeply troubled, Naisan experienced Dagora's feelings as a deep pain in his own heart. He had asked him to meet them here, in Zephyra's Enclosed Garden, to see if he could discover how he might be healed.

Dagora had come only begrudgingly, and had not spoken for over an hour. As they wandered through the lovely complexity of

Zephyra, Naisan and Venus respected his wish and also kept silence.

But when they neared a still pool in the heart of the garden, Venus said without preamble, "You must not hold such thoughts in your heart, Firad's son."

He looked at her with haunted eyes. She was so beautiful! She made the garden, magnificent in its own right, seem like paradise in the shadow of her person. Drinking courage from her perfect tranquility, he said to Naisan, "You are not Mars." It was not a tone of accusation, but of anguish.

"*What* did you say?" Naisan was too shocked to be afraid. *What did I do wrong? What word or gesture betrayed me? Joab assured me this would never happen! How could I have hoped to fool the shara's intimates! What can I do now?* Trying not to look thunderstruck, Naisan sat down clumsily on a marble bench ornately carved with lions. Venus settled down gracefully beside him, as if she were as weightless as a single feather.

Dagora remained standing, facing them with his hard expression firming his youthful face into an unpleasant caricature of itself. He crossed his arms over his chest and said fiercely, "At the bath yesterday, I saw! Mars was scarred from the lion, there across his chest. And there! And there! What did you do to him?" *What were the demands of fidelity? This Mars was so much a better than the old! What was he to do?*

"Joab gave him other tasks. Will you deny me?" *Why didn't I expect this? Why did the Oathmaster lie to me? Why wasn't I prepared? This is beyond terror.* Naisan clutched Starbha tightly with one hand and Venus' arm with the other but was too busy fighting the tightness in his chest to look at her.

"I — I don't know. My honor is... But father — his spies are everywhere. He will spread this tale. Many will believe. Should I join them?" He addressed this to Venus. She smiled unconcernedly back at him, as if they were discussing the scarlet and amber orchids by the bench. Why did she not feel his conflict? Or if she did, why did it not show on her lovely, tranquil face?

"Many may," answered Naisan, trying to sound cheerful. "But will you? If you stand beside me, I shall feel no fear." This was true. Dagora's loyalty was the essence of his strength, or so he felt now. How could he succeed without him? He glanced at Venus and found her smiling in gentle amusement! Were his problems so childish to her? Well, what could he expect? He withdrew his hand and stood. Her expression did not change in the slightest: she was the perfect master now; she was the perfect master always.

Dagora could neither answer him nor anymore look at either of them. Why was this horrible choice being forced upon him?

Naisan stared at him for a few moments, then sighed, "May time aid your decision." He walked away to hide his face.

Venus commented calmly to Dagora, "Never give the mind authority over the heart, young shara of Urlad."

Dagora turned his tortured eyes back to her and cried, "Why has this been revealed to me alone? I cannot bear it!"

Venus stroked one of the orchids near her feet and said to it, "You must, Firad's son. A precious boon of choice is yours. You must decide. As will, in time, everyone of Tala."

"Why do you demand this awful test?" She made no further answer, instead gently caressed the orchid. Dagora felt the tension mounting in his breast, becoming ever more impossible to resolve. "Why!" he asked again with greater anguish. She looked up sweetly at him and, shaking her head slowly, put one finger to her lips.

Suddenly the garden was filled with harsh shouts and the sound of battle. Following a timeless instant of loss and gain, Dagora ran to aid Naisan. Venus smiled to the orchid, joyful Dagora's heart had won.

Dagora found him fighting a dozen of the royal guard. He leapt into the combat, his sword swinging.

Naisan smiled to hear him defending his back. Grateful his first crisis was past, he channeled his energy through Starbha. The assassins collapsed, their bodies paralyzed.

Joab, looking rather like he had been sleeping nearby, came strolling over to them and said, "Not bad for a first attempt. A trifle larger force of discreation and you would have been spared the expense of public executions."

"They aren't to die!" exclaimed Naisan, shocked by the concept.

The Oathmaster answered with a large smile but a stern tone, "It is Tala's law."

"Then I change it! Banish them from Sulara. I will not kill anyone." Joab couldn't support such a barbaric custom! He went so far as to watch every footstep to avoid crushing insects! Kill humans? He couldn't be serious!

But the Oathmaster understood Naisan's need perfectly and answered firmly, "I do not approve this change in custom, child! Would you have attempts on the Solar Dynasty more frequently? Such a decision encourages this! They knew their fate. Why interfere?"

"No! I refuse to let men die! They are banished!" Naisan could no longer endure his master's presence. He stumbled away, shaking, deeply divided.

Dagora, discovering his own conflict now fully resolved, looked with tearful eyes at Joab, then followed his shara.

"Joab, he fails a third time," said Venus quietly as she joined the Oathmaster. "Is our Tala thus predestined to follow Emura? Were not his failures as Barlrin and Balzor enough to teach him this hard lesson?"

Joab smiled warmly at her and answered, "The challenge of forgiveness is forever the most subtle, Almira. The path turns still as he designed it, although he said this was one of the lower probabilities. Experience will prove a bitter curative. Let us not hinder Gana's hard labors with our own forgetfulness. What hope is there for humanity if we do not hold to the One through this Rakshasa-impregnated fog that eclipses Tala? How else can Gana free himself from Irnga's poison?"

~~~

The next morning, Naisan found Venus alone in the Enclosed Garden, sitting on the marble bench by the orchids. With great sorrow, he fell to his knees before her and sobbed, "I help no one! It would be better for me to return to the forest. There is nothing here for me. I am unworthy to be adan of Tala. Dagora was only the first — they will all turn against me. I *know* this! I can't be Mars. I want to help others, but I'm useless. Joab is wrong about me. I *am* just a cowherd. I only came to say good-bye. I can't do it, Venus! I'm not strong enough to be adan."

Venus smiled gently at him and motioned for him to sit beside her. She took his right hand in hers, looked warmly into his brown eyes, and said, "Listen to me, Naisan. Give me your undivided attention now; be clear. You have this upside-down. Forget about helping others. You cannot presume to know anything about how to help another until you know yourself. You can never be compassionate to others until you can be compassionate to yourself. It's not possible to love others until you love yourself! When you know who you are, then love, compassion and understanding will blossom in your heart.

"When you truly understand there is nothing outside yourself, then and only then can you love others. Until then, pay attention to who you are! Mind your own business, completely; withdraw from any idea of usefulness to others. And forget about needing Joab or me to help you do this! Learn to awaken joy within yourself without needing anyone or anything else. Become established in your own inner strength, Naisan! We can be helpful to you only after you realize you must heal yourself. This must be your continual, moment-by-moment desire!

"Even the least self-hatred destroys all love on the Earth and in the Universe. You must love yourself, because that is all that there is to love. You need to learn that you are the Ascendant, you are the One."

Naisan, searching deeply into her eyes, said, "I don't understand you, Venus. How could I work against love by living a simple life in Alazar's Forest? Wouldn't my stability and inner peace be more beneficial to the world than this farce Joab forces me to perform?"

"You must find your stability among the worldly, Naisan! Don't you see? Until you know yourself, you aren't even capable of knowing if another person exists. How can they accept you? How can they deny you? You can't be sure of anything. You are literally blind."

"How can I learn to see, Venus?" cried Naisan with anguish. "My heart aches at the thought of this labor. How can I learn to help others?"

"There are no eyes but the eyes of love, dearest heart. All other supposed seeing is simply wrong thinking. Love is your only business here. If someone denies you, you will return love to them when you realize everyone is only a part of yourself, a projection of an aspect of yourself. If someone denies you, it simply means that part of you needs love.

"This is the practical wisdom of how to love others. But it will not become practical for you until you know how to love all your parts, to become responsible to them, to own them, to admit that everything you see is a reflection of yourself. Everyone is a part of the One. And you are nothing other than the One. If you run away now, you will have to face this trial again and then again and then again until you master it. This world, this Tala, this Sulara, is your creation, Naisan! Love it, don't abandon it! You must learn to love all the fragmented pieces of yourself. Every person in Tala is an out-picturing of a part of your soul. Only this knowledge will bring you the peace you desire. Do you understand?"

"No, Venus. No, I truly don't. But I will study this until I do. For I believe in you — if you agree with Joab this must be, I will do my best to obey you. And pray I will one day understand."

~~~

At noon, the coronation took place as Joab commanded; the Crown of Emura discovered its rightful home on the head of Naisan. Most adored their Sun King Mars, for he seemed to all eyes to be possessed of the dignity and splendor of the Sun Kings of Emura. Yet those who were more fond of a weak Julius and a corrupt shara declared that the two myths appearing incarnate daily, Venus and Joab, were false. But in truth, no one who saw them was unmoved, either by unlimited love or unlimited hatred.

~~~

Soon after the coronation, there was a second celebration in Sulara: the adan married Venus in the Temple of Kanaan-dora. This choice of site was criticized by many: the temple was quite old and very small; it had long been abandoned for newer and larger cathedrals. Joab insisted, however: "It protects a priceless seed from Kanaan-dora and three sculptures from Emura: the Black Lizard, the White Snake, and the Living Statue of Gana. The Temple of Kanaan-dora must be renovated, preserved, always guarded. This is the greatest responsibility of Tala, its best reason for existing at all, don't you think?"

Naisan, distracted by other worries, answered him without understanding, "So be it."

~~~

With the union of Naisan and Venus, some murmured, "When has the Solar Dynasty married a peasant? What good can come of this?" But others loved her as Mother: unending love and compassion were there for any who sought it.

Joab, for his part, taught throughout Tala every day on the wisdom of Rodavi's Way, the upward ascending path of life toward the One.

Naisan did not know that he was himself of much assistance to the Talans: he was too busy struggling to master his desire to leave them and return to the forest. Nevertheless, his presence had a powerful effect, firstly because of the sweet balm of the garland of Everlast that had permeated the entire city, secondly because of the supernal power of the gem Starbha, visible to all the world for the first time in nineteen centuries, thirdly because of who he was.

As a result of these energies, a remarkable change swiftly occurred in the Golden City of the Adanai. Huge numbers of provincials, rough of manner yet pure of heart, began to move toward the Sun King, into Sulara. No one asked them to do so, but they were drawn as if by a magnet, to the extreme discomfort of many of the oldest and proudest families. The response was an equally massive exodus westward, to the province of Urlad, where Firad offered an aristocratic life-style in his capital, Ixtor. Thus by the end of the first year of Naisan's reign, Sulara was wholly transformed in character.

~~~

Unlimited was the joy of everyone in the heart of Tala when Mars Adan and Venus Adaran ruled in Sulara: no one was poor, no one was hungry, no one was sick, no one died. It was not possible to find a lane in the city without the sounds of laughter and singing. Happiness was the commonplace; sorrow was nowhere. Except, of course, hidden inside the warring heart of the Sun King.

There never before had been such a time in this world, but it was the merest foretaste of Rodavi's Age of Peace to come.

Perhaps you remember?

10
Dreams

I know not what could dispel this grief that slays me
Even were I to become Master of all the gods.
— Rodavi

Mars will re-unite this sundered world.
— Mordom

By which he means:
The Burning Sea will in that age reveal its secrets.
— Joab

Mars awoke in a field of crimson anemones and golden lupines. A gentle breeze ran its soft fingers through his hair; when had he felt so good, so at peace with himself and the world?

The shara wandered aimlessly for a while, deeply breathing the sweet air, enjoying the lovely, spring-time innocence of the meadow. Seeing a small castle's silver turrets not far away, he strolled leisurely toward it.

The Sun Prince forgot then remembered then forgot again his direction a dozen times as he walked there. He was continually distracted by the soft comeliness of the land. Everything captured his attention, nothing seemed any more important than anything else.

The castle was made of silver, entirely. It was quite clean and neat, utterly serene, but no one at all was there. Mars, at last growing tired of this solitary exploration, wandered outside again. As soon as he passed the portcullis, he saw a young dark-haired woman walking toward him. She was lovely in face and body, dressed in a bright scarlet silk that accentuated everything and disguised nothing, and had plaited a double chain of daisies in her hair.

"I am Avarsha," she laughed gaily. Taking him by the hand, she ran with him through the meadow to a small stream. Giving him the sweet water with her cupped palms, she said, "Now tell me! Who are you? Why have you come? Are you for me, or do you seek momentary and casual pleasure?"

"I would find indifference impossible toward you, fair one. As to why I came, or even my name, that I do not know."

"Then you *are* a gift from Bala! How delightful! And so handsome. With such a lovely jewel!" She touched the brilliant orange-red gem hanging from his neck, then laughed to see the many bright reflections dance over her body.

~~~

A very long time later, she said, "Now come with me! We must stand within the Silent Room to record my union." She rose, dressed and led him back toward her castle.

Before they crossed half the meadow, a roar defiled the tranquil air. Directly over their heads, a huge claw tore open a tiny cloud. Beyond the cloud was not blue sky but blackness! A second claw appeared in the rent; together they ripped the opening wider as if the cloud were not made of water vapor but canvas. Through the opening thus created flew a dragon, on its back a knight in shiny ebony armor.

"A 'Dhara!" screamed Avarsha, running toward her castle. Mars followed a few strides, then whirled and drew his sword.

The knight beamed a shaft of light toward him. With a cry of pain, the shara dropped the sword and turned to run after Avarsha. But the dragon swooped down, plucked him up, and carried him back toward the cloud with mighty strokes of its powerful wings.

As Avarsha peered through the lowered portcullis at her present being carried off, a single tear slid in loneliness over her immaculate saffron skin as she sighed, "Oh well, maybe tomorrow." Then she forgot Mars forever as her cloud healed itself.

~~~

The Sun Prince struggled as would a hare caught in the steel grip of an eagle. But noting the awesome height, he decided it prudent to stop. He realized then that although unyielding, the claws were not damaging him. There was a blank period as they passed through the cloud; then in a rush Mars remembered his name and past.

Looking back at Avarsha's land, he saw only a large silver bubble surrounded on all sides by the Burned Lands. A few other domes glittered here and there through the crystal clear, starlit night. *How could it be daylight inside, dark here?* he thought with wonder.

The knight was leaning over the dragon's wing, peering at him. His armor had disappeared; he looked now familiar. Then recognition flashed — "Maitreya!"

"Of course," the rajanya replied with a wry smile. "Ho, Airavata, hand him up, eh?"

The dragon bent a claw upward; Maitreya clasped the shara's arm. Mars scrambled up, crying, "Why did you take me from paradise?"

"That was certainly not anyone's heaven, shara! I am not surprised you thought it was, you are so chained to your peculiar ideas about your mind and body. No, you were enjoying wasting your time, but were in reality differently engaged. How shamefully you choose to forget everything that matters!"

Shaking his head to help clear it, Mars asked, "Is this truly Heramann?"

"Certainly," answered the Vidyadhara cheerfully. "Flying is my favorite pastime. As I told you, the only barriers in life are those we create for ourselves. But what *were* you doing there?"

Mars didn't answer, instead tried to organize his thoughts. What had happened? The last he remembered before the brief encounter with Avarsha was the ring of fire, created by the rajanya to protect them from, from a — ? a Rakshasa, that was it. Then there was the question of whether Maitreya was the second Etan, probably 'Ishtar, still living in this world. The rajanya had replied that he most certainly wasn't, that the other Etan was Gana himself! now become an unwilling statue in Sulara, in the Temple of Kanaan-dora. No, Maitreya couldn't have said that. That was clearly impossible. But the rajanya had said something about a statue in Sulara, and that had suddenly made Mars very, very sick, and then — ? And then he awoke without memory in Avarsha's hauntingly beautiful paradise. Why? How?

They landed far to the north and the east, in a valley high in the Guardian Mountains, in the fabled Vashti itself. It was verdant even in those days of ruin, well populated by beasts and birds: 'Ishtar had protected it from his brother's destruction of Emura. He had felt this small remnant of his Isolde Garden should be spared Orah's wrath.

Long before humanity settled our world, several hundred immortals led by Uchai-sravasa and Yehokhanan-Ishtar came here from the ruin of Etan. 'Ishtar, attempting to re-create the perfection of Etan on a planetary scale, played his architectural skills to their maximum by turning the entire world into a garden, which he named Isolde after the sharan he had loved and lost. The passing of long centuries eroded his work: by the time the Asur Emperor Valin fell before the armies of the One, the Isolde Garden had been deserted by all but half a dozen of 'Ishtar's closest friends. The others had one-by-one decided to move elsewhere in the galaxy and begin their own families and worlds. Control, even of the most beneficial kind, is eventually resented.

~~~

Mars scrambled down from Heramann and looked with wonder at the perfect order of the valley. It was as much beyond any garden of his experience as Venus was beyond any woman. He started off to explore its utter beauty, but Maitreya grasped his shoulder and said, "Wait, shara. Listen; try to understand. It took us five months to find you!"

"What? That's not possible! It was only a few hours!" Again his spirit was flooded by the chaotic vertigo of his last moments with them. Would the madness never end?

He had a febrile, hunted look that tore at Maitreya's heart. "No. I already told you: you have forgotten. It would have taken us far longer to find you but for that gem you wear. Tell me, where did you come by it? And how?" His ebony eyes bored into Mars' soul.

"Hmm? Kaysta?" Here at least was a familiar object, an anchor to still the mad whirling of the world. Familiar, but — yes, where *had* he found it? His brow wrinkled for a moment as he concentrated on the stone. A powerful stability radiated from it; the nauseous rolling of the world gradually stilled. The shara's eyes flashed suddenly. He smiled at the memory and answered, "Yes, of course! Joab! He gave it me."

Maitreya and Heramann exchanged frustrated glances, then the rajanya said, "Vashti is still protected? Our Sun Prince needs to rest."

The Vidyadhara stared at him and replied, "As far as I can see, it is safe, but why — ?"

"Rest? Whatever for? I've never felt better!" This was true: the gem had filled the shara with a wonderful feeling of strength. "We must not be late to Zared!"

"I don't think you will miss your appointed dawn, Sun Prince. But even if you did, there could be worse futures than one made by abandoning our plans. Finding you was among the hardest tasks I've ever faced; I'm not sure we've succeeded even yet. . . You see, my dear Mars, Joab gave you nothing but advice."

~~~

Before the morning birds began singing their tales to the awakening world, a shaking Sun Prince placed his trembling hand on the sleeping rajanya's shoulder. Maitreya sat up at once and peered at him through the darkness.

A little huskily, Mars told him he'd had a vivid nightmare. The shara was embarrassed about disturbing him, but Maitreya woke the Vidyadhara and said, "It begins, Airavata. Watch him closely now. Tell us, shara; leave out nothing, no matter how insignificant it seems."

Mars thought Maitreya's interest a trifle overdone; the rajanya must be humoring him. But in the gray light of predawn, he saw them both staring at him with deep concern, identical expressions on vastly dissimilar faces.

The shara swallowed, ran his muscular hand nervously through his dark hair, tried again without much success to calm his heart, and replied, "I was high in the air on a narrow — and somehow moving! — spiral pathway of bright metal, a luminous silver like your sword Nuriel. . . It was unbearably hot; foul-smelling steam drenched me, drained the strength from my limbs. Raging below was fire like I had never seen, never dreamed possible: terrible, black, bright-red, sanguine, a fearsome creation of the opposite of life, of Emptiness, of nothingness. Suddenly I was attacked by a score of enormous raven-like ogres with huge fangs! and vicious claws where there should have been hands! Oh! No offense, Heramann."

"None taken where none is intended, shara. Those of Rakshasa descent bear little other resemblance to the Vidyadharas."

"They were Rakshasas? This was real?" His heart began pounding at his chest as if it wished to break its walls and be free. He was both terrified and eager his dream might be true.

"Continue," said the rajanya so earnestly that Mars shivered in spite of the humid heat.

"Truth hides behind the surface of my dream? I looked ahead and saw in the furthest distance the soft light of a new land. My heart leapt boldly in my breast to see that wonderful glow; the moving silver spiral increased its speed in response to my feeling, carrying me beyond the attacking Rakshasas and their infernal fires of Emptiness.

"Next I was walking with two others, a young competent lady — no, a sharan! Her name was — Lila. And her father — the adan Yayati, the Lunar King of — of Calantha, that was it. What is Calantha? I don't know. How could this be true? Where else is there other than Tala?" Mars paused, searching far into his mind.

Finally he looked up, frustrated, and exclaimed, "Maitreya, I don't understand any of this! What other lands are there? But I remember so clearly! My dream seems as real as this beautiful Vashti! I don't understand!"

"Continue, shara. Don't analyze. Just remember your experience. It will be all right."

"If you say it is so, I will attempt to believe it is so. This Lunar Adan, this Yayati, was feeble, ill. Sometimes he leaned on me; sometimes I had to carry him. We walked a long time, fleeing the legions of — No! We were fleeing the adan's own son, the demonic Yadu! Now I remember: the throne was Lila's by right, but Yadu thrice attempted to murder both his father and his sister. Desperate and alone, they used the last of their power to send the Silver Spiral Bridge for assistance. How did it find me?

"I journeyed with them across the plains of Calantha, high into the mountains, seeking, seeking — another gap in my memory, Maitreya — seeking an Oathmaster, someone who looked like you, though he always wore a sky-blue robe. His name was Atri."

Heramann gasped. The rajanya quieted him with an icy glance and said firmly, "And then?"

Mars looked desperately from one to the other. Seeing no answers in either the ebony or the emerald eyes, he continued, "And then I was tightly holding this gem Kaysta, riding again on the beautiful moving pathway of the Silver Spiral Bridge, burned once more by the noxious scalding vapors, passing over the fires of Emptiness, surrounded by the attacking Rakshasas. This time it was infinitely worse, a horrible living hell. Once I reveled for warfare; after that experience, never again. My mind recoils from the unlimited terror of that passage: I cannot even think of it without longing for death to be free.

"That is all I remember. Maitreya! What does this mean? It makes no sense! There is no world but Tala's."

"Your time in that Danava's pleasure dome was but the very end of your missing months, shara. Master this memory! Thus only will you learn how you came by Kaysta. Go now, walk through Vashti, think only of this dream. Report to me tomorrow."

"But the Ebony City! My task! We are not abandoning it?" The shara was surprised how deeply he yearned to abandon it.

"Do not fear, Mars. Zared will have its prophesied god. But your path has changed. You have had aid from another, greater than I; you need time to remember. And understand."

~~~

As the shara left them, Heramann cocked his head to one side, looked up at Maitreya and said with deep concern, "Do you think this is wise, stirring experiences better forgotten? Even immortals have been destroyed by the Rakshasas. What hope can there be for humans?"

The rajanya noted the Vidyadhara's tone but was too ebullient to care. "Airavata! Don't you see? He passed to the South! He found the Silver Spiral Bridge and crossed the Burning Sea! He returned to us, did he not, with Kaysta of the Lunar Race? Though how he could do so and still be more or less sane is nothing short of miraculous. None but Joab and Atri have passed Valin's fire on the equator in millennia — surely Venus is right, this shara is Gana himself!"

But Heramann had intuited the strands of time as Maitreya was weaving them and ignored his facade. "Is he the object of my concern, grandson of 'Ishtar?"

"You don't approve of my means?" Maitreya's inflection was slightly amused; a broad smile threatened to break through his excessive beard. Airavata had again proven his wisdom. How could the Vidyadharas have become all but extinct?

"How could I judge you? But our poor world would sorely miss Atri's brother."

"Each life has limits, Airavata! Why bemoan this? My son needs me no longer; this shara will finish my work with Zared. What more would you have me do? I am not afraid to depart! What difference these illusions of life and death?   The One immutable is all that I am, all that I will ever be. Do not attempt to slow me with your sad words, old friend."

~~~

For many days, Mars walked throughout Vashti, searching his mind, yet grew little closer to the nightmare's meaning. Every night it repeated, rarely changing in any way. Soon, his boundaries of waking and dreaming began to blur: the scenes of the vision became clearer and stronger until they were almost more substantial than the world around him.

It was difficult to understand how it could be anything other than a dream: the world was all but dead; Orah's fires had left precious little life anywhere. The only exceptions he knew of were Tala, Zared, Vashti and the Danava pleasure domes. It was clear the Burned Lands no longer killed from radiation as they once had; but his dream of Calantha was of an incredibly ancient yet healthy civilization! Far older than Orah's destruction of Emura! Was it all, then, just a particularly odd dream? How could it be? The Lunar Adan Yayati, the sharan Lila, the Oathmaster Atri, they were all as real as — no, more real than his past in Sulara. Yet, how could they exist? And where? Across the Burning Sea? No one could cross that and live. But if not there, then where? And what was his relationship with them?

At times, the shara was quite sure he had fallen deeply in love with the beautiful, fragile Lila. He could remember the soft caress of her lovely ivory hands, the sweet touch of her crimson lips, the giving warmth of her embrace. How could he have left her unprotected? Why would he be such a fool? She was perfection, everything he had ever dreamed of in a woman. How could he abandon her? He loved her with all his heart! It was senseless, mad, cruel beyond all reason.

Then the feelings would pass; he would be left grappling with intangible shadows. Where was there meaning, where truth? What had happened during those missing months? Was this all a particularly convoluted lesson, created by the rajanya to prove that the world was essentially a dream? Maitreya had certainly tried to tell him again and again that the world was an illusion. But if this were so, why was it so hard for him to accept it?

~~~

One evening near the end of spring, Heramann came to the shara as he sat staring into the turbulent waters of the Boiling Lake at the heart of Vashti. Even though his scales were wide open to cool him, the Vidyadhara was extremely uncomfortable in the sweltering air. Mars, realizing only urgent necessity would bring his friend to such a sultry place, looked at him curiously, but waited for him to speak.

Heramann hopped back and forth uncomfortably from claw to claw for a few moments as if the ground were burning him. Finally, he said awkwardly, "Ah, shara! Scarcely three days remain before you must arrive at the Ebony City! If we do not leave within twenty-four hours, you will be late. We must go! Have you recaptured your memory yet?" He looked up at Mars with an innocence that tightened the shara's heart into an uncomfortable knot.

Before Mars could answer, Maitreya ran down toward them, exclaiming, "Airavata! Enough! Leave the Sun Prince. I promise you, he will rise for the prophesied dawn in Zared."

Heramann turned his lizard head slowly around toward the rajanya. A single tear welled in the corner of each eye, but did not fall. Shaking his head slightly, he said, "Be it so, old comrade. If you remain adamant in your game, who am I to argue? Farewell, friend of the Vidyadharas." Heramann transformed into his falcon form and flew toward the north.

Maitreya stared after him for a long minute with an obscure expression, then knelt beside Mars and said gruffly, "Airavata is correct, shara. I hoped you would have re-integrated by yourself. Now there is no more time: we *must* proceed. Kaysta is the only tool you require."

"Kaysta? You mean…I could have, at any time…" Why did the rajanya always want him to discover everything alone? Why couldn't he have told him that weeks ago? He picked up Kaysta and stared at it. A saffron haze flowed from the gem through Mars; he began to sink inward, to fall into a state closely resembling death.

Maitreya leaned toward him, searching deeply in his eyes, then began singing a classic tale of Joab as a young man.

> *Seventeen silver birds fly in rhythm*
> *Through springtime's innocent sky*
> *Collective memories of Kanaan-dora*
> *And the youth of humanity*
> *Slumbering wanderlust*
> *Of my guarded heart's jewel chamber*
> *Fragrant silence, sleeping desire*
> *Broken! by an Eastern wind of hate*
> *Roiling across the barren deserts of Emura*
> *Strange furtive creatures of sand*
> *Scurry from shade to shade*
>
> *Sighing, I rose to seek*
> *The fireberries of Kartika's Uttermost South*
> *Growing in lost Calantha*
> *Forgotten world*
> *Of 'Ishtar's Isolde song*
> *And the hidden valley of the Northern Guardians*
> *For by discovering both the immortal fruit*
> *And the World Tree's lost seed*
> *Might I attain my heart's desire*
> *And not fear for those seeking my torch*
> *Through the dark night of the Overlords' power*
>
> *Many before have sought through unsung journeys*
> *None before have found*
> *Three only know of the Silver Spiral Bridge*
> *Crossing the hopeless black waters*
> *They do not go that way*

The formless terrors!
The awesome boiling depths!
The Rakshasas' fires of Emptiness!

I alone trod that narrow path
And desperate plucked Calantha's forbidden fruit
And returned!
Though not all unchanged
Not all unharmed by the passage of horror
The murderous fires danced 'round me
My sword singing sank deeply
Through the bodies of the flaming guardians
As they leaped and cried for my soul
Even so, I passed not maddened!
Nor did I lose my priceless burden!
And returned with half my task fulfilled
Fireberries won!
Deathlessness mine!

Long rested I with my love of rose and columbine
Content with incomplete fullness? Never!
Again set forth I
Exploring the forgotten Guardians
Seeking the World Tree's missing seed
Frozen in eternal Vashti

With a roar and explosion, the giant form of the Rakshasa materialized above the lifeless body of the shara.

Leaping back as he drew Nuriel, Maitreya cried, "It *is* you, Bala! What other would dare attack an heir of Gana!"

The Rakshasa, lifting twin swords of infernal fire, screamed his rage, "He has been mine for thousands of years, Oathmaster! Your paltry influence shall not end my reign! This despicable human child is none other than the bane of Emura, Barlrin himself, again incarnate! My promised share! Force me to form, will you! This will be your last act of treachery!"

The Rakshasa's blades were like lightning, but the rajanya knew nothing of fear. His sword pulsing with manifest power, he parried the vicious strokes again and again. "Destroyer of Emura he may have been, descendant of Pacshash. But this shara is more than you know! Was it by accident 'Sravasa honored him above all others? Flee now while you are still able; plague Mars no more. Else your life is forfeit!"

The Rakshasa's raucous laughter was like the tolling of doom, his words like incarnate death, "Have you so mastered time then, Maitreya? I tell you, your Tala is dead! My brothers have crippled the will of your false adan in Sulara! What hope your devious schemes now? Better far to leave me this fallen one; we may even yet allow you to live somewhere in Zared's world."

"It was clever of you to use a shara of the Solar Race to steal Kaysta from the Lunar Adan in Calantha," panted the rajanya as he backed up slowly, giving the impression of fatigue. "I didn't think you were so wise. Who else could they have trusted? You certainly weren't so bright with Barlrin, as I recall. We fooled you rather well, didn't we? How many of your lovely children shriveled in the flames when my grandfather's brother Orah burned Emura?"

Bala's mouth opened as far as his ears; a bellow of inarticulate rage burst from him as he lunged after the rajanya. But Maitreya was prepared: he rolled under him, striking savagely upward. The green acid of the Rakshasa's blood burned his hand and eyes, proving the accuracy of his aim.

Bala's roar changed in pitch and volume, reaching a force that would have killed a lesser adversary. His mental control lapsed from the pain; Mars abruptly awoke.

For an instant the shara was utterly confused: the infinite light of the One, the memory-visions of his time in Calantha with Lila, Atri and Yayati, the present scene of total madness — all crashed violently through his mind, challenging him to choose. Which world was his?

But then Maitreya, trying to see through his damaged eyes, stumbled into him; Mars' mind cleared.

The shara scrambled to his feet, gripping Kaysta tightly. It pulsed with a powerful saffron light that clearly revealed the ugly red and black monstrosity overhead that was Bala. Holding a claw over the long gash in his abdomen, the Rakshasa cowered in the gem's light as if it were painful to him. Mars stared at him with terror and cried, "Bala? You? How? In the name of the seven planets of man, how did you survive? I struck you through your heart! You fell to your death from the Silver Spiral Bridge! No, I see it! You could not defeat me, so you betrayed me! Gave me that false taste of victory! It was a ruse so you could steal my memory!"

The Rakshasa drew himself up to his full terrible height and roared, "Of course, fool! I have owned you for millennia; my rule is preordained to continue forever! As it has been, it will eternally be! Kaysta shall at last be mine!" He leaped over Mars, his bat-like wings unfurling. Diving toward the still blinded Maitreya, he struck Nuriel aside and stabbed him in the back with his sword of demonic fire. The rajanya fell forward like a wooden puppet with severed strings. Nuriel clattered to the ground at the shara's feet.

Shock, fear and anguish competed in Mars for dominance. Dazed, he staggered and almost lost his mind again. At the last possible instant, he grabbed for Nuriel and brought it up to turn Bala's stroke. His life was saved, but the Rakshasa's blade burned deeply into his shoulder.

"Traitor!" screamed the Rakshasa. "What can your puny childhood do! I am more terrible than your nightmares!" Bala raised his wings in a high arch and beat them with hurricane force.

Mars was forced backward step by unwilling step toward the Boiling Lake. He fell to his knees to decrease the pressure of the tempest, his mind racing. How could he reach the Rakshasa to fight him? This time he was not aided by the sentient motion of the Silver Spiral Bridge. How could he stretch close enough? He glanced desperately at the body of Maitreya; suddenly an idea burst into him like a shaft of moonlight through the dark heart of a storm.

"I do not think I shall fall again, Rakshasa! You covet Kaysta? Take it!" Mars threw the jewel at Bala's wound. With a scream of pain, the Rakshasa fell backward. Mars leaped after him, Nuriel sparking angry fire. "How can you survive, spawn of the night? You see, the gem protects me as before, on the Spiral Bridge! But now I also hold mighty Nuriel, Sword of the Adanai! My master's death shall be avenged!" The shara swung powerfully, wounding the Rakshasa again and again.

Bala, shrieking in pain, fled upward to safety.

Mars stared after him in frustration.

A scream, "Hrai!" announced Heramann's tearing dive in his dragon form. Under the weight of the Vidyadhara's fall, Bala crumpled at the shara's feet like a ruined bat. Mars brought Nuriel down with full force, severing the Rakshasa's head.

A saffron mist, vague semblance of a man, flowed from the corpse. Bowing to the shara, it entered his body below the navel.

Mars ran to the rajanya. Maitreya's eyes fluttered open as he breathed, "Help me sit." The shara raised him gently, not daring touch his wound. The rajanya motioned him away and said in full voice, "You are now prepared for your task, Mars! By slaying Bala, you have destroyed that which you long ago believed in and thereby created. That mind-created error no longer stands between you and the One. Well done, Sun Prince!

"I will see your light dawn next in Para. Never fear: I promise you, we shall rejoice together again beneath a new sun! Farewell, shara!" So saying, the rajanya brought his life-force up and out; his body disintegrated into a fine ash.

"So ends the life of the wisest of your race," sighed Heramann, breaking the awful ensuing silence. "I hope you prove worthy of Mordom's gift."

Mars stared up at the huge Vidyadhara as his mind twisted uncontrollably from red burning agony to hopeless black despair. His chest heaving, not from exertion but from fiery distress, he cried, "*What* do you say? Mordom? Mordom! You can't mean, this — he — Maitreya couldn't have been! No! *The* Mordom? No! That is impossible! Do you know what you say, dragon? The rajanya Mordom was the strongest warrior, the most perfect Oathmaster, the greatest leader in history! Surely you know that Barlrin executed him? Sailed him to his death in the Burning Sea?"

From compassion, Heramann shrank his form down a bit as he replied, "Emura's last adan apparently failed, Mars. You, however, have obviously succeeded."

The shara fell to his knees and grabbed feverishly at the ashes of the rajanya's body. Looking at Heramann through his tears, he continued plaintively, "But he was my master, Maitreya! How could he have been Mordom? *The* Mordom? By the Grandfather's curse of Lord Gana, what have I done? Every age will condemn my memory! My future is dead!"

Heramann adopted his falcon form and flew onto Mars' left shoulder. Rubbing his soft head against the shara's cheek, he said gently, "What weight a name, Sun Prince? Was he any more or less because of his role as the Last Oathmaster of Emura? You needed a deity much less than a companion: you humans revere him no less than Gana himself. Awe can check learning."

Hopping down, he gradually returned to his dragon size as he continued, "But come, we must go! Even if I fly with full speed, it will be hard to reach Zared by the appointed hour. Any ability has natural limits, shara.

"Come, I say! Why do you hesitate? You can do nothing to him or for him. Nor does he require your concern in the slightest!

This is Rodavi's Way, the eternal way of the Seven, the infinite way of the One!

"Maitreya, grandson of 'Ishtar, descendant of Gana's only son Kartika, twin born to Atri, father of Joab, student of the mysteries of the deathless Oathmasters Brihas and Matri, protector of the northern world for fifty-seven centuries, the Last Oathmaster of Emura, Mordom, knower of the One, has today returned home."

11
Forgiveness

In that season, Venus shall bear Mars a daughter.
They shall name her Peace.
— Rodavi

Peace will reign more than a thousand years,
And know her descendants unto the fortieth generation.
During her reign, the Burned Lands will again be fertile.
People will live longer and be rarely ill.
They will be devoted to the welfare of others,
To full mastery of Rodavi's Way
And to gaining knowledge of the Ascendant One.
Her reign will be remembered forever as the Age of Peace.
— Mordom

Peace will be one of the Seven, a full incarnation of Matri.
She will marry Halil, the son of the shara Mars
and the sharan Lila,
And will bear him seven sons and eight daughters.
This union will ensure the continuity of Gana's line
Until the Downfall of Para.
— Joab

Plague smote Tala the second winter of Naisan's reign; in less than two horrible months, a quarter of its people died. Only two provinces were spared: Sulara was protected by the garland of Everlast Naisan wore; Firad's Urlad, by the Rakshasas.

Naisan had by now learned to love all people; he could not understand why all should not be cured. Filled with compassion, he sought Joab throughout Sulara. After much long and fruitless search, he found him at sunset, sitting beside the calm pool in the heart of Zephyra. Without waiting to be recognized, he cried in anguish, "Father! I *must* heal them!"

Stirring the water slowly with one finger, the Oathmaster answered softly, "Now you would cure your wolves to slaughter your lambs, adan?"

Naisan stood by him, his mighty arms trembling, his strong hands spasmodically clutching the empty air. He tried to force his heart to silence, but his words burst past his restraining will, "Father! They are *dying!*"

Joab tapped the water, sending concentric ripples to the far corners of the pool. "Naisan! Have you forgotten everything? Beyond the tumultuous waves of your mind lies the fathomless peace of the eternally still One. You *know* this! Behind the thick clouds of your conclusions and beliefs burns the infinite radiance of the utterly pure, forever serene, eternally silent One immutable. That is the Reality, the only Reality there is. *Live* the Oathmasters' wisdom, adan! Give up your false dream! Let the power of the One lift you back to your true home! If you but allow it, infinite energy lies at your disposal. Only your beliefs can stop Reality, for your ego fights to uphold that which is a lie. This world is your dream, nothing more."

"I know this, Joab! I understand I have created my world. I do! But I have changed my beliefs and judgments that created darkness and evil! I understand humanity now; I no longer condemn them for their weakness! My people are dying, being devoured by a disease that rots their flesh and maddens their minds! They are in terrible pain! It's so unnecessary, Joab! I can heal them!"

"Would you consume yourself to uphold the dark corners of your nightmare before fulfilling your mission here? You are still attempting to see diamonds in coal! Naisan! Think! You know the energy of Starbha unites with the fragrance of Everlast to turn Zared's plague only against those unable to join you in your upward spiral. Let them die, lest they further harm themselves and others. What wisdom is it to judge the world as evil and then not forgive it?

"By your thoughts, you have created enemies throughout time, Naisan. You alone have made your Universe like this, a bizarre extension of a strange illusion; now you have left yourself no other way to move ahead but to destroy those parts of your dream that are false. Forgive them, Naisan; let them return to their source in your mind. Don't attempt to uphold your nightmare by healing that which has no meaning."

"But, Father! Surely we could teach them to change? Is this not the highest form of forgiveness? Perhaps it would be difficult, but in time — ?" What was forgiveness if not patient re-education? Never had Naisan felt his crown so heavy. What was the use of Kanaan-dora's healing power if he could not use it now when it was so desperately needed? Why did Joab refuse to let him cure them? They were as worthy as any of life! How could the Oathmaster stand aside and let them fall prey to this horrible consumptive plague?

Joab withdrew his finger from the water and examined it intently. Then he stood and walked away. Naisan's hand jerked to stop him, but he let it fall again unused.

The Oathmaster looked back over his shoulder and added in the coldest voice Naisan had ever heard, "There is no time. Their bodies are utterly meaningless; you act the fool. There is no plague. There is no death. Hold to the One, adan. You have no other choice. *You* are the myth-maker. *You* are the dream-maker. Illusions are just that: illusions." Then he was gone; Naisan was left alone with his nightmare of doubt and fear. Why could he not maintain his perception of the One? The eye of his mind was blind, shrouded with a blizzard of meaningless thoughts. What was he to do? Hundreds of thousands were dying! He was their adan! They looked to him to save them!

Deeply frustrated, Naisan threw himself to the ground and struck hard at the pool's calm water. *Curse this world! Curse Tala!*

Curse Joab! Curse the useless knowledge of the One! Useless,
empty, nothing! Better far never to have been born than remain
idle at this hour!

Naisan looked up suddenly: Venus was across the pool,
holding their infant Peace in her arms. Tears were flowing freely
from her royal azure eyes. He stood to go to her, but she shook her
head firmly at him. "Hold to the joy inherent in the One, Naisan,"
she sang softly as she left him. "Know that I will ever love you.
Never have I been away from you, never shall I leave you."
Venus' voice faded as she walked slowly away, but was still
crystal clear. Before she finished speaking, her faint words felt like
Naisan's own thoughts, echoing ever more quietly through his
stilling mind.

"Don't allow illusions to cause you pain, beloved. Their
changeable appearance of good and evil, of life and death, of
happiness and suffering is never anything more than your self-
created dream. Hold to the One, my only heart. This is your great
test. Hold to the One, for only love conquers all. Only love. Only
love conquers all. Only love. Only love."

~~~

The third winter after the plague, Joab advised evacuation of
the northeastern quadrant of Tala. Thus Zared's surprise attack in
the spring struck hard against nothing; loss of life was small.

The rearguard cavalry informed Sulara of an enormous army
employing weapons not used since Emura: burning light that
struck from an unbelievable distance, cannons that fired explosives
much further than any archer could shoot. The scouts could hardly
master their terror as they described the enemy's awesome power.
"What shall we do? Fair Tala will now be as the Burned Lands!"
In this, they were not correct, of course: the death of Emura had
been caused by the omnipotent hand of Orah, most powerful of the
Lords of Etan. But to a people that had known warfare only with
arrows, swords and spears, the danger and fear were real enough.

Joab counseled only patience, "Let the horde grow weary with its long journey. It will find precious little to feed its stomach. Continue the evacuation; all will be well." So the months passed as Zared's Army of Invasion marched daily closer to Sulara, destroying everything as it relentlessly came.

~~~

After twenty-one weeks of withdrawal, General Dagora's rearguard cavalry cut off a small advance group of Zaredites and defeated them. A captive was brought to the City of the Adanai. He walked proudly before the royalty of Tala, contempt twisting his saffron face into a sour grimace of distaste. But upon seeing Naisan, he cried, "Mars Adan! How — ?"

The prisoner mastered himself quickly and began again in a particularly guttural Talanese, "My Adan and God Mars bids you pagans greeting. Surrender now, or see your land burned from fire more terrible than your worst nightmares. You have no other choice." He glanced sullenly at Venus and Joab; the blankness of his expression revealed he could see the authority of neither.

"Tell your master," answered Naisan, desperately searching the prisoner's eyes for the slightest sign of the One, "Tala shall never submit. What is more! If Zared does not withdraw, it will be destroyed to the man: a dominion is here you do not know."

"Withdraw? Before such weakness?"

The prisoner's sneer distorted his face into a virtual parody of life, or so it seemed to the adan, who sighed, "Take him back; release him on the front. There is nothing, nothing! we can do for him... No, Dagora! Not you. Stay with me today, I need you. Tell me, my dearest friend, was he typical? Are they all so blind? No, it matters not: what must be, shall be, though our hearts cry out in vain opposition. Come, let us walk once more in Zephyra, speak once more of pleasant times.

"General Aldis! Inform your colonels we set forth at dawn. Even if we ride with haste, seven suns will end in stars before we reach the Valley of Tears, where Balzor met the Asur Overlords and triumphed. At last our time of waiting is over; the Hour of Tala's Doom is at hand! Let none waver in his resolve now! The future is in our hands!"

~~~

But that evening, Naisan himself stood before the Oathmaster, looking much less the Sun King than a small, frightened child. "Not healing during the plague was different, I see that now! And I agree to fulfill your desire about the army of Urlad. But Joab! Many of the good of Tala will surely die if you proceed as you plan! Why? Why cannot you destroy the Legions of Zared before even one Talan is lost? Why do you force me to act thus, I who wish only to preserve life? You know how I love even the beasts and birds! Why must I kill, see my own slaughtered? I would rather die than see one innocent slain! Why do you demand this awful test? Can't you tell me?"

For a brief moment, the Oathmaster stared inward as he reviewed the adan's past and the requirements of his life. Discovering no alternative, he left him on the precipice. "Naisan. My son. Remember, remember. Should everyone but you be forced to hard decisions? How many of your subjects have chosen you over Mars? Would you invalidate their faith? Everyone has a role in this drama. Venus' authority will manifest before the fortnight, as will mine. But this is *your* task; how you fulfill this obligation is exactly what makes your future. The balance is delicate, extremely finely set. It cannot be changed, lest all be lost.

"Don't you even yet see this is your creation, Naisan? You have dreamed this life exactly as you willed! You must learn forgiveness! Both of yourself and of everyone else. Only then can you remake this Universe in the image of the One, your deepest and only true Reality. Don't you even yet understand? Every single person, animal and thing in this world is nothing other than a projection of your beliefs and judgments. You are the dream-maker, adan! *Wake up, Naisan!*"

Joab walked abruptly away, then ordered Dagora to allow no visitors. Naisan stood unmoving, staring into his mind. Forgiveness? What did the Oathmaster mean? What did warfare and death have to do with forgiveness? Forgive who? For what? It was all senseless, mad. What was he to do? He would not, must not, would never kill! Life and death were not dreams! They were real! Everyone deserved to live!

~~~

At dawn, the army set forth toward the northeast with Venus, Dagora and Joab at its head. "Never has Tala known such a force!" the soldiers sang as they marched for the last time from Sulara. One hour passed, two, and still the last of the golden and silver banners of the first ranks had not passed the gates, nor had the Sun King come. Three hours, four, and the very old and the very young on the battlements began asking with greater concern, "Have you seen the adan? Where is Mars Adan?" Five hours, six, and the end of the two hundred thousand passed from the Golden City. And there was still no sight of the adan.

At dawn, Naisan was kneeling beside the canopied ivory bed in which slept his daughter, the sharan Peace. He had been staring at her through most of the night. Tears were running unnoticed over his agonized face: win or lose, he knew he would never see her again. So all the prophecies had recorded. *Curse them all! Curse every Oathmaster! Why did I ever study Rodavi's Way? What have I learned but meaningless mysticism? What good has my life been to anyone! I have failed at every good and worthwhile thing, save only the creation of this innocent child.*

Not wanting to say good-bye to her, the adan kissed her curly auburn locks before she awoke, then walked alone into his empty throne room. He heard the soldiers' songs as they marched forth, yet could not force himself to act. Hours slipped by as he warred inside. How could the eternally benign One support death? It was impossible. Why could he not understand? Joab had often said the world was an illusion, created and sustained by his beliefs and judgments. What did that mean? The world was obviously real. Joab had said there could not be two absolutes. Did that mean the One was false? No, the One was real too: he had experienced it far too many times to doubt it. And there was no question that its power was extraordinary. Why couldn't they co-exist?

Why was he being asked to kill? He could not! What did this impossible task have to do with forgiveness? And why was this understanding of forgiveness so important to learn?

~~~

At noon, Peace escaped from her nanny and slipped quietly into the throne room. Naisan was slumped on his emerald-encrusted chair, staring inside at his internal war, and did not see her coming until she touched his hand and said, "Daddy. Mommy needs you. You must go to her."

He looked up at her with surprise. Taking her in his arms, he crushed her to his chest and sobbed, "Your mother the Sun Queen needs nothing, darling. She is an immortal, a goddess descended for a time to heal the world. She needs nothing."

"No, daddy. You are wrong. She needs *you*. And now. You must go to her." Peace pulled away and looked up at him, her silver eyes radiating ageless wisdom. "If you don't go to her now, she will be very unhappy. She needs you, daddy. You must believe me, papa. It will be all right. See, I will wait right here for you, I promise you. You must go to her, daddy. For me, please, papa?"

~~~

Naisan ran to Victory, arguing that it meant nothing, that the final decision could come later. As the Sun King raced after his army, an enormous roaring cheer burst from the Golden City of the Adanai as his parting gift.

~~~

When he reached the front of the cavalry, Joab searched his face anxiously and Dagora clasped his shoulder. But Naisan turned his haunted eyes away from them and did not speak.

The Oathmaster said kindly, "There is a short tale I will tell you, adan. It may help you resolve this issue of forgiveness that plagues you.

"Once a strange young man wished to test the depths of Mordom's wisdom. He led the Oathmaster through Emura's capital Phedra in such a way they passed a dead and rotting monkey. Stopping by the ruined animal, the young man exclaimed, `How disgusting, this ugly stinking beast! You have told me everything is beautiful in the light of the One. Yet how could any but a madman see beauty here?´

"Mordom laughed his deep, rich laugh and replied, `Behold the shiny teeth of this little monkey, my son! Do they not sparkle like pearls? Don't you think they are the most beautiful things you have ever seen?´

"The force of Mordom's vision was sufficient to alter the carcass, adan. It transformed before my eyes, returned to life. And it was not a weak or damaged kind of life: the monkey was the healthiest and most vibrantly alive creature I had ever known. He was my pet for years. From that day, I knew there were no limits to the power of the One. No limits except those we artificially impose from our beliefs in the false reality of our created dreams."

Without looking at the Oathmaster, Naisan abruptly reined in Victory to ride beside Venus. *What does this have to do with forgiveness?* he thought with anguish. *Why does Joab insist on this insane war?*

Venus entertained him that long afternoon with Songs from Kanaan-dora, but his internal struggle drove him deeper and deeper into his mind: he could only imperfectly hear the dulcet voice that always before so well soothed him.

~~~

At sunset, the adan and adaran turned to ride northward, leaving Joab in command. "Good fortune be with you," said the Oathmaster, "But for no reason tarry! Battle will join by dawn of the sixth day hence; you must not be late!"

"Do not fear; I will be there," answered Naisan, attempting without success to sound confident. It sounded hollow even to his own ears. The icy wind roaring through his chest was dulling his senses, numbing his heart, freezing his mind. Joab was asking the impossible! He would not, could not kill! Everything of his life had increased health, furthered existence! He must not violate that! He would not, could not, must never kill! What in death was even vaguely forgiveness?

Dagora was pale, yet he too wished the adan success. Naisan wondered sadly how much he had guessed.

~~~

Venus rode the dappled mare Joy, the only offspring of Victory and nearly as ideal a horse. None others could have traveled so far so quickly: on the evening of the third day after leaving the army, the adan and adaran reached their destination, a wide valley just south of the highway between Urlad and the eastern provinces. Naisan's call had been well answered: thousands of the elephants, lions and wolves of Tala awaited them there.

Far from firm in his decision, the adan said with melancholy, "It is so hard, beloved. You know I care for many as dearly as myself. Yet were I to lose everyone — Julius, Dagora, Aldis, yes, even you and Peace! — but still have Joab, I would be content. His smile makes the entire world sing; his frown causes all creation to be angry with me alone.

"Others give me themselves, I love them for it; but Joab gives me myself. Venus, my beloved adaran. Is there sense in this? Any at all?"

"I am satisfied, my Lord, with your turning of this wheel. Trouble yourself no more. You *will* succeed." The alternative was far worse than death. What more could she do for him? What simple words of love might help him surmount this barrier? He must understand forgiveness from the perspective of the One! Else all his labors throughout these eighty-two millennia had been wasted; he might as well never have drunk Irnga's poison.

"Rest in peace tonight, blessed adan. The morrow shall require all your strength, all your wisdom. If you sleep, dream only that ever will I love you, ever will I believe in you. As it is in our shining sphere, so is it forever everywhere. Never can I leave you; never shall I be apart from you.

"Dare not ignore Joab's counsel: when your work with Firad is completed, hasten eastward. For no reason delay longer than dawn of the day after tomorrow.

"Farewell, Venus' true heart. Look only to the light of the One; you will not fail."

Once more, Naisan felt the warmth of her love enfolding him. Once more, he saw her radiant world, as clearly and perfectly as the wondrous day he had met her.

Once more. But a moment later she was gone, a single star setting in the west; he was in darkness, alone again. As utterly alone as if she and Joab had never been. As terribly alone as if he were the only human in a world of beasts.

Naisan felt as if his spirit had flowed out of him, leaving a hollow and valueless shell. The Sun King sat heavily and felt his awful solitude. Victory stood behind him to ensure his privacy. It was not necessary: the animals of Tala respected their master's wish.

~~~

All that night Naisan's head was buried in his hands as the memory of his life played before his inner eye. *When he was very young, really still a baby, an eagle carried him to its nest. He watched a chick crack its shell and come all wet and new into the spring world.*

He was not much older the first time he healed a broken wing, that of a barn swallow. The small bird followed him for years afterward, fearing no one, as it was favored by Naisan.

There was the season of black agony when his father Sanel died. Naisan sat alone in their home for three weeks, refusing even to see the animals. Finally, a small woodland creature, a chipmunk, drew him from his despair: it stood on its hind legs and rapped again and again on the shutter with its tiny paws; Naisan, laughing in spite of his dark mood, followed him out into the vibrant health of the living wood.

He met Joab the next spring. The Oathmaster stepped from the forest as abruptly as if he were a tree miraculously entering into life. Or so it seemed to Naisan who, from his first look, was torn between the desire to flee in terror and to fall at the old man's feet. Being thus suspended, he did neither; instead, he stared gaping at him and thought of absolutely nothing to say.

Soon after that was the lion's attack of Mars, when he first discovered Victory. After he healed her, she never failed to come to him whenever he called her with his mind. At times, they had been seen far off, flying like the wind; it was rumored throughout Sulara a god had bewitched the mare, this was why neither the shara nor anyone else could any more mount her.

Then there was the day Venus came to him at the pool of the rainbow fish. He was staring at the water, idly wondering and half wishing if he might one day enter Sulara, when the bushes across the pond moved suddenly. How could it be? He was fully aware of the life of the forest; no being of that size was nearby. It was Venus, staring at him with infinite love shining through her azure eyes. His world at once transmuted into a vision of perfection, a miraculous emanation of the One's transcendental light. Never had he dreamed of such wonder, such glory, such beauty. Never had he dreamed the One was so magnificent, so unequalled by anything of space or time.

That experience repeated again during the Annunciation of the Adanai of Emura. Then for the first time he fully realized there was great meaning in his leaving Alazar's forests to accomplish the strange task of ruling Tala. Then for the first time he accepted Joab's installing him as heir apparent as something other than a peculiar quirk in his master's omniscient brain.

And then Peace was born. For a short season, Naisan felt as if he fully understood Rodavi's Way. For an all-too-fleeting moment, he felt that he was sharing in the Golden Age of Peace, that he was not doomed to the handful of years remaining to the Sun King Mars.

But then came the plague. His unrelieved anguish for the suffering of the Talans marked the end of all illusions about his destiny. He realized then the ancient prophecies about the short reign of Mars were most assuredly about him and no one else. He realized too that the next three years were going to be the hardest of his life.

And, echoing over and over, he kept hearing the roaring cheer of his people as he raced after the army four days before.

~~~

As the visions repeated, another part of his mind desperately sought alternatives. He must not be forced to kill! There had to be another solution! Had to be! He loved life! He worshipped it in all its forms. Once he had had contempt for humanity, it was true, but Venus and the Annunciation had changed that! He loved all humans as himself! Those sleeping an hour away were traitors, working to destroy Tala, but what of that? Such were the mistakes of children! Those of Urlad should be gently re-educated, not murdered!

And deep inside Naisan's mind, silently witnessing the memories and the inner struggle, was the eternally still One. Silently witnessing, forever at peace, infinitely patient, never judging, never criticizing, never condemning, never accepting the existence of any reality other than its own absolute perfection, the One waited for the only possible outcome. Silently witnessing, silently waiting. What difference if it took another eighty-two thousand years? What difference if it took another eighty-two million? The One had all eternity to wait for Naisan to remember. What difference did it make when the adan awoke to himself? *Silently witnessing, silently, silently waiting.*

The mare Joy carried her mistress tirelessly westward: at dawn five days later, Venus stood on a lonely high mountain overlooking Urlad.

"Alas, my poor land," she murmured as the tears trickled from her royal azure eyes, "how diseased you have become. Would I have had my beloved Gana land first here had I looked so far ahead? So fair you were then! Ah, the Grandfather is right: *Time alone is supreme; Time alone destroys all.*"

Her curse projected a billowing amber mist that in less than an hour covered the whole of Urlad.

Slowly, slowly, Venus' right arm began to rise. As it did so, Ixtor and Barafel and the hundred and seven cities and villages of Urlad began to burn, began to burn with raging unquenchable maelstroms of fire.

By noon, Urlad was destitute of all life. Not one blade of grass was spared the sacrificial conflagration. Slowly, slowly, Venus' right arm lowered; the ashes of Ixtor and Barafel and the hundred and seven cities and villages of Urlad began to sink.

Slowly, slowly, Venus' left arm brought the ocean roaring northward. By sunset, Urlad had become a dark, roiling sea.

~~~

The smoke and ash from her work covered the heavens for years after the passing of Mars Adan; the people remembered those twelve years of winter forever after as the symbol of their loss. It was not until Peace ascended the throne of the Adanai that the clouds from Urlad's death vanished from the sky.

Using the One with such authority as had not been since the ruin of Emura could not leave Venus unaffected. Her body was no longer corporeal: her weight was gone; her feet no longer touched the ground. Setting her face toward the east, she floated toward the Valley of Tears. Joy whinnied once after her mistress, then retraced their path down the mountain.

12
The Valley of Tears

I behold a fierce war in that season
The Sun battling the Sun
For supremacy of the world.
— *Rodavi*

None but the most fortunate shall survive
The war before the Age of Peace.
— *Mordom*

Mars' third death will bring
Salvation or damnation to my Tala.
— *Joab*

No experience of hell can last forever: one hour before sunrise, Naisan pulled Starbha from his breast and screamed, "No more! My God, no more!" He threw the gem to the ground and jumped up and down on it in rage.

Victory whinnied gently and softly nuzzled his cheek. The Sun King raised his hand to strike her, but she looked at him with love filling her warm brown eyes, fearless of his intent. His hand froze in space for a timeless instant, then darted to the ground. Clutching Starbha again to his heart, he leaned into her, weeping.

In that moment of catharsis, his struggling mind stilled; the memory-visions and the incessant questions melted together into the silence of the One. In that sudden tranquility, he glimpsed the motion of the larger wheel. Two powers warred for supremacy in his heart and in Tala. There was the One — the infinite silent essence of light, of Truth, of Beauty; the fundamental reality of every Oathmaster since the first, Solon; the Source of both Joab and of Venus; the glorious and self-luminous root of all power, growth, progress, evolution, life. And there was the antithesis of the One — a dark force of hatred, structured by Emptiness, a hideously deformed authority that led forever to stagnation, degradation, devolution, death. He knew then that Emptiness was an illusion created by his ego, given form by his judgments of good and evil, fostered by his perceptions of life and death, maintained by his complex intellectual beliefs in space and time.

In that instant of Ascendant Silence, Naisan saw that by his inaction, he was giving the victory to the illusion, to Emptiness!

A violent tremor tore through the adan, starting from his feet and shooting upward through his spine. He leaped onto Victory's back, screaming, "So be it!" Roaring his rage with the animals of Tala, he surged with them in one mass northward.

At dawn's first light, they reached the sleeping army of Urlad. The traitors had not the slightest warning: at one moment, they were dreaming sweet dreams of conquest and plunder; at the next, they were being brutally torn, gored, clawed. They were fell warriors, having covertly trained for many years, but were no match for these savage beasts, fierce with feral rage: by noon, only two humans still breathed in the valley.

But soon Victory found Firad, shara of Urlad, hiding among the corpses; without a word, the Sun King slew him with a single stroke of Mars' sword. And then no man but Naisan lived in the Valley of Urlad's Blood.

The adan did not rest, but began healing the wounded animals. As he worked, his eyes misted with tears: many died before he could reach them; every loss cut deeply into his soul. Not only was dawn of the next day past, the sun was far toward day's ending before Naisan ordered the last of his wild servants eastward. Mounting Victory, he cried to her, "Now race as never before, the Hour of Tala's Doom is at hand!"

As the Sun King faded into unconsciousness, his mare proved again she was as the horses Gana saved from Martanda: so untiring was her gait, all but the swiftest beasts were overtaken, even those Naisan had sent forth immediately after the massacre.

Yet even so, it was well past noon of the sixth day after leaving Joab and the army before Naisan stood on the rim above the Valley of Tears and looked over the battle raging below.

Joab had led the army with all haste northward and arrived in the Valley of Tears in advance of the enemy.

The evening before the battle, the Oathmaster bent his mind westward. He could see Venus steadily riding Joy toward the Mountain of Destruction; he could see Naisan racing eastward. "But so far," he murmured in dismay. "And so tired! Did he have to heal every red fox? He has over-burdened himself! How will he survive the morrow? The largest part of his task remains undone!" Sighing in resignation, he thought, *But what will be, must be.* And carefully, the Oathmaster Joab planned the Last Battle of Tala.

~~~

Just before dawn the next morning, a messenger burst into Mars' tent and cried, "My adan! The army of Urlad is destroyed!"

"What did you say!" exclaimed Mars, almost more astounded by the pale and shaking appearance of his servant than by his words.

"Firad's Legions are destroyed! I met their scout last evening, but his entire body was torn! He died in my arms! I have killed three horses to bear you this tale!"

"You have done well. Go, lose yourself in the pleasure tents, rest. Tell no one else this tale, lest the army becomes despondent."

~~~

Mars stared at the small mirror on his camp desk, lost in thought. Zared carried not only seven hundred cannon but the last operable lasers from Emura, sixteen in all. Even in terms of numbers, Zared outnumbered Tala more than two to one. What difference the loss of the fool Firad?

The adan of Zared struck hard at his table in rage.

~~~

At dawn, Mars ordered the lasers to fire. But Joab was prepared: the Talans had so polished their shields they were as mirrors. Guided by his unequalled mind, the shields flashed into place at the correct instant and angle. They melted, killing the shield-bearers, but enough coherent light returned to its source to destroy the weapons.

~~~

"What say you now, adan?" cried the general Kurudon, enraged. Kurudon was dark, handsome, vain, cruel. He was foremost of Zared's Inner Council and had been absolute ruler of the Ebony City until Maitreya's improbable prophecy about an incarnate god had so strangely been fulfilled.

That long-awaited day, the Inner Council stood at the predicted hour on the roof of the Council Chambers, the highest building of Zared, and surveyed the horizon.

"I see no one," Kurudon said with great satisfaction. Now that this foolishness was properly over, they could return to the business at hand. "The solstice is passed; let us return below. I have a report on our plague virus — "

At that instant, the Vidyadhara came roaring from the east. On his back, Mars shone like a second sun: Nuriel and Kaysta burned with intense fire, aureate and saffron.

Heramann circled three times over the Ebony City before alighting on the steel pyramid that made the highest part of the Council Chambers. The shara dismounted; Heramann shrank to his falcon form and hopped onto his shoulder.

All bowed to Mars save Kurudon, who cried, "Prove you are the Awaited One, you who dare come like a god!"

Mars stared back at him, using Kaysta to amplify his power. Kurudon fell prostrate against his will as his voice was forced from him, "You — are — the Lord!"

From that day, Kurudon well played the part of the obedient servant. But never did his spirit bow to this pale-skinned impostor; he watched him constantly, seeking always the means to destroy him.

"What is your command, Mars?" asked Kurudon with barely masked contempt. "It will take hours to position the cannon. We were fools not to do so already. I say we must use the gas."

Mars, evenly maintaining expression and tone, replied, "Would you kill our own with the poison, Kurudon? That is madness. As I told you yesterday, I say again today; let them fight as of old! These Talans are weak, unused to warfare. Their trick will only serve our greater glory — now will our invincible strength manifest! Yet for security, bring forth the cannon. They will not be able to play such pretty tricks with our artillery. And doubt not: have you forgotten Maitreya predicted our absolute victory if my commands are but obeyed?"

Kurudon left, but also ordered the poison gas prepared. For too long had he been this one's puppet. As an afterthought, he sent an aide to find the last messenger from Urlad.

~~~

Zared's cavalry surged forward then, but the archers slew most before they reached Tala's line. Those who survived could not break through the shield wall; the handful who jumped over came down in a hornet's nest of swords and spears. But behind the cavalry steadily advanced the army of Zared: half a million men and women in rank after endless rank. The valley floor looked like a moving black sea of death; the flights of arrows from the opposing armies were like thunderclouds in the heavens.

Throughout the morning hours the defensive line held. Tala was entrenched in the upper ground; Joab removed casualties and brought in reinforcements with the grace of a master dancer. The Talans had well trained during these last four years: even though there had been no war since the Solphglen Rebellion seven centuries before, few fled the battle. Tala steadily lost ground, pushed backward by the sheer mass of the enemy, but the line broke nowhere.

~~~

This was the situation when Naisan appeared on the rim of the valley. He was exhausted, emotionally and physically drained; his golden robes were torn, fouled with dried blood. But the Talans cried with joy, "The Sun King! Mars Adan is come!" Many had doubted when he left with Venus; now all were filled with hope and fought with renewed strength.

Naisan held the beasts until more should come and because he feared their inability to distinguish friend from foe. Instead he lifted his bow. He had filled his arrows with fire and wind; each was delicately attuned to his mind. Only Naisan had had the time and strength of spirit to master Kanaan-dora's art of war: as he bent his bow, he surveyed the battlefield and projected the future positions of a thousand of the strongest and bravest of the enemy. Loosing the arrow, he divided it with his mind into a thousand as it flew. His targets fell, mortally wounded. At such a distance, there could be no return fire; Naisan released forty such arrows, reserving only his last and most powerful. After he was done, forty thousand lay dying from his work alone.

His efforts well succeeded: Zared was retreating. But in spite of Joab's efforts to restrain the Talans, they were chasing after the enemy all along the front.

~~~

"It becomes a rout," screamed Kurudon. "Fire the cannon!"

"No!" cried Mars. "Wait until we have withdrawn far enough. Let the fools follow us far into our trap." He restrained the Inner Council as long as he could. No mistakes were now acceptable: this battle was much more delicate than he had dreamed it could be.

At last he gave permission for the artillery to fire. The signal flag fell; within seconds, the explosions began, spreading mindless fear among the Talans. But the barrels of most of the cannon exploded, killing many of his own army. "Treason!" he cried.

"Stop firing! Inspect the others! Bring me the Colonel of Cannon! And his staff! At once!"

~~~

The largest part of the Talans had panicked and were fleeing in abject terror. Those few who were holding their ground were as besieged islands, surrounded by the pounding thunderous waves of the resurgent enemy.

Naisan saw Dagora fall, pierced by a dozen of the enemy's spears. Filled with rage, he cried, "Joab! There is my reward for following your will? This is Rodavi's Way? Such is your plan for the salvation of the world?" Fitting his final arrow, the adan bent his bow to a full circle, attempted to channel the destructive power of the One, then released it. He tried his best to control it, but his mind was not sufficiently matured. Of humanity, only Gana at the height of his power would have wasted none of it; of the Lords of Etan, only the Archer, Krishanu: as the arrow flew, it divided into a thousand, then each part divided as much again. A full million arrows descended onto the battlefield. The effect was chaos and despair to Zared: seventy thousand were killed, as many more were severely wounded.

~~~

"How can this be?" screamed Kurudon. "We retreat again! Do my senses lie? We must use the gas! The wind has been favorable all day. We must act!"

"Are you insane, Kurudon? I forbid it. Only at the last moment. Urlad approaches. Firad will descend upon their rear with eighty thousand men. Patience. But to be cautious, let it now be prepared."

"We must use it now! As soon as the retreat is completed. The gas is ready!"

"Whose authority," growled Mars, half-drawing Nuriel.

Before Kurudon answered, an aide passed him a message. The general's color turned livid; he leaped to his feet, roaring, "Urlad's army is destroyed! *And* our adan was told at dawn!"

Mars fought his way through the Inner Council, killing Kurudon and most of the other generals before being himself slain. The unfortunate truth was that, unlike Naisan's Starbha, Kaysta of the Lunar Race was of strictly limited value against human enemies.

~~~

Naisan stared helplessly across the Valley of Death as the vermilion clouds mushroomed over his army. The gas canisters were few, Mars had sabotaged most; but even one would be sufficient to end all life in the valley. While the poison strangled the Talans, the Sun King moaned, "How easily the Oathmaster could change the wind! Why does he not act? Why has he betrayed me? Why has he abandoned us all?" Naisan moved into his mind, trying to use his limited ability with the One to alter the currents of the air.

Long before he succeeded, the Wind Lord Boreas, ordered by a different and higher authority, reversed his direction; now it was the Legions of Zared who were dying.

The gas was slightly lighter than air; a modicum of both armies was spared.

The many years of training in the Ebony City proved fruitful: Zared was the first to regroup and charge.

But now Naisan loosed his wild subjects: they came roaring, trumpeting, screaming forth to hideous battle.

~~~

There was no joy for Tala in this victory: of the two hundred thousand who had marched from the City of Gold a week before, scarcely twenty thousand lived. Of these, over half were fighting a losing battle with death.

For thirty-six hours, Naisan labored, healing. In the thirty-seventh hour, at the same moment Venus began the destruction of Urlad, his body could endure no more. He had returned exactly five hundred from the Temple of King Death.

All that day, the warriors stared with growing concern toward the strangely darkening west; the glorious hues of Orah's setting spoke eloquently to many that a new age was upon them.

~~~

The remnant of the army gathered before Naisan's pavilion the next day at noon. Within an hour, Venus drifted in from the west, sighing over and over to herself as a dirge, "Urlad is no more. Gana's Urlad is no more." She floated to where Joab was standing, lost in thought.

The Oathmaster started when he saw her. Clasping her hands, he kissed them, then ordered the attendants to bring out the adan of Zared. They protested, "He has been dead since the battle!"

"Nevertheless, bring Zared's Adan. It is time the truth of this age be known."

When they saw Mars' body, the soldiers cried, "So like the Sun King! How is it possible?"

The physicians carried Naisan from his tent. He was as pale as death itself; a moan went up from the assembled ten thousand.

The Oathmaster touched the Sun King's foot; Naisan shook once violently, then awoke. His breath coming in painful gasps, he said hoarsely, "Father, promise me — do not deny me! — promise me... you will care for my Tala always. And not withdraw again from Sulara... until Peace masters a perfect understanding of the One."

"You request difficult boons. Yet is the will of the Seven in accord with yours. I will not leave Tala until the Downfall of Para." Raising himself up to his full height, Joab cried the Death Prophecy, "`La — hai! When ten thousand children attain the wisdom of Mars Adan and the love of Venus Adaran, only then will Joab abandon this Earth. On that day, this world shall end!'"

Naisan, staring at him with longing, breathed, "When?"

"When time is fulfilled, Sun King! The saying for Zared's Adan is this, `When this sundered world joins in unholy war, when the Living Statue walks, when Mars and Venus come in forgetfulness to protect the Lost Generation of Five Hundred, then know the Ten Thousand of Kanaan-dora have returned!'" The Oathmaster would say no more, though the Talans questioned him at length.

Naisan raised his hand; all speech ended. He commanded in a powerful voice, fading echo of the beloved Sun King, "Bring me Zared's Adan, that our age may end." He saw now his final sacrifice.

They brought the corpse to him. Naisan touched Starbha to its heart and whispered, "Life shares with life. Death be masked by my love, masked to claim us both henceforth." With a choking rattle, Mars' breath flowed, his gelid flesh warmed, color returned to his face.

A roar went up from the host, "The Sun King wakes the dead! Zared's Adan is reborn!"

Mars, slowly opening his eyes, looked long at Joab. At last he said weakly, "I did my best."

As the soldiers murmured their astonishment, the Oathmaster replied, "You have succeeded, adan; all is well at this ending! Zared and her legions are no more." Mars gave a heavy sigh and settled back. *Thank God,* he thought weakly. *Thank God.*

Joab continued, "Some others are here for you, Mars."

The sharan Lila of Calantha and a young child were standing behind the Oathmaster. Mars motioned her forward; with a sob, she ran eagerly to him.

Falling onto his chest, her tears wet his tunic as she cried, "Shara, behold thy son! Halil, behold thy father!"

Mars stroked his son's ebony hair and stared with longing into his auburn eyes, opened wide with wonder. He pulled him to his side and held him with all of his meager strength as he rasped to Lila, "Your father?"

She answered with anguish, "Yayati Adan has re-entered Almira's shining world, my Lord! My evil brother Yadu descended on us with the full might of the Calantha Legions, even as Airavata arrived to carry us away. Father died in my arms! Atri forced us to leave! Laughing without fear, he alone faced the invading thousands. Now do we, homeless and unprotected, seek asylum in this foreign land."

"There can be no fear in that, sharan," responded Joab gravely. "Halil will attain to maturity with Peace; in time, he will drive his usurping uncle from the stolen throne. I promise you: your heirs will rule in Calantha until the return of Gana."

Heramann came forward, tears shining on his emerald scales. "This planet grows the warmer for me, adan, seeing you thus entering the Long Ice. If Atri did not carry my solemn vow to aid your son, today I would leave this accursed world forever. No, do not fear! Halil shall know my devotion, and what is more! that of the whole of the Vidyadharas! Yadu will not long resist us, not even if everyone of Calantha stands behind him and the Rakshasas lend their full power!

"Hrai! The Vidyadharas shall again honor our life's pledge to Kartika's Lunar Race, protectors of the Sacred Hatching Ground in Calantha! Yayati and Atri shall be avenged! It shall be as when Gana with the Lords of Etan faced Navril Hagar and threw him from his diamond throne! We will come burning from the sky as we did then! I, Airavata, fourth born in Calantha, pledge this to Mars Adan today! Whatever is left of my race, none of us shall enter the Long Ice until the false scepter in Calantha falls!"

~~~

Naisan, feeling the world fading, with difficulty removed the garland of Everlast and handed it to Lila, saying, "For my daughter. Be her mother, sharan, I adjure you."

She took the wreath saying, "Be it so, adan. I shall be the mother of Peace."

Naisan sighed deeply, then removed Starbha and handed it to the Oathmaster. Fighting hard to stay conscious, he whispered painfully, "Joab. Father. I have always longed to ask you... I must know this, now at the end... Joab, Lord of my soul, do you love me?"

The Oathmaster, unmistakable emotion shining through his gray eyes, softly answered, "Doubt not, adan. As I have preceded you from age to age, so will I forever. We shall one day rejoice together again under a new sun. For this truth is eternally so: I love you."

~~~

Mars, understanding Naisan at last, followed his lead and gave Kaysta to the Oathmaster. With a great cry of sorrow, he exclaimed, "Lila! Halil! Airavata! Remember me! Though all eternity separates us, I promise you! I shall find you again!"

~~~

Venus placed a hand on each adan and exclaimed, "Farewell, good people of Tala! Follow the Oathmaster's counsel always! We shall return at the Ending of Days!"

A golden shower of light flowed from her shoulders and, forming the appearance of two mighty wings, began pulsing with vibrant power.

As she raised one majestic wing of light over each adan, the three began slowly rising, leaving the Talans below with upturned faces, shouting in wonder.

Peace and Halil

13
The Death of Love

Trembling I sit day and night, my friends are astonish'd at me,
Yet they forgive my wanderings. I rest not from my great task!
To open the Eternal Worlds, to open the immortal eyes
Of Man inwards into the Worlds of Thought, into Eternity
Ever expanding in the Bosom of God, the Human Imagination.
— Blake

As soon as they were out of sight of those below, Venus moved
her hands together. As she did so, the two Adanai drifted together
until they were touching. She clasped her hands; Mars and Naisan
merged, becoming as before: one body, one mind, one soul.

~~~

Thus was my consciousness recreated from those divided: my memories of Earth flooded back just as do the waters of a lake when a dam breaks. My dual life-experiences in Tala had only obscured the present without extinguishing it, just as clouds cover the sun. The light of the Ascendant, reflecting through my two nervous systems, had created my apparently separate minds, just as one mountain seems two if viewed from different valleys, or as the sun on troubled water appears many.

I was back in the cave in the Himalayas, sitting on the stone outcropping next to Sharon. I was still holding her hand; the declining sun, not yet quite moved beyond the mountain peaks, caressed her golden hair, lighting brilliant ringlets of glory around her radiant face. No time had elapsed! I had lived two complete lifetimes as Mars and Naisan, mastered the First Sphere Compassion Technique, experienced love and glory and suffering and death and no time had elapsed!

My mind was shocked, terrified, confused, maddened. I had heard of such time-compression events before but never believed them possible. How could it have happened? This was not simply a dream or an illusion. My experiences in Tala were real, as real as my current life; they were sequential, painful, joyous — as Mars and Naisan, I had struggled, lived, loved, died.

As my friends and companions Ascended peacefully together in the cave, my mind played whirlwind with impossible memories attempting to find a stable home in my rapidly evolving present. Was I going mad?

I resolved to tell no one until I had come to a clear understanding of what had just happened to me.

~~~

But that night as I struggled without success to find sleep back in my own cave, I found I could contain my words no longer. I rolled over in my sleeping bag and whispered, "Edg, are you awake? I need to talk."

Steve's gentle snoring continued without break, but Edg at once replied, "Sure, I don't sleep much up here. It's too clear, the Ascending. What's up? Something got ya'?"

"Seems to. Outside? Steve's wiped out from the climb — or maybe too many nights climbing on 'Dite."

We dressed and entered the Himalayan night. A half moon floated above the mountains; it was clear and quite cold. As we wandered down to a hot spring near the stream, I said in my best humble tones, "Edg. I feel I must apologize. I've felt uncomfortable with you since the day I met you, because you represent a power which I've never understood, a power I've always been afraid of and avoided. I'm sorry. I was wrong."

"It's nothing, my friend. But I don't think you'd mention this now if something hadn't changed your mind. What's up?"

"New experience. Last evening, when we were Ascending in the group cave, I had the most extraordinary vision. Part of it consisted of a long experience with three Black Ishayas."

"Really? Tell me!" His excitement was contagious; I eagerly relayed my lives in Tala, with special emphasis on my time with Joab, Maitreya and Atri. Speaking it out helped to stabilize me; I began feeling better than I had since before my visions began.

When I finished, he said slowly, "You know, that is what I envision the Black Ishayas' role to be here — a kind of supervisory function. They stay in the shadows as long as Isha's Teaching proceeds according to St. John's intent and only emerge when something is out of alignment. Or when they wish to move the Ishayas in a new or adjusted direction. That sounds exactly like the Oathmasters in Tala, doesn't it?"

"That makes for an interesting theory," said someone neither of us had noticed, sitting in the moon shadow of a large boulder, not seven paces away. It was one of the local hermits — a very old man with no clothing other than a loin cloth to keep away the bone-numbing chill of the Himalayan night. How did he manage to resist the cold? His matted locks hung almost to the ground; his beard was thick and full; he had a timeless quality about him that made his age impossible to determine in the moonlight. By his accent, it was obvious he had been well-educated before he devoted his life to the recluse path.

I had not seen him earlier that day, but Edg knew him from previous visits and replied, "Kailasa-ji, I did not see you in the shadows. How much did you hear?"

"Most of it, I think," he replied warmly. "Enough to recognize that your friend here has been chewed on by the Destroyer."

"What do you mean?" I asked curiously.

"Your visions. Lord Gana is pulling your chain, young one. If you survive, you'll be a great one, a Maharishi. Once the Destroyer starts playing with your mind, you'll either join him in the highest consciousness or end up quite mad. There are no other possible futures for you now."

"You know of Gana!" I exclaimed, my heart racing. "How could you possibly?"

"Everyone in this small valley knows of the Supreme Destroyer, Lord Gana. And everyone knows of his mind-created world Para. Even in the world below our secluded valley, most have heard of Gana, although they usually call him by one of his other names — Rudra, Shiva, Isha, Christ. The same energy in different parts of the world has different names."

"How is it," I began slowly, trying to find a thread of meaning to stabilize my once more whirling mind, "that the Destroyer aspect of God is identified with the Christ? That doesn't make a whole lot of sense to me."

"Lord Gana is also known as Nandishvara, the Lord of Bliss, boy. The Lord of Love, that's Shiva. When the supreme destruction occurs, all of Narain's created dreams melt away — all the created Universe vanishes back into the one True Reality — all of multiplicity returns to the Absolute Unity of the pure Ascendant One. Destruction of ignorance is Gana's supreme role. And then pure love rushes in. Rather, when ignorance is destroyed, the awareness of pure love returns. It was never truly lost, just shrouded by false and painful beliefs."

"So the supreme Black Ishaya is Christ who is Shiva," said Edg, sounding highly pleased.

"Of course — the ultimate destruction destroys your false Universe and returns you to your true home, the Ascendant. No greater act of love could exist."

"That must be extraordinarily painful," I said, mostly to myself, vividly remembering my death as Mars.

"Doesn't have to be. That depends on how life is lived. The more free you are from attachment, the less pain there is when your dream-life is cut away from you. Let me tell you a story I have always liked. It might help you understand this."

Once Indra, the king of the gods, was cursed by an Ishaya to forget who he was. Indra was at once reborn as a wild boar.

The gods were frantic without their ruler — the upward current of creation was everywhere dammed up and subverted by the demons and Rakshasas. They searched everywhere for their king but found him nowhere.

Finally, Agni, the God of Fire, recognized Indra wearing the body of a pig. The gods approached him and beseeched him to return to his throne. But Indra was not interested in their words: having forgotten everything of his past, he told them he was perfectly content with his life as a boar — he adored his pig wife and pig children; what use did he have for their words of glory? They had no meaning in his life.

From desperation, the gods decided they had no choice — Yama, Lord of Death, was dispatched. One by one, everything Indra loved was taken from him — his sons and daughters, his wife, everything he cherished was destroyed. And yet still he clung stubbornly to his life as a pig.

It was only when Yama killed the body of the wild boar that Indra awakened from his peculiar dream. Only when every attachment was broken did he reawaken to his true status. Joy for himself and the Universe dawned that day. Destruction led to Heaven for him, you see.

"I have heard this story at the monastery," said Edg. "It was one of the clues that led me to think there must be another kind of Ishaya in the world. A destructive kind."

"I'm not surprised," replied Kailasa. "I learned it from my Teacher, the last Custodian, Maharishi Krishnanand Ishaya."

"So you were an Ishaya once!"

"Still am. All the hermits here once followed the White Ishaya path. We retired up here when the duties and routine of the monastery life began interfering with our growth."

"You're Black Ishayas, then?" I asked, amazed to find Edg's improbable theory being fulfilled.

The old ascetic laughed for a long time then replied, "None of us would be so bold to claim such a title! I suspect the Son of Thunder Boanerge might begin to consider himself one of the Black, but he's had almost two thousand years, working on it. The last real Black Ishaya I'm aware of was Isha himself. But that is certainly the aspiration of everyone here. Someday we will attain that level of consciousness. Someday we'll unite completely with Isha, with Gana. And then we'll be of the Black too."

"I'm confused," I said weakly. The unexpected confirmation of Edg's beliefs was settling poorly in me; I felt as if I were in the middle of a war as my visions of Para and Tala battled for supremacy with the normal Earth world of my past. "I no longer know who I am, nor even which world is real. Which is the Truth here? I have had two extraordinary visions, one of a world of supermundane perfection, Para, a world as like to Heaven as I can imagine; and one of a world not so different from this one. This second world might even be this Earth, but it was so long ago no one any more remembers any of the events or characters of my vision.

"These experiences have grown stronger in me; they are as real or more than this everyday world, more real than you, more than the mountains, more than the stars, more than the moon above — I'm lost, confused, alone. So alone. Who can help me now?"

"Ultimately, only yourself," began Kailasa.

But just then Sharon ran down to us, greatly excited, and said, "Found you at last! I've wonderful news! I've just seen Boanerge!"

~~~

Sharon, Edg and I walked alone up the mountains, heading to the glacier at the head of St. John's valley. Boanerge had apparently spoken to Sharon for a long time and given her specific directions: for some reason he did not make clear, the three of us were to proceed alone up the glacier.

Before we left the valley, Nanda gave Sharon and me the Second Sphere Love Technique, the Earth Technique. This was the opposite of the First Love Technique and completed it: instead of causing energy to flow down into me from the Ascendant, this technique flowed energy out from me into all of Creation. I liked it more than any other of the Second Sphere Techniques; it felt very healing to my heart and to my relationship with the world. As soon as I received it, I began to feel stable and calm again. Perhaps everything was going to work out after all?

It was a glorious, clear high Himalayan day. The sun glistening on the compacted snow and ice sparkled in myriad reflections of beauty. The view over the valley below, lightly misted in the early day, was exquisite. The rugged peaks all around were as beautiful as any mountains I had ever seen anywhere on Earth — they were almost as wonderful as the eternally white mountains surrounding Dawn Mountain in my vision of Para. Or perhaps my memory of Almira's World had begun fading — how could any place of our world compare to the unequalled wonder of the Source Universe?

By noon, we were hot: the sun reflecting off the ice felt quite warm in spite of the altitude. Boanerge's instructions to Sharon had led us here but no further: he had said we should receive the technique from Nanda, leave the valley by mid-morning, climb until noon, then wait. We had received the technique from Nanda, we had left the valley by mid-morning, we had climbed until noon; now we sat on the glacier and ate the fried eggplant, mung dahl and saffron rice our cooks Hari and Lal had insisted we bring in our packs.

"What now?" I asked both of them and no one. "Why are we here? What are we waiting for?" I was beginning to feel a little foolish; I would rather be Ascending in the caves with the new techniques or else focusing on my visions.

Neither of my companions could think of an answer.

Sharon suggested we Ascend; we could think of nothing more logical and agreed.

This time it was quiet and peaceful for me, a pleasant contrast of normal experience after the intensity of my visions of the past two days.

~~~

After an hour or so, Sharon excused herself, saying she wanted to go a little way off for a few moments for personal reasons; we said we'd look the other way.

"What do you think, Edg?" I asked him quietly as she trudged away. "What's going on here? What's with this bizarre day? Do you think Boanerge really appeared to her?"

"Don't know. I've never seen her so withdrawn. She seems as if she's hardly here at all. The lively spark of her joy seems completely shrouded, all but gone."

"I don't like this at all. What's with her, anyway?"

"Haven't any idea. Maybe she's so self-absorbed because of her vision? Though, now that I'm thinking about it, I have seen that kind of look before — she reminds me of Swenson when he left Patmos."

"Ollie — " I began, but my words died in my throat as we heard Sharon scream.

Leaping up as one, we raced after her.

There was a narrow and deep crevasse in the glacier. It had been glazed over with a thin film of ice. Sharon hadn't seen it; when she'd stepped on it she'd broken through and fallen. She was caught on a ledge about a third of the way down. The angle of her leg made me think it must be broken, but I didn't think she'd fallen far enough to be killed.

As these perceptions flashed through me, I felt a wave of anger for Boanerge. Why had he told us to come up here today? Surely he had foreseen what would happen. Why was he doing this to us?

We called to Sharon but she didn't move or answer.

"Can we reach her?" I asked Edg doubtfully.

"Sure. The crevasse is narrower over there, see? We can wedge our way down easily enough. Getting her back up is going to be trickier. I wonder how strong that ledge is? It might not hold all three of us. Better let me go alone."

"No. I'll go. If something goes wrong, you go back for the others, OK?"

"I should climb down," he replied. "I'm in better shape than you." That was undoubtedly true, but there was no way I was going to be a spectator when Sharon's life was at stake.

"Doesn't matter. That's not a hard climb. It'll be easy enough. Nothing compared to hanging plywood on a steep roof. Look, I'm already gone." I walked along the edge of the crevasse.

Edg began to protest again, but just then Sharon stirred, moaned, looked around and said, "Oh my."

"Be right there," I called down to her as I began the descent. Going down was even easier than I thought, but the ledge was narrower than it looked from above and seemed extremely fragile.

"Sharon," I said, "this looks pretty delicate. Can you slide toward me? I don't know that this can hold both of us."

"I don't know. I'll try. I think I broke my leg, but I'm OK other than that." She inched toward me along the ice, slowly, carefully, painfully.

I was tightly wedged into the narrowest part of the crevasse, but I knew I could easily pull her out once she reached me.

It was agonizing, watching her cautiously slide toward me, but there was nothing to do but wait.

The last of the ledge was the narrowest and most dangerous — it was little more than a half arch over the dark depths below. Sharon boldly started out on it, then saw how very thin it was and stopped from fear.

"I — I don't know if I can do this, my love," she breathed.

Edg called out from above, "Why not back up onto the wider part? I'll climb back down to the valley and come back with rope and the others."

"That'd be more than four hours!" she replied. "I'm getting chills: very cold. I'll be all right. Just give me a moment. Used to be terrified of heights, you know? When I was a kid my dad actually did the horrible thing you hear about — had me climb up a stepladder, then said, `Jump to me, Sharon. Don't worry, I'll catch you.´ So I did. He moved aside at the last instant and let me fall onto the floor. Then he said, `That's to teach you never to trust anybody.´ Took me a while to get past that. Hard to keep faith, you know?"

"Sharon," I said, trying to sound calm, "here, I can get a little closer. The ledge widens out again at this end. See? I can almost reach you. Just a couple more feet and you'll be with me, see?" I stretched out my hand to her. We were close, almost touching. "Reach for me, darling. I'm right here. I'll get you. I'll hold you."

"Oh my," she breathed. "Oh my." She started slowly crawling toward me again, closer, closer — I pulled off my glove; our fingers were touching; I stretched forward to grasp her hand...

Suddenly the vision of Para intensified and began once more eclipsing the world. "Not now!" I cried. "Not now!" But there was no stopping the inward pull of its power. The crevasse and Sharon drifted backward in my mind.

As the world faded completely, I saw the ice of the ledge breaking beneath her, saw her falling — did I have her? I struggled to hold onto her and to the world.

Was I falling too? I no longer knew, I no longer could see anything of Earth. I heard Sharon crying out to me, "Ever will I love you, ever will I believe in you!"

Were we falling? Did she say that? Or was it only vision-memory?

14
Visions in Eternity

For all are Men in Eternity. Rivers, Mountains, Cities, Villages,
All are Human, & when you enter into their Bosoms you walk
In Heavens & Earths; as in your own Bosom
you bear your Heaven
And Earth, & all you behold, tho' it appears Without it is Within
In your Imagination, of which this World of Mortality
is but a Shadow.
— Blake

The seven rainbow wheels danced before Gana, but now the lower three burned with perfect clarity. Had they not always done so? He could not remember. How long had he been floating here, watching them? He could not remember that either. Suddenly the emerald wheel, the fourth of the seven, expanded around him. For a timeless instant he was confused as infinite verdant emotion engulfed him in light and sound. In another moment, the light divided and multiplied...

~~~

The shara returned to himself in a body walking outside Para's Dome of the Spheres. Almira was at his side, her thoughts singing rapture through his heart, *My Lord! Your first three tasks are ended! Forgiveness completed the victory. The first three of your mind-created enemies are no more!*

Standing now before three of the seven huge weeping willows beside the lake were statues. The first was of Vasuki, dressed in scarlet robes. As Gana stared at it, the first Perfection clarified in his mind. With a roar of triumph, he cried, "Come forth!"

Instantly, the shores of the lake were crowded with every species of animal, every one of Kanaan-dora, Martanda and Emura as well as all those of his idlest daydreams. The air above was filled with opalescent birds and butterflies, filled so completely there was not the slightest tint of blue above. The lake teemed with fish of all varieties; everywhere nearby the fields, forests, waters and skies were alive with the motion and color of the newly returned residents of Almira's world.

Simultaneously they cried with their many voices of their elation and wonder in life. The sound was like thunder; from its stentorian might came its meaning, "We return!"

The beasts bowed to him in their various ways; the birds dipped for him in their flight; the fishes leaped for him through the water; then all moved joyfully away, spreading though the forests and waters and plains of their new world.

"Well done," commented Almira. *I knew you would discover Vasuki's gift in time. Creative power follows quickly in the wake of freedom from the fear of death.*

She led him to the second statue. It was of Mordom, wearing saffron robes. As Gana gazed at it, tears filled his eyes. *Why?* he thought. *Why did he leave me?*

Almira chuckled gently and brushed her hands over the stone; the statue melted into life. The rajanya stood there, beaming at them.

"Maitreya!" gasped Gana with joy, embracing him.

"So I was there," laughed Mordom, greatly pleased with him. He paused while the shara integrated his memories.

"What is happening to me, Maitreya?" asked Gana, for the moment wholly the young shara Mars again. "Why did you leave me in Vashti? Zared was a hell the like of which I never dreamed possible. I needed you. Desperately."

Mordom laughed the deep rich laugh the shara had thought ended for all Eternity and answered, "There is no death, Mars! It is all an illusion, a cunning dream of time and space."

"Why does it appear so real!"

The rajanya laughed again and answered, "You are expressing your hidden inner personalities, shara. As Gana, you repressed several aspects of yourself you judged unworthy. Your impractical Naisan-side, for example — a gentle lover of the world, but not helpful to other humans. Your dissolute Mars-side, for example. Such passionate drives! So forceful, so useless!

"The problem with your repression was that you also lost the brilliant gifts locked inside those aspects of you. This is why you have had to out-picture them, so that you could recapture that energy which you buried away from your awareness."

"You mean the lifetimes I lived after Gana were simply to learn to love myself?" asked the shara.

"Exactly! And the out-picturings have been numerous. The more extreme the better, for then you could the more easily see them and master them. The furthest limit of your repressed energy created the Rakshasa Bala and the shara Firad, as the two most recent examples."

"*I* created Firad? *And* Bala?" asked Mars, incredulous.

"Of course," chuckled Maitreya. "Who else could have? Look into your heart. Don't you see them there?"

"But Bala! He was so inexpressibly evil! A Rakshasa, Maitreya!" Gana didn't want to accept that kind of responsibility.

"Everyone does this, shara! All people everywhere repress the largest parts of themselves. But what is pushed down here, pops up over there — life is resilient, and denial is never possible in the Universe. Everyone's dream world is populated with repressed sub-personalities... And very little else," he added with a deep laugh.

The rajanya held forth a vial filled with a brilliant, iridescent fluid and said, "Take this, Mars, drink. This is known as Soma; it is a symbolic form of my Perfection enlivened now by your evolving mind. You will better understand how you have populated your Universe later. A few unavoidable experiences more. Farewell for now."

As Gana tasted the liquid, the rajanya transformed back into the statue. The shara's body began glowing with a gentle saffron light, but nothing else at all happened.

"Mastery of the body is a gradual process," commented Almira gently. *There is no need to feel disappointed. You will fully understand each of the seven gifts only when all your tasks are fulfilled.*

"I would like to know now what Maitreya has given to me!" exclaimed Gana, frustrated in spite of her soothing words.

Oh, your appreciation of the Authority of the Second of the Seven will come soon enough. It will not take long before you begin to perceive and communicate with the subtle beings working for you throughout creation, the celestials and elementals. But first let me introduce you to another of the Seven.

The third statue was of Joab, wearing golden robes.

"Joab! I should have realized he was one of the Seven. Would that he were with me here!"

The Oathmaster's voice boomed from behind them, "Am I not with you, Naisan, now and always?"

Whirling around, Gana beheld him, but a Joab he had never known in Tala: the light radiating from him was almost unbearable, brilliant and golden; on his head was a crown of fulgent fire; there was no sign of age on him or about him.

"Joab! You, the Third of the Seven! I should have known! And yet, why are you here? Do you no longer care for Tala and my daughter Peace as you promised me?"

"Sun King, I care for your heirs and people still: the authority I am allowed there would be baseless did I not live forever here. But what is more: because you ventured there, the best of Tala is also here: everyone you knew and loved there has preceded you here. Naisan! The whole of Tala is in Para, transmuted, a part of the Cathedral of the Sun!" So saying, he took Gana by one hand and Almira by the other; instantly they stood before a new palace Zephyra in a new and perfect Golden City Sulara.

"The hour of your crowning is come once again, shara! This is the gift of Joab the Golden." As the Oathmaster led them forth, Gana recognized Dagora and the others who were killed in the battle, as well as all those who had died since his simultaneous births in Tala. As he saw them, he recognized he was a part of them: he knew there was no distinct line of individuality between him and any of his subjects.

"Many will come later, of course," commented the Oathmaster. "All will need your guidance: this world of your creation can seem much at first entering. You must aid them all. By your age-old choice, this is your eternal duty as the Master of Para."

As they entered New Zephyra, translated (as was all of Tala) into purest light, a shout went up from the assembled thousands, "Hail to Mars! Hail to Venus! Glory to Joab!" Taking the crown from his head, the Oathmaster placed it on Gana, then knelt before him. The Sun King entered into perfect union with him: from that moment, he knew he was an indivisible part of Joab, just as Joab was a perfected part of him.

The people cheered, "Victory to Gana, the one true adan of Para!"

~~~

New Tala was in Gana and Almira's world, but it was in that part known as the Cathedral of the Sun: the sun shone there, as did the moon and the stars; there were days and seasons and years. It was as if this part of Para was midway in the evolution of worlds: more wonderful by far than Kanaan-dora or Martanda or Earth, not as perfected as the larger part of their mind-created paradise.

One day, Gana reasoned this must be true for the New Talans themselves; Almira answered him, *Yes, they will one day leave the Cathedral of the Sun. Only by journeying once more into the outer Universe will they gain permanent residence in our world.*

"Then I also must once again leave?"

As you now play the part of adan of New Tala, our world will be less to you — more like the worlds of your recent past. This will be so until your seven words are fulfilled. This was her only answer, yet it did not disturb him: his life was full, guiding his many subjects. There was little time for doubt.

~~~

"Almira," said Gana pensively, "Why have I not yet discovered anything of Maitreya's gift to me?" It had been a year since the rajanya had given him his boon. The adan had as yet experienced nothing of its power and understood nothing of its intended use. He could still feel the iridescent Soma liquid Mordom had had him drink, vibrantly coursing through his veins; but even after a year, he had found no application for it.

It is time, my Lord, her thoughts softly flowed through his mind. *Come with me; I will show you what happens to those who defeat the mind-created illusions of their second wheel.*

With no transition, the adan and adaran were walking together through the matchless cedar forest he had first discovered in Para. The animals and birds that wandered freely everywhere else had not yet entered here. Was some other force keeping this one forest isolated from even the most beneficial kind of entropy?

They walked, seemingly aimlessly, for a very long time, enjoying the cathedral nature of the vast silent forest. Gana wondered again what Maitreya's gift was; at once Almira motioned for him to sit on a marble bench, ornately carved with angels, set in the hollow of a particularly enormous tree. The inside of the tree was so vast it contained a small meadow with scarlet snap-dragons, golden lupines, and a deeply emerald grass. Almira knelt beside him, watching him intently.

Gana smiled at her, then began to look around at the small meadow. What was Mordom's Perfection? Almira had told him it involved communicating with different levels of Creation. What did that mean? How could he imagine that which he could not conceive? Engrossed in thought, the adan stretched out his arm to touch a small crimson snap-dragon. It seemed particularly lovely, more alive than the others.

It took Gana several moments to realize that he was not staring at a flower but a small humanoid figure, clothed in the colors of its stem with its leaves as arms. He knew he did not create this little being as he had Para's animals; nor was it a vision born of intense concentration as when he had focused continually on his memory-dream of Calantha in Vashti. No, this delightful little creature had been invisible a moment before solely because his senses had been too narrowly defined.

Gana stared entranced until he noticed some other peculiar motions near his feet. Looking around, he saw that all the flowers were now also human. Even the blades of grass had humanoid shapes, with their arms raised above their countless heads, bending now this way, now that in the gentle breeze.

Every plant was human! Every one different, every one unique, every one beautiful. The cathedral cedars were the best of all: venerable and wise with majestic personalities slowly matured through their long growth. In delight, he cried, "It's too marvelous!"

You see now that all lives! In the most personal sense of the word. Each and every grain of sand has a unique existence, an individual reality in the One's light.

"There is more," she laughed as she took his hand and led him through the forest. At first he was so entranced by the human appearance of every object — every flower, every tree, every stone — as to be oblivious to all else. *If this is the whole of Maitreya's gift, it is truly wondrous,* he thought, but then he beheld a tiny face peering at him from behind a large rock, and realized he was looking at no plant — it was a tiny, independent being. The only word that came to mind was, "fay"; as she turned and flew away, startled to be seen, Gana's vision expanded, he saw the others: tiny brownies and pixies and elves and larger naiads and dryads and gnomes and dwarves peeking at them from behind leaves, stems and tree trunks, playing in the forest around their feet.

A light shower of golden rain passed over; every drop was human. A mild wind blew; the breeze was alive, a wind spirit — gentle now, but capable of vast strength. In a stream, sprites and water-nymphs danced on the waves and dove and sparkled in the water. By thought, Almira created a fire; salamanders, fire beings, maintained the existence of each flame, joyfully played in the light.

All natural laws maintaining the integrity of Narain's Dream have humanoid counterparts. Even if never seen, they have always existed. And always will, even if the ability to know them be one day lost.

"Say not so!" he cried as a baby elf swung on his little finger. "Tell me rather that I will know these delightful creatures always!"

In this world of our creation, you shall. And of greater than these, beloved, for these are the elementals, which have lesser intelligence than the average human. But there exist also celestials, more evolved than most of human descent. Look at your Guardian Mountains now!

On each peak appeared a radiant humanoid face, spreading energy outward. Above them all was the ruler of the entire mountain range. She was more majestic than any of the others, beaming extraordinary wisdom and supernal light to all of creation.

Almost overwhelmed by his new vision, the adan cried, "There are so many levels! And knowledge and power increases in each! Is there an end?"

Almira paused a long moment before her thought came, *Full understanding of this will come later, after your seven tasks are fulfilled.* But during that moment of silence, everything, the entire world — all the plants, animals, elementals, celestials — melted into the pure light of the One. Almira alone remained, but transfigured: the whole of Para, indeed, the whole of the Universe appeared within the gentle radiance of her eyes.

~~~

Long they walked entranced by the beauty and happiness of the elementals and celestials.

Gana asked her finally, "Why can't I hear them?"

"You cannot?" She asked, surprised, then touched his ears; at once he was inundated by a multitude of tiny and great voices, ranging from the delicate tinkle of baby flower fays to the loud resonant booming of huge tree gnomes.

Soon you will master their languages and learn much from them. Her thought was cheerful, but he recognized the doubt lingering in her eyes and wondered silently.

The joy of his new perception banished all questioning moods. They chanced upon a grove of flame trees, dancing in fast rhythmic seasonal cycles, similar to the grove of vine maples in the heart of the orchards. Their play appeared more ecstatic than that of the vine maples: with every change, from spring to summer to fall to winter, a new group of elementals came and lowered or raised a curtain of multi-hued light. No tree would bud until the spring elves called forth the sap; none would rest until the fall sprites danced to herald the withdrawing of the leaves.

Gana discovered he could now see many more buildings: temples, huge meeting halls covering leagues, small homes for elementals and their families. One structure high on a distant mountain was brighter than any other; Almira answered his unspoken desire, "We can if you like." *But you must promise caution! Exactly there your rashness led to your fall.*

The building was spherical, not large, yet pulsing with a different and fuller energy. There were no entrances; Almira explained, "These bodies will not suffice." She touched him; he transmuted into a golden sphere, subtly marked with crimson. She transformed into a silver mist, slightly azure. They floated through the wall.

They were immediately engulfed by music, every melody unfamiliar but pleasant, coming from all sides, above and below. There were innumerable strains of song, each complete and self-sufficient, yet perfectly harmonious: each individual movement produced a necessary part of the euphonious whole.

There were soloists, choruses, orchestras, dancers — most humanoid, but transparent and wonderfully radiant. Some had four arms, some, many; some had two heads, some, many; some were simply a geometric form, as if they had grown tired of maintaining a complex body, or else had found it unnecessary or meaningless. Some were completely formless, brilliant vapors of light, pulsating with rhythm and sound. There was no end to these musicians in any direction: the walls had vanished. Or perhaps they had no inside surface, perhaps the building had only been a doorway into this higher dimensional realm. Did this place extend forever?

Almira's thoughts glowed softly in him, an integral part of the mosaic of sound: *Yes, you did once attempt to find the limit of this, the Grandfather's Hall of Music. You traveled with the infinite speed of your mind to discover its uttermost ending. After centuries of racing through this endless region, you recognized your failure and returned, angry at your defeat. Thus did your pride inspire you to refuse to bow to the Grandfather on that fateful day, causing your fall from his curse. There is no end in any direction! To leave, we must alter our level of being: this Hall of Music exists everywhere, always.*

Each singer, dancer, musician resonates on the subtlest level of relative creation. Therefore every sound, every movement manifests grosser levels of reality — commonly perceived as stars, planets, universes, bodies, natural laws.

All here strive for the Ideal Perception of the One — to perfect their individual part of the already perfect Whole. A result of this is the force of evolution in the relative worlds.

When the young ones rest, as they must at first, their material creations dissolve. When they awaken, their Universes are again created. Although you no longer remember, we two who created Para are older. Therefore we rarely sleep. Your long absence has been your only recent opportunity to do so. You re-awaken now;

our world rebegins. Perhaps you and I shall never again need to withdraw; Para will remain undecaying forever! There are such developed beings, such eternal regions. Narain and his Ocean make one example; the Grandfather and this Hall of Music make another.

"Could I meet them?"

"No!" *Not yet. You are not yet ready. First, you must complete your seven tasks...Come, one experience more before we return to New Sulara.*

The Grandfather's Hall of Music vanished as their bodies transformed; they stood again in the Dome of the Spheres. Gana's new vision also functioned there: each of the Seven Regions of Light was human, as was the Universe itself. Every galaxy had a human form; each sun was a distinct individual. The Earth was a fair woman; every continent was alive with humanity.

Almira told him to look more closely; his body in the chair opened around him, every organ was human as was every cell. At the subtlest level, the seven rainbow wheels appeared. The bottom three were still and clear, revealing their humanity: Vasuki, Mordom and Joab. The upper four were still rapidly spinning, fiery suns of color; it was not apparent whether human shapes hid within them.

Gana wondered why Almira had brought him here; in answer to his thought, he saw that connecting each of the seven was a golden thread. Slowly the thread magnified, revealing another form. At first it appeared as a staff of light with two serpents, one white, one black, twining around it and upward: it formed a caduceus, traditional symbol of the Healing Arts in every civilization.

Two hands appeared on the staff: the right, holding the white serpent Sesha, the left, holding the Vidyadhara Heramann. Onward still the staff transformed, becoming at last a human form. It was human, it was feminine, it was Almira.

"Yes," she said from behind him, "it is I." *I give you this, I give you all.*

Behold here our shared peril! These fiery spinning wheels are the seven centers of life in you. These seven centers give you the experience of the One, they give you the experience of all things. When they function as they should, I pass infinite energy through the Golden Thread; thereby you experience our mind-created world and the highest and most expanded levels of your Self.

But the seven should be still and clear! They spin and are multi-colored because you have allowed limitations to exist in your mind. These false judgments and beliefs, accepted by you from time long past, have gained enough strength to take on external forms: you have created enemies throughout space and time! Constantly they seek to destroy you, for then they would have true existence. At your expense! They are aspects of you, are nothing other than projections of your seven centers, but already each has gained sufficient power to enslave you.

If any of these seven projections learns enough of the subtle science of the Oathmasters, they could force entry into the Golden Thread. We would once more be violently sundered; never again could you gain my presence. And if the Golden Thread or any of the wheels were thereby damaged, you would become insane! Even death would not free you then! How far backward could you be thrown? Would Narain's Garden, our world, our Universe, survive the subsequent ruin of your Downfall? We have only one path, which we have been following since that long ago day of the Grandfather's curse: you must re-learn the correct use of each center. Each of the false limitations of your omnipotent and omniscient mind must be transformed into its true, its unbounded status. Only then, when you have finished each of these seven tasks, will I be able to pass infinite energy through the Golden Thread eternally; we will be united forever in Para.

You see how the lower three are still and clear, radiant and perfect jewels? This means you have mastered your first three tasks; only the last four remain. You progress well!

As Almira's thoughts flowed through him, the cabin around his alive-dead body began rapidly changing. The priceless gems Kaysta and Starbha disappeared from around his neck; on his right hand materialized a statue of a white snake, modeled after Sesha; on his left hand appeared a perfect representation of Airavata in the form of a black lizard; a throne of solid gold was placed under his sleeping body. As he stared entranced at the seven wheels, the cabin in Emura was torn apart, the Temple of Kanaan-dora was built around him.

Of these many changes, Gana saw only that the first three wheels now burned perfectly clear. If he had seen, if he had allowed himself to know, would his future have changed? Surely he would not have left his ten thousand without seasoned guidance: his son Kartika, although a brilliant youth, was of immature understanding when the poison claimed his father's breath. Hard indeed it was for him to withstand the subtle perversions of his cousin, the Valin-enslaved Irnga.

But Gana did not see, did not know that time moved very strangely in this unique interface between his mind-created world and the material Universe. He did not understand the full extent of his moment-by-moment decision; therefore he permitted his immortal body to sleep while everyone he loved lived the natural course of their existences, aged and died.

Shara, shara! Your long unbroken sleep caused by Irnga's poison! Would Calantha have forever divided from Emura if you had lived? Would Kaystarbha have remained broken, the equatorial fires so long continued? Not all the twisted ones were destroyed when the Seven burned Kanaan-dora, nor were all killed in the Rakshasa wars with Valin on Martanda!

Almira, knowing full well her adan saw and yet did not see, smiled inside as she moved her mind to touch his, *You are tired, my Lord. Come, let us return to New Tala. You will have as much time as you need to study your new abilities.*

~~~

"*Mirabel, why does Almira allow Gana to remain deluded about his true fate? Why did she capture a few moments of his life and expand them?*" *Malinda glanced up at her sister curiously from the tapestry they were weaving. This thread was quite unusual, unique in her experience.*

"*One body was chosen to fulfill the need of the Universe,*" *Mirabel answered without looking up from her work.* "*One mind must fully expand. One spirit was marked to bear the destiny of all worlds.*"

"*Is this not true of everyone?*" *asked her sister Mirabeth curiously, stopping the swift flow of her loom.* "*Is there more than one spirit? The existence of the One implies there is not. There is only the One; therefore, there is but one consciousness in creation. Why then did Almira steal Gana from his home in Emura?*"

"*The shara is infused with the infinite light and presence of the One, my sisters,*" *Mirabel answered, now also stopping her work.*

"*Is not everyone?*" *persisted Mirabeth.*

"*He has the strength of spirit to manifest in our Universe the Seven that predate creation.*"

"*Surely everyone does!*" *exclaimed Malinda.*

"*No, Gana alone can fulfill the seven impossible tasks required to rescue the whole of humanity. But if and when he succeeds, everyone throughout space and time will be able to follow. Someone has to be first, you see.*"

"*Yes, but can he succeed?*" *asked both her sisters at once.*

"*That, I surely do not know. Pull your skeins, if you wish. We can jump ahead and see.*"

15
Minstrel of Kanaan-dora

At day's end comes
Peace
Love
Silence
But not throughout the night
Not until the One is mastered.
— Rodavi
Suffering through the Soul's dark night
Is the fate of all until Reality is known.
— Mordom
There is no expansion without contraction,
There is no going without return,
There is no life without death,
There is no joy without pain,
Until the Ascendant is perfected.
— Joab

One day some fifteen years later, the adan and adaran walked through New Alazar's Forest and chanced upon the pool of their first meeting in Old Tala.

"Look, Venus! How lovely, the water. I wonder if the rainbow fish live here still, would again dance for me?" Gana knelt by the quiet pool and gently touched it. The fish were there; their dance was even more beautiful than he remembered.

Almira showered him with light and love as her thoughts laughed their expanding joy, *My Lord! For eons I considered the Grandfather's curse senseless: I knew no reason for your banishment, for your loss of godhood. But now I learn you have both lost and gained through your many passings. Somewhere, you lost the blind pride that inspired you to insult the Grandfather of the Spheres that fateful day. And in its place, humility has blossomed, making you the more beloved of celestials and humanity. In this way is Rodavi's wisdom demonstrated: "That which is full cries to be emptied, that which is empty cries to be filled."*

Gana smiled at her rather vaguely. He was thinking, *Rodavi. Who is this Rodavi?*

~~~

That evening, the adan and adaran sat feasting with a merry crowd in New Zephyra: it was the sixteenth anniversary of his crowning. A young minstrel girl, very beautiful with long, flaxen hair cascading over her dark emerald robe, stood and asked permission to sing.

"Of course," Gana replied, wondering how he could have forgotten one so lovely.

She began in a melodious voice filled with compassion. As she sang, the adan not only heard but saw her song, so marvelous was her skill.

> *Seventeen ships of silver-green*
> *Golden prows front the empty west;*
> *Wave-foam from their carven bows*
> *Breaks over rushing black water;*
> *Filigree structures of intricate height*
> *Speed balanced life toward the final promised haven:*
> *The Seafolk of Kanaan-dora!*
> *Their home forever, forever lost,*
> *Forever lost 'neath the triumphant wave.*
> *"Alas for Kanaan-dora the Sacred!*
> *No more shall homeless wanderers walk your blessed lands,*
> *Nor climb the Sanctuary Mountains of 'Ishtar,*
> *Nor gaze into the bottomless depths of Solon's Pool!*
> *Lost! All, all are lost*

'Neath Ocean Untamed.
An eternal curse be on those forgetful ones
Who thus destroyed our peaceful land!"
So sing the sad mariners as they search;
Search, though time and world should fail;
Search, through this distant empyrean, far beyond thought;
Search,
Search for new land, an unknown realm
Remembered,
Remembered in misty tales from the Forgotten Years;
Remembered around the morning fire
Remembered best by blind men and old women,
Memories told to thoughtless, uncaring children;
Memories now the last vital hope of desperate lost seafolk,
Searching,
Searching for salvation in the ancient vision of a new land
Of rich brown earth and singing waters.
Silently,
Silently they stand, staring to the west;
Silently, hoping still their dream may yet be
And new life blossom 'fore all precious breath is lost.
Silently, but —
No sign of freedom!
No sign of hope on this starless world of flat water!
Only the ancient whisper from a more innocent youth of this,
Necessary journey taken, always taken, forever to be taken,
From the fallen, evil lands destroyed,
To the new, prepared for nourishing growth.
"How many times homed?
How many times homeless?
Only the Pillar of Kanaan-dora could tell us,
But now it is forever, forever lost
Forever, forever lost
Forever lost 'neath the triumphant wave."

Minstrel of Kanaan-dora

As the last lingering chord fell from her lyre and her final melancholy words faded from the hall, the adan turned to Almira to ask her what Kanaan-dora had been. She was not there. How could he have been so captivated? He bent his mind throughout New Zephyra but could feel her nowhere. He asked Dagora (as always, sitting nearby), "Where has the adaran gone?"

Dagora smiled back at him and asked laughingly, "Who?"

"Almira, my Sun Queen?"

"Who?" Dagora asked again, this time obviously perplexed.

"The Lady Venus, of course! Almira! Why do you look at me so vacantly? Are you all right?"

"I have never felt better, my Lord. But this Lady? I have never met her. Is she a celestial of the air or fire you have neglected to introduce to me?" Dagora's eyes revealed only sincerity; the adan sat back, astounded.

The faces of his dearest friends revealed not the least comprehension of the words Almira, Venus, adaran, Sun Queen.

"Leave me. All of you. I must think. Aldis! Find Joab; request his presence here."

What happens? One moment, Almira and I share perfect peace, infinite love; the next instant, even her memory is erased from my subjects! How can this be? He sent his eyes throughout the whole of New Tala, then in expanding anxiety throughout the whole of Para: she was nowhere.

As the adan thus searched every place they had shared in joy, Joab entered, bowing. "Why do you summon me, Naisan? I am hardly different from you: all that I am you are."

"Father! You forever remain my superior in wisdom! You are certainly more than I; where else might I turn in doubt? Joab, beloved Oathmaster, where is my Almira?" He looked at him with child-like innocence.

"Who, my Lord?" Joab asked with a blank stare, as if Gana had mentioned a perfect stranger.

"The Lady Venus, of course! What! Has everyone gone utterly mad? Who is Gana without Almira? Can the sun exist without its light? Can the mind experience without the senses? *Do I not have an adaran?"*

"Naisan — "

"No!" he cried with rage, striking the table so violently it burst into fragments. He covered his eyes with shaking hands and continued, "No. I'm sorry, I see she is no longer in you. Forgive me, father! This evening — I do not fathom it. Let me explain." He told the Oathmaster of his life as he remembered it. When he mentioned the song, on impulse he sent an aide to find the minstrel.

Joab responded slowly, as if with great effort. "The events of my memory are... *similar.* But I have no knowledge of your Almira, other than the natural functioning of Life within you. I perceive the truth in you: I see you believe your memories. But I am afraid I do not know how to help, other than by the rather obvious suggestion this may be related to your fourth task. The ways of the heart are exceedingly subtle; the Emerald Oathmaster is known to use bizarre methods to fulfill his ends. But what Vaga could mean by erasing such a supernal being from the Universe, or by — "

"Yes. Of course. This must be what you think, what any would think. That I am wrong; that I have had my mind filled or changed! Very well! I accept this challenge! Either Gana Adan remembers falsely, or the whole of Creation is in error! One only can be the victor — there cannot be two absolutes, one author only can imprint the pages of Eternity! Be it so! Where do I begin? I suppose I must meet the Emerald Oathmaster Vaga. How may I find him? Never has he or his three superiors made themselves known to me. Where should I look?"

"Again, I know not. As he is greater than I, he never informs me of his whereabouts. If any would know, it would be Narain."

"Narain? Surely you play with me! Long have I sought him, never have I rediscovered him! How can I find such a one to tell me how to seek another to teach me how to discover my missing beloved? It even sounds ridiculous!

"Nevertheless, what other course do I have? If not even *you* have the faintest memory of her, who can aid me? The rocks have never felt the caress of her soft feet; the air whispers with no scent of her sweet breath! Joab, Joab! Meaning has flown far from me today! My work for these years appears as the play of a spoiled child, the ravings of a mad fool! Of what value my realm, of what use my knowledge and power? That which is most precious was stolen between two thoughtless words, between two careless heart-beats! How could I be so weak to let my attention wander?"

"You cannot guard your life-breath as you would a priceless gem such as Kaystarbha, Sun King! A moment's carelessness can ruin a life, it is true; but your error (if you made one!) was not of this nature."

"Then what? Can you tell me? Why did I first fall? What is my mistake now, what my wrong thought or deed?"

"What has plagued our Universe since time began is none other than the conflict warring in you now, my Lord Mars. You have experienced, you have seen, you have known. Yet you are not free. You say you have lost that which is dearest. I say that is impossible. Regardless of the existence of this Almira, you can never be touched by the dualities of life if you hold to the One. You know this! Yet you have not realized it deeply enough: you are still affected by the meaningless."

As if to comment on his words, the Oathmaster closed his eyes; his breath stopped. A nebulous mist drifted from his throat, gradually coalescing through the colors of the spectrum until it became a man in a flowing sky-blue robe.

"Atri!" exclaimed the adan with great surprise. "You do me unequalled honor, great sage! How can I serve you? Anything mine I give you: all my world is yours."

"I have no need for such, Mars; I come to offer you my advice. Vaga the Emerald cannot delude me as he does the most part of your subjects. I am not permitted to interfere with his project by resolving your dilemma, but I will freely share my knowledge. There are two methods to discover any lost objects, be they animate or inanimate. The first is to seek the aid of those who are wiser. In this case, Narain, the Grandfather, Matri, Brihas, myself, or Vaga. The second choice is to enter the field of the never-changing One and there pose your question."

"If the One is non-changing, how then could I ask anything? And where can I find it?"

"As the One is not localized, shara, it can be found anywhere at any time. The method is simplicity itself: renounce or forget everything else. But for you, since you have become so devoted to action, I recommend the other path. Find your hidden connection to Vaga or one of the others. This is my conclusion."

"Where must I look?" inquired Gana earnestly.

But the Oathmaster was already dissipating into mist and floating back into Joab. "Don't let appearances deceive you, Mars! Truth wears innumerable faces; inside, it is always the same. Above all else, remember this."

Aldis entered the hall now, exclaiming, "My Lord! No one knows how to find the minstrel; indeed, no one ever saw her or heard her sing before last evening!"

"What? Impossible!" Gana bent his mind again throughout Para, but could find no trace of either Almira or the minstrel. This time he touched many of his subjects with his awareness, leaving a message describing both. When he finished, Aldis was long gone; Joab was patiently waiting.

"That was wise, my Lord. While you were so engaged, I requested Aldis to meet with those present last evening, write out the minstrel's song, and discuss any other odd events which may have occurred. They have finished; Aldis once more approaches."

Aldis returned, carrying a parchment scroll. He kneeled before Gana, handed it to him, and commented, "Here is the poem as she sang it, my Lord Mars. We all agreed on the wording, but that enchanting melody that so moved us? Somehow no one could remember it. We hope this is satisfactory."

The adan took the scroll and glanced at it. He was about to thank Aldis and dismiss him, but the words stuck in his throat, for this is what he read:

"Hamsah."
"Hamsah," whispers the snow as it drifts to the ground;
"Hamsah," pours the rain as it rushes past,
thawing the frozen lands;
"Hamsah," chuckles the stream playing down two sides of the
emerald field;
"Hamsah," cry the babies in their nest in the lilac near the wisteria
in the Inner Garden;
"Hamsah," dreams lovely young Mira as she sleeps
through the dark night in the Eastern room;
"Hamsah," she sighs in the early air of bright morning
as she gazes at the distant white mountains
with a half-understood, half-denied knowledge
growing in her heart;
"Hamsah," she smiles, radiant at breaking of fast
as she remembers her silent communion
with dawn curling over those distant peaks;
"Hamsah," she laughs as she runs
down the dusty trail eastward, ever eastward;
"Hamsah," she prays as she lies in the soft-needle bed of a
dark-silent forest as the sun sets far, far to the west;
"Hamsah," she cries as she dances
with soft-nosed deer in the quiet gray-time just 'fore dawn;
"Hamsah," she runs and plunges her golden locks
into the icy stream flowing from the vast peaks towering overhead;
"Hamsah," she laughs as she rolls in multi-colored meadows

> *of alpine flowers hidden in forgotten valleys*
> *of the Mountains of Eternity;*
> *"Hamsah," her life joyously expands onward*
> *to the One that is her source and goal;*
> *"Hamsah," she sings of the all, of the One,*
> *of the ultimate secrets of space and time;*
> *"Hamsah," her echo comes reverberating*
> *to us imprisoned dwellers in flatland*
> *who cannot or will not follow;*
> *"Hamsah," her echo comes and always will come*
> *as a hope, as a signal, as a warning to complete us;*
> *"Hamsah. Hamsah. Hamsah. Hamsah."*

"My Lord," whispered Aldis; Gana started as if he had been awakened from a dream: how long had he been absorbed in the poem? "My Lord, we were also asked if anything unusual occurred last evening. All anyone could remember was, ah, your question about an *Almira*. We thought perhaps you were testing our creative powers to see if any of us had visualized the *Mira* of the song. Some said they were successful: they described her as an exceedingly beautiful sharan, empathetic, compassionate, wise. Was this your purpose, my Lord Mars?"

"Hmm? Ah, yes. You have considered well. Thank you. Thank all of you. Ah, you may go, Aldis... No, wait! Meet again to discuss this: `Where can Mira be now found? If nowhere, where in all this world can her echo be heard?´ This should suit her reality in your minds... Also, see if any of you knows of an historical precedent for this song."

As Aldis left, the strangeness of this reality burst forth, "Joab! This was not the song! No, not even close! How utterly bizarre!"

"Not the song? *Not* the song?" The Oathmaster's forehead wrinkled; for a moment he looked exactly like an eighteen month old discovering salt is rather different from sugar. "Are you sure? Then what? Do you remember?"

Gana told him her exact words: they were deeply imprinted on his mind. "Tell me more of Kanaan-dora," he added when he finished. "What is it? It must be important in this."

"*You* ask *me* of Kanaan-dora? You can't be serious — surely you — no, I see you..." The concern was too strong to be kept from his face. Was Gana thus pre-ordained to fall again? And further?

Joab turned toward the window and looked over New Sulara as he continued, "I suppose it may help to remember the past. That tale was the oldest history in Emura when I was born there. It told of the settling of the world by a handful of refugees from the ruin of Kanaan-dora, annihilated by Lord Brihas, master of the Seven, due to the evil of its people. Led by the shara Gan — ah, led by the last sharas of the Starlord and Gemstone Council of Kanaan-dora, ten thousand only completed the journey to the West before the final doom struck the land. The Oathmasters preserved the treasures of Kanaan-dora throughout Emura's history, but the common folk considered the tale a myth. There is no second continent; the land mass is contiguous in the northern hemisphere. Or, that is, I mean it was. Was until Venus smote Urlad with fire and — "

"What did you say!" Gana practically screamed at him.

"Yes, what was that?" The faintest of memories flickered in Joab's eyes. "How strange. For a moment, I pictured your Almira; she was destroying Urlad. But now the proper memory returns: Orah rains his fires on the corrupt land."

"No! The other is correct! Please don't! Don't let it fade! Surely you remember her presence in Tala! Don't you recall the birth of Peace?"

"The birth of Peace I remember well, adan. But of course her mother is your cousin, Firad's daughter, the sharan Daralyn. I'm sorry, Naisan," he added, seeing his face.

"If it's gone, it's gone," the Sun King replied heavily. He drifted into a silence that spawned a new idea, "Could the ocean the mariners crossed be of a different nature? Could it not be space itself; their seventeen filigree ships, starships from a destroyed world?"

"That is exactly how it was, of course..." replied Joab, staring at him with growing concern.

Gana noticed Joab's anxiety but ignored it in his excitement: "Then the tale of Kanaan-dora must be real! And that must mean that Kanaan-dora's shadow still exists. The minstrel sang of the `Pillar of Kanaan-dora´ and `Solon's Pool.´ What are these?"

Joab beat back the rising wave of doubt and replied as if he were speaking to someone who had never seen them, never known them as intimately as Gana now knew New Sulara. "Legend tells us: in the Sanctuary Mountains of 'Ishtar there was a deep pool named Solon after its creator, the Oathmaster-shara who founded Kanaan-dora. In the water could be seen an ivory pillar, a projection of the all-knowing field of the One. Any question asked to this pillar would be answered. But what good does such knowledge do you, as Kanaan-dora has been lost for eighty-two millennia?"

"I don't know. But there must exist somewhere a logical solution to these difficult riddles. Does not Kanaan-dora's shadow fall in other ways?"

"Why, yes! It does! Even here, in New Sulara! There is a small building, the Temple of Kanaan-dora, containing some treasures. Do you know it?"

"Know it! I married Venus there! On your advice!"

"Indeed? Your memory thus significantly marks it. Let us go there."

Outside the entry to the Temple of Kanaan-dora, Joab explained, "This was built long before the fall of Emura around the Living Statue of — ah, hmm.

"'Ishtar restored it and built Sulara around it when Tala was founded. It contains the last treasures of Kanaan-dora, excepting the diamond staff the Oathmasters have always used; the twin gems Kaysta and Starbha; the Silver Spiral Bridge kept by the Lunar Race in Calantha; the sword of the Adanai, your Nuriel; and the Crown of Emura."

Inside, Gana saw the image of himself, the alive-dead body of his distant past, but considered it only a statue. He glanced at it briefly, but was much more fascinated by the two sculptures placed on its hands.

The one on the right hand was the purest white and was in the form of Sesha as a tightly coiled serpent. Gana picked up the other, a representation of the Vidyadhara Heramann in a wholly black lizard form. "How mysterious are these!" he exclaimed with great interest. "As I recall, in Old Tala, neither can be separated from the statue's hands. Yet here they are unattached."

"No, Naisan, they are unconnected there as well, but are too heavy to move. Tradition is unfortunately silent concerning them. All we know is that they came from Martanda. We don't know why the sharas carried them. We don't know what they are for. And most significantly, we don't know why they are so heavy."

In the statue's lap was a red book, imprinted with a gold embossed image of an Oathmaster holding the diamond staff. The adan put the Black Lizard sculpture down and picked up the book.

"That is Solon's *Book of Mystery,* source of every prophecy concerning life in accord with Rodavi's Way. It was when Barlrin destroyed the original in Emura that Mordom concluded we no longer had a choice and ordered me to kidnap the adan's infant son, Aharon Hanif."

"Can you read this?" asked Gana, curiously turning the pages.

"No, only Rodavi and the earliest Oathmasters knew its language. Strange it's here. It must possess an extraordinary degree of power to be in New Tala after its destruction in Emura."

"This I will take," Gana said, putting it in his tunic. "Of that which is here, this alone is wholly lost to the old world. I conclude that if Venus had any purpose in placing it here, it must be for my use now, in New Tala.

"Are there other memories of Kanaan-dora?"

"Only one, my Lord Mars." Joab opened an oaken chest carved with a three-branched tree and took out an oddly shaped object, apparently formed of solid gold. It was the size of Gana's hand and vaguely resembled a seed. "This is the only product of the World Tree of Martanda, Vanaspati. As such, it is the most important treasure in Tala. Yet what to do with it is a mystery. There is one clue: hold it in front of your forehead."

As the adan did so, a thought entered him, *When Time's End nears, I must sprout in Vashti.*

"You see some cause for its being held in awe. Discovering this seed in the Guardian Mountains I consider my greatest accomplishment; carrying it to the Temple of Kanaan-dora was the hardest task I ever faced, harder even than crossing the Burning Sea and discovering the immortal fruit of Calantha. The opposition from the Rakshasas made the passage to the south seem a child's play. Rodavi wrote that the seed of the World Tree had to be reunited with this White Snake statue of Sesha and this Black Lizard statue of Heramann for his vision of the future to be fulfilled. They are like the three sides of a triangle; none is complete without the other two. But no one understands why. And I am afraid that bringing the seed to the Temple of Kanaan-dora was one of my life's deepest disappointments: it accomplished nothing."

"Let us return to Zephyra, Joab," Gana said wearily. "I am burdened by enough mysteries now without uncovering more lying far off in space and time. These statues and this golden seed make me feel old. Old and very, very tired."

16
The Downfall of Para

Last before the End of Time
Comes the Downfall of Almira's Shining World.
— Rodavi

When the Downfall is imminent,
Gana will forget his past.
When Almira is betrayed, the destruction of Tala
Can be numbered in hours.
— Mordom

There shall come a day when the Rakshasas' strength
grows so great
They shall attack and destroy Para.
When the Downfall thus comes, the nature of the human
Throughout the Universe shall be immeasurably weakened.
The Oathmasters' powers will wane;
The subtle abilities of humankind will deteriorate for everyone.
Average humans will be plunged into suffering and misery,
Their lives will be as far from Rodavi's Ideal
As it is possible to conceive.
— Joab

Aldis came to them when they returned to Zephyra; he made this report: "My Lord Mars, here is our conclusion. If Almira exists in this world, she would be in the Guardian Mountains; these parallel the 'Mountains of Eternity' that so enchanted the song's Mira.

"When we quested a precedent, Dagora remembered this tale from Tala.

Alexis was a wealthy young shara, deeply in love with a commoner, Mira. Without giving the slightest warning, she disappeared the day they were to be married. It was rumored the shara's father had gone in secrecy to her and forbade her to marry his son. Filled with grief, Alexis offered a regal reward for information leading to her discovery.

Reports came to the shara of many who claimed to have seen her. Many tales were false, but those which rang true always shared the strange fact that Mira was seen alone, surrounded by wild animals, high in the mountains.

Alexis' father told him he would disown him if he sought her. The shara waited for a year, torn inside; at last he renounced his birthright and set out to find his beloved.

Alexis roamed the wilderness for many years, seeking Mira during the warm months, seeking rumors of Mira during the cold seasons. He heard many tales in the valley villages; thrice he was convinced he saw her: on a distant peak, on the far side of a wide ravine, across a raging river. But he never found her: each time she vanished before he could reach her.

Finally, enfeebled with age, Alexis gave up and returned home to die. On his way down from the mountains for the last time, he chanced upon a cave one late afternoon. Winter was coming soon; he knew it would be severely cold that night. He huddled deep in the cave through those long dark hours, praying to understand why his life had been such a disastrous waste.

Alexis later swore that during the night his prayer was answered: Mira, still as young as spring, came to him and told him his life's quest would be fulfilled if he returned to that cave with the last breath of winter.

Alexis waited through the frozen months with feverish anticipation. As soon as the snow began melting, he set out one final time. He never returned to his father's people, nor was his body ever found. Some of the mountain villagers claimed, however, to have seen him, young again, dancing with Mira through the high meadows of alpine flowers, usually among herds of deer or elk.

The story passed into mythology, my Lord; it is responsible for the common sayings, "Alexis and Mira bring youth to those in love" and "Mira blesses those who care for the animals." It was also mentioned that our words, "mirror" and "mirage" probably came from this story of Mira.

"That is all of the tale," concluded Aldis. "And, I'm afraid, the best we could do, sire."

After he left, Gana said, "Joab! This tale stirred my memory! Years ago, just before my lives as Mars and Naisan, Almira mentioned a cave near Dawn Mountain. She said we were eternally united there. I must go in search of it! There I will find the key to discover my lost adaran."

"Perhaps," commented Joab. "But I wonder if this is what Atri meant? It seems rather — "

The Oathmaster was interrupted by a soft tapping on the window. When he opened it, in flew three elementals. They were wood elves, dressed typically — in ochres, auburns, verts. But they were flying in a triangle so tightly woven that Gana thought for a thoroughly strange moment they were physically joined.

The three landed before the adan, continuing to maintain their tight triangle. Only their golden faces turned toward him as they spoke.

"My Lord!" began one in his high, reed-like voice.

"We have — " continued another in identical tones.

"A message!" concluded the third in the same voice.

"Good," Gana replied warmly, amused that their unique mode of communication reinforced the impression they were a single being. "Is it important?"

"Very!"

"Yes!"

"Terrifically!"

"Ah? And just what might it concern, my three fine friends?"

"The adaran!"

"Venus!"

"Almira!"

"What!" cried Gana, his light pleasure replaced by the vital passion of his desperate need. "What? Joab! Can these three elementals alone know of my missing beloved? Such worthy souls! Let me have it!"

"We can't — "

"Exactly — "

"Let you — "

"Have it," they finished in a melodious trio.

"No? Do you have a message for your adan or not?"

"Yes! But — "

"It's not an `it´ — "

"Rather, it's a — "

"Who." The three separated and began to wander around Gana's meeting room, looking for any and every object of wood to enliven with their unique interpretation of life. But where they had stood was now revealed a tiny yellow flower fay. From extreme modesty, she had wound her wings so closely around her that only the tiniest area of her face still showed.

"Do not be afraid, my pretty lady," Gana said gently: he deeply loved the simplicity and beauty of the flower elementals. "Do you have something to tell me?"

She unfolded her dappled wings just a little before answering in a voice like the tinkling of tiny silver bells, "Oh, dearest adan! I am as you see me, a very small being; normally my only task is to bring life and dew to the buttercups and clover blossoms and to feed nectar to the baby seeds in the spring and only to the clover and buttercup seeds, mind, never others; and this is all I do and I enjoy it very much! and try my best to do it well. But I heard that the High Lord of the Fays commanded we were to watch for any sign of a certain minstrel lady dressed all in pretty green and for an adaran Almira, the Lady Venus! and that if we saw or heard or remembered either one, then we should at once stop our work and make it known before the adan himself! And that scared me for, oh dear me! I did remember such a one, or rather, did remember both, for I saw them both not long ago, walking together hand-in-hand, talking sweetly, laughing gaily. And the Great One, the one dressed like an adaran, all in whites and pretty yellows with a beautiful golden crown of fairest filigree stopped before me! and as I curtsied most carefully to her, she touched me on my head so it grew larger inside somehow and then she said that when he requested memories I should find the adan! and that scared me, but she said again that I should go to the adan when he requested memories and tell him, `Our world retains the record of all times and places, hidden in the Guardian Mountains´; and she made me repeat it seven times! just to make quite sure I had it just right. And then she said I should tell the adan this when he called for information, and when I heard the High Fays' message, I remembered! and then I asked everyone how to find the adan, and a very old tree, the wisest one I know, all covered with the largest burls of brown knowledge you could even imagine, the wise old tree said he knew three wood elves who knew how to find the adan, and so I sent a message to them and then they came and found me and they said they would take me to the adan and oh! Oh! I hope I've done the right thing! I hope I have! And please, please mister adan sire, may I go back to my clover blossoms and buttercups?"

"Little sharan, I am very grateful to you," said Gana. Bowing low to her, he took her tiny hand and kissed it. "You have helped your adan more than you could have ever dreamed." At this, she turned very, very scarlet and folded her wings back about her so closely that only the smallest part of one eye was visible.

"Take her back to her flowers; guard her well. She is a precious jewel, a Starbha among fays."

"At once, your majesty!"

"Immediately, sire!"

"Of course, your Excellency!" So saying, the three wood elves picked her up, found a break in their work and flew away.

During the fay's long speech, the three had been enlivening the wood of every chair, every table, every ornament in the hall. Trees were by now sprouting all over the meeting room, leaving very little room left in which to meet.

"Most marvelous," commented Joab, sitting in a young and growing sapling that a few moments before had been a maplewood chair. "How do you understand this message?"

"Were we not just discussing how to use Solon's Pool in lost Kanaan-dora? Now the answer comes, `The memory of all times and places is hidden in the Guardian Mountains.´ Joab! She guides me still! This must be my fourth task, there can no longer be doubt! I must find this record; when I do, it will doubtless reveal the knowledge I need! Will you come?"

"You know well I cannot. If this is truly your fourth task, you are required to walk now alone."

"So be it," answered Gana sadly. But as he turned to go he added brightly, "Well, do me one last favor. Call in some carpenters to bring this meeting room to order?"

~~~

The adan stood again on Dawn Mountain above the high waterfall, once more deeply moved by the beauty there. Sighing, he sat and began expanding his awareness through the mountains, seeking both the record and the Cave of Union.

Before he had really begun, a celestial appeared beside him. By his helmet and ebony uniform, he was an officer of the warrior caste. Bowing, he said with great agitation, "My Lord Mars! Our world is attacked!"

"Impossible! Who would dare attack this hallowed place, protected by Almira?" Gana replied, but realized at once his error. Looking toward the dawn, he saw the air darkened by the battle of the celestials and the invading demonic legions.

"A Rakshasa Lord, Setha-klesha, has been granted unprecedented power due to the fierceness of his austerity! My Lord! They taunt us that the Grandfather has granted him invincibility! We bend before him like grass in an autumn tempest! What are we to do? Para falls!"

"Find the exact words! No boon could be eternal for such as these! It had a beginning; there must be a flaw, there must be an end! Find it!"

The officer saluted and vanished. *Now I have no time! I must find her quickly: without Venus, Mars is powerless.* Again Gana let his mind flow through the mountains. Almost immediately, he found a cave; Almira's command entered him, *Search first here for knowledge, all will be well.* Eagerly, he let his vision run down the cavern. But it was stopped by some power he did not know; even with his full will, he could not move it farther. He would have to go there bodily!

Concluding this would take too long, he began to seek the cave where he and Almira were eternally one. It did not take much longer to find it in a nearby mountain. Another duplicate of his body was there, in a trance similar to the life-sleep in the Dome of the Spheres. But this body was both male and female!

Hermaphrodite! This is what she meant? Once the surprise of his perception passed, Gana realized that although double-sexed, the hermaphrodite was not grotesque; rather, it was simply what it was. At one moment, it seemed a beautiful golden woman; at the next, a magnificently handsome man; at the next, a couple in intimate embrace; at the next, a being of no sex at all.

When his awareness touched it, the hermaphrodite emerged from its trance and floated to him. Bowing, it said, "Command me, my adan."

At that moment, the celestial warrior returned. With a long side glance at the hermaphrodite, he said, "My Lord! We captured one of the foe and forced him to speak. As reward for a thousand years of arduous austerity, his master 'Klesha was in fact granted invincibility by the Grandfather. The exact words were, *Indestructibility by any male, female, or eunuch.* Thus he conquers the Universe; he sweeps our invincible forces before him like so much dust! What can we do?"

"My Lord Gana!" exclaimed the hermaphrodite excitedly. "I can certainly defeat these and their ruler: I am neither male nor female nor eunuch. Indeed, it occurs to me that this task, so impossible for others to accomplish, must be the sole reason for my creation."

"So be it," exclaimed the adan, relieved. "Take Nuriel, take Kaysta, take Starbha. Protect the Universe, offspring of my soul." *That should solve this,* he thought gladly.

But as the hermaphrodite flew off with the warrior to join the celestial army, the world suddenly decreased in color: the omnipresent light faded, an earthquake shook the mountain. Gana surveyed his land in doubt, then hurried to the first cave he had discovered.

A short emerald flame was burning in the cave's entryway. When the adan reached there, it coalesced into a tiny man, scarcely as tall as Gana's knees, clothed in a very dark emerald. Shaking his finger at the adan's face, he said, "You are not doing well, not well at all, not at all, not at all." He slowly faded away, but his "not-at-alls" continued echoing through the air like an eternal anathema. They seemed to be coming now from deeper in the cave; as Gana moved into the mountain through many turnings and down, ever down, the "not-at-alls" stayed before him, becoming progressively fainter. As they faded, so did the light. And so did the adan's memory.

At last the echo was entirely gone; it was utterly dark. Never before had Gana experienced such a pall of gloom. His ability to float vanished with the light; he began to walk. An inner voice shouted, "Go back, fool! Go back!" But a gentle warmth radiated from the book pressed to his chest, reminding him of his purpose. Love for Almira drove him stumbling on.

I must be lower than the plains, he thought, yet on he continued, deeper and ever deeper into the mountain. He began to feel he had moved there forever, that there was no other world than this unending cavern of silent nothingness.

By the time he had forgotten everything not only of Almira but of himself, a faint chartreuse light appeared ahead. Slowly but continually the cave became brighter as he moved onward and downward.

He emerged from the passageway into a verdant light as bright as sunlight. He was in a huge corridor, two leagues wide and one high, with no visible end in either direction. It was filled from floor to ceiling with books of all sizes and shapes, neatly shelved, all in varying shades of green.

Gana wandered aimlessly to his right, glancing at the titles, but could not read any. There were many kinds of print, many types of letters, but none in any language he knew.

Before very long, a wizened old lady appeared far down the corridor, scuttling toward him as if she were descended from a crab. She was bent nearly in half; three huge warts were her dominant feature: one on her grotesquely protruding chin, one on her hideously deformed nose, one that covered her otherwise repulsively indented forehead. She wore a shapeless short dark-green dress; her skin was a thoroughly nauseating verdigris, which fact made the adan suspect that in any light she would be green. A more ugly person he could not even imagine. But Joab had taught him that any form can clothe a heart of purest gold; he further believed that sometimes a soul chooses a homely body to perfect humility. He had also vowed to hold clear Atri's parting advice not to be fooled by appearance.

Bowing to her, Gana said, "My Lady, where am I?"

"Indeed," she creaked in a voice reminiscent of a rusty iron gate forced open after decades of disuse, "this inquiry is common among philosophers of all times, ranking second only to, `Who am I?´ But you seem to intend it rather more directly? I thought so, although the deeper might have served you better. Well, my role is not to choose the query, only to answer.

"This is the Universal Library. Anything happening anywhere in Narain's domain is herein recorded. In our small way, we mirror the absolute perfection of the never-changing truth of the Eternal One. The entire endless range of the Guardian Mountains is laced with these corridors. And I am Letha, one of the nearly infinite number of librarians placed here by the Grandfather to assist those who wander this way. You desire, I presume, a specific memory?"

They continued walking as she talked. The light began slowly decreasing in verdancy. With the change, Letha appeared a little less ugly, even a fraction taller.

"I wish to study the records of Solon's Pool in the lost land of Kanaan-dora."

"Well," she mused, "there are millions of Kanaan-doras existing today; an uncountable number that existed and were destroyed in one way or another: by fire, plague, war and so forth. But since you come from the small portion of Para that contains New Tala in the Cathedral of the Sun, you must be questing the Kanaan-dora whose refugees survived Valin and Martanda and settled Emura and Calantha? This makes it rather easier."

"Your knowledge is astounding!"

"Not. If the archivist does not know the seeker's needs, how can he find? The subject, however, is still quite extensive: every thought and deed at Solon's Pool are herein recorded. I assume you are only interested in, `Questions to Solon's Pool'; more specifically, those posed in the correct way to be answered?"

As she spoke, she decreased in ugliness, grew straighter, taller, less green; her voice became ever more pleasant. The light also continued subtly changing, although they stopped walking and stood before a wide branch corridor.

Fascinated by the marvelous changes she was undergoing, Gana nevertheless answered, "I seek knowledge of how to speak with Narain."

For the first time, his guide seemed surprised. "You travel around the world to see the nose on your face?" Letha chuckled, mostly to herself.

But then she smiled and added, "Yet sometimes that which is most obvious is hidden best of all. My Lady Matri, deathless master of the seventh wheel, once said:

> *The stream of life has many turnings:*
> *Now it rushes swiftly through narrow ways,*
> *Now it is caught in slowly turning pools.*
> *At times speaking in many voices,*
> *At times forced into silence,*
> *It travels always to join the larger water,*
> *The goal sometimes forgotten, sometimes known,*
> *Yet always there, waiting with infinite patience.*
> *And when two journey together to their final home,*
> *They merge to become one river with two shores,*
> *Stronger and greater than either in isolation.*

"I shall find the record you seek, my adan, though you choose one of the most difficult of paths. In ancient Kanaan-dora, one only was wise enough to ask this of Solon's Pillar, a minstrel girl named Lina. Let me see the book you carry!"

It was again his turn to be surprised. Was this librarian omniscient?

"I thought so! One chapter is exactly what you seek — you are carrying her history with you! As well, I might add, as the answers to several other questions you could (and perhaps should) have asked.

"Come, sit beside me while I translate Lina's tale for you." She sat on an ivory bench, ornately carved with exotic fruits and flowers.

Letha told the story in a voice that became more and more musical, more and more filled with life and health. All the while she spoke, her body increased in beauty, became more radiant, more soft, more tall, more perfect. *As if someone were needed to make her live,* thought Gana in amazement. *How long has it been since any came here?*

In the latter days of Kanaan-dora, there remained a few who could see and speak with the subtle beings of creation, the elementals and celestials.

Such was the sharan Lina as a child. Unlike many of her generation, she danced and played with the angels of the air, water and forests. Like many of her generation, she lacked no material thing. Her parents were very good to her, yet perhaps too good: she felt ever more stifled by their endless but shallow gifts.

Something of her long hours with her celestial companions merged with her spirit: Lina grew wondrous in beauty and voice. Many thought her singing magical: whenever she sang, they could see the images of her songs. Her fame spread widely and quickly; she performed throughout Kanaan-dora. The Starlord and Gemstone Council was especially fond of her; they requested her presence again and again. In time, her success eroded her innocence: her ability to see and hear the elementals and celestials gradually decreased and eventually was lost.

But before it altogether vanished, Darien, an eminent wind celestial, became enchanted by her music and person and fell hopelessly in love with her. He requested a human form in order to win her; after much long entreaty, he received it. "But only for seven days," commanded his Lord, "then you must return to your duty. What! You would permit blizzards in May?"

Gratefully accepting his new body, Darien descended to mortal flesh to woo Lina. He found her in a garden of indigo lilac and crimson wisteria; she was instantly overwhelmed by love.

They spent one joyful week together. At the last minute of his allotted time, Darien revealed his true nature. "Then I too shall become a wind celestial," she sobbed, "even if I must die to do this! I am yours forever!"

Darien reached out to hold her once more, but his moment had fled: he vanished in a cool breeze.

Lina sang no more from that day. Her sole interest was in finding the least scraps of knowledge of the celestials of the wind. Most thought her mad; many said she had entered one too many times into her magical songs and could no longer come out.

After years of discouraging wandering, Lina chanced upon an old Oathmaster in an ancient and all but forgotten valley. "I have been moved by your devoted search, my child," Rodavi's master Trita told her. "I will therefore tell you the answer you seek. You must be in Solon's Valley in the Sanctuary Mountains of 'Ishtar when the moon is full. There will appear in Solon's Pool a pillar of light. You must then ask how to meet Narain: he alone in all the spheres can fulfill your desire."

Filled with gratitude, Lina journeyed to the forgotten pool, but arrived one day late: although she was entranced by the water's quiet beauty, no pillar appeared. She built a small thatched hut and waited for the month to pass, staring all the dark hours at the pool to be safe, living on wild fruits, nuts and roots.

At the exact moment of the next full moon, she gazed into the water but beheld no pillar! Confused, she looked up at the moon. The Oathmaster had spoken so plainly! How could she have misunderstood him? Trita had said there would be a column of light in the water when the moon was full. But there was nothing!

Frustrated, Lina walked around the pool. She nearly despaired, but when she was directly across from the moon, she laughed in joy! For it was reflecting perfectly on the water, forming a column of light! And within the column appeared an image of a man's face, an Oathmaster, wise beyond any human she had ever met! Eagerly, she asked, "How may I see Narain?"

But Lina's heart was not entirely pure: she doubted the pillar because of a tiny seed of vanity for her marvelous beauty. She *received no answer but an enigmatic smile and the statement, "Appearance is meaningless."*

Sadly, Lina waited a second month, living mostly on water, trying hard to regain her youthful innocence. At the correct moment, she asked the Oathmaster's face in the pillar, "How may I talk with Narain?"

Lina still possessed, however, the faintest measure of pride for her extraordinary voice. There was no answer but a slight shake of the Oathmaster's head and the words, "Singing of the One is not the same as knowing the One."

Filled with remorse, she passed a third month, living mostly on air. At the correct moment, she said to the pillar, "I must meet Narain!"

This time, her heart swelled with love and certainty; at once Solon's answer entered her mind, "Go to Narain's Temple at the ocean. Sacrifice there your most precious possession. He will come."

Lina went to the temple at the ocean, took a dagger and without a second's hesitation ended her life.

Narain came to her and said to her spirit, "Never in Kanaandora have I known such a one as you! You are highly blessed, sharan; your wish is granted. Join to Darien as his wife; let your beautiful voice be a joy to all lands and peoples." Narain not only transformed her into a celestial, he made her music more enchanting than before. Her echo is still heard in forests, in stringed instruments and in seashells, my adan.

"Simplicity! Simplicity itself! Now will I be able to meet him." Gana thanked Letha warmly and stood to go. But she seized his hand and pulled him into her. He was shocked to see how absolutely free from imperfection her face and body had become.

In a low voice of sublime mastery, she said, "My adan, my adan! Would you rather not stay here with me, in the Home of All Knowledge? What could we not be together? What else in life has meaning?" Letha's passion was overpowering: listening to her for so long had captivated him. Her emerald eyes pulled him into her, closer, closer, closer...

At the final instant, his individuality's deepest root rebelled; its "No!" grew louder and stronger, reverberating inside him, until he shouted it. Her spell was broken; his spirit was loosed from her enrapturing will.

If he had not spoken, would he still be there, neatly shelved with an emerald green binding?

With his freedom, Letha transformed into the minstrel!

"You are Lina!"

"Once I was. And you were the celestial Darien I loved. Gana! This part is accomplished! Know that I am also Almira; this is but one of my unending forms!" She transformed once more into her radiant self. But as he moved to embrace her, she cried, "No! We must hasten, our time fails! You have made a grievous error."

The library vanished (was it only illusion?); they moved through the mountains as if the rocks were shadows, heading with the speed of her mind to Narain's Temple in the Cathedral of the Sun.

Gana was joyous to feel her presence everywhere! And the memory of her restored to everyone! But Para had become grey; he dreaded a terrible evil had befallen it during his absence.

"Not yet, my Lord." *But it impends. The army of Rakshasas was improperly destroyed. They were the mind-created enemies of your fourth wheel, the center of the universal nervous system which is your heart, Para itself. They had to be unmade, even as you corrected the ego-created beliefs of your first three centers: the Asur Overlords, Bala with the Legions of Zared, Firad with the traitors of Urlad. That was why you lived as Balzor, Alazar, Mars and Naisan.*

But you awoke our physically unified body too soon! This was to have happened only after you discovered me, hiding in the foundation of this world. This was the message I left at the cave's entrance! "Search first here for knowledge, all will be well." I could not be more explicit: you alone had to decide. My Lord, you chose wrongly! Setha-klesha alone was to be killed by our hermaphrodite body, that only after the destruction of the enemy host by our celestial armies. As it is, 'Klesha is dead, but so is our double form! What is infinitely worse, several Rakshasa lieutenants escaped our army and entered the energy channel which carries life from the fourth center to the fifth!

"Behold the Golden Thread!" A massive golden column of fire erupted from the ocean and shafted upward to the sun. High above, three Rakshasas were *inside* it, racing toward the solar disk. They were surrounded by thousands of celestial warriors, but they could not be touched, for they were inside.

"How — ?" began Gana in great and mounting confusion.

When the true ruler of our world, the hermaphrodite, was killed, this passageway blinked open. The sun was to be the site of your next task; but you are in no way ready for the fifth wheel's trial. Gana! If even one of those Rakshasas enters the doorway to Orah, all will be lost! Your life-sleep will end with your madness, for your fifth center will be permanently damaged! Para will be destroyed: our sun will nova! You must stop this! You alone can do so!

"But how? What can I do?" What was happening? What had he done? This couldn't be happening! What was going on? It was such a small mistake!

The world began spinning around him in faster and faster circles of light; he was ever more confused, ever more frightened by her thoughts.

You must fulfill your task: you must here destroy your most precious possession. You must break the Golden Thread! Naisan! You must kill me! I am the Golden Thread!

"What? Never!" He was warring against the terror in him now, battling with all his will the waves of horror that alternated wildly with waves of fear. Each rising impulse was more gripping and powerful than the last! His mind was failing before their onslaught! His heart was being torn apart in his chest!

There is no other way! You must do it! This suspended moment will be lost, but your life and sanity will continue. You will break the passageway to the sun when you break the Golden Thread, thus protecting our world forever. The lower three wheels have been purified, they will give it energy eternally: Para will be isolated from space and time so it can never again be attacked! Trust me! And remember, Narain will come to you! But you must hurry: see how closely the Rakshasas approach Orah!

"You must do it, Mars! *NOW!*"

She handed him a silver kris; he gaped at its jagged serpentine blade as his mind whirled chaotically through visions: Almira dying, lost to him forever; Joab's teaching, "Bodies perish, those indwelling, never"; the Rakshasas entering the sun; death raining on their world; all their people destroyed, from the mightiest celestial to the smallest flower fay.

With unlimited anguish, already completely demented, he sobbed, "This must not be!" and plunged the kris deeply into her.

"Victory forever to Gana, one true adan of Para!" she cried as she fell dying at his feet.

A silver shaft at once cut the golden column of fire: the sun and five hundred celestial warriors vanished. The remaining celestials fell upon the Rakshasas. But Gana was only certain two of them were killed — the last might have vanished with the sun and the five hundred celestials.

~~~

In the Temple of Kanaan-dora, the Living Statue of Gana shivered once violently, then fell forward to the floor. There it lay ominously still. Trickles of blood ran from its mouth, nostrils and ears.

~~~

From the wound in Almira's heart emerged a small green flame which rapidly expanded into a man: the Oathmaster Vaga.

He said sternly, "You have triumphed in your fourth task, adan, but at the expense of your last three. This world of your creation is eternally protected, but will sleep forever unless you again awaken. One boon I grant you in hopes of your eventual success: complete memory of all that has befallen you. Almira's moment has ended with her life; you no longer have a home here. You must therefore *Go now.*"

Instantly, Gana's awareness expanded again: all of Para became a small part of his heart in an infinitely larger body. The seven fiery wheels appeared before him, but vastly changed: the fourth wheel burned clear, but the connecting link with the upper three was broken: the top three wheels blinked out.

Almira once told him the seven wheels were the seven centers of life not only in his body but in the universal nervous system. What would her death mean for his life and for their Universe? That the seven were no longer functioning correctly was obvious. Were they permanently damaged? What could he do? How could he have committed such great evil? Why had he listened to her insane counsel?

~~~

The expansion continued; Gana found himself once more standing before the boundless ocean. The magnificent form of Narain reclined still on the serpent; uncountable billions of Golden Spheres, each containing a perfect Universe, surrounded him on all sides. The Sun King bowed to him; Narain raised one cerulean hand in blessing, smiled and said, "Never fear, shara."

The expansion in Eternity continued on: Narain, Sesha, the spheres, all the unending cosmos melted into the infinite light that was more than light of the One. At the apex came the thought which was not different from the experience: *Truth.*

~~~

Then implosion. Faster and ever faster Gana shrank and fell as his awareness and power became less and ever less. The last thing he experienced was a shattering of his mind into thousands upon thousands of fragments, as though he were a mirror dropped onto rock from the top of a cliff. One of the larger pieces re-entered his bleeding statue-body in Tala. The Temple of Kanaan-dora collapsed around him in violent earthquake; all of Sulara was in flaming ruin.

Gana knew no more.

17
A Black Ishaya

I stood among my valleys of the south
And saw a flame of fire, even as a Wheel
Of fire surrounding all the heavens: it went
From west to east against the current of
Creation and devour'd all things in its loud
Fury & thundering course round heaven & earth.
By it the Sun was roll'd into an orb:
By it the Moon faded into a globe,
Traveling thro' the night; for from its dire
And restless fury, Man himself shrunk up
Into a little root a fathom long.
— Blake

I awoke at the bottom of the crevasse. Sharon's crumpled and lifeless body lay beneath me, still warm but stiffening quickly in the cold. Amazingly, my mind at first remained clear and calm; I observed these facts without the slightest emotional involvement.

Edg was gone from the rim above. When he saw us fall, he must have returned for the others. How long ago? I had no way to tell. When would he return? Before dark? I didn't know. Was I all right?

My body was stiff but broken nowhere. Perhaps I had fallen onto Sharon; Sharon had broken my fall. Sharon!

The loss of Almira and the loss of Sharon flooded through me like a curse of damnation. I cried my agony to the uncaring ice, screamed my rage to the uncaring world. Why had Boanerge betrayed us? Why had I been so insane to listen to Almira's mad words in Para? These worlds were exactly paralleling each other!

What was going on? Why was my life being destroyed? Why was I such a fool?

I lay on my lifeless beloved's breast for hours, sobbing in misery.

After what seemed days, Boanerge's voice (sounding exactly like Joab's) whispered to me, "Ascend, child."

I did not care to listen. Why had Boanerge betrayed us? He had promised me there would be no more accidents! How could he not have forewarned me of this? No! He had set this all up — set her up to die! He told Sharon to come up here today! Told her to climb up here, knowing she would be killed! Why, God, why?

I felt a hand on my shoulder. I looked up through my tears — it was Boanerge, appearing to me now that I was fully awake. Or was I? I had felt awake the first time I met him, but that had ended as a dream.

"No, I'm really here," he said, answering my thought and smiling warmly at me.

"How? No! *Why* did you permit this? You know Sharon was the best among us. Why, Boanerge? You promised me there would be no more accidents. You promised me! Why?"

"This was no accident, shara. She set this all up long before this lifetime to assist you, to bring you to the Ishayas, to me, to the memory of your past."

His words lashed into me — he had called me shara! The two halves of my experience collided within me — which was vision, which reality? The crevasse began spinning around me; I felt an intense vertigo, a nausea born of competing worlds.

"What is going on here?" I sobbed. "Who are you? Who am I? Why me? Oh, God, why me?"

"It is time to learn your Second Sphere Cognition Technique, my Lord Mars. It will heal your mind completely, bring you endless peace. It is built of surrender to the Will of God."

"I have no desire to surrender to the Will of God, Boanerge!" I answered stubbornly. "If God could permit these senseless tragedies, why should I dedicate my life to that?"

Boanerge laughed. It was not malicious, but came from unbounded joy moving. But it felt like blows to me.

"Naisan, my Naisan, this game is far from over for you, you know. Once begun, once dedicated to the Healing of Time, a soul will do whatever it takes to be whole. Disfiguring illness. Crippled, deformed body. Death of children or lovers. A thousand-thousand bodies may fall away, yet onward the questing soul marches. You dedicated yourself to the healing of humanity, my Lord Gana. Long, long ago. I have watched you and guided you and played with you for countless lives. This game continues now from the weight of our shared past. You might dream that you wish to stop it now, but that is impossible. What is left of your ego is like a tattered cloud before a desert sun. Truly now, truly: do you wish not to know the Second Sphere Cognition Technique?"

"Damn you, Boanerge! I have nothing left. Nothing left to lose. Almira is gone. Para is gone. Sharon lies here dead. What have I to lose? But is that enough to motivate anyone? Why should I go any further with this Teaching? The more I learn, the less I have. Why should I want this? Why should anyone?"

"You're only losing your dreams, child."

"Doesn't feel like it!"

"Nevertheless."

"Will it heal me?'

"Of your current crisis, certainly... in time. Of your remaining trials, probably not — but then, we have five Spheres left, do we not?"

"Damn you, Boanerge! You play with me like a cat with a mouse."

"Assuredly so, my friend. It is my task to awaken you to your status. You *will* be a Maharishi, fully established in Unified Perpetual Consciousness, or die trying. And if that happens, rest assured, we'll pick up again elsewhere and later — we will rejoice again together beneath a new sun."

"Why are you doing this to me? Who am I?"

"That will be clear to you when you've mastered the Seven Spheres of Isha's Teaching. And I'm doing this for you because I care for you: you are my son."

"Will I ever remember anything? How could I have made such an insane error in Para? Why did Sharon leave me here? It all seems so senseless, so cruel."

"You will never understand until you master surrender, Mars. Your limited, ego-based will must die. Then you will understand the meaning of everything that has befallen you — and you will understand the great battle we are fighting for the mastery of all worlds and all times."

"Boanerge, Boanerge, I feel so unworthy, so ignorant, so helpless. I'm just one. What can I possibly do? The world is so large."

"You can do what any human can do, Naisan. You can love. And you can Teach. And you will Heal. Together we will save this world, and from here — all others. But one step at a time, OK? And your next step is for you to learn to surrender your limited will in all things to Cosmic Will."

"How can I do this thing? Cosmic Will pays no attention to our small pains. We live, we suffer, we die. God cares not. How can I surrender to that? It's senseless, cruel."

"It's neither senseless nor cruel. But you will never understand the movement of the larger wheel until you have grown fully in consciousness. There comes a point in every soul's evolution when one must decide whether to stay with the ego or go with faith. The ego has an agenda for you, an agenda that desires to keep you bound to the beliefs and judgments of the waking state. It will kill you to defend that agenda. It will torment you and destroy you if you dare challenge its authority."

"Could that be any worse than this torment I feel now? Could its destruction be any worse than yours?"

"That's where your choice must be made! There is no help for you until you learn that all choices come from you. You are creating your Universe in each and every moment. Once you've understood that, you will recognize that surrender to Cosmic Will means surrender to your own higher Self. There can be no loss that is real after that."

"It all sounds like words to me, Boanerge. And yet here lies Sharon, dead, growing colder. Why not just heal her? You promised us all immortality, remember?"

"She chose this path, Naisan. Not me. Why would I wish to invalidate her free will?"

"Why would she choose to die here, now? It's senseless, cruel beyond belief. I don't believe you. I don't think you know any more than I do. Maybe you've lived a long time. Or maybe you're just a fantasy of my deluded brain. I don't know anything. But I do know that I don't want any more instructions. No more techniques. It's all too painful. Everything is being stripped from me."

"You can stop anytime you choose. But if you continue on now, you will have the answer to your question, to all your questions: you will understand who you are, who I am; you will understand your destiny and the fate of this Earth. You will become a Healer, a Teacher, a Worker of Miracles. And our suffering world needs you to be you desperately."

"Do I care for others enough to renounce my own pain?"

"Your question answers itself, doesn't it?'

"My arguments are futile against you, Boanerge. I have no choice here, not really. Of course I have to go ahead. Kill me if you must, take everything I treasure from me, yet still onward will I move. I don't have any choice."

"Of course you do. The fact that it appears you don't proves my point. You are here for one reason only: to learn who you are and then communicate the Truth to others. But don't take my word for it. You will know it soon enough by your own direct experience."

My protests had grown feeble. I was enraged at him; I was sure he had lied to me and might well be lying to me now, and yet I knew I had no hope of ever understanding anything at all about life without knowing the Seven Spheres of Isha's Teaching.

As I lay next to my lost beloved to practice the new technique, I asked Boanerge, "More visions coming, then?"

"You bet," he replied, smiling and winking.

"Not too surprising, that. You're sure: there will be an end?"

"You will awaken, my son. And together we will again be as one. We are with you always!"

~~~

I must have already been slipping inward from the power of the new technique, for I thought I saw Sharon standing now next to Boanerge, and she was Almira.

Her lips formed the words, "I love you."

And then once more I was gone from our Earth. Would I again return? And what more would I lose this time?

18
The Well

The surface shows calm
Where the river runs deep.
— Rodavi

All power is yours
In heaven and on earth.
— Mordom

Only a fool mistakes
Innocence for ignorance.
— Joab

Jacob stood by the well. He was no longer young: his flowing beard and hair, once flame red, had long ago turned to charcoal and were now streaked with ash. He wore a plain woolen robe, gathered around the waist by a strand of rope. On his feet were the simplest of sandals, each made from a single piece of wood with rope for a thong. No ring ornamented his hands, nor was there anything else on him or about him other than the robe, rope and sandals.

Jacob stood by the well his father had dug, silently stood as he had every day for so very many years. His sole purpose in life was to let the bucket down whenever someone came by and then bring it back up, filled with the clear, cold water. This he did, day after day, year after year, through all the seasons: during nature's youth, as his humble eyes smiled for every sign of the reawakening world; during summer's heat, as he stood in the shade of an old tree his father had planted the day Jacob was born, an unfailing source of crimson harvest fruit; during the coldest of winter, after he pushed a trail through deep snow so he could stand vigilant through the few daylight hours.

Jacob stood by the well today as every day of his long life, but again today not one came to drink! The peasant sighed, "The seventh day! How shall I live if I receive no grain for the sweet water?" He heard the animals whispering that a grave danger approached the land, but Jacob had never been afraid. Nor did he ever trouble his silent peace with politics: he did not know whether his country was democratic or tyrannous. Nor did he care to know: he never asked any who sought the water for news, nor did he listen if they talked of the ways of the world.

Once an itinerant scholar, pitying the peasant his simplicity, tried to teach him of the great, wide world. Jacob was standing by the well (as he always had and always would) when along had come this child of bitterness (as Jacob thought him), a man not half his age, but so bowed and careworn as to seem years older. Jacob had listened patiently, but throughout the learned discourse, he thought only, *None of this is for me! I stand by the well to draw water. This is life; this is all.* The wise scholar, despairing of helping such an ignorant fool, had gone away cursing. But Jacob soon forgot him, just as the boundless ocean absorbs the waves of any boat passing over its surface.

Once also a popular saint chanced by the well. This one was famous world-wide, not for the power of his mind but for the healing authority of his heart. He came to the well as Jacob was busily working, lowering and raising the bucket for travelers. A soft glow began to spread over the saint's face as he watched him; when Jacob turned to him with a bucket of the perfect water, the saint fell at his feet and kissed them, saying, "Blessed are you among celestials and men!" and then went away, singing joyfully.

For a few weeks, Jacob had more work than usual: those who deified the saint found his behavior at the well quite fantastic. But since nothing else at all ever happened at the well, the people stopped coming just to see the peasant: the most remarkable thing about him was the total lack of anything whatsoever remarkable about him. He spoke only to answer questions about the water or direction. And on the second topic, his comments were of hearsay only: he had been born in the hut of his parents and had never gone beyond the hills around the small valley which contained the well.

Of the thousands who passed by Jacob's well during the eighty years he raised the clear, sweet water, only these two, the scholar and the saint, took any interest in him — the one to improve, the other to approve. Everyone else drank the water and looked at Jacob with as much interest as if he were the rope attached to the bucket.

Thus the long years passed through Jacob's silence. The peasant knew neither luxury nor want, desired neither a better home nor riches, missed nothing of the many things for which other men of the great, wide world fought and died.

But today, as Jacob stood by the well and no one came for the water, he thought, *All is not well in the world. If the people do not drink, what will become of them? Perhaps I should go see what has happened. But then, what would become of the well, if no one draws her?*

Shrugging slightly, Jacob said, "Good-bye house. Good-bye well. Good-bye, tree." For the first time, the peasant strode out of the valley of his fathers, not once looking back, never to return.

It was spring when Jacob left the well; the days were warm, the nights still cool. He walked all that day but met no one. Past the valley's small hills, the land was flat, treeless plain. The dusty trail continued straight ahead with neither curve nor branch. As the sun set in a glory of crimson and aureate and darkness quickly came, he lay in the soft grass and watched the stars appear.

Jacob had often slept outside and was deeply intimate with the firmament. Many times, he identified so strongly with its silent procession that it took him a few moments in the morning to remember that he was Jacob, not the Grandfather's empyrean above.

Rising at dawn, Jacob continued on. Within an hour, he came to a grouping of houses and thought, *This must be the village so many said was such a friendly place! Surely now I can learn what happens to the world, why nobody comes for the sweet water.*

No one at all was there. It was an ugly, cramped place and stank; he did not wish to stay long. There were some dried figs hanging from a wall and a loaf of bread that was still fresh on a table; he took these and ate them.

Out of the village, Jacob came upon a fork in the road. Stopping, he fingered his beard as he thought, *Now, what is this? One road becomes two? Why do they need two? Is not one enough? Where could they possibly want to go?*

While he stood confused, a red fox leapt from the grass, turned a somersault in mid-air and landed neatly in the middle of the fork. He cocked his head and sat looking at the peasant with his bright, sharp eyes.

"Hello, red," Jacob said. Although he didn't love the foxes so much as some of the others, he had no aversion toward them and gave them the water when they asked for it.

"Hello, Jacob," laughed the fox, for he had visited the well before. He scratched his ear as he added, "Where are you going, leaving the sweet water?"

"I seek the other people of the world. Do you know where they have gone?"

"Do not. But I saw them all going, not all at once, yet every day a few, until the last left just yesterday in a frantic hurry. They were most careless about it: some even forgot a few chickens. Very kind of them, I thought." He licked his paw as his eyes gleamed with the memory of plump hens. "The humans, if you're really interested (though for the life of me, I can't imagine why), went down this road." He lifted his whiskers at the wider branch.

"Then, I must go that way," said Jacob, walking on without another thought of the fox. But the small beast had nothing better to do that fine spring day; he trotted beside the peasant and chuckled tales about rodents and rabbits and hunting. Jacob had no interest in those things; he gave him no answer. As the fox was very fond of his own voice, however, and furthermore rarely had anyone to talk to, he accompanied him for a long time. The sun was approaching mid-afternoon when the fox stopped suddenly, pricking up his ears. The next instant, he bolted back the way they had come, ears pinned back, tail flying straight behind.

Jacob soon heard what had so startled the fox: a distant, vibrating thumping, steadily becoming louder and louder, so that the ground began to shake. When he reached the crest of a little hill, he saw below more people than he had ever imagined. They filled the plain for leagues, as far as he could see.

I did not know there were so many men in all the world! What can they be wanting together? They would drain the well! How do they eat? Some were on horseback, but most on foot; all were dressed in gray. Some looked angry, some sick, some afraid, but most dull. Asleep from the hopeless sameness of their lives?

These could use the clear well: hardly do they live at all.

A mounted officer spurred over to him and shouted angrily, "Why are you still here? This province was ordered clear last week!"

Jacob looked at him with wonder and answered, "I didn't know." Why would they send everybody away?

"Well, go now!" the officer cried, then jabbed his spurs into his gelding's flanks.

Jacob called after him, "Where?" but the soldier was already beyond hearing or caring.

Few others looked at him. Only one more spoke to him: a youth, little more than a child, stepped out of file to tie his bootlace. He was one of those who seemed mostly afraid; when Jacob asked him, "Where do you all go?" he stared at the old man in astonishment.

"To defeat the invaders, of course! To war! You truly have not heard the demonic Salazian Legions defile our sacred soil?" Without waiting for an answer, he ran to regain his place.

After the columns of men came cannons, then wagons filled with munitions and provisions. Last of all were four carts filled with women.

~~~

Jacob walked on until the stars were well out, then lay down for his usual dreamless sleep, perfect imitation of an innocent child's.

The next day had hardly begun when a brilliant golden moving light appeared in the far distance. Almost before the peasant knew it was indeed a horse *and* a rider, they were beside him. The stallion reared to a sudden, unexpected halt; Jacob stared in amazement: never had he seen a nobler animal; the man on his back, carrying a drawn sword of opalescent fire, shone with a fulgence rivaling the sun. The horseman cried with stern majesty, "Jacob! You left the well!"

"Lord! The people stopped coming! I wondered how I was to eat? So do I seek them, thinking all cannot be well in the world."

"What strange doubts inspired you to abandon your sole charge! Now what will become of the well? You can't believe your efforts feed you? None lives in isolation; always are we nourished by our Mother. Have you not seen the animals, learned their secret?"

"I know them. But I always thought a man must be different, must be more consciously active to fulfill his duty."

"How so, foolish child! Jacob, because you left your one task, a different well is now given you: continue onward to the city Falon, three days further down this road. There share the new water with the people: many die from thirst daily."

The peasant protested, "Where is the new well?" But the stallion raced away: war had come again to the west; many were to perish in the days ahead.

~~~

Jacob came to Falon on a market day; a large crowd, not only of the city but also of the surrounding villages, was gathered in the central square. The peasant looked over the noisy throng and thought, *What have I to do with these?* But then he remembered the Golden Rider; a wave of strength swept through him. Climbing onto a stone fountain, he cried, "Brothers, hearken unto me!"

Some laughed in surprise (such things were *not* done in Falon). Some cried with anger, "How dare that peasant call us his brothers!" and turned away. But some, grateful for any novelty in their unchanging days, looked at him curiously.

Not knowing how, not knowing what he would say next, Jacob spoke in a strong voice that came from his heart and touched the hearts of many. "My brothers and sisters! I am sent to quench your thirst! I heard you have never tasted the well; indeed many of you have already perished and cannot receive the clear water I pour freely for you.

"Come! Let us sing together our joy in Love. Does not the Mother bring forth in warmth and silence? Is not the fertile Earth ever-growing? Is there not pure water enough to satisfy all desire? When has the sun failed to shine since first you breathed the sweet breath of life?

"With this fair world of green-blue and golden brown, why is there pain? Why do you suffer? A garden is planted to bring joy! For how long will you dwell in darkness, you children of Light and Truth? Why do you strike your kind Father? When in your short and troubled lives have you not doubted and turned from the well?"

Most passed on, not understanding, not caring to understand. But some few stayed, a painful hunger in their eyes, deeply moved by the peasant's simple phrases.

Two hours later, when he ran out of words, several asked, "Teacher! Where do you stay?"

"Teacher?" he chuckled softly. "The peasant has just come from the valley. He has no place but the open air. What more does he need?"

But Sanel, a dealer in foreign cloth, said, "Please come to my villa, sir! I have a pleasant home and garden near the edge of the city."

"I should like to see a garden," said Jacob, and at once started off with the merchant.

But others cried, "Wait! When do you speak again? We must hear you speak again!"

"When do the people gather?"

"Here, every third day."

"Then let it be here, in three days."

As they walked to his villa, Sanel told him, "For many years I have felt a certain darkness in my life, a kind of emptiness, hard to define, hard even to understand. I have a wonderful wife and baby girl; my parents left us enough we need never worry. Yet there is a hole in my life. I have studied all branches of knowledge, all seem incomplete. Even Joab's *History of Lord Gana* fills me only with knowledge, never with the experience of Reality. I have heard many discourse on the nature of truth, but it was not until today that I thought, `Here is a man *living* his Teaching! Here at last is one who not only speaks, but knows!´

"This is why I asked you to our home. And sir! If I can aid you in any way, please tell me!"

Jacob discovered here something he had rarely seen. The merchant was cloaked with a certain awareness, a vibrancy of life discoverable in others mostly by its absence. He made most of the Falons seem lifeless wraiths by comparison.

Jacob's heart went out to him; Sanel felt an intense flood of peace engulfing him.

~~~

The next day, Jacob walked alone through the great city Falon, astonished equally by the many huge colonnaded stone buildings and by the misery on the faces of the people. Coming at noon to a commercial square, he was surprised to see an old flower vendor who couldn't walk.

"Why don't you move about like these others?" Jacob asked curiously.

"Alas, sir," answered Aldis sorrowfully as he peered up at him through his honest but tired eyes, "I have been lame since birth. Never have I had the use of my legs, never known the simple joy of moving about easily."

"There sits a marvel! Not to walk, not to use the legs given him by his Mother and Father! Do you think you are a snake, thus to crawl on your belly?"

"Cruel man! You mock me!"

"What do you mean! Do you believe your Parents wish you to suffer?"

"No? No, I do not understand why they should. Still, I do not walk."

"Do you not? Do you not, indeed? As the Mother is Love and the Father, Forgiveness, I say you have no choice but to stand, a Living Man!"

Aldis stared at Jacob for five full minutes, his face changing from sandstone to granite to sandstone again. A violent shaking vibrated through him, rising from his feet to the top of his head. Then slowly, hesitantly, with a peculiar admixture of fear and faith, he stood. Jacob chuckled and passed on; Aldis walked throughout Falon, the tears flowing over his time-worn cheeks as he cried, "The eyes! His eyes! Look at me! Everyone, everyone look! I walk! *I walk!*"

~~~

That evening, Sanel eagerly sought Jacob throughout the villa. This was the second time the merchant had tried to approach him. Last night, as Jacob sat in the small courtyard garden, Sanel had knelt beside him and plied him with question after question, seeking to fill every gap in his understanding of life. But Jacob had responded with an imperturbable silence, accentuated only by his broad and perfectly serene smile. Sanel, abashed, vowed to leave him alone until he again volunteered information. The merchant had succeeded all day, but the rumors about the flower vendor broke through the wall of his restraining will.

Sanel found him now, sitting before the fire in the study. Throwing himself into an adjacent chair, he said brusquely, "Is it true?"

"Is *what* true?" countered Jacob, smiling at the fire.

"Everyone is saying you healed old Aldis, the flower vendor of Commerce Square! Did you?"

"I healed no one. I asked him why he wasn't like everyone else. That's all."

"But he never walked before! Why suddenly now?"

"Perhaps he never tried. Perhaps no one ever asked him. Who knows? He does now; surely it is enough?" Jacob looked up from the fire with a child-like innocence that somehow drained away the merchant's curiosity, leaving a confused but deep serenity in its stead.

Mumbling, "Well, good night, then," Sanel stumbled off to an early bed.

~~~

The next morning, as the merchant passed the peasant's room, he saw that Jacob had not slept there. Hurrying to the study, he found him sitting exactly as he had the evening before, staring still at the ashes of the fire. The peasant was completely still; for a fearful moment, Sanel thought he must have died during the night! Jacob looked up at him suddenly, surprise widening his gray eyes, then shook his head firmly. Sanel was too startled and confused to bother him again.

But that night, his wife Leora conquered her own fears and quietly approached Jacob as he sat in the study, staring at the fire rekindled for the cool evening. The peasant moved his gaze slowly from the flames to her, then smiled warmly.

Taking three deep breaths for calmness, she tightly clutched the back of the chair and said a little huskily, "Sir, last night my daughter Susan ran to me, crying in terror, and said she had seen a wild elephant! When I asked, `Where?´ she replied, `Just there! There he goes!´ and stared into the moonlit garden. This was not the first time she's had such visions; her fantasies have many times been vivid to her. But last night she was so afraid she could not be calmed until I looked into the garden and assured her there was nothing there. I was wondering if you could — "

Jacob stared at her with surprise as he tried to understand. Finally the strangeness of it all burst forth: "What! You truly did not hear the trumpeting of that fear-stricken beast, quite enough to awaken the dead, let alone the sleeping? Nor that huge lioness chasing him, screaming her awful rage?" Jacob's perennial smile was replaced by a slight tightness around his mouth; his forehead wrinkled a little from the strain of trying to comprehend the strangely limited senses of this otherwise stunningly beautiful person.

"My Lord! I neither heard nor saw," Leora answered, her lovely ebony eyes wide with surprise.

"You are so full of the world you do not see the beings of light? Can it be possible? I never dreamed, dear one... Leora, Leora! What then would you do if a messenger from your Father appeared in your entryway? If you can neither hear nor see, how would you know of his coming?"

"I — I do not know, Jacob," she stammered with deep sadness. But she brightened as she asked, "Is there hope for my being one day as my Susan? Can you teach me?"

"I can teach no one anything! But you can perhaps regain what you have lost... So long ago you have forgotten who you are... Given enough time." The peasant looked back at the fire, surprised yet mildly amused by this discovery.

~~~

The next day, Jacob stood again on the fountain's rim in the marketplace. The crowd was larger: many had heard of Aldis. Some who had attended before were saying Jacob was in wisdom like the Oathmasters of Emura and Tala. But others laughed,

"What similarity is there between the wise Joab or the superhuman rajanya Mordom and this noisy peasant?" And others scorned them, "Here? In this modern day? A myth walking the world? How utterly mad!"

Jacob looked up through the bright azure sky at the many small spring clouds racing overhead, fleeting memory of last night's storm, and thought that today he might share the new water with many like Sanel.

Jacob drew deeply from the new well as his voice boomed over the assembled thousands, "I have a crystal cup, cut from a single diamond of imperishable beauty! Let me fill it with the golden light of the living well! Drink its fire, let the power of the One course through your bodies of clay! Drink! to remember you are the sons and daughters of Father Sun! Drink! to sing together in the coming dawn!

"Oh my lost children! Weep no more in loneliness! Live no longer the sad emptiness of your private night! Let your gates open to my fragrant draught! Orah's chariot but awaits your permission to battle the demons of doubt and greed! The Sun yearns to carry his fire into your frozen hearts!

"Hear my voice, crying to you from your own soul! Show me there is still life inside your rigid dying bodies, show me you can still see through your purblind eyes, else I must despair and turn to others! For if you are already dead, of what use the sweet water I pour freely for you?"

An older man, at once moved and terrified by Jacob's deeply penetrating voice, cried, "Teacher, you pierce my heart! I long to share your cup! But my mind struggles to reach you; I am confused! You say life should be all joy? You say suffering is not meant to be in our lives?"

Jacob gathered a fold of his robe and peered at it as he answered, "There stands one who hears with both ears."

"I believe the Grandfather originally ordained life so! But the labors of Navril Hagar, the Asur Emperor Valin, perverted his intent and now life is married to death, happiness to pain, health to disease! Consider, for example, the passing of babies who have experienced nothing of life! Where is the all-embracing love, the divine joy in such tragedies?"

Jacob, staring intently at his robe, asked, "Is it possible any should die early?"

Some exclaimed with disgust, "Why listen to a peasant so ignorant of life!"

Jacob looked up from the wool with a wild look of surprise which some misconstrued as anger and answered them, "You grieve for the Living! If an infant returns early to the Mother and Father, should it cause pain? You think you create life! Never has it been so! You reflect the soul of Narain, the light of the One; this also mirrors in your children. You can't believe you own them? They are not your goods, not your chattel; your responsibility is to cherish them, to protect them as a sacred trust. Where, then, the grief? If a poor man comes into vast wealth, does his family mourn?"

~~~

When the shadows climbed Jacob's robes and caressed his lips, he ended abruptly, "When shall we meet again?"

Many shouted, "Tomorrow! Let it be tomorrow!"

"What of your daily tasks?" he laughed gaily.

But they answered him, "Nothing matters but seeing you and hearing you speak!"

"Then let it be tomorrow," he smiled as he walked off with Sanel.

A young nobleman named Arthur, very tall and fair with profoundly azure eyes, hurried after them, crying, "Teacher! Hold!"

Jacob had noticed him earlier — an improbable reflection from the declining sun had for a time played over the youth's golden head alone while all others were in shade.

Arthur, swallowing with difficulty, said, "Teacher! For years, I have prayed for guidance, begging the Grandfather to reveal meaning in this harsh world. Many times, your face appeared before me in vision. The last time — just last night! — there was also a voice like the crashing roar of a great ocean, `Follow this man. He will teach you of the One.´

"At last I have found you; never will I leave you!" Arthur threw himself at the peasant's feet and kissed them.

Chuckling softly, Jacob raised him. "If you would go with me, who will stop you? Come, eat with us."

Thus did Arthur come to Jacob, the same Arthur who would one day protect the Five Hundred from the Salazian Legions.

~~~

Late that evening, Jacob sat in Sanel's study before the fire, contemplating its flames. Sanel and Leora, Arthur, Aldis and a few others were there, hearts full with his silence, minds straining to understand him.

A sharp knock brought the merchant abruptly to his feet. He hurried to the entryway, thinking, *Who could come at such an hour?*

Opening his door, he discovered a shabbily dressed young man. The visitor stared at him fervently for a long moment and then exclaimed raucously, "There is a teacher here! I must see him." The light from the gas lamp behind him made his unruly sable hair appear almost demonic.

"He is here," whispered Sanel, perplexed by such intensity of word and form. "But he has not spoken all evening; he only smiles at the fire, thinking private thoughts. I would recommend you wait until tomorrow and — "

"Sanel!" boomed Jacob's voice from the study. "Bring Steven to me; never deny or even postpone entry to those who Live!"

"If you would go with me, who will stop you?"

Although his wild appearance well masked him, this visitor was a shara, eldest son of an adan of a distant country. At the age of twelve, he had concluded the highest value of court life was in its absence and had left home, desperately seeking an alternative. He had discovered many with much learning during these past nine years, but as of yet, not one who could fill both his heart and mind, not one with sufficient integrity and personal power to meet his high expectations and desires.

Today, however, he had heard of the peasant Jacob, a man who spoke of life differently from others, with strength and wisdom and manifest love. There were many stories racing around Falon about fifteen remarkable cures that had taken place while the peasant was speaking; many of the credulous were saying he was a Miracle Worker of unprecedented power.

Steven eagerly sought the merchant's villa, but stood outside, divided in mind, for several hours. There were so many false teachers in this impoverished age! What if — again! — this peasant were only another? At last, he gathered his courage. Certain he would be disappointed, he requested entry. And now he was being led, his heart beating against his chest like a newly caged lion, into the heart of Sanel's villa.

How could he have known my name? he thought, even as the presence embodied in the study began flooding through his spirit.

Jacob, staring still only at the fire, said warmly, "Welcome, my son! But where is the child Deborah?"

Steven discovered chaos. How could this simple looking peasant know of the urchin who had dogged his heels for the last month? Long had he cursed himself for sharing the crust of bread that earned him her loyalty. It had taken him until that very morning to escape her watchful eye. *Could he have seen us together? I have never met him before! How then, can he know of Deborah?*

As Steven's mind raced through multitudes of improbable solutions to explain this peasant's impossible knowledge, his mouth dropped open in disbelief. Reaching the only reasonable explanation, he decided he must have dreamed the question and asked in a tone that implied he expected no answer from such a simple-looking old man, "What is the ground of all knowing?"

Jacob, looking still only at the flames, moved his awareness fully to confront Steven. The effect on the shara was to split his mind between the vision reported by his eyes that the peasant had not moved and the deep intuitive perception that he had and was now staring at him.

Jacob, pleased to discover how well Steven perceived this manipulation of the One, said with what appeared deep sadness, "You desire more life when you squander what you own? I ask you again, shara Steven, eldest son of Johannes of Celamir and Ambarina of Selorina, *what have you done with my lost daughter Deborah?"*

The shara could deny the pressure on his heart no longer. His mind a chaos of wild confusion and passionate hope, he fell to his knees before the peasant, choking, "My Father! Forgive me! I — I left her this morning in Samora. But — "

"But? But? You come back to me with excuses? You expect the Mother's grace if you deny those who depend on you? *Go from my presence, dare not return without the child!"* Jacob's eyes moved slowly from the fire; the power of his gaze for the first time thrust deeply into Steven's auburn eyes. An intense light burst into life in the shara, paling the room.

"I go at once!" he cried. Leaping up and giving an awkward half-bow, he ran from the villa. Nor did he stop running until he had almost reached Samora and found Deborah asleep in the grass by the side of the road.

Taking her in his arms, he cried gladly over her; the child awoke with a laugh, "Oh, Steven! Steven! I knew you could never leave me!"

Thus did Steven first come to Jacob, the same Steven who would lead the Five Hundred after Jacob's death.

~~~

Nearly three thousand broke their daily routines to listen to the peasant in the closed market the next morning. The empty stalls and booths seemed to him a fitting symbol: the energies of the world appeared as a finely tuned balance he alone had been given the ability to adjust. Knowing it was his last speech, he held back nothing: for twelve hours, he gave of the fullness of his spirit as his powers of expression grew without limit. His voice, at first beautifully resonant and full, gradually transformed to become so perfect as to be more than verbal: almost it seemed as if his thoughts were passing directly and distortion-free into the listening minds without the medium of the mild spring air.

These were the final public words of the peasant Jacob in Falon:

"My people! I ask you one final time, why do you turn from me? What impulse of perversity closes your hearts, we who were joined in the Eternal Light and Song of the One in the Beginning?

"Why do you deny both the Nectar and the Bread? Is the clay grown so thick in your ears you cannot hear me crying, alone in a city of the Dead? Have your judgments and beliefs so dulled your senses you can neither taste nor smell, but touch only?

"What can I do so you will eat my wholesome grain? Must I break this old body before you will listen to me? My soul yearns for your presence; my hand stretches forth to grasp again your love, flowing in rivers from your melting hearts!

"Have you so forgotten the Joy? Was not one taste from the Cup enough to reveal the vibrant life of the One?

"Why do you search in the desert for water? Why do you crawl through the weeds seeking the bread?

"With the Burnished Gold in your hands, why do you barter for the mirage?

"Your daily poisons have blinded you! You have sacrificed Truth to the idols of a degenerate mankind!

"Of what use your hearts without strength! Of what use your lives without Love!

"In the dawn of Creation, your will was manifest! Why let this twilight of superstition cloud your dreams? The Source has returned today! Rejoice with me! Forgive yourselves, forgive the world, dance in the light of the One!

"Will you not share the sweet water? I tell you this truly: the Darkness and the Light become now more intense. The Darkness, to be rooted out and forever destroyed; the Light, to triumph for all time.

"My people! Do not awaken the fourth day hence and find yourselves among the stubble after the reaper has passed! I tell you now in plain speech, the fate of Falon is fire!"

Startling himself, Jacob let his mind slip inward, challenging the awful truth he had just discovered. For ten minutes he wrestled with his doubt as his listeners looked at him with increasing confusion. What was he doing? Was something wrong with him? He was staring above them, over their heads; those who were close enough saw his eyes move quickly, as if they were watching something or someone. These craned their necks to follow his gaze but could see nothing but the limestone of the bank across the square and, above that, the flawless azure of the spring sky.

Finally Jacob trembled once and, looking back at the Falons, cried in full voice, "Be it so! The moving script continues on! Let none oppose its violent decree! At the fourth dawn hence, I will lead forth those who are Alive; only the Dead shall remain.

"Leave behind everything, save only the clothes you wear, one blanket, and enough food for seven days. You must all come: after the peasant's final walk, this seven days' journey, you will be delivered from the city of the Dead into a new and superior world."

Many cried, "See! The peasant *is* mad!" But some remembered the war to the west and were deeply troubled. And some, those most moved by his presence, decided without hesitation to go.

~~~

That evening, three of Falon's leading officials met in the administrative offices of the largest bank in the city. The maroon velvet carpeting and rich wall hangings were placed to accentuate rather than hide the thick limestone. The owner of the bank loved permanence; he always felt a powerful force of stability radiating from the rock, quite thoroughly opposed to the strange temporal weaknesses of common humanity. He leaned back in his swivel chair and ran his hands through his decreasing hair as he made his point once more, "No! I say again, we are being fools. Do we not control Falon? Why should we allow a *peasant* to disrupt business? Three thousand today! Why tolerate such slothfulness? A terrible day. The worst this quarter. I tell you, he must be banned."

The mayor stopped pacing to stare at him. Why were bankers always concerned only with the size of their pocketbooks? What was important about business when the essence of Falon's future was being poisoned? He said brusquely, "You have completely overlooked this Jacob's importance. Prevent him from speaking publicly, he will continue in private. We have only one way to keep him from corrupting the youth. That which has always worked before will not fail us now: he must be executed."

"You can't be serious!" exploded the captain of the police, angry with both of them. *A harmless lunatic shouts in the square and our leading citizens think it important. No wonder the diabolic Salaz nation conquers the world,* he thought with contempt for his race. "He is obviously a troublemaker, quite probably mad. But he said today he will be gone soon. We need only patience. And please, half a measure of common sense."

"But many will go with him!" cried the banker and the mayor in one voice.

"You don't think so? Who would leave his home to follow a raving lunatic? They have merely found an excuse for a holiday. Believe me, twenty-four hours after this peasant is gone, no one will remember a word he said."

"At the very least, I agree we must forbid any more of those logically absurd speeches," grumbled the mayor, far from satisfied with this solution, but seeing no way to penetrate the captain's firm indifference.

"No sense in allowing this illegal holiday to continue another working day," agreed the banker sourly.

The police came to Sanel's villa and told the merchant Jacob could no more speak in the market or anywhere else in Falon under penalty of death.

The peasant nodded serenely at the fire when Sanel told him the news. The merchant, as ever eager to help this strangely silent giant, said, "I have a field of young barley to the west of town. We can meet there, it will hold many thousands."

And Arthur said, "I could speak to my uncle. He is captain of the police. He could over-rule this."

But Jacob laughed with deep amusement and answered them, "No, they have been told enough. They must choose whether to Live or Die. The simple truth is: I never had anything at all to say."

19
The Living and the Dead

Pain is the thought of evil
Wreaking havoc with your perfect mind.
— Rodavi

We all create our own world.
Happy or sad, healthy or sick,
Wealthy or impoverished,
We live as we choose.
There is no one to blame.
There is no one to thank.
There is no one but ourselves.
— Mordom

The Five Hundred will choose life
When death appears the straighter path.
— Joab

As Jacob spoke that day, the last retreating remnant of the army that passed him the week before was surrounded and destroyed to the man by the invading Salazian Legions.

The victorious generals met together that evening inside their young empress' tent. It was barely large enough to hold the twelve of them: Avera matched her soldiers' austerities in her own life. She ate as they ate, dressed as they dressed, slept as they slept. The fanatic devotion of the Salazian military was no accident.

The laudations were well-spoken and long. But Avera's youngest general, Golranel, did not join the others in their acclamations. He stood moodily in the back, impatiently awaiting his empress' attention.

Avera noted this small disharmony but saw no good reason not to let her ranking officers congratulate her and each other to the limit of their desire. But when even the most ecstatic and the most verbose began to pause in their rhetoric for suitable metaphors to describe the greatness of the Salazian military and the brilliance of the empress, Avera looked with rage at Golranel and said coldly, "You do not rejoice in our small victory, young general?"

Golranel gazed steadily into the ebony eyes that terrified half the world and answered slowly, "This victory was well and good, your Excellency. But truly, what have we accomplished? Not one of the barbarians escaped to report our superior science! What advantage our prowess if we fail to use every means to end here and turn the legions to the western war?"

"What do you suggest?" Avera asked with greater interest. She began idly fingering the golden gem Starbha hidden beneath her uniform. Golranel would as usual have some horrible but wonderful scheme. It was his extraordinary brilliance coupled with his extraordinary ruthlessness that had advanced him so far so quickly. He was her elder by a mere three years!

Golranel, smiling inside but showing only his usual grim intensity, pushed through the generals and faced Avera directly. He put both his hands on the map table between them and leaned toward her as he said in a low voice, "Mass fear. This is what I see, Avera. Terrify the barbarians. Their armies will not fight if they understand the terrible powers we have wrested from the old books of the Oathmasters. Look — there. See it? A squalid capital of this pathetic region. Falon, I think it's called. Let us descend on it with full fire. Let a few hundred only survive — just enough to scurry eastward and spread the tale of our superior might. Then, we need only wait. Can there be doubt they will quickly submit?"

Avera looked long at the lanterns' shadows playing over the maps on the table. All the generals leaned toward her now, curiosity about her response stilling any other thoughts. Avera felt their concentrated attention and used it to help focus her mind. Even so, her decision was long in coming. It would be a mistake to think even a faint compassion for Falon's hundred thousand slowed her. Logic was her only god, terror for speed a practical tool. Yet still she hesitated, for she felt a strength hiding there, an unknown power that might create future complications. What was it? Martyrdom, perhaps? She well understood the effect of symbols — part of her meteoric rise was due to her father's murder. The fact that she had herself committed patricide never in the least clouded her perception of the assassination's effect on the public. *Will turning Falon to rubble serve us well? Or might it unite these pale inferior breeds?*

Avera clutched Starbha tightly in her strong hand, rejoicing again to feel the profound mystery of the gem's unfailing power. Laughing gaily, she cried, "Be it so, Golranel! Your lovely thought appeals to me. I would quickly leave this accursed land of chalk-white devils. See to the details and proceed."

~~~

At dawn of the fourth day following, fifteen hundred met before the north wall of Falon. Many came from fear of the prophesied destruction, some from love alone. Those staying behind leaned out their windows, jeering, "Do we look dead? That peasant said only the living would walk away today! Why do you follow that madman? Are you well, or has this last winter driven you insane? To think we thought of you as Falons!" A few turned back because of such words from their life-long friends and neighbors, but most could not be dissuaded; they gathered in the chill air of dawn.

Steven, Sanel and Aldis went among the fifteen hundred and told those who had brought more than their clothes, one blanket and food for seven days to flee Falon toward the east.

Many of the thousand who were thus commanded complained bitterly, "That is unfair! Must we walk unprepared into an unknown future?"

But when Steven answered them, "Have you so little understanding of who Jacob is? Are you so hopelessly blind?" Some, ashamed, cast away their swords and jewels and cash boxes and joined the five hundred who were following the peasant northward.

All that day, Jacob led them slowly up into the foothills. He halted just before sunset on a plateau; the Five Hundred watched with aggregate emotions as Falon's lights began burning in the far distance. Not a few longed to return and doubted the peasant. It had all been so sudden! Where was he leading them? Anywhere at all? Were they being fools?

Jacob broke the day's silence: "Light no fires tonight! Rest now, rise early, behold a city of the Dead!" He lay down and was immediately asleep.

Most did as they were told, but Sanel sought out the shara Steven and asked, "Why does the Teacher neither eat nor drink? He has brought nothing for himself!"

Steven looked at him with anguish and answered, "Did he not say the Seven Days' Journey was the Last Walk for the Peasant?"

"Surely he spoke in metaphor, as so often before the masses!"

"Perhaps, Sanel. Perhaps." Steven rolled himself in his blanket and turned away. But after the merchant left, the shara stared sleepless at Falon for the rest of the night.

~~~

Just before dawn, the Five Hundred awoke to a distant rumbling, as of thunder. Looking back at Falon, they saw a terrible black smoke of death and destruction rising in raging billows toward the lightening sky. Those with the sharpest eyes said, "Salaz has surrounded the city! They fire continually! Where is our army?"

That entire morning the Five Hundred watched, mouths agape in stupefied horror.

At last Jacob said, "It is no more. Now are the Dead dead. Let us continue on." He walked toward the mountains; slowly, all stumbled after him.

An hour passed in a dazed silence broken only by the soft sobbing of those who had lost dear friends and relatives that morning. Suddenly Leora cried, "That dust! It comes this way! A cavalry! We are betrayed! Flee!"

Jacob made no reply. Neither did he change his pace, though the Five Hundred surged past him like an angry sea. As soon as all but Steven, Arthur and Deborah were in front of him, he called to them in a loud voice, "If you run, you will die. I cannot protect you if you leave me."

The Five Hundred reluctantly stopped and waited for him: questioning his prophecies no longer seemed particularly wise. Yet even so, it must be noted if their subsequent fate is to be understood: all but three doubted him in the next few hours. Had they escaped the death of Falon only to be butchered in the open fields?

~~~

By mid-afternoon, the cavalry was within a bowshot of them. Jacob, living the perfection of the power of the Golden Rider's new well, held up his right hand. The cavalry stopped, exactly as if it were composed of so many dolls and he had pulled the one string activating them all.

"It is abundantly clear," said the captain to his major, "that fool was badly mistaken. We have ridden all day and seen no sign of a band of refugees. Nor could any now escape our sight since we crossed that last crest. Certainly he mistook rocks for people in the smoke-filled light of dawn."

"You are certainly correct," said the major to his captain. "Let us humbly suggest he be skinned and boiled then fed to Avera's lion for wasting our time. Signal the return!"

The cavalry rode back as it had come. But one of them did not move as their wave broke around him: a minor officer held his mare rock still as he stared in disbelief back and forth from the retreating cavalry to the refugees, standing in plain sight not fifty paces away.

Jacob walked through his people to him and said in perfect Salazian, "Welcome, lieutenant! We have been waiting for you.

Thank you for hurrying to us." He led him to Sanel and said, "Speak to David of the One. Out of the vast Salazian horde, this child alone is Alive."

Thus did David first come to Jacob, the same David who would be the Last Living One of the Five Hundred.

~~~

Shortly after the beginning of the sixth day of their journey, Jacob led the Five Hundred off the main trail onto an ancient and all but forgotten path. Each day, they had walked from dawn until dusk, pausing for only an hour's rest at midday. They had made excellent progress: the snow-capped peaks of the Guardian Mountains were all around them.

The peasant had kept silence since he turned the cavalry; many were concerned for him. Many also seriously doubted their own fortune: their food was almost gone. They regretted abandoning all their weapons and tried to catch rabbits and wildfowl. But Steven forbade them, "If you break his commands, how can you hope for his protection?" There was considerable worried murmuring, but most of the Five Hundred based their hopes on the peasant. No one was yet brave enough or afraid enough to disturb his silence.

All that day, they walked along the rough trail as it followed a swollen stream through a virgin evergreen forest. The valley, at first quite wide, shrank gradually into a narrow gorge, dangerous but lovely: many cascading waterfalls ran down the high cliffs to join the rushing water far below.

As the sun slipped past the mountains, the path emerged from the canyon and ended in a large, verdant meadow, surrounded on all sides by the mightiest of the Guardians. The Five Hundred had climbed very high: only a league above, there was snow even on the southern slopes; they had already crossed many patches lingering in protected places. The children had thoroughly enjoyed that; they played in it with careless springtime laughter while their parents doubted ever more earnestly. *When will they learn life is at best hard and frequently cruel?*

The stream they had followed all day fell from high above into a deep pool. Jacob knelt by it and gazed at the water. All left him alone except Arthur, who never left his side for any reason. The young nobleman sat down beside him to be available to assist him in any way.

Not very much farther away waited the child Deborah. Since she had first seen Arthur, she had been as loyal to him as he was to Jacob: she found Arthur perfect in every way. Steven had at first been perplexed by this sudden transference of her devotion; but when he thought about it, he felt it a fine way for her to keep out of trouble and approved of the change. It was not clear if Arthur liked having this constant red-haired shadow, but probably he was too engrossed with his continual study of Jacob to notice her unfailing, one-pointed attention.

~~~

As the Five Hundred ate their evening meal, a few approached Steven and Sanel and said, "We have food left for one day only! Tomorrow our children starve! We must understand his intention."

"I do not know his mind, I do not question him!" Not trusting his eyes, the shara strode from them. The merchant, however, was emboldened by their fears: concern for his family was an ever-increasing burden. He agreed to approach Jacob.

The peasant still knelt by the pool. A chipmunk was on his shoulder but ran off when Sanel came. Before the merchant spoke his doubt, Jacob exclaimed, "Sanel! Are you truly still so full of fear? Why do you burden your mind with care and your heart with worry? Your only requirement in life is to give yourself wholly to the One. Do you feel more for your beautiful Leora and your adorable Susan than does the Mother? Why then do you doubt Her all-embracing love? You must learn to master the movements of your mind! Else its vagaries will lead you again and again into doubt and despair, even on the threshold of paradise.

"Sanel, that small chipmunk told me of a rabid bear, terrifying this small valley. Give me your dagger!"

The merchant's face burned: Jacob had ordered them to bring no weapons. But he had worried for the safety of Susan and Leora and had secreted a kris in his tunic. As he brought it slowly out, its silver blade shone lethally in the moonlight.

"If there is danger from a bear — !" exclaimed Arthur.

Jacob answered him quietly, "No one will suffer from it." He took the dagger with a strangely wistful expression, then ran a finger slowly down its serpentine blade as he murmured, "Every act is matched by a perfect and just compensation. Still, it is curious such a blade should be the one to pay the debt." Shrugging slightly, he slid it under his girthing rope then looked up at the merchant. A violent fire raging in his eyes, he ordered him, "Sanel! Listen carefully now. I called you to me — yes, I called you! You could not have approached me had I not.

"Tell the Five Hundred to rest early tonight and not squander these dark hours in idle chatter: tomorrow will be the hardest day for the Living since the Downfall of Para — when their share in this labor began."

Jacob stared dreamily at the pool again, letting the weight he had artfully removed from Sanel settle to unite with the others taken from most of the refugees. After a long while, he shuddered and continued in a voice so full of melancholy the merchant at first thought he must be discussing the death of someone dearly beloved, "Also, build a simple but sturdy bridge of log and stone down from this pool, there where this stream is narrowest. And Sanel! Have you not noticed this water is not cold?"

The merchant had indeed noticed the stream warming as they followed it, but had concluded nothing from this curious fact.

"There lies the answer to the doubt burning in you, martyring your peace," Jacob ended, staring still at the water.

~~~

The peasant did not move again until two hours before dawn. Then he rose suddenly and stole silently from the sleeping Five Hundred. Arthur was up and after him at once: he never ate until

Jacob ate, never drank until Jacob drank, never slept until Jacob slept. He hurried after him now, afraid of losing him in the darkness.

There was no need for fear: Jacob was waiting for him just beyond the knowing of the others. He spoke softly out of the night, "Arthur, Arthur, beloved child, exceedingly bitter will this day prove for you."

"How so? When I am with you, all is light and joy!"

"You have given the reason. I must go now; you may not follow for long years: much life remains for you in this great, wide world."

"I will go with you!" Arthur was frightened for the first time since he had met him.

"You cannot. Despair not, I will not forever forsake you; we will one day rejoice together again under a new sun. Trust in the perfect order of life! You must learn to love me more abstractly: as you see the workings of the Seven in all of Nature, I will grow fuller and more complete in your heart. Give me your word!"

"You ask my lips to blaspheme my soul! I shall follow you!"

"You shall not!" The peasant raised his hand; Arthur fell to the ground. Jacob knelt beside him, took his head and held it to his breast. Weeping, he kissed his forehead, then straightened his tangled golden hair. "My dear, lost son," he murmured.

Suddenly Jacob looked into the bushes and said, "Do not fear, Deborah. Your Arthur will awaken with the dawn. Come here, child; I must speak with you."

~~~

At dawn, the Five Hundred were torn from their sleep by a roar from the rabid bear. Leaping up in fear, they saw it racing toward them down the mountain! A few more bounds and it would be upon them! A chaotic impulse toward safety, away! flowed through them all. At the last instant, Jacob leapt from an overhanging branch onto the back of the charging beast. The kris rose and fell swiftly; the forward rush of the bear changed into a crashing roll as it struggled to dislodge the attacking human.

Suddenly Steven was beside Jacob. He had awakened early, intuiting much of the peasant's sacrifice, and had sought him earnestly for the past hour. He had soon found Arthur, sleeping peacefully, but only moments before had at last discovered Jacob.

As the bear shrieked its death, the peasant shakily rose to his feet and shouted in full voice, "Stop! Do not climb up! All is well!"

But Steven, seeing his wounds, exclaimed, "Teacher! Lie down!"

Jacob whirled toward him, his eyes huge with victory or surprise and cried, "It *is* you then!" The words resonated inside the shara, instantly distorting space. Jacob seemed to grow enormous; the peasant's hands as they slowly, slowly came closer looked like two huge trees, stretching down toward him from a mighty mountain of Jacob. Ever more slowly the hands approached, expanding larger and ever larger as they relentlessly came. And then they were touching his head; they were as searing lava, burning away the last vestiges of everything that had once been Steven. The shara screamed; his knees buckled under him as he fell backward onto the still jerking corpse of the bear.

Jacob smiled a little crookedly at him as he said, "You must guide them now." Then he turned back to the Five Hundred and shouted, "My time ends! Steven is appointed your leader. Ever do his will, even as if he were I! Doubt not: on the second day, your past and future will manifest!" He fell to his knees, clutching his chest.

The Five Hundred cried as one and raced forward. But before any reached him, a brilliant golden fire flowed from his heart and a gentler but sublime argent mist came from the deep tears in his back. In an instant, the Oathmaster Vaga, clothed in a dazzling emerald robe and wearing a crown of fulgent gold, stood on Jacob's left; the eternally numinous Venus in radiant silver was on his right.

Only the peasant and the shara heard her words, "My Lord! You have succeeded beyond all hope," and his, "Well have you turned the wheel, my son." Lifting Jacob as if he were no heavier than a single feather of goose down, Vaga looked over the Five Hundred and added in a voice so loud and full the ground vibrated, "Never — violate — Steven's — will!"

Venus meantime was adding her soft power to Jacob's by flowing a portion of her spirit into the shara. Steven felt a healing force of calmness reintegrating his mind as her thoughts sang through him, *Never fear, shara! Always are we with you.*

Then the light grew more and more painfully bright until all but Steven had to turn away and shield their eyes. Thus no one else saw what next happened. But when the brilliance abruptly ended and the Five Hundred could look again, only the shara remained. He was still lying on the bear, but was now apparently unconscious.

Sanel cried in fear and desolation, "Woe for Jacob! Why did I not seek that bear last night!"

Aldis shouted with rage, "What! You knew of it? Yet you did not tell us! Why — ?"

"Yes, condemn me! I deserve your hate. Yes, I knew! Jacob told me. But he said no one would suffer! Woe! For now I perceive he meant no *one*, but all together! Woe, woe for our lost Teacher!"

"No, Sanel!" cried a voice not unlike the Oathmaster's. Looking up, the Five Hundred saw Steven, standing now. But he was transfigured: ethereal light radiated from his face and body: he appeared almost as glorious as had Venus. "Your first understanding was correct! Jacob suffered no more from his wounds than does the Sun from the dust of space! How can we mourn, when our Teacher has returned to his Source! No, my brothers and sisters, we must rejoice today! The well overflows now; we can, nay, we must! continue drinking."

Steven climbed down from the ledge, passed through them as calmly as if he were a gentle breeze and they a stand of oak, then walked across Sanel's bridge and started up the mountain.

No one moved until Arthur, who had awakened with the bear's first roar, said dully, "We must follow. It was my father's last command." He crossed the stream; gradually all followed, dazed, shaken, crying softly. Last of all came Sanel, his head drooping.

20
The Cave

There is not now
There has never been
There will never be
Anything but the One.
— Rodavi

The Lost Generation of Five Hundred?
The world's one hope to escape
The incarnate Rakshasa's iron heel.
— Mordom

The Five Hundred will be powerless until the World Tree blossoms
In the presence of the White Snake and the Black Lizard.
Then only will the Ten Thousand remember their meaning.
— Joab

Steven led the Five Hundred in gradual curves up the mountain. It was a beautiful, clear day: wisps of cloud were caught by two or three of the Guardians, but other than that there was nothing above but the almost translucent blue of the high mountain sky. For the first few hours, a gentle breeze wafted upward from the valley floor, massaging them with soft forgiving fingers. This gradually stilled; the mountainside was silent but for the steady trudging of a thousand feet. The world seemed to be expectantly waiting, joining the refugees in their silent anticipation of an impossible future.

Steven walked slowly, calmly, rejoicing in the strength and wisdom of his new mind. With his rapidly evolving senses, he could clearly see the path Jacob discovered, formed ages ago by the wise men and women who had also come this way. When? The rocks did not sing to him of that. But the shara was certain it had been several thousand years since any followed this route.

After climbing for an hour, Steven started to push through deep snow. Almost as compensation for the increase in effort, his mind expanded more quickly; he learned he could now read the future as easily as the past. With grim surprise, he discovered the potential loss of several of the Five Hundred in the next few hours! Were there alternatives?

~~~

The refugees followed him with an almost mindless hope. A few attempted to understand the changes in their new leader; most were simply obeying Jacob's last command. But two who had been most filled with anger for the loss of Falon turned their minds ever more irreversibly toward hatred.

~~~

Four hours up the mountain, Jonathan, a youth of sixteen, daydreaming of his recent losses, missed his footing and slipped on the compacted ice. A dozen hands grabbed for him, all failed.

"No! Jacob! My God, no!" he screamed in terror as he realized he was lost and certainly going to die. But his pleas did not slow his accelerating slide down the steep slope. And at the end of the slope was the high cliff down which tumbled the stream's waterfall!

The Five Hundred stared in horror, paralyzed by the unfolding tragedy. Their trail doubled back and was directly beneath Jonathan, but all were already past: no one was there to break his fall toward inevitable death.

In defiance of all logic (and caution), one near the end dared push past Sanel and Leora and sprint back. He knew as he ran it was an impossible feat: no one could race so far so quickly. He could see the boy's rate of fall, could see the distance he must cover to reach him in time: it was obvious he would be too late. It was impossible, a mad quest; yet on David raced, dividing his gaze between the falling boy and his own dangerous route.

As he ran, the Salazian lieutenant kept one thing firmly in mind: the boy safe in his arms, grateful, alive; he refused to accept the reality of any other thought. The power of his concentration distorted time around him, stretched it so his race became a slow-motion dream. Space followed time and tunneled around him: he could no more glance at his own path but only at Jonathan, hurtling ever more slowly down the ice toward his certain doom.

The Five Hundred stared as if they were frozen to the ice. Steven alone continued to climb calmly upward. And in his expanding silence, he adjudged both Jonathan and David worthy of very long lives.

At the last instant, time and space returned to their normal flux: David caught Jonathan around the waist. It still was a dangerous balance of conflicting forces: his well-toned body was barely strong enough to keep both of them from tumbling over the cliff.

David peered over the edge and wondered when he had learned to be so bold. Holding the boy to his chest, he leaned back on the snow and sat down heavily. Jonathan followed him without resistance, hardly yet believing he was alive. Shaking so violently his teeth chattered, he thanked the Salazian for saving his life.

"Jacob saved me!" laughed David as he stared with new eyes at the majestic azure, white and verdant world below. "Never could I repay him for freeing me from Avera's cruel army, even were I to rescue ten thousand from untimely death."

~~~

As David and Jonathan walked back to the others, Steven chuckled gently to himself: now the strands of time could be woven to save almost all the Five Hundred. Almost all.

For the first time that day, Sanel also felt a lightening of his mood. Most others of the Five Hundred had scorned David because he had served in the Salaz army. Only the merchant and his wife had been kind to him: Leora enjoyed talking in her native tongue; Sanel had long ago conquered national and racial prejudice when he married a foreigner. He had also enjoyed this rare opportunity of practicing his Salazian: his pastime was the study of the various current and ancient languages of the world. His mind craved the different logical patterns of foreign symbols and meanings. David was a vintage wine to him.

~~~

At noon, Steven stood before the mouth of a cave, high above the valley. Not far below, the stream gushed from the mountain, then cascaded in a series of small cataracts to the high waterfall. Living ever more fully Jacob's peace, he smiled in his heart.

The shara raised his arms over the valley and shouted to the Five Hundred, "Now comes the final test! There will be no more light for you. Place your hand on the shoulder of the one before you. Dare not delay! At sunset, this passage closes!"

Without further explanation, he entered the cave.

Arthur, who all morning had walked behind him in a daze, suddenly understood the shara's request and stopped stock still. Staring at the darkness of the open cavern, he was terrified to the furthest reaches of his spirit.

Aldis studied him briefly, then hurried past him to catch hold of Steven.

In a burning anguish of dark dread, Arthur stood paralyzed as the rest of the Five Hundred followed into the cave. Everyone else was also afraid, but most did not hesitate long, their fear of losing the connection to the human chain being the greater.

At last all were gone, save only Arthur, David and Jonathan. As the others had entered, David had walked more and more slowly and finally stopped altogether, also paralyzed by the horror of this dark entryway.

Jonathan waited patiently for a few moments before saying softly but firmly, "You must not fear! Jacob led us here only because light lies ahead."

Shaking as violently as had Jonathan a few hours earlier, David answered, "What dread this! How can you know that? How can

Steven possibly know where this leads? That looks like my death! Never have I known such fear."

"This?" asked Jonathan, looking at the cave curiously. What could be frightening about a hole in the rock? They had nearly died today! This was nothing. "Come with me — see, I will hold onto you. You needn't fear."

"You will help me? You promise not to leave me alone?" The lieutenant stared at him desperately.

Jonathan looked him squarely in his dark eyes and answered with absolute sincerity, "I so promise."

"Then, if you go before me, I will follow you." David closed his eyes firmly and clenched Jonathan's shoulder tightly in preparation for the dark terror.

"What else can we do? And you?"

Arthur said nothing, instead stared at the cave as if entranced. Jonathan waited a moment with decreasing patience, then cried, "Come! Why do you wait? Surely you heard Steven? I can hardly see them anymore!"

Still there was nothing but the terrified silence.

"Stop this! You must not remain! Will you not come? No? David, what can we do? We must go! They're gone! Arthur, dare not wait! Remember Steven's warning!" Jonathan entered, David following as closely as if they were born connected in the womb.

Arthur did not follow.

He had been born with a fear of closed places, of being buried alive. *This test on the day of Jacob's death! It is unfair!*

Follow!

I cannot!

You must!

How can I?

The afternoon slipped by as he struggled, but Arthur did not follow.

One hour since Jonathan and David went in; he berated himself loudly and long. Still Arthur did not follow.

Two hours, shouting imprecations at his stubborn flesh, cursing himself and the world, Arthur did not follow.

Three hours, the sun slipped behind the Guardians. He shivered in the sudden cold air yet could not make his body obey the stern command of his will: Arthur did not follow.

Four hours, he cried, "On you fool! The day is ending!" and slapped himself all over. But he was a statue: Arthur did not follow.

As the sun crossed the rim of the world, he at last gathered the last sundered sparks of his courage and bolted into the cave. Too late! He felt before he heard the rock slide, forever blocking the Five Hundred's path. Running forward through the dust-filled air, he clawed at the settling rock as he shouted, "No, my God! No! The end!" He beat his fists against the uncaring stone until he collapsed to the ground, crying, "First Jacob, now the Five Hundred! More than I can bear! Too long in this insane weakness — too long in this mad world! Alone, alone again! Miserable, ill-formed, railing fool! Depart far off! You are ruined! Nay — damned! Damned for all Eternity!"

~~~

The cave was utterly black, clammy and cold. But the ground was not particularly rough; Steven walked *very* slowly so the human chain would not break. After an hour, he started gradually upward. There were few bends; he alone knew where there were branches. The roof was generally out of touch, except for one horrible place where all but the smallest children had to crawl on their hands and knees.

Two hours into the mountain, the cave became warmer; the rock began glowing faintly phosphorescent. It gradually brightened until it was no longer necessary to maintain physical contact. Steven still ordered single file; he knew there were deep cracks in the rock.

One disobeyed and was lost here — Razael's mind was beyond Steven's influence — passionately twisted by hatred. She had fled

Falon from fear alone and had deeply resented Jacob for not speaking more plainly. All her family, all her friends except her brother Morgan who walked before her now — all were dead, solely because that *peasant* had not told them everything he knew! And now this boy ordered her to walk in line like an animal! Why should she listen to him?

Razael walked off into the darkness to relieve herself. The next in line tried to stop her, but her brother Morgan who shared her mind said, "She'll be back in no time." But Razael had no more time: she stepped into empty space and hurtled screaming to her death.

Steven was at Morgan's side an instant later, hoping in spite of his foreknowledge to turn him to union with the Five Hundred. The shara held both his arms firmly and stared intensely into his eyes, wide with grief and terror.

"Let me go! I must climb down for her." Morgan twisted against the shara's strong grip.

Steven did not release him. "It is too late. Her thoughts destroyed her. You must turn back to us now, lest you too fall."

"Why!" cried Morgan in rage. "Who do you think you are! You lead us into this sunless tomb to destroy us all! How will we ever find our way out again? My poor Razael will prove the lucky one: we are all going to die in here! Lost, alone, starving to death! Unmourned, unburied! A better fate to have died at the hand of those black devils than to let her lie there! We are not like the evil Salazians: we bury our dead!"

"So do we," muttered David, but Steven answered him:

"No, Morgan. It is as it must be. Her hatred alone tore her from us. Do not partake of her false and fearful judgments! You must become as the others. Her ruined body is meaningless. It would be better to forget it ever existed. And remember her with joy."

Morgan protested with greater anger, "You are as mad and uncaring as was Jacob! My entire family is ruined! The two of you have murdered us all!"

Steven released Morgan's arms and said calmly, "You can be helped only if you wish it, Morgan, Kabil's son. The choice is yours. Join us if you can."

The shara walked back to the front of the line. With varying degrees of hesitation, the Five Hundred followed, haunted by Razael's echoing scream, but now even more unwilling to disobey their new leader.

Morgan cursed them all yet saw no choice but to follow. He walked now far behind the others, vowing vengeance as his anger festered ever more irreversibly in his dying mind.

The walls receded as the Five Hundred entered a vast cavern. A steaming stream crossed before them and disappeared into the ground. When Sanel saw it, he whispered to Leora and Susan, "There runs a partial answer to the riddle of the warm water below! Yet still our larger question remains unanswered. No one could live here long. I wonder, wouldn't it be better if we returned to the world and — "

From far ahead, Steven laughed with unabashed joy and cried, "Sanel! Will you never learn to trust the One? Surely you recall Jacob's warning, `Do not in pride rely solely on your own strength?´ Remember? Truth is never far from you if you keep your heart open to it.

"My people! Here we rest tonight. Finish your poor food from Falon; by tomorrow evening you will think of the outer world only as a bad dream. *Now!"*

Marking or answering his command, there was a deep rumbling groan and shaking of the mountain. The Five Hundred looked at the shara with sudden terror, but Aldis cried in a loud voice, "The entrance closes, as Steven foretold!"

Morgan, reaching the last limit of his mind, shouted in rage, "You are as insane as he! Who can anymore doubt we are going to die in here!" He stalked back the way they had come, his heart twisting into a hard knot of doubt and despair.

~~~

After most of the Five Hundred were sleeping, Sanel scurried up to Steven. The merchant, wishing to compensate for his continuing doubts, had visited all the refugees to inquire of their well-being, and had discovered the surprising news which he now breathlessly related, "Steven! Steven, neither Arthur nor the child Deborah are here! Steven, did you hear? They never entered the cave or are lost somewhere behind! What should we do? Arthur and Deborah aren't here!"

The shara opened an eye and looked thoughtfully at the merchant. He had been sitting quietly, searching his new mind for knowledge, attempting to learn if there were a foreseeable end to his growth. He had found none: there were no longer inner walls of any kind, no restrictions to his knowledge of the past or future, no limits to his abilities, no boundaries to his ever-expanding awareness. This, then, was the effect of the One fully unleashed in the mind?

The shara looked at the merchant for a long moment, then answered quietly, "Don't bother to seek them, Sanel; they are still outside. Didn't you notice how her loyalty transferred from me to him as soon as she met him? Jacob told her to hide in the forest when the Five Hundred crossed your bridge, for he foresaw Arthur could not enter the cave. Deborah will be the perfect helpmate for his task. Let's see — in the seventh year hence, they will parent a daughter. They will name her Jacobi in honor of the peasant. Jacobi will mature to be a master of the subtle sciences, an Oathmaster of unprecedented power.

"And there will be a second child born two years later, a wonderful soul of light; a ray of Almira, actually. They will name this one Ste — oh, never mind."

Sanel, thinking, *I do not understand this man,* mumbled something incoherent and stumbled off to find Leora and Susan.

~~~

The next morning, Deborah followed the Five Hundred's track up the mountain and found Arthur sleeping in the rubble at the slide's base, his golden hair charcoaled with dust and grime.

She woke him gently, saying in her sweet voice, "Lalasa, dori! Do not be sad! It is a beautiful, clear day. Come see how gloriously Lord Orah shines on the mountains!"

He looked up at her through his misery and wondered if she had come as an angel of death or rebirth. But when she led him out of the darkness into the bright sunlight, he discovered the world had not yet been destroyed by his grief. The Guardians stood still, as majestic and untouched by his passion as if his losses were less important than the moving shadows on their eternal glaciers.

In spite of the stern disapproval of his mind, his heart smiled for the beauty of the world. He answered her tenderly, "Jacob must be with us still, Deborah. You are right, it *is* a lovely day."

~~~

In the unchanging twilight of the cave, time was only a remembered concept. But it was before most of the Five Hundred were awake that Sanel screamed in fear and then shouted, "Morgan! He's dead! Morgan murdered himself! Steven! Morgan is dead!"

The shara waited until all gathered, then sailed his infinitely calm ship into the heart of the sea of chaos. The impassioned crowd parted before him as effortlessly as young bamboo before an enormous bull elephant. Kneeling beside the corpse, he closed its eyes, then said in a voice without inflection, "Who will return this to the world of the Dead?"

David and Jonathan stepped forward to carry the body to the stream. Steven looked up at them sharply, his mind whirling through an unexpected series of transformations. There could not have been more contrasting pall-bearers: David's birth gifted him the ebony skin and hair of the Salazians; Jonathan was of the Dimen race of near albinos: his eyes were blue, but his hair and skin were white. Steven stood slowly, understanding the meaning of their symbol. Now he knew why they had been the last to enter the cave; now he knew their destiny.

As David and Jonathan cast the corpse into the stream, the lieutenant sang the Salazian burial hymn:

At the waning of the moon,
At the failing of the wind,
At the setting of the sun,
They have placed me in my grave.
Broken my arrows, vanished my dreams!
No more will my love enfold me,
Nor my son fill me with pride!
No more shall I sing of my victories,
Nor caress my lyre with my swift, sure hand.
All my works are faded:
My world is a statue of dust.
I say to you, still walking in the living air,
Think sometimes of me!

"What did you say?" asked Jonathan curiously.

"That is how we honor our dead. He deserved this much to have followed Jacob so far."

Jonathan looked at him with doubt and said flatly, "I don't know if I believe that! Is it reasonable that everyone who fled Falon deserved life? Perhaps he had to die to purify us."

"Careful, young foreigner! Such thoughts are dangerous. Were all those killed by my army murdered for the benefit of our Five Hundred? Did your own parents deserve their fate?" David regretted his rebuttal at once: the look on his friend's face tightened his heart.

As he weighed his grief on the scale of his innocence, Jonathan found no easy reply. Finally he dropped to his knees by the stream and, looking up at David with brimming eyes, said with sorrow, "I begged them like this! On my knees! But they would not even come to hear him. Ah, I have been a fool! Why should anyone ever have to die? It is senseless, cruel! We Dimens have been decimated by this war. My family came to Falon as refugees. And now they are all gone, slaughtered by those Salazian demons! Those — " Jonathan stopped abruptly, his face imitating the ruby shade of his blood.

"Forgive me, my friend! I didn't mean — "

But the lieutenant laughed softly and, kneeling beside him, lightly stroked his hair. "No, lalasa, no. Your words do not touch me, only your deep pain, which I share. The Salazian people are not free. Avera strangles them as surely as she will the whole of our world if she is not stopped. It may have been better — far better! for your family to be killed in Falon than to live in slavery." He pulled Jonathan gently to him. The boy resisted for a moment, then collapsed onto his chest, his long sobs working to release the anguish of his wounded heart.

The Five Hundred laboriously followed Steven along the stream for several more hours. The water continued to warm, but the dull twilight remained constant. They walked steadily, trusting still, but most increasingly despondent about this unending trek through the slowly changing cave. There was no food left! No means for gaining more! Was it possible Morgan had seen the truth and chosen the only alternative to Steven's insanity?

But shortly before noon, Susan looked up and cried excitedly, "Daddy! I see blue sky! *Sunlight!*"

Shouting with fervent excitement, the Five Hundred ran forward past Steven, still walking sedately. What can compare with the wonder of daylight after so long in such a cave, not knowing, only hoping, there would be release? Sudden liberation from slavery? Miraculous recovery from a terminal disease? Perhaps these might inspire a similar ecstasy. But here there were no lingering chains or weakness, only joy!

The Five Hundred raced forward, screaming their wonder. Their failure, therefore, was the more terrible. They could see, but never reach: the cleft in the rock far above was at the apex of a convex and smooth surface. Their flaming hope burned in an instant to a gray, cold ash.

The shara laughed gently and said, "Too eager, too excited! Calmer minds will be better suited for the returning product of your evolving minds. Look there!" He pointed toward the faint light ahead. Almost they surged ahead again, but he held them with his words.

"Wait! There is no falseness there: you will emerge into your new home in the brightness of noon. But to prepare you for your new world, I must tell you the one history that will create your future."

For the next two hours, the shara stood in the sunbeam from the false opening, moving slowly with it as he summarized part of Joab's *History of Lord Gana* to the Five Hundred.

Come!
Listen!
Hear first my song of Gana,
Immortal father of our race!
Gana the shara, Gana the one true adan!
Gana the damned!
Murdered by his sister's son
Before the World Tree's seed was lost
Or the Sundered Gems stolen
From the Living Statue's hands!

21
The Statue's Dream

The seven rivers call to me
from my lost home
twilight voices of yesterday's dreams
When did I last see your timeless face?
When understand your infinite ways?
Almira, Almira!
How did I come to you?
Why did I lose you?
The fire in the rainbow wheels has died now
Yet again and again I question my sundered soul
Why?
— Gana

As Steven began his history, a remarkable change began in the forgotten but living statue-body of Gana, buried deep in the ruin of what had once been the glorious Golden City Sulara of the Adanai. For the first time in ninety-four millennia, he began waking up.

At first only partially aware, he beheld visions.

Gana, hiding behind the sunbeams, saw the Five Hundred huddled in the cave, listening with wonder to Steven's strangely timed tale. Every single one of them was amazed their new leader would pick such an odd moment to stop their search. What lay beyond the cave? Only the shara knew, and he was stopping them here, on the threshold of release, to tell them Joab's story of the mythical founder of Emura! It was simply too strange; it made not the slightest sense.

But Gana, looking down on them with the eye of his mind, understood Steven's meaning. He knew the fate of the Five Hundred; he knew who they had been and who they would be; he knew their relationship to himself. *Curious,* he thought sleepily. *I hadn't realized...*

His first thought after so long catapulted Gana's mind backward. Through the founding of Emura, through the wars with the freed Asur Emperor Valin on Martanda, through the destruction of Kanaan-dora by the omnipotent Brihas, Lord of the Seven, Gana wandered backward in memory and vision, ending finally at his youth in Kanaan-dora with the kind old Oathmaster, Rodavi.

Gana paused there for an hour of sweet innocence. Then an enigmatic smile from Rodavi sent his mind whirling backward once more. Further still Gana flowed through his endless memory: back through uncatalogued births in lands all of creation has seemingly forgotten, back beyond stellar systems now nothing more than so much scattered cosmic dust, back to the source of the earliest humans before the first solar furnace of our present cosmos exploded into life.

Of many of these memories others have spoken, written and sung. But of that primordial beginning of Gana's endless labor, I have never seen nor heard a record. Until now.

~~~

It was a golden and silver dawn when the Seven walked eastward singing, following the Azure Star as ever before.

The united liquid-essence that was humanity's spirit was drawn after them, at first as a few isolated drops, then in rivulets, then streams, then rivers, then floods, until they flowed toward the Path of Travel twelve billion strong.

The boundaries of space and time were broken; joining with the Seven, the twelve billion stepped beyond the relative Universe in their return to the One.

Of those who crossed over, a unique soul wondered why it was necessary, thereby questioning the authority of the Azure Star inside the perfection of the One.

Thus Shatarupa created the possibility of return.

Her desires were incomplete, unfulfilled. She loved the old Universe and had wanted to remain behind. But the other half of her spirit, Swayam, clearly remembered the Path of Travel and carried her with him. Thus duality was introduced into the singularity of the One. This had never happened before, but it was for exactly this Almira had long planned and dreamed.

Others who wished to come were not so fortunate as the twelve billion.

Vasuki, the miller's son, could not follow the Azure Star — his father chained him to the wheel. He died that day, so great was his grief.

Malinda was imprisoned by her false husband and treacherous sons until it was too late. She raced after the others, but they were gone; she knew she could never discover the way alone.

Her elder sister Mirabel found her at dawn and shared her misery on the slow walk back to their planet's surface. She had been far away when the Azure Star came, had not realized the Path of Travel was opening once again. She had been lax in her study of the One; it had been so very long since the Azure Star appeared the last time. Then she had been only a child! But in those days of completion, everyone had known what to do: not even one had been left behind. It was still remembered as the Perfect Path. And now she was trapped on the wrong side of the Azure Star! Circling a dying sun! Would the Path open again before the inevitable end of worlds claimed their home? So far already had her memory decayed in the absence of the twelve billion. So far already had her spirit congealed into matter.

~~~

Many felt rather than saw the Azure Star — it was a subtle wave of joy inside, pulling them eastward.

Some heard it as a rhythm of unsurpassed enchantment, coming from the Eastern rim of the galaxy; some saw beams of pulsating azure and argent light; some both saw and heard; a few also tasted, touched, smelled. All these went joyously, without pause or question.

But the sad truth was that the vast majority refused to acknowledge the Azure Star's pulsations of the One: the Path of Travel had taken too long to re-open. What value could there be in leaving their home worlds for an unknown end?

The Seven wondered that long hour if they should have come far earlier as Lord Gana had so urgently requested. But the Immortal Council had never been moved by one only; therefore, they had waited through measureless Eternity until others would share his belief.

At last the Seven had stood as one and the Path had opened. Gana held his anger as he waited for the earliest. He knew they were far too late, yet he of all would give first to those making the attempt.

But after the twelve billion were present and the Path again closed, Gana strode in wrath to the Council and cried, "So be it, my peers! Who will now cast down the Fallen Ones?"

Who could answer? So many, many more than ever before had remained behind.

Brihas looked up slowly from his omnipotent hands and said quietly, "It does seem, my son, we have tarried over-long." A dismal, gray rain covered the Council to mark his words. Brihas was the foremost of the Seven, known by himself to be the oldest, known by all to be the wisest of the Council. Yet he was never unwilling to admit a flaw in logic, even when the flaw was as diabolically well hidden as this one had been. "What do you suggest now?" A ray of light opened the storm and shafted onto Gana.

"What difference what I suggest? What can be done? Our Universes lie in waste before Indifference; our Eternal House is become a musty creed of faith." Gana sat heavily into his throne, his face a horror of dying souls' despair. He raised a hand lethargically; the darkness returned as the clouds closed.

"Perhaps not, my Lord!" exclaimed Almira with joy. "For I volunteer to return for those Forgetful." She stood deliberately, gracefully, and stared up at the thrones of the Seven Suns with an innocence of perfect love and radiant beauty. The clouds vanished as if they had never been as the Immortal Council bathed in her splendor.

Gana stared in amazement at her: he had always considered her a minor celestial, hardly before worth a moment's notice. She was glowing brilliantly now, golden, white, iridescent, extremely beautiful, expressing more energy than he had thought she possessed. "Hah? But what alone could you do, Almira?"

"Who can declare the endurance of a branch before it is tested? But will I indeed go alone, my Lord Gana?" Her piercing look stirred his slumbering anger just as does a human a dying fire.

"No... By Narain's unending dream, no! You have ignited my heart, Almira! My place among the Seven I renounce until I set this matter right! My indolence seems now to have been inspired by Emptiness itself. For had I argued as forcefully as I believed, we would have sent the Azure Star many ages of the human earlier. I hold this error mine alone."

"Well done, my Lord!" cried Almira, her joy that her plans were so well succeeding for the moment overshadowing her caution. Realizing her error, she continued hurriedly, lest any of the omniscient minds of the Council discover her full intent, "Will any others journey backwards to repair the evil of our neglect? One more would be useful."

Silence was her only answer. Silence for so long that Almira despaired of further aid. How could she create the new order without the full influence of the Seven?

Silence extended in self-luminous radiance through measureless Eternity...

Suddenly Matri raised her staff of light and said, "It is good your magnet has two poles, Almira! But for the completion of your labor, there must also be a connecting rod. I too will accompany you, taking with me a ray from each of the Seven, in this way to atone for our Council's strange error. We three will suffice — too much energy in the lower spheres would work against our desire, I believe.

"I suggest we begin now, seeking first Narain's counsel for guidance." As she stood to go, her ebony robe scattered stars like so much dust over the Council of Immortals.

"My thanks to you, Master of the Seventh Wheel!" exclaimed Gana, deeply moved by Matri's selfless gift. "But first let us ask the ruler of the Council to pronounce his foresight."

Brihas' eyes drifted closed. He sat silently for a long moment, then began in a slow, rhythmic voice of power, congealing space and time into a new Universe of name and form, "Difficult will be your path: the fallen children have grown far from us, especially since those who could answer the Azure Star have already done so.

"But out of hidden and forgotten places, a new race will be born, a New Star will rise for the Lost... Many close ones fall... Worlds die... Suns, nay, galaxies will be destroyed... The cry of the Mother for her lost children...

"Your loss in the second year will be compensated by unexpected victory in the fourth. The fire-despair and storm-wrath of the fifth will prune your tree, for the Grandfather himself will curse you, my son Gana, for your pride in early swift success. This will in time prove a blessing, for many who were otherwise lost will be found when you are forced to return to the lowest levels of the relative worlds to rediscover your lost meaning.

"The full fruit will be harvested no later than the sixth, if the pestilence and repeated indifference of the desperate fifth do not first destroy it." Opening his eyes slowly, he continued, "Gana! This is no small task. Hard labor lies before you. You have but one cycle of a Universe: six of our years, no more. Then we shall again send the Azure Star and re-open the Path of Travel. If they do not remember their heritage, if they again reject the Azure Star, we will have no choice but to revoke their Universe of free will and re-assign them to lower spheres. You understand and agree?"

"I do, my father. But I speak for myself only."

Matri said, "I will of course abide by these parameters." She left to begin.

But Almira said, "All perfect; all true. Yet I may ask for an extension of one more year at Closing." A shocked silence exploded through the infinite Regions. Who but the Grandfather and Narain had ever dared challenge the immortal Lord of the Seven?

Brihas' eyes narrowed for a moment, but then he laughed with joy, "Your astounding spirit may yet prove the deciding factor, young one. Go; if you need your year, ask me then. But this additional charge I lay on you, for thus doubting me: find him who dares oppose the Seven's will and bring him here with you when you return.

"May Narain be with you through all your labors." At the mention of the Grandfather's Father, the Immortal Council melted into the Unbounded Milk Ocean where Narain can at times be found.

Gana and Almira shared silent thoughts with the Father until both were content with his guidance. She vanished first; Gana began to follow, but then for a moment reconstituted his body. Taking a handful of water, he molded it into a brilliant opalescent gem. "Kaystarbha," he said softly as he affixed it to his breast. "Thus will my mind ever be connected here, to Narain's World."

The ocean lingered awhile in their memory before melting back into the One. Narain smiled to himself at the wonderfully complex dance Almira had so cleverly begun. Novelty in Absolute Perfection was unusual, all but impossible. This should make an interesting Universe.

~~~

Almira and Gana stood before the twelve billion who had followed the Azure Star up the Path of Travel and asked if any would be bold enough to return. It was an unlikely and unprecedented request, but this was an unlikely and unprecedented task.

Two rose without the slightest pause: Solon and Rodavi. They would become the first two Oathmasters — the first to establish the Path of Return, the inner road to the One for all of humanity throughout the Cosmos.

Shatarupa stood next. She was young on both sides of the Azure Star; although she felt the new powers wonderful, she yearned for the old Universe. Swayam could not let her go alone, of course: he too stood, but reluctantly. Thus was the sharas' line secured for the new work; the order of their rising further established the normal directions of householder men and women throughout all future time.

No one after these four moved for a long time. But then the wise young Mirabeth rose — she had been watching Almira closely, now her final doubts were gone. She also missed her elder sisters Malinda and Mirabel, wished to free them from the spheres of time and space. It was a vitally correct gift: these three sisters every age has remembered as the three immortal goddesses of life. As Matri has said, "Wherever there is Truth, Beauty or Love in this Universe of the human, there are the footmarks of the three, Mirabeth, Malinda, Mirabel." These sisters together constitute the triple source of destiny: fate is woven of the threads of time on their triune loom.

Next a young man stood slowly, calmly, assured of his power, secure in his wisdom. "Seventeen times have I followed the Azure Star since my first birth. How many Universes have I seen destroyed? I cannot even begin to count them. And never have I been asked to go back. Yet Narain once hinted at such a peculiar possibility for me. So do I volunteer myself — although I was quite old on the far side of the Azure Star."

"You need not fear, Airavata. Undying youth will return with you." Almira was well pleased; she felt this one worth thousands:

although Airavata did not yet know it, he was a full manifestation of the Grandfather. Now would creative inspiration be firmly established. *We are complete,* she thought. *My Universe is going to work.* But she asked, "Are there others? The end is doubtful; the path dangerous." She did not expect more — who else would leave the perfection of the One for an entire cycle of a Universe?

Yet one more did stand. He was not the least to take the backward road, but many have since said it would have been better far if Navril Hagar had not volunteered. Why did he rise before the host that fateful morning? Was it, as his descendants and followers have ever claimed, because of the task's magnitude, because he believed his strength could be well used for the furtherance of humanity? Or was it, as his enemies have forever held, because he desired to control others: how could one who had followed the Path and returned not be among the credulous?

Perhaps both theories are correct, yet not complete even in their union — Navril Hagar was no doubt at once more and less than those who loved him and those who hated him felt — strong in the task, yet with areas of deceit far deeper than any could have expected in a comrade. From him, humanity gained passion, greed, anger, as well as most achievements of courage and genius. From him also have probably come the strange understandings of death and life, of mortality and immortality of our current age.

Navril Hagar stood and said, "Then I make the seventh. Is our number now complete?"

Almira and Gana gathered the seven into them then said in one voice, as if they were now one being with two bodies, "Seven is a final count, echoing well Reality. Yet ten would serve us better — but it seems no more are now ready. Listen, humankind! This Door of Return will remain open for four of the Grandfather's years. Until then, three, seven, or nine more may come — but only in groups of three or more, never alone. And after the fourth year, no more will be permitted to Return, for the Path will become too steep.

"Wish us well! Narain willing, we will come again before six of the Grandfather's years have passed with your families and friends. Farewell!" Almira and Gana led their seven through the golden doors.

The twelve billion dispersed slowly throughout their newly created home. Twelve lingered: these also had been moved by the task, but had doubted. Now they looked curiously at the passageway, divided in mind. They drifted together eventually, realizing a precious boon of choice had been given them.

The twelve built a perfect circle of stars before the golden doors, then waited for some sign to clarify their destiny. Two of them, Mordom and Atri, asked them to meet before the common junction of potentialities every few months to discuss possible futures.

~~~

Gana's dream ended; he awoke fully to his body for the first time since his nephew Irnga poisoned him. This waking robbed him, however — all memories vanished back into the infinite light of his consciousness save one.

A fully developed immortal's body was his final possession now, as his lungs tasted again the breath of raw infancy.

Nature had been kind in her ruin of Sulara: the buried Temple of Kanaan-dora was connected to the modern surface by a narrow but adequate passage.

The Living Statue made his way out and stood naked, blinking at the setting moon, as a passing shower started the labor of cleansing the dust of lost centuries from him.

Following a profound but blind intuition, Gana started walking toward the site of the City of Coral, Phedra, first capital of Emura, crying in the long forgotten tongue of Kanaan-dora, "The sixth year! Fools, do you not hear? Will you not listen? This is the end of the sixth year!"

22
Vashti

What need has the One for thought or care?
Everything that is was created
In an instant from nothing at all.
What need has the One for thought or care?
— Rodavi

A life lived in the light of the One
Accepts no boundaries of time or space.
— Mordom

Of all the true and wonderful visions of 'Ishtar's Isolde
The most wonderful and the most true was Vashti.
— Joab

Steven led the Five Hundred from the cave into the last surviving remnant of 'Ishtar's planet-wide Isolde garden, Vashti itself, preserved still from the changing world. An impossible mystery to some, an improbable myth to others, now this final memory of the perfect science of Etan was the promised reward for a handful of ragged refugees.

"There are no passes," laughed the shara, enjoying their wonder, "so we needn't expect unwelcome guests. Go, enjoy! Do not fear the fruit, though its appearance may seem strange to you. There is only one law in Vashti: for no reason go near the Boiling Lake."

With glad cries, the Five Hundred ran like children into their new home. Almost Sanel joined their rushing entry; almost he united with them in their re-awakening innocence. But for too long had he studied life without living it: the shock of the beauty of the valley after the awful nothingness of the cave seared into his heart like the sudden ignition of a sun in the intergalactic void.

His legs froze beneath him as he thought, *This is impossible!*

Leora waited for him, but it was the hardest gift she had ever given him: she longed with all her soul to run into Vashti, to be one with the others at last, to be free from the awful stigma of her race. She stood by him, staring at him with increasing anguish, loyally respecting his agonized immobility, deeply torn inside.

Susan waited between her parents quietly, holding and slightly squeezing their hands. She could feel their conflict, but it did not touch her. Life was full and complete now, always, forever.

The anguish of the couple mounted in intensity to an almost feverish desperation. Were they to be excluded from paradise after all?

Steven chuckled from behind them, "You still don't see, Sanel? The heart of Vashti is volcanic: it is an enormous boiling lake, which keeps the air here forever pleasant. Tropical fruits — papayas, mangoes and varieties extinct in the outer world grow near that; slightly farther away are banana, avocado, then citrus and almond orchards. Higher, where seasons begin, are peaches, plums, walnuts and other fruits and nuts, then apples and cherries. Higher still come the grasslands, free from snow only half the year; above these lie the alpine meadows. Highest are the ice fields, rarely affected by the thermal masses rising from the lake."

"But, but! It is impossible! Who could deserve such a gift?"

"Deserve? Who could ever deserve this? Did Gana deserve Almira? We are here to enjoy!" It was Susan who spoke; Sanel and Leora looked at her with amazement.

~~~

On the third day, Steven called the Five Hundred together; they gathered in a natural amphitheater in the high meadows. Some were wearing the huge gems — rubies, diamonds, emeralds, sapphires — lying everywhere like so much cut glass. The incomparable jewels braided into their hair or tied into rough garlands or sewn onto their aging cloaks would have seemed a fortnight earlier to have been a poet's dream, an idle fancy of unproductive hours. But the gems were in fact the least of Vashti's wonders.

Some of the Five Hundred had formed close ties with the tame deer, sheep and goats that grazed Vashti's grasslands. It was already common to see humans and animals wandering together throughout the valley; many of the Five Hundred brought their new companions with them to this meeting and sat with them amid the delicate alpine flowers, gently stroking their fur.

Some, the most advanced of Steven's new students, were too filled with the wonder of the celestial sights and sounds hiding in Vashti's waterfalls, trees and gardens to notice the jewels or play with the animals.

But a handful were not adjusting well to their new world. Even the wonder of Vashti had not defeated their life-long habits of belief in good and evil, of analysis, of judgment. It was for their benefit Steven called this meeting: the shara knew there were five who desperately needed his assistance. The others could safely progress at their own rates. There would have to be some universal problems to join them all completely to his will, but those could come later. For now, these five must be reached.

Aldis was one of these. His had been a brutally hard life until the wondrous day Jacob cured his legs. He could see the peace on the faces of most of the Five Hundred; he could feel their awe for their new world; he intuited something of the ever-increasing ecstasy transforming them from the inside. But try as he might, he could not stretch his mind to sail with their soaring spirits.

As soon as most of the Five Hundred had gathered, Aldis said brusquely, "Steven! I'm bored! Could I build some shelters?"

Steven smiled serenely at him, but waited for the final few to gather before answering, "Why not sleep under the stars? If you grow cold, move closer to the lake. What difference if it rains on you? But there are also several caves you may use if you desire. Sanel can show you where."

Aldis, realizing he had asked the wrong question, began again, but Sanel was already asking if they could shear the sheep and milk the goats. The one-time merchant no longer felt as isolated from the others: his life-study of Joab's *History of Lord Gana* was providing several remarkable clues about the why and how of this valley; this was beginning a bridge to the innocent hearts of the others. But as this was only from his mind, he still felt his aloneness; he wished to perform some useful service to prove his worth. To himself.

Steven, wondering what would make the best way to weave the merchant's powerful intellect into the evolving spirit of the refugees, glanced at him but then caught the thread of the moment and, quickly looking away from him to a man named Simon, answered, "If you wish, but never deprive a goat's kid to gratify your desire."

Simon was as agitated by Steven's sudden attention as if he had just discovered he was sitting on a nest of fire ants. He leaped up and cried, "Steven! All my life I have molded wood! Could I make a statue of Jacob?" He had wanted to ask the shara this for three days; Steven's gaze coupled with the simple power of his answer to Sanel had inspired this short speech. A quiet, strong man, Simon had all his life shunned crowds, had never before uttered a coherent phrase before more than three or four. And now he had spoken in front of so many! Staring with embarrassment at his large hands, he felt at once freed and fundamentally changed by his action. Steven's answer was almost redundant.

The shara rejoiced at the ease with which his troubled five had reduced to four as he answered, "Cut no living tree! But there is some standing deadwood; all your desires have been anticipated." He glanced at the woman at Simon's side, Elizabeth, then, frowning, looked away.

Elizabeth was eldest of the Five Hundred. Her life until the day Jacob came to Falon had been one of routine; of simple, mindless desires floating around the topics of flowers (she had a large garden), books (she was a librarian) and what she should prepare for dinner. She was in the market the first day the peasant spoke; one penetrating look from him had been enough to change her world forever. Casting aside everything of her past, she followed him with her heart.

Elizabeth gazed at Steven with hope, but saw him frown and turn aside. His withdrawal forced her to the precipice: gathering her courage from the distant reaches of her past, she exclaimed, "Why! Who orders this valley? Everything is in its — it's hard to say — its *proper* place. There is an abundance of everything needful, nothing that can harm! Why? Why are the animals so tame? Even the birds have no fear! Why does the temperature remain constant? How is it the volcano does not erupt? Why, Steven? Why?" Failing to find more words, she stared desperately at him for understanding.

The shara neither answered her nor even again glanced at her. His attention was now riveted on the iridescent butterfly that had climbed down his arm to dry its wings on his hand. He gave no sign he had even heard her speak.

The silence stretched long enough to become painful for several of the Five Hundred. Elizabeth, quietly sobbing, buried her head in her hands and moaned, "Oh, Jacob. My Jacob."

Leora broke first. She had been a virtual outcast for so long in Falon simply because she was born Salazian; now that she was one with the Five Hundred, she could not bear the thought of any being excluded from the wonderful wholeness of Vashti. Crossing to Elizabeth, she put an arm gently around her and said, "I know the answers, dear heart. Jacob would rejoice that my eyes learn to see! The living beings here are many more than I believed possible a week ago. Am I not right, Steven?"

The butterfly, now thoroughly airworthy, stretched its wings and flew upward toward heaven. Steven answered softly, "You know you are. The pleasant truth is that all will soon see the celestial gardeners of 'Ishtar's Vashti. Let us therefore leave such

questions, Elizabeth, until you discover our allies for yourself."
The shara now turned his warm brown eyes toward her; a flood of
peace came from them and raced through her. With a little shriek
of ecstasy, Elizabeth stared back at him with unalloyed joy. For the
first time since early childhood, her heart relaxed back from the
courtroom of judgment to the temple of silence. *Four becomes
three,* thought Steven with gratitude.

But Aldis felt even more lost from this mystical reply. "Steven!
I am more confused daily! I haven't the foggiest idea what you're
talking about. Nor have I since you sat us down in that foul cave
five hundred paces from this paradise and told us that long tale of
the legendary shara Gana. Who are you, anyway? Why did you do
that?"

"It is a little strange, isn't it?" chuckled Steven, giving him an
enormous grin. "A man born to himself but twenty-four hours
before stops you at the last instant, on the verge of fulfillment of
your desperate desire, and tells you one of the oldest tales of
mythical Emura. Most peculiar, wouldn't you agree?"

"Yes, confound it!" sputtered Aldis, far from soothed by the
shara's words. "Why don't you ever tell us anything clearly?"

"All right Aldis! Here is the simple truth. I stopped you all just
there because it was Jonathan and David who carried Morgan's
body to the stream that empties our Boiling Lake. That was a
message from the One to me, a statement that you were all
beguiled by oppositional states of duality and would have wasted
your lives here if I let you go ahead without more knowledge. Or,
here is another way of saying this: Gana needed your combined
attention just then to re-awaken more or less sane."

"You're laughing at me!" cried Aldis, on the verge of tears.

"I most assuredly am not," answered Steven. "You can only
hear what you are ready to hear. Words are clumsy tools compared
to experience. You need only calm your mind, Aldis, Darmin's
son. Then the light of understanding will reveal itself to you from
inside your own self. No one can resist Vashti for long. Even your

hard past will not long stand against its gentle benevolence." Concluding his phrases had planted the desired seed and the three would be two soon enough, the shara turned toward Sanel and exclaimed, "What did you make of the history of Gana?!"

Sanel started violently: why was Steven questioning his mind when it was his heart that was empty? Why did the shara want him only to think about life? What he needed was action! He wanted to contribute something real, something tangible, anything but more dry information! Swallowing with distaste, he answered, "The old books recorded that Gana returned to our world several times: as Barlrin and Aharon Hanif, to destroy Emura; as Balzor and Alazar, to found Tala; as Naisan and Mars, to save Tala from Zared and begin the Golden Age of Peace. The Oathmaster Joab wrote that these lifetimes were related to Gana's first three tasks."

"Did he? What else did Joab say?" asked the shara merrily. He was happy now because he was thinking that only a few more manipulations of Sanel's mind would be all that were necessary to meld Sanel with the others. And then there would be only the last and hardest to pull into the shimmering magic that was the congealed consciousness of the Five Hundred in Vashti.

Sanel saw that Steven was not exactly laughing at him, but his eyes were dancing in amusement. Why was the shara forcing him to say these impossible things? Nobody ever read Joab's *History of Lord Gana* anymore; few knew anything of these old epic myths. Sanel had accepted these histories only with his mind, never with his heart.

"Joab said that at the End of Time Gana would come again with Venus and the Ten Thousand of Kanaan-dora to protect the Lost Generation," he answered, scowling.

"Did he? Do you by any chance remember the number of the Lost Generation?" Steven was widely grinning at him now, thoroughly enjoying the changes in Sanel's face.

"I do. Of course I do. But surely you can't think that — !"

"What difference can it possibly make what I do or don't think! I have nothing to do with it, as you will all one day realize. The number is five hundred, of course. One way of understanding your reason for being here is to discover why Joab named you `The Lost Generation.'" The final stroke was so very sweet. Sanel looked a different man: younger, at peace with the world, wide open, innocent. Steven wondered with a rush of gratitude if Jacob left him thcsc few challenges so he could grow further into this infinite mind. *One more...*

"Surely because we have lost the world," said David, sure of his answer.

"Have you, David? Where are you then?"

"I meant we are lost from civilization," answered the Salazian, still certain of himself.

"Are you, David? Does this make any sense? Think of your life until a few days ago. Isn't it more logical that all the Five Hundred were killed outside Falon by the Salazian cavalry? And isn't it more likely that you alone opposed the slaughter and were butchered with them? Wouldn't you have to agree this is much more probable than what you believe happened?"

Steven abruptly stopped, shocked. He was not reaching David at all! His words were rebounding from him without the desired effect! Even the concentrated attention of the whole of the Five Hundred was not pulling the Salazian into his influence! Given the speed and momentum of his expanding mind, this felt like running into an invisible and invincible wall.

David could think of nothing to fill the sudden silence other than to stare open-mouthed at the shara. Steven, amazed to discover a limitation in his mind, showed only his usual calmness as he continued, "Enough. Perhaps too much already. You don't need me, you don't need more words. What each of you needs is to study your own hearts. You have all the tools you require.

"Go, enjoy Vashti. Listen to its waterfalls and breezes; play with its tame beasts; enjoy its precious stones and magical gardens.

Or think of Joab's teachings. Or tempt Sanel to tell you more of the lives of Gana in Emura and Tala, particularly those of Mars and Naisan. And those of you who have already learned to see the celestials, work with them always to learn more.

"Rodavi's wisdom might prove useful to some of you: `Life, like a many-faceted crystal, fractures the infinite One into versicolored beauty.´

"Do not forget the one danger in this last memory of 'Ishtar's paradise: *Dare not venture near the Boiling Lake."*

Quickly the unequalled air and water of Vashti melted the limitations of all: everyone of the Five Hundred discovered the valley's protectors. Even Aldis. Everyone, that is, except for Elizabeth. For sixty days she tried, without the slightest flavor of success. Perhaps it was her desperate effort that caused her repeated failure, perhaps it was her life-long habit of judging herself as unworthy. Whatever the cause, even though the others vividly described the remarkable joyous beings everywhere, there was nothing visible to her but an occasional shimmering in the air or water.

At the last, thoroughly frustrated, she came sobbing to Steven, "I should not have come! I should not! I cannot even rise to the initial stage!"

Steven held her for a long moment and gently stroked her silver hair. Then he grasped both her arms and, staring intently into her soft gray eyes, answered firmly, "No, lalasa, no. You are wrong. Nothing can stop the power of the One. Nothing save past denials has the authority even to slow it." Releasing her, he turned and walked slowly away.

"Steven, you are right. I have denied myself," she began, from habit speaking her fear. But her mind was already whirling through a chaotic rush of sudden color and unexpected meaning. Her words gradually stilled; within a moment, she was lost within her new world. She could see! See! For the first time in her eighty years. Everything before her was ablaze with moving light. Her eyes evolved quickly now; soon all the varied beings of Vashti, from the tiny flower elementals to the mountain celestials, as large as the Guardians themselves, were visible to her.

"Oh my! Oh — they're beautiful! So beautiful! So happy!" She gasped as two the size of children of seven or eight ran up to her. They were as intrigued by her — grasping her hands, they ran with her down the mountainside through the meadow until she fell, screaming with laughter, kicking the air with joy as if she were once again no more than Susan's age.

On the hundred and thirtieth day in Vashti, the Five Hundred reached the first crisis designed to mold them into a single mass of consciousness. On the hundred and thirtieth day in Vashti, Jonathan reached the natural end of his life's contract. On the hundred and thirtieth day in Vashti, Jonathan died.

He was with David by the Boiling Lake that day, talking and eating tropical fruit. They had spent a particularly fascinating day with a mountain celestial, learning of the Seven Regions of Light that enfold our Universe with radiant beauty. These are the natural homes of the Seven, the deathless ministers to humankind who in every age endeavor to remind us of our lost heritage and aid us through the jungles of this earthly plane.

David and Jonathan were discussing (one might more accurately say, arguing) whether or not Gana's perception of the many levels of creation in the Dome of the Spheres could be shared by anyone or could only be experienced in Para. Jonathan had just adamantly (and, he felt, adroitly) upheld the latter view when he chanced to see a particularly beautiful mango — red, yellow, obviously succulent and ripe — hanging far over the steaming water.

He was up and after it in a minute. David was meantime arguing that of course *any* reality could be experienced by *anyone* at *anytime* and was too engrossed by the flow of his logic to notice his friend's foolhardy danger.

Jonathan, stretching his weight carefully over the branch, answered his stream of discourse, "No. It is obviously impossible. From their mind-created World only could you view our Universe from the outside. How could anyone possibly see the entirety of Creation from the outside when you are inside it? It makes not the slightest sense. You are clearly mistaken."

David, realizing where the boy's voice was coming from, leaped up with concern: "Jonathan!"

Too late! The branch broke; Jonathan fell with a cry of surprise into the water. He surfaced once, screaming in agony, beating the water erratically, too mad from the pain to attempt to reach the shore.

David, wildly seeking a tool, saw a little tree nearby. Forcing it to the ground, he whipped it back and forth to tear it from its roots. The tree cried to him to spare it; David heard its terror but was too mad with fear to seek another solution.

The trunk ripped apart; thrusting the tree into the scalding water, he pulled Jonathan to the shore. Not noticing how he was severely burning his own arms, he lifted the boy from the water, crying, "Jonathan, my brother!"

"David," he rasped as his eyelids' mad fluttering marked the last pulses of his failing heart. "Tell Steven — " And then, with a long sigh, he died.

~~~

Simon was seeking the ideal wood for his statue of Jacob when he heard Jonathan's fearful scream. He was therefore the first of the Five Hundred to learn of the tragedy; with fierce anguish, he ran through the valley, crying the tale to the others, "Find the Teacher! Jonathan fell into the Boiling Lake! Steven! Find the Teacher! Find Steven!"

All the Five Hundred scurried throughout Vashti, but it was Leora who needed him desperately enough to find him. The deep roots of her lonely past had not yet been wholly severed; the shara felt her the best messenger for his response.

Discovering him high on the southern slope, Leora shouted as she climbed up, "Steven! Steven! Come! Oh, Steven, come quickly! Jonathan fell! Into the Boiling Lake! Steven!"

The shara continued his leisurely stroll through the copen, amber and violet alpine meadow without turning toward her until she reached him and panted, "Steven! Jonathan — "

He whirled around, grabbed her arms fiercely and stared at her, his eyes burning with what she thought was rage.

"Leora, Leora! Why this terrible alarm? Suddenly our valley becomes a hell of worry, fear, sadness. Would you make this last fragment of Isolde become as the forgetful outer world?"

"But Teacher! Jonathan — "

"Is alive, as well as any of you. Go back and tell them, `No one may die in Vashti until all have understood why Joab called the Five Hundred the Lost Generation.´ I will follow directly, but... but there it is! Look at this tree! I must study it before that storm breaks... Go! Why do you wait? Hurry! Mustn't be late!" Steven knelt by his small discovery, examining it intently. Not so easily would he be distracted from the slender silver thread of light that had led him here.

Leora, trying to remember Steven's words but failing from the terrible pressure of the moment, ran back to the sad crowd at the lake. All the Five Hundred were gathering there; some of them had placed their most precious gems at Jonathan's feet; seven of the deer knelt in a circle around him. David was still embracing him: no one's tearful entreaty had yet convinced him to let go. Yet everyone knew the boy was dead.

Leora cried with anguish, "David! I found the Teacher, but he didn't come! because he said Jonathan was all right and no one would die — but oh! I see he is — "

"Where is he!" screamed David, releasing the body at last. Rising with wrath, he glared at her.

"The south slope! He was — " David sprang off like a hunted deer. " — examining an odd little golden tree," she finished with a sob. She straightened Jonathan's ivory hair and closed his eyes.

David found Steven exactly where Leora had left him, kneeling by the little tree. The Salazian did not waste any breath shouting as she had, but concentrated on his race up the mountain. When he reached the shara, he cried, "Steven! Why! Why in the name of Jacob ..."

"David!" exclaimed Steven with passion. "Be careful! This tree is extraordinary! I do not know if another of her kind ever existed in this world! How fortunate we found her before the storm broke! How could she have come here? Perhaps her seed lay frozen in the ice for millennia, waiting — "

David looked incredulously back and forth from Steven's eyes, burning with wild fire, to the little golden tree, standing brave and alone in a small patch of emerald grass. At last he gathered his mind and roared, "Steven! Jonathan's *dead!*"

"For this very summer, this very day! How wonderful! David, dig her up. Very, very carefully. What shall we name her?"

"Steven, Steven! Did you not hear me? My brother is dead! Woe to have saved him from that falling death only to see him boiled alive now! Why? My God, *why?*"

"Would you have denied him these months in Vashti, David? Who else in this world has been so rarely fortunate? And who in this world can determine a life's span? Which of our race has the authority to so control the loom of the triple ministers of fate?

"But I say to you now, my friend, this death occurs only the better to demonstrate who you are. For this reason only has Jonathan fallen from life a second time. David! You remain a slave to the false appearance of this world! Even in your past in Salaz, you have heard of those who healed the sick. If they had more completely lived the power of the One, would they have found it more difficult to raise the dead? I think not.

"Well, we are still in the prelude of a very long tale. David! That storm descends over the Guardians with ice and death for this small being. *Dig me this tree!*"

David was deeply insulted, wildly angry, crazy with fear, yet fervently desiring to believe. He stood a moment more, wrestling with his raging emotions. There was, however, no way to resist Steven's last command. Diving at the ground, the Salazian scooped savagely at the moist earth until the tree came free. "There, curse it!"

Steven was already strolling down the mountain. "Bring Vanas cautiously, David," he called over his shoulder.

~~~

By the time they returned to the lake, Jonathan's body had been covered with flowers and jewels by the children. All the Five Hundred were morosely awaiting the shara. Many were crying, some were praying, a few were staring at the lake or into space, struggling to master their feelings.

Steven passed through them like a mild spring breeze, stepped over the corpse without glancing at it, then knelt by the broken sapling. "Why, David?" he asked with deep melancholy. "Why did you murder this small being? Replace him with Vanas! Her nature is suited to a tropical climate. How amazing she should have sprouted so high!"

The Five Hundred looked on dumbfounded as David meekly dug a hole and placed the little golden tree carefully in it. As he finished, his hands and arms raged with pain. He screamed in agony: not until now had he felt his severe burns.

"Leora," demanded Steven sternly, "why did you not repeat my message?"

Leora stared at him through her brimming eyes and tried to understand what he was asking of her. Did he not see this horror? "You mean about Joab? I... I must have forgotten. I — I'm sorry. When I saw Jonathan I thought I must have heard you wrongly."

"What did you see? Only the lie reported by your eyes about your false belief in the importance of bodies. Why should physical states possibly matter? Is one woman better than another because she is more beautiful? Is one man better than another because he is stronger? Is anyone better than another because he is richer?

"Why do you allow your beliefs to block your perception of Jonathan's Reality? You believe in suffering, in death, in pain, therefore this is what you see. If you believed instead in the never-changing Reality that is the One, you would see no suffering, no death, no pain, because these do not exist in Truth.

"Tell them now what I told you, Leora! Perhaps we may yet begin to undo your strange network of beliefs."

"You! ... You told me to say that no one would die in Vashti until all have understood why Joab called us the Lost Generation." Why had he forced her to say this? The boy was dead! Why say such a thing now? The words burned her throat like gall.

Susan, much too young to understand the tragedy before them, asked in her delicate high voice, "Oh, Steven! When will we understand the last Oathmaster Joab?"

Leora tried to hush her, but Steven was already turning to confront her. Would he be angry? Leora looked at him with fear, but he was smiling broadly at Susan, his eyes sparkling with mirth! What was wrong with him! Had he not loved Jonathan?

"At least there is one who remembers! Well done, child! For you and the others like you, a decade may teach you the secret of Joab's riddle. But for some of these others, I wonder if even fifty years shall suffice to undo the wrong thoughts of their unhappy dreams."

"Then some of us will never understand his mysteries," said Aldis, coughing to mask the pain in his voice. "I am already seventy-nine."

Steven said to David, "You would have felt nothing from your burns had you not killed a tree. Come! Jonathan has rested long enough. He least of all would like such a pathetic, woebegone crowd. Pick me a leaf from Vanas."

Wincing in anticipation, David gingerly touched the little golden tree. Surprised, he exclaimed, "The pain is gone!"

"Of course," replied Steven, taking the golden leaf. He bruised it, breathed on it, then rubbed it over Jonathan's heart. The boy shook all over; a great convulsing shudder moved from his feet to his head; his breath flowed again.

"He lives," whispered David, then shouted with mad delight, "he lives! My brother lives!"

Jonathan's eyes fluttered open. Seeing first Steven kneeling by him, he exclaimed, "Oh! Did I sleep long?" He recognized David next and said, "I think you're right after all. The Seven Regions of Light can be seen anywhere. I've just had the most amazing dream — " Then he saw all the Five Hundred gathered around and added with happy curiosity, "Everyone's here? Is it a meeting?"

Steven stood, rubbing his hands gently together to remove the vestigial effect. David embraced Jonathan, for the second time that day, his tears flowed fully.

"Vanas is a most unusual tree," murmured Steven.

~~~

On the anniversary of Jacob's death, Sanel came to Steven and said, "Teacher, I find that I am confused." He stopped, embarrassed. Steven never volunteered knowledge; it was always a questionable matter, trying to learn from him. It was not that the shara was ever curt or unfriendly, quite the contrary! It was just that there was always *something* most unsettling about those forever joyful eyes that looked through you into the heart of your soul. And his answers were usually so enigmatic as to make one wonder why he sought instruction.

Steven looked at him thoughtfully, but made no other response. Taking a deep breath, Sanel continued, "At times, I see people I do not recognize! Neither elementals nor celestials; human beings, but not of the Five Hundred! Yet when I look again, they are always gone!"

"Interpretation?" This was good, but still far from their need. Perhaps they were ready for more?

"I wonder if this valley were created by its custodians? The celestials maintain the order here, but — "

"Sanel, you are right. Although Vashti *could* have been created by subtle hands, it *was* not. The memories of the earlier humans, Vidyadharas and Lords of Etan are everywhere. As your vision evolves, you will more clearly discover the impressions they left in the subtle recording matrix of the One. In truth, no experience is ever lost. This valley has been a major junction with the higher dimensional worlds for many thousands of years. Here Joab discovered the lost seed of Vanas when Emura still ruled the world. Here the rajanya Mordom fell, sacrificing himself to defeat Mars' mind-created enemy, the Rakshasa Bala. Many others have lived full lives in Vashti, though there have been none for a long time. But finding Vanas growing here last fall convinced me we are to be the last to use this route. I am now certain Joab was not speaking a metaphor. I believe the days of this world are numbered."

"The Earth? To end? What? What is the number?" asked Sanel's mouth, but his mind was hammering at him, *As always! I ask for a spoonful and receive a gallon; I ask for a pound and receive an ounce! I do not understand this man!*

Steven grinned back at him without answering, thinking this a sufficient problem. For now.

~~~

At midday, a feast was held in honor of Jacob. After the meal, Simon stood and said, "I have an announcement. Rather, a small unveiling." He pulled the cover from his carving.

"Jacob!" gasped everyone, and not just to be polite. Somehow Simon had recreated the peasant: his form, his color, a familiar expression — pausing in the middle of a profound yet simple sentence — his hair, his eyes. His eyes! How perfect in life, how perfect here! They followed you everywhere and expressed emotions: love, authority, peace, forgiveness, joy.

Immediately a goldfinch perched on its shoulder and a chipmunk jumped into its lap. But Susan's response was best: "It's him! It is!" she cried, then ran to the statue and put her small arm around its waist.

Tears blurred Simon's eyes; he stumbled from the banquet.

Aldis looked at the statue with a peculiar mixture of joy, longing and sorrow. Even after a year, he was still struggling to be as the others. Simon seemed a perfect model of the kind of man he wished to be; to see the sculptor's moment of triumph was at once an inspiration and a painful reminder of his own limitations.

Clenching his hands tightly on the fifteen carat emerald he used to help focus his mind, Aldis stood and said, "Steven! I have a question." The many individual conversations ended immediately: Steven had not addressed the Five Hundred as a group for some months; he preferred to speak quietly to individuals or groups of no more than two or three.

The shara gazed with an unreadable expression at the old man but said nothing. Swallowing with difficulty, Aldis looked around desperately at the Five Hundred, seeking support. They stared back at him with eager curiosity, wondering what might happen next. Except for Susan: she was squeezing the hands of Simon's statue, telling it of her past year. Aldis wondered with a touch of vertigo if he should instead mimic her. But no, there was no other way to regain his self-respect; he must become bold to be worthy of Vashti.

"Steven. Ah, Steven. We've been here a year now! And, well, Steven. That is, I was wondering if the water, or maybe the air, or that is, could you... Confound it, Steven, none of these beautiful young ladies has had any children! I want to know why!"

The shara made no reply; the silence grew deeper as many looked hastily down at their banana leaf plates.

Finally Sanel stood, his face flushed, wondering why he so frequently was the one who tried to interpret Steven. "Aldis. Ah, speaking for the *men*. Is there ever a moment when we are not surrounded by elementals and celestials? And — "

"Don't you believe a word of that!" cried Leora, jumping up in shock. "Everyone knows better. Our love is so full, our joy so complete, our every moment so perfect; there just doesn't seem to be any point, any desire to... lesser..." Her voice trailed off.

Aldis, surprise overcoming reticence, exclaimed, "Hah! I only wish I were a few years — "

"Whatever the various reasons," interrupted Steven, content now with him, "the fact is: no children will be born in Vashti. You might consider this, Aldis: one way to gain something is to give something else up. Create a vacuum, it will be filled."

David asked eagerly, "Is that it, then? Discovering how much the Lost can lose?"

Steven laughed so uproariously the tears ran from his eyes. "So you make a beginning! But of what importance this compared to remembering what you lost before you were born into this world? Remember, Joab named the Five Hundred the Lost before the Downfall of Almira's World, before Gana was thrown from Para."

~~~

Seven years after the Five Hundred entered Vashti, Susan eagerly sought the shara throughout the valley. Although a girl of only eleven springs, she was the unrivalled favorite of everyone: as lovely as Leora, she was more filled with the innocent wisdom of the One than anyone else.

Steven knew she was far ahead of the others: more self-luminous, more aware, possessing a greater understanding as the natural by-product of who she was becoming. Filled with the vibrant excitement of hope, he stood quietly in the bright sunlight of the high meadow, awaiting her.

Susan climbed swiftly up to him, her eagerness belied by the grace of her movements. Wondering if she were being too bold, she knelt beside him and stared at the crimson and gold alpine flowers until he stroked her hair gently and asked, "You have seen Her?"

So he knew already! How could she have doubted? The Five Hundred were as weeds in his garden! "Today! At my favorite pool. It's on Laughing Creek — you know, it runs from the Big Blue Glacier into the lake near the Golden Tree Vanas?"

"Well I know it."

"It was there, in a small cedar grove. The brook comes playing down a little fall into the most lovely, quiet pond, which has the prettiest rainbow-colored fish in it. I was feeling so good, so, I don't know, so light, so alive; everything was so bright; the humming in the air was so loud. I looked up suddenly, there She was!"

"Who, beloved?"

She gazed up into his warm eyes, seeking confidence. But he felt it imperative she find her own strength and looked away. She tried to answer but found she could not. Closing her eyes to gather her spirit into her center, she said in a small voice, "Almira." The name and memory inspired her to greater mastery: in a rush came the rest, "She was so beautiful! All dressed in iridescence with long rainbow hair and a silver tiara, so glorious! So beautiful! And Steven! She walked across the pond and *into* me! And now I see Her everywhere, behind or inside, or on top of — it's hard to say exactly — *with* everything, all the people, all the trees and flowers, all the animals and birds, all the elementals and celestials, in *everything!* What does it mean! It's so wonderful, so beautiful! I love Her, I do!"

"You are correct, lalasa. She is the Mother. Your perception will develop quickly now. Has She talked to you?" At last! It was beginning!

"No. Or at least, I have not been able to hear Her." Now she spoke with the confidence of an equal. The last barriers between them were gone, melted by the dual influence of the shara's love and her belief in her Self.

"Soon She will; much of wonder will you that day learn. You are nearly home!" He kissed her gently on the forehead; a wave of warmth rushed through her, causing her vision to become more acute, brighter. She laughed in ecstasy, then ran joyfully back to the valley.

~~~

In late summer five years later, Susan and some other young people were picnicking on the north slope, near the base of the Great White Glacier. They had just finished the fruit and nuts they had gathered, one of the girls was opening a rare treat — a cheese! — when suddenly Susan stared in horror at the glacier above and screamed in terror. At that instant, a wall of ice broke loose and fell roaring down the mountain toward them.

Steven was walking that day with Jonathan and David on the southern slope, high above where he had found the Golden Tree Vanas twelve years before. It had been the driest and hottest summer since they came to the valley; new areas were opening on all the mountains, gladdening the shara's heart. He loved the highlands more than anyone else; he felt there was still much knowledge they were holding for him.

Today he had brought the two inseparable friends here to show them a curious white sculpture the receding snows had just uncovered. "Look at it closely," he told them, staring fiercely at Jonathan. "Do you recognize the style or letters?"

David wondered why Steven was so interested in it. What could be so fascinating about an old statue? With a shrug for the mysterious nature of the shara, he bent to pick it up. He tried with increasing effort, finally pulled at it with all his might, but could neither lift it nor even move it.

"I don't understand! It looks light enough! It must be connected to something underground."

Steven turned his ecstatic eyes toward him and cried, "It is not! Yet neither can I move it. But let him try."

David stood slowly, wiping his hands on his robe. They felt oddly chilled, almost as if they had been holding ice. But the statue had not felt cold when he touched it: it had been warm, heated by the sun. Shaking his head with doubt, he stepped back.

Jonathan looked at him curiously, seeing his confusion without understanding it. Steven did not seem to be acting peculiar: the shara's eagerness had inspired him with a powerful urge to understand this little white statue. Kneeling by it, he gathered all his strength in his attempt to force it from the ground. He was thrown over backwards when it came up with no effort.

"Yes!" cried Steven with even greater enthusiasm. He was right! One of the immovable statues from Sulara's Temple of Kanaan-dora had somehow found its way to Vashti with the seed of Vanas! "I thought so! Of all the Five Hundred, you alone can bear the White Snake! Can you also read its message?"

"I cannot," answered Jonathan, holding and examining the statue with a similar feverish excitement. It was filling his body with raw power and his mind with wave after wave of joy. "Never have I seen such a script. But, what do you mean? This is not heavy. It is all but weightless."

"So to you," said David, equally frustrated by this strange statue and the equally strange behavior of his companions. "I wasn't exactly playing with it. Let me see it. No! You hold it." He stared at it for a long moment, then said, "It *is* meant to be a snake, isn't it? And the lettering is like an inscription I once saw in the Salazian capital Rhodos, an inscription that dated back ten thousand years, to Tala! How strange. Tala was supposed to have been in Caremia, across the Ocean of Urlad! How could it have come here? I wonder what it says."

"I certainly don't know. But I want you to carry it to the lake and ask Sanel to study these letters — " Suddenly the shara whirled around and stared with horror over the valley: he felt the same terror entering Vashti as was Susan at this same moment.

"What is the matter — !" began David, but his words died in his throat: Steven had vanished.

~~~

The shara regretted leaving that way. *Another tale about my greatness,* he thought sadly. *Surely, this is not their need.*

But then his mind was absorbed in the invasion. He was now on the far side of the valley, above Susan and her friends, facing the mass of falling snow and ice. A fire, brighter than five hundred suns, flashed from his forehead. Not only did the avalanche disappear in vapor, but most of the glacier as well.

The shara fell to his knees, pale, shaken. Susan ran up to him, crying in fear, "Steven! Steven! What — who — what was that! *She* was not in it! Not in the slightest!"

"The Emptiness? It was a Rakshasa, dear heart, a Rakshasa. Odd it could enter here. Best to forget it. There is no longer reason for alarm. It is dead."

Steven was much more worried than any of the Five Hundred could guess. An undercurrent of doubt had been slowly maturing in him over the past year — something unexpected was happening outside their protected valley, some momentous change in the world for which he was not prepared. How could an invader have come so soon? Surely the world was deteriorating, but how could Vashti's Guardians have failed already? He was not ready! The Five Hundred could not support him properly, could not channel the limitless power of the One to aid him! If the balance had slipped, he would stand alone against the servants of Valin! He needed more time!

~~~

The next day, the shara Steven walked alone up the mountain past where the White Snake had lain exposed by the retreating ice. Crossing a little crest, he entered a small, unknown hollow. A second statue was there, sculpted like a Vidyadhara, but wholly black and without lettering. He bent to study the Black Lizard and found it as immovable as its white counterpart. With a wry chuckle, he left it there and continued up the mountain, insisting on better answers to the doubts diminishing his peace.

~~~

It took a full day for the Five Hundred to realize the shara was missing, but just an hour for them all to forget their various routines for the high excitement of the search. It was fortunate that Susan found his footprints on the snow first: she posted herself as sentry to keep anyone from following. "He has gone to meet with his Father," she told the others firmly. "He will return to us when he has finished."

The curiosity of the Five Hundred grew as large as the Guardians, especially since an ethereal light radiated at night from the mountain where the shara had disappeared. Nevertheless, they were wise enough to obey Susan's adamant will.

She stood there, waiting through eleven mild days and eleven bitterly cold nights, steeling herself to her Teacher's service, purifying her mind by her action in preparation for his return.

The morning of the twelfth day, she saw him coming slowly down through the crimson-gray stillness of early dawn and ran to him, crying, "Steven! I've been waiting!" But when she saw his face, she could only stare at him, thinking, *You are He.*

Steven pointed back up the mountain; she ran there, hoping to see Jacob. He was not there. Disappointed, she turned to leave, but then saw the Black Lizard. Picking the statue up with no effort, she ran to catch Steven.

~~~

The shara could do nothing but sit by Vanas: for three weeks he neither spoke nor ate nor even drank. All who looked at him were astounded, although most could not yet see as well as Susan.

At sunset of the twenty-second day, he said suddenly, "Bring Sanel to me."

"She stared at him thinking, You are He."

Elizabeth was squatting nearby, eating a banana. To hear him speak again after so long catalyzed an enormous leap. Realizing her route would end in a scalding dip in the Boiling Lake, she twisted in mid-air, clawing at space. The result was a dramatic display of gymnastic skill that barely saved her person from being scorched.

Steven chuckled, "I thought I must be watching one of the children, Elizabeth! Such feline grace would be extraordinary for a teenager!"

Sanel came running up, shouting excitedly, "I've done it, Steven! I've done it! I've read the White Snake! Ah, I'll never begrudge those many hours devoted to ancient Talanese again! Don't you hear? I've deciphered Jonathan's statue!"

"Is that right!" shouted Steven back at him. "What does it say, what does it say!"

"The White Snake reads, `United with my ebony brother and the golden flower of Vanas, Mars will lead the Ten Thousand to victory over the numberless hordes in protection of Vashti.´"

Here Steven began quoting with him, "`Then will descend celestial fire; the Lost Generation of Five Hundred will return to their ancient home under Almira's wings. I, Joab, have written this!´"

"Oh," said Sanel in a small voice as he realized the shara had been speaking with him. "How did you know?"

23
The Message

Take not gain or loss to heart:
These are minor thoughts.
Conscious purpose never succeeds:
Only innocence attains its will.
— Rodavi

Mark well the End of Time!
Look for Mars and Venus
And the Ten Thousand of Kanaan-Dora
When this divided world is joined by unholy war!
— Mordom

At first I was melded with others
As a rock of a granite wall.
But nature and perverse will broke them all.
I alone remained:
Embattled,
Yet firm in myself.
A single stone,
A weathered statue of adamant resolution.
— Joab

The same day the Rakshasa forced its entry into Vashti, the Empress Avera, having long ago conquered the entire northern hemisphere, began her invasion of Calantha. Her scientists covered a fleet of steamships with an insulated steel; the Salazian legions crossed the Burning Sea. But Avera's technology was not yet advanced enough to defeat that adamant ancient civilization: Salaz was repulsed. Although Calantha had not grown in martial knowledge, much of Kanaan-dora's wisdom had been retained there through the long ages: Avera found that venerable oak too hardy for even her fell axe.

The Empress threw the full might of Salaz at Calantha three more times and failed three more times. But Avera had never learned to accept the reality of failure; forced by her unbending will, her servants eventually created her the necessary tools: they learned to fly machines through the air.

In the thirtieth year after the Five Hundred entered Vashti, the Salazian Empress Avera descended with sudden death from the skies on Calantha. The descendants of Gana's only son Kartika fought as fiercely as cornered beasts, but were no longer a match for the technological prowess of the North: within three weeks, that great nation which had known independence since the landing of the refugees from Kanaan-dora fell to the brutal power of the Salazian Empire. Avera had succeeded in her life-long quest to be Empress of all the world.

~~~

Steven stood alone in his high meadow, feeling the waves of terror enveloping the world like a cocoon of death. He knew he could wait no longer: prepared or not, the three must depart from him. Those three were the most developed of the Five Hundred — the closest to fulfilling their roles in the difficult requirements of this age — yet even so, he feared for them: their tasks would be the hardest, the most violently opposed by the nearly omnipotent forces of Emptiness. Was it reasonable to hope their still limited mastery of the One would save them? Even with the full support of what was left of the celestials?

Sighing deeply, almost bitterly, Steven called the three to him. They gathered to him eagerly, their minds bright with the excitement of this invitation to approach the shara. Steven was usually in meditative silence; only when one of the Five Hundred reached a barrier that could be surmounted in no other way would he come quietly to them and touch their minds with ideally chosen and rarely failing words or actions.

To be asked to join him was rare; to be asked in a group of three was unprecedented. David and Jonathan and Susan approached him with eager joy, then knelt before him in perfect submission.

Steven danced in their minds briefly, asking himself again if they were ready. Susan, as she had been for nearly thirty years, was the closest to perfection of any of the Five Hundred. If this extraordinarily lovely woman had lived in the common world, she would surely have been revered by now as the greatest wonder of her age. Few of her desires went unfulfilled: as one example, her mind-created sculptures, almost more alive than the beings they mimicked with consummate artistry, were common throughout Vashti. Ever since she had carried the Black Lizard, she had been more Steven's partner than his student: the difference between her and Almira was one of degree, not of kind. The shara's fear for her was that she might attempt to bear too much; thrice already he had cautioned her not to take on more of the Five Hundred's weight than was required.

Jonathan was not so far from her degree of perfection. Steven had often felt he would have been his successor if the requirements of their age had differently ordered their tasks. As it was, Steven rested most of his hopes for the success of their journey on this deep-chested giant of a man. The shara's concern for him was that his love for David might become oppressive when they must part.

No, of the three kneeling before him now, David was the only enigma. And this was an enigma the shara had no way of resolving! He did not know whether or not the Salazian was prepared, no way of ever knowing: of all the Five Hundred, this stunningly handsome man alone had never been within the scope of Steven's all but infinite mind. David reported experiences similar to everyone else's; from all external tests, he appeared on a par with Jonathan and Susan; but Steven simply did not *know,* would never know, could never know. The pivotal crisis of the age was forming around David, twisting its fibers of the One and of Emptiness toward him like a mighty vortex of fate; the outcome was nothing less than the future of the world; and yet Steven did not know if David were even close to being prepared.

Sighing again for this one empty place in his mind, the shara told the three they must leave Vashti and carry a message to Arthur.

"What?" asked David, assuming he must have heard incorrectly. "Why leave? Arthur spends his time by the Running Creek, on the west — "

"No, David. Not Shawn's. I meant the Arthur left outside the cave with Deborah, thirty years ago. Remember?"

"But Steven! Surely that Arthur long ago — " What was troubling the shara? Why did he look so concerned? He had never seemed so sad. In fact, he had never once evidenced even the slightest sadness. Was he ill? Was that even possible?

"He and Deborah live there still, following Jacob's teachings in their small valley."

David, increasingly confused as awareness of what he was hearing penetrated his mind, tried once more, " But! Arthur failed the Test of the Cave!" What in the name of the Seven was Steven talking about? Leave Vashti? If the outside world still existed was less than meaningless. What difference did it make to him, to any of the Five Hundred, what became of the world? That place might as well be dead. Surely no one worthwhile could still live there — everyone there must be more akin to the animals than to the wonderful unity of the Five Hundred. The memory of Arthur was still in him, surprisingly clear after so many years — a tall, handsome blond youth, always tagging after Jacob as if he were his puppy — but he had never entered Vashti! He had failed the last test!

Steven sent calm impulses of love and order to the One in David's heart. But, as always, the unreachable nature of the

Salazian shattered the shara's extensions; they rebounded back as if they were striking against a mirror rather than a conscious mind. Frustrated by this one failure of his subtle power, Steven tried again to reach him with inadequate words, "Arthur did fail at the cave. But only because it was not *his* test. The simple truth is that he is another aspect of my Self: there is no real difference between us. He does not, however, know who he is.

"When Gana was thrown from Almira's World, the Golden Thread was damaged, thereby shattering his consciousness. Jacob had to pass either to Arthur or myself the one connecting fiber that contained the missing parts of Gana's mind. He chose to give it to me, for he knew that in Vashti we might succeed in replicating that fiber.

"Almira foresaw this task when Gana was poisoned by his nephew Irnga: planning for his eventual re-integration, she created the two immovable statues, the Black Lizard and the White Snake, to carry his mind forward through the illusion that is time. Joab fulfilled her intention when Para was destroyed by bringing the two statues and the seed of Vanas here. And now the three of you must complete this work we have all labored on so long: you must convey the fragments of Gana's mind to Arthur. At dawn, you will cross the mountains: Susan, carrying the Black Lizard; Jonathan, the White Snake; David, the golden flower of Vanas."

"So the Tree's one bud is blooming at last!" exclaimed Susan joyfully. She at least was thrilled by the thought of seeing the outer world. If any lack existed in her nearly perfect mind, it was the slightest sadness for having entered Vashti too young to remember anything else. This would be a great adventure!

"It blossoms this night. You must deliver it and the statues to Arthur before two days have passed." It sounded so simple to say! Yet what chance did the three have against the infernal might of the Rakshasas?

"And after we find him?" asked Jonathan. His feelings vacillated between David's and Susan's: at one moment, he was excited by the possibility of seeing the world again; at the next, he was deeply saddened by the thought of leaving the Five Hundred. But of course to fulfill a request of his Teacher made all other concerns irrelevant.

"Then, you will have more and harder tasks. Even the society of the Five Hundred will be lost to you. Tonight I will teach you and Susan a special manipulation of the One that will help Arthur and the others protect Vashti. Your primary work from now will be to master this ability. And David, your task may prove the hardest. You must re-enter Avera's army — "

"What! Surely my ears lie to me today! That witch can't still live! By Narain's Dream, Steven! There must be another way!"

"If there were, I would tell you of it. There is not. No one else can accomplish this, David. To create the victory, you must leave here, rejoin the Salazian army and as quickly as possible work your way into Avera's Inner Council."

"How will I even find her? It is a large world!" It was a weak excuse, but seemed ideal to his desperation. Was the peace of Vashti now to be his only in memory? What evil had he committed that his life should take such a painful turn?

Steven smiled, a little wryly, a little bitterly, and answered, "Today she is with her armies in Calantha — "

"Calantha!" cried Jonathan, at once entirely sharing Susan's feelings. "Then Sanel's tales of the shara Mars are literally true? There is a world beyond the Burning Sea?"

"There is. This very spring, Calantha has fallen to Avera, ending its millennia of independence. The Salazian Empire has united the northern and southern hemispheres."

"But, Steven!" exclaimed David, ever more frustrated. "So what? What can this possibly have to do with us? What difference to us who rules the outer world?"

"David, David! Have you not understood the tales of Gana, of Mars and Naisan? In thirty years, have you not yet discovered why the Five Hundred were termed the Lost? No one lives alone!

Vashti would shrivel like a moth in the Rakshasas' fires of Emptiness if the celestials lost control of this world. Never is a living being isolated from any other! Never can any live alone — Lieutenant."

Hearing his rank again after so long was like a physical blow: David recoiled as if he had been struck. Was he thus fated to lose them, to rejoin the enemy? Was he to be a slave again? Did he not have free will? Could he not simply refuse to leave them? What wrong turnings had divided him from the Five Hundred? It was true he had not yet learned to hear and see Almira dancing in every particle of creation as did Jonathan and Susan, but few others had yet accomplished this either: in fact, only Leora and Simon. What sins in his youth had earned him such a hellish fate?

"What have I to do with this!" he cried, more angry than afraid. He looked desperately to Susan and Jonathan for support; they returned his gaze with compassion more than offset by their eager anticipation of their journey. Finding little solace in either friend, David sighed heavily and looked over Vashti. He could see many of his friends below, joyously going about their evening tasks, oblivious to the suffering he was enduring. *Why? Why me?*

Steven answered slowly but with warmth, "David! Trust in the way the Seven have ordered our age. Believe me when I tell you that there is no choice. It has to be you: you are the lost key! Even now, the celestials and the Rakshasas war for your spirit. You feel almost nothing of this because of the beneficial power of the One in Vashti."

"What is that supposed to mean?" asked David without looking away from the valley. Never had he felt such anguish! To have lived in such bliss for so long, now to be forced to return! The thought of his impending damnation was worse than awakening in hell.

"Let me explain. Before Avera mastered even her original country Salaz, the Rakshasas gave her the gem Starbha, wrested from Joab when Almira's World was destroyed. They saw in her their best hope to conquer the Earth and free their Lord Valin.

"Joab managed to hide Kaysta from the Rakshasas, but the day approaches when Avera will also own that gem. Her possession of the two halves of Kaystarbha is not by itself sufficient for her to free Valin, but she will in time also discover the diamond staff of the Oathmasters!" Steven paused, looking at David to encourage his comment.

But the Salazian was still moodily gazing at Vashti and gave no sign of comprehending Steven's words. Susan, however, understood them fully. She looked at Steven with love and said simply, "Then. We are dead."

David and Jonathan stared at her, but Steven could not help smiling for her wisdom. "Soon. But the Empress will not at once gain full knowledge of the staff. You are right, of course: were she merely to break it, every one of the Five Hundred would die — instantly.

"David, you must understand: Gana partially failed in his fourth task. Therefore the radiance of Para has ended; its peoples entered a trance-like state similar to sleep. When Gana was thrown from the world he created with Almira before our Cosmos began, the Golden Thread of the universal nervous system was damaged. The only tool in creation judged powerful enough to prevent the Universe from immediately ending was the diamond staff of the Oathmasters, for it embodies the beginning and end of the power of creation. The whole of the life of the Universe now flows through that instrument! David, you must stop Avera from destroying it until we are prepared to restore Gana to himself. This is your second task. The third and the hardest is to have her break it at the correct instant, then take it and Starbha and Kaysta from her and return to Vashti."

"And then?" David was not following Steven well. Nevertheless, he could not help being fascinated by the mention of Gana. If only he were a witness rather than a participant! Suddenly he looked hard at his mind: what was the source of that thought? What else could possibly be important in life other than aiding Gana? He should be grateful for this! What was causing these doubts? Was Steven correct about the celestial-Rakshasa battle for his mind and heart?

"And then? Then all will end correctly. The staff and the twin gems are the final requirements, but only if you bring them at the right moment to me in the presence of Vanas. Then the Five Hundred will return to Almira's World, which will re-awaken unto itself; Gana will return to full sanity. The nervous system of this Universe will be repaired; Gana's error in his fourth task will be corrected; Almira will continue with her plan for the evolution of our Cosmos. But if you fail and the diamond staff breaks before we are ready — "

"Then everything has been in vain," finished Susan. "Gana and this Universe of his creation would have to begin again. Almira told me this! Yet even She does not know any other way to gain the Oathmaster's staff, David. Aiding Gana directly in his higher tasks is forbidden even to Her."

"But, *why?* Why me? There must be so many ways to accomplish this." David was not having much success in stilling his doubts: they kept arising as if he were being filled with someone else's desires. Never since entering Vashti had he experienced such mind-distorting confusion. The many jewels of Vashti below sparkled lovely joy in the moonlight, but David could not see their gentle beauty: he was too busy wondering if his life would ever again be ideal. *Why? Why me?*

"No," answered Steven slowly, watching the Salazian closely to see whether they had already failed. But David was inscrutable, as unreadable as he had always been, a perfectly opaque consciousness, untouchable by the shara's mind, invisible to his intuitive comprehension. It was exactly as if his living essence, part and parcel of the One that breathes through all of creation, were surrounded by an impenetrable wall of Emptiness, impervious to the shara's power. Why?

"No. Out of all the uncountable billions of the Universe, only two still have the ability to lift the diamond staff. The identity of these two is well known. One is the chief instrument of the Rakshasas — the Salazian Empress Avera. And the other, David, is the one who carries Victory or Damnation for our age and for our Universe in his hands. That one is none other than — you."

David felt the pressure of this knowledge pushing at his mind like a hurricane flood eating away at an earthen dike. His eyes closed and his head bowed forward as he tried to master its force without damaging his mind. He could not deny its awful presence, could not ignore it, could not move its course in any way: its frenzied power kept mounting in intensity until he felt his skull must surely burst from its terrible might. *Why? Why me?*

~~~

At dawn, Steven ended his instructions with the command, "Descend now to the Boiling Lake for the statues and the flower. Bear it carefully! Not one petal may be damaged before it reaches Arthur."

When they returned, David was carrying a large golden flower, every one of its hundreds of petals radiant with its own internal light. Jonathan exclaimed, "I could not pick it, though I tried with all my strength! Yet when he touched it, it fell into his hand!"

Steven laughed with joy to see the One now so clearly on David's face. Surely the blossom of Vanas would complete his journey to the celestials! "Now you understand why you three must bear this three-fold message to Arthur."

David looked at him with clarity and said calmly, "I will do my best to fulfill your will, my shara. But before I leave this paradise of 'Ishtar's creation, I would have your explanation of Joab's naming us `the Lost.'"

"Have you observed the number of humans in this valley is five hundred and four?"

"Yes, of course, but what importance that? Surely Joab was giving an approximation."

"No. When the Oathmaster said, `The Five Hundred,´ he meant exactly what he said. The three of you and myself are not of their number. In the final instant when Gana was thrown from Almira's world, five hundred celestials were drawn downward into this Universe with him. These are our Five Hundred; the evolution of their minds back into the One is the most powerful tool we have to return Gana to himself."

"If we are not of the lost celestials, then who are we?" asked Jonathan, surprised.

"You may have difficulty understanding this answer for some time: it is not an easy knowing. You and Susan are the right and left hands of Almira! You, Jonathan, *are* the White Snake, Almira's copy of Sesha; you, Susan *are* the Black Lizard, Almira's copy of Heramann. But who are you, David? That I do not know."

"What!" the Salazian exclaimed with astonishment. "Why?"

"I don't know! And it is not for lack of trying. From the day we entered Vashti, I have attempted to move my awareness into you. There is a block in my mind — a restriction that keeps me from understanding you. From our first moments here, I have been unable to touch your spirit, to know you as I do the rest of the Five Hundred, to meld your consciousness with theirs into a single mass of light and power. Of all in the valley, you alone are forever beyond my ability."

"Why?" asked David again, confused.

"I tell you, I don't know! I theorize you are connected with the break in the Golden Thread, the break which keeps Para frozen, the break which keeps Gana wandering in a mad imitation of life, the break which keeps the forces of the One in this Universe so weak before the forces of Emptiness. This is why you alone can bear the flower of Vanas and the diamond staff.

"I can say no more, I know no more! But you must leave now: by midday, you must pass the summit, else you will be caught in the bitter cold of night, unprotected on the high slopes. Simon made you these snowshoes; they are filled with the power of the wind, they will make your journey light. He also made this maplewood jewel to hold and protect the flower of Vanas.

"One final advice I give to you. Remember it well: *Do not in pride rely solely on your own strength. Do everything together while you can. A three-fold cord is not easily broken.*"

Susan, her brilliant mind coloring her words radiantly golden, said, "Steven, before we go, there is one thing I too would ask you."

"You know already, don't you?" No one else would ever so fill his mind and heart. She was the perfect embodiment of Almira in human flesh; full mastery was within her grasp. The Five Hundred were as children to her. Would another world, would another age blossom with her return? Would she one day come striding back to him over emerald hills, yellow and blue-cloaked in the new beginning? He had never loved another more — nor would he ever.

Susan, feeling their sundering as deeply as he, gazed at him with tears filling her eyes and answered softly, "Yes, beloved. But I long with all my heart to hear my shara say it. Steven, will you tell us plainly at this division that *you* are Lord Gana?"

He smiled bitterly and replied, "You have said it, lalasa. Arthur and I labor to complete Gana's fifth task. Jacob spent his life at the well, raising the radiant energy of life, Almira's manifest power of the One, from the fourth center to the fifth. In this way our damaged Universe began to be reconnected to its Source. From love of humanity, Jacob abandoned the well; his innocent act endangered the whole of creation. But because of who he was, he had sufficient skill to create an alternative. He externalized the connecting link: he created Arthur, the Five Hundred and me to bear the burden of continuation. And now your sacrifice in leaving your home will make the first scene of the final act that will restore Gana to himself."

The shara watched the three messengers race up the mountain, their flying feet almost but not quite touching the snow. He sighed, oppressed by the weight of his future. *Now there is a scant twenty years for the rest to become as these three. What a labor! I wonder, will it be possible for me to achieve my small part in this age?*

Elizabeth came running up the mountain and broke his doleful reverie before it really began: "Steven! Thank you for letting me approach you! I'm one hundred and eleven today! Can you believe it? Do I look a day over twenty? And I, that is Aldis and I, well we — he has asked me to marry him! Do you approve?" She smiled at him with eager hope, hardly daring wish he would consent to their silliness, yet fervently desiring that he would. It would make Aldis so happy!

The shara grinned broadly at her and said with intense warmth, "Elizabeth! Thank you for answering me." And he gave her such love from that moment she never again doubted Almira lives as completely and beautifully in her heart as she does in the heart of everyone...

~~~

Shortly after noon, the three messengers stood high on the mountain slope and cast a long, pensive look back over Vashti, their home of thirty years. "Farewell, Oathmaster Steven," Susan whispered, surprised the unfulfilled longing in her breast was continuing. What had she to do with such a feeling? Hers was not a life of the world! Turning her mind from the unfamiliar emotion, she added in full voice, "Fare you well indeed with your many! Come, brothers!" She led them quickly over the flank of the mountain.

United in mind and heart, Jonathan and Susan and David returned to the great, wide world.

They did not go alone: surrounding them on all sides were tens of thousands of celestials. Their golden, silver and multicolored energies filled the sky with supernal beauty as far as the messengers could see. This was the largest gathering of the forces of the One in the Universe since the day the shara Gana with his Ten Thousand joined the Vidyadharas and the one hundred and eight Lords of Etan led by Orah, 'Sravasa and 'Ishtar and cast Valin from his diamond throne into his endless bondage.

But in those earlier days of completion, the forces of Emptiness had been far weaker: they had only partially recovered from their unexpected defeat on Martanda; Valin's walls of Asur fire fell with relative ease. Gana reached the new world without losing even one more of his refugees.

But today, the balance had shifted: the Vidyadharas were extinct; the unsurpassed wisdom of Kanaan-dora was all but lost from the world; the Lords of Etan were working in other regions of the Universe to further the Grandfather's intention. The celestials were still a mighty force, but from the day Gana was poisoned and the Solar Race effectively ended, almost none of our world even knew they existed. And no one knew anything but rumors and myths of the Oathmasters' science for communicating with and strengthening our allies on the subtle levels of creation.

The celestials were therefore cut off from the heart of humanity; their primary source of nourishment was gone. For as wonderful, long-lived and wise as the celestials are, without the lively interaction of humanity with the One, their power in the world decreases from age to age.

The forces of Emptiness had therefore become the virtual masters of our world and of our Universe; this was particularly true since the Downfall of that glorious bastion of the One: Almira's transcendental world Para.

To restore her Universe, Almira designed this message the day she led the refugees from Kanaan-dora to our world. Planning for the eventual re-integration of Gana with a higher understanding, she formed two statues from her person and breathed life into the seed of the World Tree.

Joab, understanding her intent, commented in his *History of Lord Gana,* "When the golden flower of the World Tree and the immovable statues move from Vashti, the End of Time begins."

But it was not clear whether either Almira or Joab had foreseen how the long lapse of time would so favor the forces of Emptiness...

The Rakshasas also knew what successful delivery of this message might portend for their future rule. They did not know exactly when the three would pass outward, for they were still barred from Vashti. But when Avera's destruction of Calantha was certain, they knew it would be soon.

Therefore the moment the messengers left the protected valley, they were detected. It did not take much longer for the Rakshasas to gather and attack the celestial army protecting them. Diving in wave after wave of Emptiness, they came on and on, sacrificing life after life in the hope of freeing their imprisoned master.

The celestials were not as they had once been, yet still were they mighty in the use of the One: a golden hemisphere of protection formed around the three as they raced through the mountains, tightly clutching their precious burdens.

Perhaps because of the level of mastery of the messengers, perhaps because they had so well learned of their connection with that which underlies and pervades all of creation, twice only that day were they directly assaulted.

One of the Rakshasas knew David from before. The Salazian had seen action in Avera's wars; he had taken lives. He had not fully forgiven himself for this. The Rakshasa recognized the faint fiber of Emptiness connected still to David's heart and followed it unerringly to its source. For a moment, none could withstand him: he fought his way through the celestials and dove at the running humans. Flying past Jonathan and Susan, he struck David with his flaming sword of Emptiness.

The celestials recognized the flaw in David and weakened his connection with it. No longer attached to the human, the Rakshasa was defenseless. The celestials filled him with their arrows; hissing like a snake, he fell dying near Susan's feet.

Shuddering, she leaped over the smoking corpse and ran to David. He was lying where he had fallen; there was an ugly, deep burn across his back and shoulder. Taking a golden leaf from inside her robe, she crushed it, filled it with the power of her mind, then rubbed it into his wound.

David's eyes fluttered open; he said quietly, "The flower. Where is the flower?"

"The maplewood container fell down there!" cried Jonathan, pointing at a narrow, deep fissure. "Can you rise?" The wound had closed and seemed to have healed, but something about David's calmness seemed false; Jonathan wondered if the leaf of Vanas had neutralized all the Rakshasa poison.

"I'm all right," answered David, sitting up and rubbing his shoulder gingerly. He stood slowly, feeling giddy. "Can we climb down there?" He looked doubtfully over the edge. The awesome height made him feel dizzier. He leaned back, rocking on his heels, moaning. The Rakshasa poison was strengthening his connection to the weaker part of his past. In a collage of moving color, every wrong thought and deed of his life flashed through his mind. With a sickly feeling of despair, he remembered the most horrible of his acts as a Salazian lieutenant. How could he have been so evil?

"It is perhaps not necessary," answered a celestial, brilliantly silver, alighting near him. "Now that we have driven back the offspring of horror, we can be of more assistance. What is your need?"

"A portion of our message fell below!" exclaimed David, feeling ever more lost.

The celestial started toward the crevasse, but Jonathan cried, "No! Only he may carry it."

"Then, I will carry him." The celestial picked David up; together they floated downward. The moment the celestial touched him, David felt the Emptiness strengthened in his heart. He could not help but weep for the terrible wrongs he had committed.

Jonathan and Susan saw his tears but Jonathan thought he wept in gratitude for his returning life and Susan felt he was joyful to be touched by the celestial.

The jewel container was unharmed. David opened it quickly, fearing the worst. The flower of Vanas was all but intact: only one petal was broken.

Sighing with gratitude, David briefly felt again complete, whole. There must still be hope!

But there was none, he was betrayed: the celestial was no celestial but a Rakshasa, skilled in illusion. Revealing his true form, he leaped on David and struck him through his beating heart with his dagger of infernal fire.

~~~

"What can we do! The leaves do not revive him!" Jonathan had never experienced such an agony. "Why did we let him go alone! Steven ordered us never to part! We have betrayed him, we have betrayed Gana, we have betrayed everyone!"

"We must use the broken petal!" Susan also felt the horror, but was firm in her decision. What choice did they have?

"But the flower must arrive whole!"

"It cannot even be delivered if he remains dead! I will do it. Full responsibility is mine." She crushed the petal and rubbed David's chest.

Two minutes of steady work, there was nothing. Concentrating all her energy, she cried, "Almira! Now, if never before! Now, so the world may continue! Now, in response to our vital need!" Susan pushed the petal into the deep wound in his chest.

With a choking rattle, David's breath moved again; he assumed once more the burden of life. His eyes burst open with anger as he cried, "You dare recall me? I was free! Almira welcomed me home! But hearing your call, she ordered me to return, to serve in the final struggle for this Universe. Then the sweet scent of Vanas sought me out and carried me with it. I have come back to darkness, losing Beauty, losing Truth, losing Life, for one reason only. Do you know it?"

Jonathan was too full with joy to follow his emotion, but Susan understood his words and kept a troubled silence. Had she destroyed herself?

~~~

The messengers were well protected for the rest of the day: David's sacrifice had cleansed the last fibers of Emptiness from his spirit. He was free from the Rakshasas now, therefore all but invisible to them. With no hold of self-condemning belief among the three humans, the Rakshasas had no effective weapon against the celestials; therefore the successful completion of this stage was all but assured. The celestials formed a mighty arch of light over the three, large enough and high enough to be seen for many leagues.

In Vashti, the Five Hundred beheld the glorious light of a perfect rainbow, high above the southern mountains; Steven rejoiced to learn David had mastered his first task.

~~~

By sunset, the messengers were below the tree-line, running downward through an alpine meadow. "That hemlock grove?" asked Jonathan with an enormous yawn. "I don't know about you two, but I'm exhausted." David and Susan followed his lead without comment; soon the three were settled in the soft needles for their first night in the outside world.

Even though only one had a peaceful rest, none of them heard the watchers stealing toward them. At dawn, they were awakened by a shout, "Ho, Jacobi! Here they lie!" The messengers stared upward at the points of twenty drawn arrows, held by twenty identical and magnificent red-haired women of perhaps twenty autumns, dressed as they, in simple woolens.

David said with a certain wry amusement, "We mean no harm, but come with a message for Arthur." He stared at one of the twenty as he spoke. His focused attention was enough to shatter the illusion: the twenty melted into one.

She lowered her weapon and looked at him with an amazement that verged on veneration. "Forgive me!" she exclaimed, kneeling before them. "Your mastery was veiled! I am Stevana, Arthur and Deborah's younger daughter, yours to command."

A huge golden-maned lion leaped into the hemlock grove from uphill. Stevana raised her hand to it; the lion came to her and touched her. She whispered to it; the lion vanished and in its place stood another woman. If possible, she was even more beautiful than Stevana, with golden hair cascading in glorious profusion around her perfect features. She looked at her sister for a moment, reading her thoughts, then stared at the messengers. "How could it be that two Salazians are among the Lost?" she asked in a stern but slightly tremulous voice. "In Joab's writings, there is mention of only one, the Last Living One; father explained this must certainly be the lieutenant known as David. Who, then, are you?" Jacobi could perceive the radiance and power of the three, but her study of the mysteries of the Oathmasters had increased her caution: the Rakshasas were ingenious in their perverse twisting of human senses.

Susan smiled warmly at her and answered, "My mother Leora was born Salazian. She was the daughter of an ambassador and lived most of her life in Falon. She was Sanel's bride."

"Sanel!" exclaimed Jacobi, reddening. She also fell to her knees before the three. "I beg your forgiveness!" she cried in a voice that manifested increasing light and power. "We hear from the Five Hundred at last! I do obeisance to the Lost."

"Jacobi, my elder sister," said Stevana, slightly amused by her excessive emotions. "Seeker of the mastery of the secrets of the Oathmasters rather than the lore of the world. But perfectly right in her interpretation of last night's storm, that much is certain."

"Your journey from Vashti could not be at a more auspicious time!" exclaimed Jacobi joyfully, uplifted by the fulfillment of her belief. "Father has reached the ultimate crisis of his growth — "

"Then take us swiftly to him!" interrupted David, casting an uneasy glance to the southwest. A huge force of Rakshasas was gathering there, resembling nothing so much as a vast thunder cloud.

~~~

As they walked together, Susan asked Stevana and Jacobi of their lives. She could not remember any who were not of the Five Hundred: these two were the perfect answer to her desire for knowledge of the world.

In spite of her feelings and words, Jacobi was still cautious: her belief was that the enemy was capable of any deceit. But Stevana believed in the three without question; she eagerly told their history: the simplicity of their childhood, the martial training of their youth, the growing complications of the recent years as more and ever more Outsiders tried to explore the mountains.

She added with a peculiar mixture of calm certainty and feral passion, "But of course we always stop them." As she spoke, she stroked her bow as if it were alive.

"We have done our best to keep Vashti a secret," added Jacobi, glancing at Stevana curiously. How her sister enjoyed war! It was to Jacobi at best an unavoidable evil. "We succeed with difficulty; it grows progressively harder. And if the rumors are true Calantha has fallen — "

"They are," said Jonathan, as an unconscious aside. "Avera is now Empress of all the world."

The sisters looked at him with anger and curiosity: the one finding her deepest fears confirmed, the other discovering more of confusion than doubt. Jacobi's hand moved to the hilt of her dagger as Stevana began to ask how the Lost could know anything of the outside world. But before either could speak, to challenge or to question, Susan cried, "Hold! Someone comes!"

"I hear no one," countered Jacobi, sure of her hearing. But within a moment she crimsoned and added, "I am humbled. Forgive me again." Soon all could hear the racing horse.

"Here, just here; let's stand here," said Susan distantly. Her mind was expanding with powerful impulses of life. Only the approach of a perfected Oathmaster could produce such an effect. But who in this modern world?

Jonathan, almost paralyzed from the intensity of light bursting forth through him, commented distantly, "Yes, this small amphitheater makes as good a reception hall as any available."

David felt the approach of the rider as fully as did Jonathan and Susan, but his recent departure from our Universe had given him (at least temporarily) a larger mastery than the others. He alone noticed that Stevana and Jacobi did not know an ally was approaching. Smiling to himself about a younger David, he said gently, "No, Stevana. No, Jacobi, do not spread your illusions now. You could not delude that one by such. And I don't think you would survive his wrath."

The five of them were not far from Arthur and Deborah's small valley: its waterfall had been visible from the last crest. As they waited with eagerness, assurance and doubt, Stevana thought, *What horse could race up such a slope?*

Quickly, unbelievably quickly, the huge white stallion bounded over a boulder and halted, steaming, facing them. It was the same horse and rider that had met Jacob on the Falon Road thirty years before, but now Nuriel was sheathed.

The five stared at the Golden Rider with amazement, their minds overwhelmed by his manifest power, their hearts bursting with awe, their bodies frozen from the pressure of his presence.

David integrated the massive in-flowing of life sufficiently to say, "The messengers from the Lost surrender their lives to the Master of the Age. Our tools are yours; our message is in your hands." He opened the maplewood jewel and offered the one flower. Jonathan and Susan followed his lead and held forth the statues.

The Golden Rider leaned toward them and smiled. His resonant words moved into their minds almost as if they were their own thoughts: "I recognize you, as you do me. Once I wore the Oathmaster's cloak; close indeed did I come to bringing perfection to our world.

"Close indeed did I come, but the hurricane of despair destroyed my garden in the end. Since the Downfall which diminished us all, men have called me often, Death, but occasionally, Life. But before my frozen despair, in time past you all knew me as — Joab."

24
Gana Damned

You do me wrong to take me out o' the grave.
Thou art a soul in bliss; but I am bound
Upon a wheel of fire, that mine own tears
Do scald like molten lead.
— Shakespeare

My mind!
My mind burns in hell!
How can I see again, how to breathe in peace again, how
to be again, how ever again with all lost!
The pain!
The pain of damnation!
Damnation eternal!
A presence defiles me —
A presence which leeches corrupt civilizations
A presence which feasts on murdered worlds.
"No, shara!"
Rodavi? Speak not again!
"There is a movement in deep waters,"
I must not hear this!
"A spirit of fire and Cosmic regions,"
Curse you! Why do you torment me!
"Living forever in the light of youth and dawn."
Depart, fool!
You sin against me to awaken me from my tomb!
My friends revile me!
My enemies ridicule me, rejoice in my fall!
My path is narrow cut between Emptiness and undying
hell-fire!

Hope lost
Lost...
All, all are lost
All
Kanaan-dora
Martanda
Krishanu
Para
Almira slain again and yet again
Forever
All burned all destroyed all ruined all desecrated
In the destruction of every world.
The pain!
The raging, burning pain!
Break earth, devour my rotting flesh!
What my mind
What my beloved people
What was —

*What was — the passage... Yes, that makes for sanity —
that scene Rodavi loved so well from my Bethmac play, that
may even now turn the wheel —*

Yet again and yet again and yet again
Crawls this miserable worm from morn to morn
To the last breath of discarded Eternity
And all our pasts carry poor simpletons
A lonely hour to inevitable death. Die, die, brief flame!
This world is but a passing dream, an impoverished actor
That cries and moans a moment in its play
And then passes forever more. It is a drama
Sung by a madman, replete with power and glory,
Meaning nothing.

Gana wandered blindly into a camping ground of Avera's cavalry and slew the Salazians in a sanguine rage before they could realize he was anything but a foul and drunken nightmare.

His slight wounds calmed his mind for the first time in these long years, bringing a measure of peace into the unending storm. Recognizing his humanity and nakedness, he sat among the dead and tried to order his mind. Who was he?

Three strands of thought flowed through him: he remembered, as vividly as if it were yesterday, the death by his own hand of a loved one — his wife, or someone as close; there was a pulsing warning by an Oathmaster he did not otherwise know about a six-year limit; and from a deep and silent witnessing center radiated the firm belief that there remained only the smallest fraction of that time.

It was such an impossible, mad reality: Gana saw within himself the whole of creation, oppressed from all sides by a strange vacuous nothingness. The Universe struggled to live on, but was all but conquered by the ascendant Emptiness. And hidden on a minor and externally insignificant planet, the final battle was shaping, relentlessly growing like a giant cancer. And he himself was the not quite sane solution to the entire complex riddle.

One unextinguished ray remained in this desolate sea of Emptiness — a thin triple fiber of golden-silver light spiraled through him, through the planet, through the Universe, through the surrounding Regions of Light, through a transcendentally perfect world that he could almost remember creating with his slain wife.

A handful only attempted to preserve this triple thread, extend its dominion, increase its power. But the rest of the planet's life (indeed, the vast majority of energies throughout creation) were working to destroy it. Most acted unconsciously, through excessive dullness, apathy, false judgments and beliefs about themselves and others. But some were laboring to sever this slender triple thread by active malicious intent.

And there was another force, impartial to both powers, silently watching, silently waiting, fully capable of ending the universal conflict at any time, but consciously choosing to not do so for reasons of its own. Benign? He did not know.

Gana cradled his head to ease its pain.

He did not intend to sleep, but fatigue coupled with his wounds claimed his breath once more: the shara entered again his death-sleep, for the first time in these thirty years.

A dream played before him. Gana was with Rodavi in Kanaan-dora — it was his sixteenth birthday; his master had taken him aside following a particularly vicious attack by some others of the young sharas: they were jealous of Gana's understanding of the ten vows, the vital essence of Oathmastery.

Gana asked him earnestly, "Why? Why is there pain?"

Rodavi smiled warmly at him and gently touched him on the forehead. Instantly, the shara's mind blossomed outward to infinity, experiencing the whole of creation in the expansion.

One thing only he lacked in that fullness: knowledge of whether this experience of the Ascendant was open to any, or was in fact gifted only to a chosen few.

Rodavi never answered that. His silence and enigmatic smile for years after infuriated the shara. But in time Gana learned to enjoy that mysterious response as one of the Oathmaster's highest teachings.

Pulsating white light from a self-luminous sphere alternated with an unbounded awareness that was not flat but contained all of creation, turned gold, then brilliant silver, then melted back into the formless One. Gana's breath started for a moment; he rasped once hoarsely; it stopped again.

His dream changed: he relived now his final hours with Almira in Para. It was no ordinary dream: he felt he was actually there, in their mind-created world, yet he also knew he slept. Rodavi might have said such duality was a good sign, a sure sign of coming release. Perhaps. Madness and genius often appear as a coin's two sides.

Gana dreamed of his last hours in Para, but now the ending changed — when Almira handed him the kris, he instead threw it into the ocean. The result was that he regressed to Lina's Song of Kanaan-dora and relived his last hours there again and then again and then again, endlessly.

The silent witnessing haven of his sanity questioned through this perpetual recurrence, *Why did the fire flame high, only to be smothered? Why was I chosen? Why did I fall? Is it possible to be worthy once more of my priceless lost gem?*

And then, deep inside, one more idea began forming, began growing slowly like a tiny crystal in a vast underground cavern, an idea that eventually expanded and rose in power until it eclipsed all others with its unanswered facets of hope and despair, *Could there have been a different ending?*

There was the mistake on Dawn Mountain, when I awakened the hermaphrodite instead of seeking Almira. But was not the second error the same, only of higher degree? On the Mountain, I put the safety of the world above the search for Almira; in my final act, I put the safety of the world above her life! Was this not madness? Even when no one could feel her presence, was she not everywhere there? How could any world exist for even a moment without Almira? She is Truth, she is Beauty, she is Power, she is Life!

Was her death, therefore, avoidable? What if I had turned the dagger on myself instead? I would have been lost to our world in either case, but she would not. Could there have been another way to destroy the Rakshasas in the Golden Thread without killing her?

As this flowed through him, he was anguished by remorse: agonies of self-hatred rolled through him as vile circles of madness, recurring ceaselessly through his Eternity of self-imposed hell.

~~~

Eventually, Gana slipped back into true sleep. And then the repeating regression of his final acts before the Downfall began again. Over and over again, endlessly. But at last, from some unknown source, came a change: when Almira gave him the kris, he began expanding through space, chasing after the Rakshasas inside the column. He reached two and slew them, but the third escaped into the sun. And then it was exactly as she foretold: the sun exploded; death rained on all his helpless peoples.

Gana flashed again back to Lina's song of Kanaan-dora. But now the churning question had gained new power, *What if I had been faster? What if I had destroyed all three first? Or what if I had expanded enough to protect the world even though the sun was lost? Yes! Or — could I reverse the flow of time? Para is a mind-created world! It moves to a different temporal pulse than this Universe. Perhaps time, then, can be altered? Did she not once tell me, millions of years here may equal but a moment there?*

Or ... perhaps the mistake was not truly made! Might it not have been another level of Vaga's illusion, designed to help me complete the fourth task?

But her death! And the Downfall! The rending implosion into non-entity! The shattering of my mind! How can I, the tiniest portion of my former self, solve a problem I could not when I possessed all my power and wisdom? Yet if I cannot, why did Vaga grant me memory of all I have been and done?

But my madness now! And this other throbbing memory —

"You have only six years — six years — six years before we send again the Azure Star —"

Is this all delusion, born of a weakened body, a wavering heart, a disturbed mind? Am I anything but an idle thought in someone else's dream? Answer me, Rodavi! Who have I been, who am I now to consider myself blessed, gifted, even sane? Tell me!

"You have only six — six — six years before the End of Time —"

~~~

The dream ended a final time with Almira's death by his hand. With a sigh that carried the weight of the world, Gana awoke for the second time since his living death began. Seven more years had passed, he was now in Avera's capital Rhodos, on display in the Imperial Museum.

His mind, clear for only a moment, was quickly buried again by the incessant hammering of the "six years" refrain.

Breaking his steel chains as if they were clay, Gana smashed the glass enclosure and pushed his way through the screaming riot he thus created, heading back to a city that had not existed for nearly fourteen thousand years, crying his truth to the uncaring world, "Fools! Why do you not listen? Will you not understand? The sixth year is over!"

25
The Queen of the World

Let us sit together and drink together of life
My diamond goblets
I fill for you with the golden water
Of the sun-berries from the Uttermost South
From Calantha of ancient song
A thousand-thousand men in steel gray suits
Marched through my garden today
Heading, I fear, to the terrible fires beyond
The one-time voiceless mountains of my Eastern border
They carried bright banners of sanguine and ebony
And sang of my distant past
But I had no desire to follow.
I went that way once
I climbed the dark grim mountain teeth
Far enough to see the unhappy lands and peoples
Beyond my garden wall
Oh my brothers!
They will find no sun-berries there
Nor maidens of fair form to ease their burdens
Their life-breath will be chained in clay
The measureless power will steal their eyes' humanity
They will die again and yet again Forever
— Arthur

Kerem, adan of Salaz, was as ambitious as he was crippled. As is often man's way when life does not fulfill individual desire, Kerem prayed for a son to expand his work.

But Kerem was honored by only one living child from all his eight wives. And that one was a girl.

Thinking the gods could not so easily thwart his will, Kerem raised his daughter exactly as he would have a son: he provided her with the best instructors money could buy in all branches of warfare and science while simultaneously crushing any and all feminine desires. Kerem taught her to view all life as a battle to be won at any cost.

Thus all the sharan knew was learned in a twisted way.

At sixteen, she murdered her father, then inaugurated her reign by publicly executing any who might ever have the will or ability to oppose her.

Not content with Salaz, she created a fanatically devoted military, general led by an extraordinary collection of scientists. They provided her with ever-more advanced weaponry and ever-deeper knowledge of the mysteries of the Oathmasters.

Even so, the sharan might have remained a minor footnote in the history of the world. But the Rakshasas recognized in her the answer to their long quest and gave her the golden gem Starbha of the Solar Dynasty of Emura and Tala.

Within two years, Avera began to expand her dominion: at first, by conciliation, treaty, bribery; then, as her powers grew and limitlessly grew, by sudden murderous war.

If there had been a concerted opposition in her first years, she could not have succeeded. But in those days of division, the myriad small nations did not band together soon enough. By the time the peasant Jacob left the well, the Last Alliance opposing her absolute dominion of the northern world was crumbling. With the demolition of Falon, the weaker eastern countries learned her science had defeated them; it did not take her too much longer to subjugate the remaining nations to the west of the Salazian Empire.

As unchallenged ruler of half the world, Avera bent her thought across the Burning Sea. Eventually even sweet Calantha was crushed beneath her iron-shod heel.

~~~

Avera eyed her new possession with a strange mixture of attraction, repulsion and a deep fascination that seemed more than a statue should warrant.

"Golranel," she said with pyretic passion, "what is the source of this wonderful art? Who carved it? It cannot be old, yet it seems timeless — perfectly sculpted by a master the class of which does not live in Our domain. Explain it."

The major-general looked at her curiously, surprised to hear such emotions in her voice. Could human feelings still be generated by that mechanical heart? He had long ago concluded it was impossible.

"I am not convinced, Excellency, that it is a sculpture. I think it the remains of an actual man, perfectly preserved by some unknown art. Touch it, you will find that there is some warmth always with it. As indeed, is a softness like living flesh." There was only one way to explain such an improbable thing. But the explanation itself was impossible!

"This was once alive? We are the more intrigued. If this were once a man, We rue the day of Our birth for never having met him! Never has there been one more noble! We have been blinded by the poorly made men around Us! Our senses have longed for such fulfillment — never again shall We be content with the puny slaves of Our realm! This would have made a true adan — nay! an emperor to share Our throne! What is its history?" How could a statue so move her? She had not felt such passions in years. But then, this statue possessed such incredible beauty... Avera yearned to know it. And felt increasingly frustrated her desire could never be fulfilled.

"It was a treasure of a governor in the Eastern Sector. That cavalry division, killed to the man six years ago, remember? This was found in the midst of the dead, almost as if the bloating corpses strewn about were thrown by it. The governor thought its presence too bizarre to be included in his report. Then too, he was afraid it was a machine — "

"What foolishness, this? Which of the lost civilizations could have built such a thing?"

"I agree, it is improbable. Yet is this statue improbable. Its condition resembles a coma, yet it cannot be — there have been no breaths since it was found."

"Then what, Golranel? Surely you know something."

"I *know* nothing! There is one strange history from Tala. I hesitate to repeat it, for it is clearly impossible. You know how they aggrandized their world, filling it with gods and miraculous Oathmasters. They invented unlikely myths to explain their genesis, never accepting the simple truths that life is an accident and humankind descended from the apes. The Oathmasters said we are not native to this world. Joab recorded that in the Temple of Kanaan-dora in Sulara, there was a `Living Statue´ of Gana, mythical founder of Emura, a God-like human of extraterrestrial origin. Yet when we unearthed that temple last spring, there was nothing."

"Not the Black Lizard, not the White Snake, not the Golden Seed, not the diamond staff! We wonder still if Taman excavated the right temple!"

"He is a supremely cautious archaeologist, Avera; both the Caremia and Urlad maps confirmed the site. The Board of Supervisors rated the probability at over ninety-eight percent. Still, it is hard to understand how immovable statues could have been moved. The staff, of course, might have been taken."

"If it were ever there. Only Deldorzian of the historians said it was."

"Yes, but Deldorzian was the last of the Talans and has been verified accurate on their Civil War many times."

"We must again visit that place... But if this is the Living Statue, how it traveled fifteen thousand leagues is beyond Our poor understanding. We order it placed in the Imperial Museum. Enclose it well, even chain it, lest it decide to go a-roaming again. And research Sulara again and more thoroughly. There is something most peculiar in this." Was this the frozen memory of a god?

"There is a second extraordinary riddle this morning, your Excellency. A young minstrel is here, wishing to sing to you. Normally, of course, I would not consider bothering you, but she sends this as greeting." Golranel untied the knot in the cloth he was holding and let the supernally brilliant jewel roll slowly onto the table.

Avera clutched for the gem under her robe as she cried, "What! Can there be doubt! It can only be Kaysta! Or, Starbha."

"Kaysta, surely: it is saffron, crimson, glorious. Starbha was supposed to be of a simple golden hue, was it not?"

"Whatever its name, it is as beautiful as the tales have told! See how it burns with its own fire, more beautiful than any gem of this world! We shall see this purveyor of myths! No, Saxona! Leave Our new statue a while longer; I wish to — ah, examine it more thoroughly before it is displayed."

Stevana entered, bowing and smiling. Avera was struck by her beauty, but that was hardly a point in her favor. Stevana wavered when she saw the frozen body of Gana: its appearance moved her as much as it had Avera. But unlike the Empress, she could use the power radiating from it to calm her heart and clarify her mind. Breathing deeply for stability, she said boldly, "I would sing to you, oh Most Exalted and Brilliant Ruler of the World, the tale of the shara Gana."

"More myths for idle minds?"

"A poem... Or, a dream... Or, perhaps, an exact history. The listeners will decide for themselves. That gem I delivered to you from my father is only the first part of his message to you, your Excellency. The second is this epic song."

"Your father is — ?"

"He is called Arthur, your Excellency. He is a simple cowherd, but a man of subtle understandings, pure with the lyre, an expert in the ancient writings of the Oathmasters. He bade me quote Mordom of Emura to you:

> *Can these histories be true?*
> *I say, Aye. And Nay!*
> *Nay: I myself created them from the void.*
> *And aye, with many more and more remarkable still:*
> *For these are limited, finite,*
> *But Nature, infinite in her complexity.*

"On which lines my father commented, `In an infinite Universe, every thought must exist somewhere, sometime as a physical reality. Every dream of every human is therefore literally true.´

"He also instructed me to repeat Joab's Fifth Staff Prophecy to you:

> *When the Ruler possesses both Kaysta and Starbha,*
> *Can my diamond staff be long removed?"*

Stevana's look was piercing; Avera felt her hand reaching for the concealed gem. She willed the motion to stop, instead smiled coldly and said, "Let your tale proceed, child. Saxona, triplicate recording, please." What kind of day could provide such mysteries?

Stevana, grateful for such early success, began Arthur's dangerous gambit, weaving for Avera the tapestry of Gana's rise and fall.

Listen!
"Hear first my song of Gana, immortal father of our race!
"Gana the shara, Gana the one true adan! Gana the damned!
"Murdered by his sister's son before the World Tree's seed was lost or the Sundered Gems stolen from the Living Statue's hands!"

When Stevana finished her tale with the Downfall of Para, Avera, feeling as if she had drunk poison, said in a half-strangled voice, "Did she succeed?"

"What?" asked Golranel, amazed by the pale and shaking appearance of his empress. *By Marzia, she looks like a half-breed. Was she having a stroke?*

"Who?" asked Stevana, surprised equally by the appearance of Avera and the subtle changes in Gana she had seen during her recitation of Joab's history.

"That being you called a Rakshasa. Did she enter the sun?"

"She? I know not. No one does. Father reasons: when the Golden Thread was cut, there was a contraction of the space-time continuum that pulled the last Rakshasa and the five hundred celestials into a lower sphere. Perhaps even here to our world. But of course it is only a conjecture."

"So the ultimate answer is one of doubt. That at least is gratifying. What happened to the seven wheels after Gana murdered Almira?"

"Perhaps you recall Joab's First Staff Prophecy?

"My diamond staff became a thread of silver light, passing through seven spinning rainbow wheels of blazing fire. A wave of expanding golden light rushed upward through the first four, transforming them to stationary jewels of flawless clarity. But when the wave passed the fifth, the staff broke! The top turned dull and black. But the bottom with the lower four remained bright."

Avera, shaking her head to clear it, demanded, "Tell me the meaning of humanity!"

From anyone else, it would have seemed a strange transition. But Stevana was prepared and answered simply, "The cow, your Highness. Selfless service and life are her willing gifts."

"Not Arel's hawk or Gurion's lion?"

"Never. Humankind works painfully through lower phases to triumph over its bestial nature."

"Why were there seventeen ships, then?" Avera refused to be angered by a child. She would be dead soon anyway.

"The Oathmasters recorded: seventeen classes of humanity escaped Kanaan-dora. There were four divisions from each of the four continents plus the entirety of the Solar Race."

"Who decided who would live?"

"The sharas' Starlord and Gemstone Council voted for the crews and passengers."

"What became of the rest of the Solar Race?"

"They were captured and murdered by the Asur Emperor Valin on Martanda."

"And what happened to Martanda?"

"Valin's prison of Emptiness exploded. Perhaps its remnants circle a nearby sun, perhaps they are our own asteroids. All the ships fleeing Kanaan-dora were lost there — except Gana's."

"Who could require an entire planet for a prison?"

"One only in the unending worlds requires such a wall. It has been the burden of our peoples since the dawn of time to ward his cell. Sesha chains him elsewhere now; yet his agents strive forever to free him."

"What aid do they require to succeed?"

"Kaysta and Starbha reunited and possessed by a civilization advanced enough to twist open the space-time vortex of his prison."

"Could the Salazian Empire do this?"

"If the Empress of the World so chose, she could make the attempt. But finding the prison is the real challenge for those who wish to oppose the One."

~~~

Avera changed her mind: instead of ordering the minstrel shot, she had her followed. That her enemies had now challenged her was abundantly clear. Where was their fortress? Probably the

legendary Vashti. But who were they? The prophesied Five
Hundred? Or the Ten Thousand of Kanaan-dora, miraculously
returned from their ancient graves?

It hardly mattered: whoever they were, they felt confident
enough about their powers to reveal their knowledge. Let them
rave! Giving her Kaysta was the ultimate of stupidity! Their over-
confidence would destroy them. She had both halves of
Kaystarbha! Held by a single hand for the first time since Irnga
and Kartika took them from Gana's frozen body! Soon the
diamond staff would be hers; its secrets and powers would belong
to her alone. The fools!

Yet to ensure her reign, she must discover the hidden valley
fortress. She did not doubt Vashti existed: the Oathmasters had
been right about her rise to power and conquest of the world. She
must destroy the last memory of opposition. Joab's Seventh Staff
Prophecy haunted her through every waking moment with its
sinister threat:

If the Last Living One from Vashti
Grasps my broken staff
The Ten Thousand of Kanaan-dora will rise
And the blasphemous scepter fall.
Then shall the Last Living One enter unto Vanas
And the Lost Generation will be as before.
Here end all Prophecies:
Our world shall that day be destroyed by the shara's fire.

To map the planet from the sky, Avera poured the Empire's
full resources into the airships. Where was the valley? In which
range? Every area must be photographed. She would not lessen the
pressure on her scientists until her machines could do it. She must
reign forever!

Yet with even the Empire's full wealth channeled by her
indomitable will, it was seven full years after the fall of Calantha

before the first jet propulsion system was proven effective; three more years passed before it was widely applied and her equipment sufficiently refined to conclude the photographic work.

"Well," she said sourly to her new aide, "does Vashti exist, or was Joab guilty in the end of wishful thinking?"

"There seems to be no such valley," answered David sadly. "Or at least, no photograph shows it."

"By the accursed diamond staff! Their fortress must be underground." Avera rose abruptly from her desk and strode to her window. Clasping her hands tightly behind her, she stared darkly over her huge gray capital.

"It must be, your Excellency. Joab has never been proven wrong before. And he made no less than sixty-four references to Vashti." David paused, cleared his throat, then added, "Ah, your Highness. I also have a report on the missing children in the Eastern Sector. Do you wish it now?"

She did not move and made no answer. David waited a few moments, working hard to master the revulsion he always felt in her presence, then continued, "As you know, your Excellency, the first babies were stolen shortly after the fall of Calantha. To date, approximately ten thousand have disappeared. I have plotted a distribution on this map. Would you care to see it?"

"Ah, hmmm? Yes, you may approach Our person, Colonel."

David hurried to her from the Council table. "There is a concentration here, in this minor province, where — "

"Not there! Was that not the home of that chalky insurrectionist, that false Oathmaster, that — what was his name?" She returned to her throne: she never liked to be too close to anyone.

"Jacob, your Excellency? The same. I have researched his Movement, as I reasoned there could exist some relationship with the babies."

"You are thorough, aren't you?" she mused in a vaguely malicious tone. She lightened it almost at once, considering the young Colonel not worth the trouble. "But, that is good. There are too few truly competent officers on Our staff. Remind Us of this peasant, this — what was it? — Jacob?" She picked up and began spinning a small globe slowly, apparently much more fascinated by its moving color than her new aide or his words.

"Yes, Excellency, Jacob. He was a — a simple man who appeared in Falon, the Blasted City, a few days before it was leveled. He inspired fifteen hundred to leave before we destroyed it."

"A wise action!" she exclaimed gleefully, spinning the globe faster at the happy memory. "That alliance of white devils surrendered soon after that."

"Yes, your idea was a paramount strategic device. Now, this Jacob led five hundred — "

"Five hundred? Did you say *five* hundred?" interrupted Golranel, leaning forward in his chair and peering intently at David through his thick horn-rimmed glasses.

"Yes, five hundred. It is of course remotely possible these could be the Five Hundred of the Lost Generation, but it is not very probable, is it? Jacob led the refugees northward; none of them was ever heard from again. Probably they perished from starvation, following the madman. Or perhaps they degenerated into a tribe of nomads. There are many such in the area.

"Whatever happened to them is a mystery. But Jacob sent the other thousand eastward. Some of these compiled his Teachings, proclaiming him a modern Oathmaster. His words have spread through all the provinces and are, in my opinion, a major cause of inefficient work habits.

"The kidnapped babies have not been traced to this sect. But why not be cautious? Let us stiffen the laws against them everywhere. And place a stronger emphasis in that province on precise interpretation of our decrees."

"You are comfortable making Our laws, young Colonel?" Avera stared without winking at her new aide, examining him as intently as if he were a particularly fascinating insect she had just discovered underneath a rotting log. The globe in her hand gradually stopped spinning; she did not turn it again. David stared back at her, fearing to speak, fearing to not.

Golranel looked back and forth from the observer to the observed for a few minutes with a mirthless grin. Finally he coughed and said caustically, "David! I am not satisfied with your account of the missing five hundred. Five hundred disappearing adults, then ten thousand disappearing babies in the same province forty years later! These coincidences of number are amazing enough, but that Jacob could have known in advance of our attack on Falon is nothing short of astounding." He walked around the table to view the map. "There could be an underground valley. If so, it would be in this branch of the Backbone Range — the, ah, Guardian Mountains." He put a corpulent finger down exactly where Vashti should have been showing.

"Logical," agreed David, grateful for any diversion from Avera's attention, "if it were possible their descendants still existed. Perhaps a land investigation?"

"Be it so," Avera answered, slamming the globe down so violently it cracked. "But, Colonel! Let Us caution you to restrain your cleverness. We would hate to lose such a promising young member of Our staff through an unfortunate — rather, an excessive zealousness."

"Certainly, your Excellency! My one desire is to serve your exalted throne! In fact, I would like to use this moment of your undivided attention to request a transfer to the Translations Council."

"What? You astound Us, boy. You wish to quit a department where you have shown such promise for a — to be gracious — dubious future among Our scholars?"

"Exactly so, your Excellency. The air corps is not my great love, although it made a useful ladder to your throne. For years, I have studied Talanese. Major-general Golranel feels I might be of some assistance to him."

Removing his glasses and setting them on the table, Golranel settled back into his chair, folded his huge hands over his enormous stomach and said with a deep rumble of satisfaction, "This is my idea, Avera! This Colonel is nothing short of brilliant; his knowledge of the old languages is astonishing. He has already helped me understand portions of Joab's riddles; he may be instrumental in the discovery of the diamond staff itself."

Avera looked from one to the other with decreasing interest. Shrugging slightly, she said to the air between them, "Very well. We don't like to restrict Our personal council, but prefer to see natural inclination play its full role. But, David! Be careful around Our Golranel! He has the fangs of a lion, the claws of a tiger and the appetite of a wolf. Only We can control him." Avera was moderately pleased. *This will end this young fool. He rises a little too quickly, is a little too smart. The major-general will make a short meal of him.*

~~~

In the forty-sixth year after the Five Hundred rediscovered 'Ishtar's Vashti, Golranel stumbled over an uneven place on the floor of what had once been Sulara's Temple of Kanaan-dora. Within an hour, he was talking via satellite with Avera.

The Empress flew there at once; the diamond staff virtually leaped into her hand, at once regaining the brilliancy that had failed ten thousand years before.

"Joab was right again!" cried David, ecstatic to see the staff alive at last. "Did he not say in his Third Staff Prophecy, *Only two will be empowered to lift my staff at Time's End, the Ruler and the Last Living One?*"

"David! How it burns with authority! What a priceless boon, this quintessence of the Oathmasters' lost art! I wonder what mysteries it —"

Before she could even begin to examine it, an aide ran to them, shouting, "Excellency! Calantha revolts! The entire southern world is in flames! Six divisions are destroyed!"

"What! I'll *boil* them all!" she screamed, striding in wrath from the now valueless Temple of Kanaan-dora.

David did not immediately follow: he sat exactly where Gana had through the long ages. Rubbing some dust between his fingers, he smeared it on his chest. Laughing in his mind, *Strange. Why did I do that?* he hurried after the empress.

~~~

Because of the rebellion, Avera's detailed analysis of the ancient tool was postponed. She drilled a small hole in the staff's handle and chained it to her wrist, the more easily to spend every free moment studying it. Because of the ferocious tenacity of the Calanthan revolt, there were precious few such moments. But the constant presence of the staff was by itself sufficient to transform her: soon she no longer needed sleep; her body gained the invulnerability of steel; her sharpness of intellect and senses increased almost without limit, yet not quite enough for her to hear or see the Rakshasa servants of Emptiness working tirelessly for her.

Also because of the rebellion, Avera concluded this was her final test, Vashti must be in the southern hemisphere, in Calantha. She therefore did not object when David quietly cancelled the overland explorations in the Guardian Mountains, which had discovered nothing: any climbers nearing Vashti usually met with fatal accidents. The area was well known for its treacherous slopes and unreliable weather. But for nothing else.

26
A White Snake

In time to come
There will be one solution only
To every mystery of creation.
— Rodavi

There is only one solution now
But most find it easier to believe
In multiplicity than unity.
— Mordom

I am a Messenger of the One.
I cannot suffer, cannot be in pain.
I cannot die or experience any loss.
I never fail to do all the One asks me to do.
— Joab

It took four years to crush the Calanthan revolt: Joab and Jacobi had prepared it well. During this time, the Oathmaster and his disciple did not return to the north; but at the close of the fiftieth winter after the Five Hundred entered Vashti, they abandoned the last remnant of the ruined Calanthans and used the Silver Spiral Bridge for one final crossing of the Burning Sea.

Jacobi came to the Council Meeting at the exact moment of the spring equinox. Her sister was already there, sitting quietly in the firelight, but David had not yet come, nor had Joab returned with Arthur.

Stevana was wearing a peculiar garland — a white and very alive snake. As it coiled in unhurried spirals around her neck and over both shoulders, its fiery eyes radiated intense light. Before Jacobi could ask of it, her sister began sending her mental images of someone who was beautiful, powerful, majestic, wise, someone who was —

Jacobi thrust her hands forward to stop the visions. "What can you possibly mean! Gana sits statue-frozen in Rhodos! You yourself saw him there!" It was difficult to tell in the flickering light of the fire, but Stevana seemed oddly flushed. She couldn't have succumbed to passion? Didn't she understand the terrible demands of their age? What time was there for human love?

"No, Jacobi! Gana awoke again and journeyed eastward. He rescued me, using this serpent which he revived. This is Sesha! Can't you understand he is Gana? Who else could return life to the Serpent King?" She stared earnestly at Jacobi, urgently desiring her understanding. And approval.

Jacobi felt Stevana's need; her heart longed to accept her sister's impossible belief; but her mind rejected the idea. In love with Gana? It was preposterous! And yet — and yet, there was *something* about her sister's emerald eyes, wide with love and impassioned belief that spoke more eloquently than her words or mental images. "Stevana! How can he be Gana? Is he an Oath-master like Joab, capable of stopping his breath? Or a shara like Solon, full master of the One?"

Stevana poured more and more of her spirit into her sister's heart. She must convince her! Only if the Council aided her with willing belief could Gana complete the reintegration of his mind! She needed them all!

Gazing fervently into Jacobi's deep azure eyes, she grasped her hands and answered fiercely, "There is nothing beyond his power! 'Sravasa gifted him immortality after Valin was imprisoned. You must believe me! He is not an Oathmaster, but a true shara, last of the Starlord and Gemstone Council of Kanaan-dora. Surely you remember Mordom's prophecy, *The Living Statue will breathe again at the End of Time?*"

"Of course I remember!" cried Jacobi, pulling away from her. "But apparently you have forgotten Joab's comment that Gana would wander insane until he met his reborn wife, the sharan Almira of Kanaan-dora, murdered by Valin on Martanda!"

"I haven't forgotten," Stevana said quietly to the ground, blushing in spite of her certainty.

Jacobi leaped up, staring at her sister with horror, her eyes flashing savage rage, "Almira! Have you gone utterly mad! This can't be your thought! The Living Statue, no longer frozen, just happens to wander into Stevana's arms, Stevana who is none other than the sharan Almira herself? I cannot fathom this! How can your lover be Gana? Was he not reborn as Mars in Tala? And does not our own father remember his life as Mars?"

Stevana looked up at her calmly: she felt this outburst must surely mark the dissolving of the last obstacle preceding belief. Or at least preceding acceptance of her own belief. Which was almost the same thing and would have to do. "As Mars *and* Naisan, sister. In this way, Gana is unlike common men — he lives in more than one body, he is so saturated with the understanding that he is the One. Therefore our father Arthur shares that existence. But my shara is the original! If we can use his knowledge, what hope will Avera and her tawdry empire have?"

Jacobi began again, "I can't accept — !" But the last image from Stevana was so powerful, so flawless in its display of the possible, she instead sat down again, wholly lost in its wondrous splendor. Gana reintegrated with himself, ruling the world with benevolence and love! It was too glorious and beautiful to deny. She smiled as she allowed her own brilliant power to flow fully with her heart's desire. "No. You are not a child. I suspend judgment. For now. Tell me this tale."

"Thank you, dearest one! You have blessed me with a magnificent gift! He will join us soon; I'll be brief, showing you more than speaking. Since you are so much with Joab, learning the ways of the Oathmasters, it has been my habit to hunt alone. No! Never think I begrudge you his choice, sister. You have always loved the arcane more than I, just as I have always loved the wilderness more than you: you know I am happiest when I wander alone on a task for father. Even the company of the Ten Thousand seems shallow to me compared to the pregnant life of the fields and forests, the silence of the Grandfather's empyrean above.

"Last spring, father ordered me to pursue a fierce being who was terrorizing the nomadic tribes: slaying any who crossed his path. I was certain he was some hideous new invention of Avera: I could never see him clearly because of the veil of Emptiness around him. I thought he was protected by hordes of Rakshasas. Only later did I learn they were attacking him, not aiding him!

"The trail led me far to the north by last summer — as far as the land of the night-time sun. Yet stretching ever northward were his tracks in the snow.

"Feeling a change in the air, I took shelter in an ice cave near the foot of a glacier. I dared a fire: I was certain none of the enemy would brave the coming storm.

"My reflection in the ice was oddly distorted; following a deep intuition, I dug into the cave wall with my sword and uncovered a frozen white snake. It looked exactly like the statue Jonathan carried to father! I set it by my fire and asked it what it knew of Vashti. Then I laughed at myself, wondering what you would think of me, sharing my dinner with a frozen serpent.

"Just as I drifted to sleep, two dozen of the enemy attacked. You know they have sought me ever since I sang in Rhodos of Gana's Downfall. Apparently now the Rakshasas' power is grown enough that even common men can penetrate my illusions."

"That makes a poor sign."

"Indeed! I desperately fought, but my defenses were crippled — hundreds of Rakshasas were fighting for them. The humans wanted me alive, but the agents of Emptiness were less generous: their infernal swords and daggers of fire did not spare me.

"When my last illusions were shattered, my last hopes faded like a waking dream, my last thoughts stilled to failure, suddenly — from nowhere! A giant serpent with a dozen hoods rose above me, screaming its rage. Its flames devoured men and Rakshasas alike but felt strangely cool to me.

"My wounds drained my failing awareness from me. My last vision was of the serpent — men falling torn from its dripping fangs, Rakshasas by the dozen withering in its flames — bathing me with its healing fire...

"When I awoke, the bodies of the enemy were neatly stacked outside the cave. My wounds were crudely but well dressed; I was surprised that I felt no pain. A stranger wearing a silver robe with this serpent coiling on his shoulder was sitting by the fire, staring at me. He was the most handsome man I had ever seen: the light of the One shone from him in multi-colored glory, more powerfully than I had known was possible from a human being. Sixteen celestials were distinctly visible in the beams radiating from his forehead, seven more in the concentric circles of light flowing from his heart.

"I said, `Well, my beautiful wizard, you are an excellent doctor!´ He smiled warmly at me, pointed at himself and said in a wonderfully rich and melodious voice, `Swayam Gana-shara´; suddenly I understood my long hunt had ended...

"He had come so far northward in the hope the cold would aid his struggle for sanity. Combined with my fortunate discovery of Sesha, it has succeeded.

"I asked him here to meet the Council, sure that our combined power will finish stabilizing his mind. He was reluctant to come so far south; therefore we waited through the winter, thus to preserve the delicate balance he has with such difficulty — "

At that instant, Gana leaped from the shadows, stark naked, once again utterly mad. The One and the Emptiness alternated in wild patterns of blinding light and utter darkness from his face and heart; at one moment he was surrounded by thousands of radiantly beautiful celestials, at the next, by equally vast numbers of hideously ugly Rakshasas.

"No!" Stevana cried. "Gana-shara-reg! No, my God, no!"

"Ika! Fila-fila savanu! Ika!" He shouted, then jumped over their fire and disappeared in the gloaming.

Stevana was after him at once; Jacobi only moments later. Her last doubts had fled from one look at his face.

~~~

They searched the whole of that somber night, but he was gone.

At dawn, the sisters met by the ashes of their fire. The track of Stevana's tears through the grime on her face tightened Jacobi's heart. Why couldn't she have believed her sooner? Holding her sister close, she stroked her hair and said softly, "Lalasa, dearest. Believe me, all will end well. Hold to the One with faith and hope...Tell me, what did he scream? Did it mean anything?"

"No. Or, maybe it did, I don't know. Oh, Jacobi, what am I to do? I am lost! He's gone! Why did I leave him alone so long! He — he said, `Beware! The sixth year is over! Beware!'"

~~~

That very morning, Avera reaped the fruit of her years of patient analysis of the staff. Before her stood, bowing, the chief Rakshasa of the world. "Who, what are you?" she cried, her amazement colored more by curiosity than fear.

"Your humble servant, Excellency! At last your eyes and ears are opened, we can aid you directly! This is a great day for both of us: you are the agent of our deliverance! You alone in the long history of the world have amassed sufficient power to free my Lord Valin!" He explained the Rakshasas' understanding of history and how they had long worked always to further her interests. He also told her many secrets, including the exact location of Vashti...

~~~

"Curious," said Joab. "Rather, astounding Sesha has been found. How did she come by it?"

The Oathmaster was sitting with Arthur and David on a small plateau not far from the Guardian Mountains. Before them on the ground was the white snake Stevana and Jacobi had left with David. The serpent had coiled itself into a pyramid; its hood was raised, cobra-like; its fiery, unwinking eyes stared intently at the three humans. In the absence of its Lord, Sesha maintained unwavering quiescence.

David, fascinated by the serpent's steady gaze, answered, "It was frozen in the Arctic. Gana awoke it, used it as a channel to save Stevana from a combined Rakshasa and human attack."

"Such was ever his ability. This makes unexpected good fortune! I don't know if you fully understand who (or rather what) Sesha is. When the Seven burn a Universe, the ashes are swallowed by the Serpent King. In this way, the residual potencies of every life are preserved through the dissolution between creations. Sesha contains the future ashes of our Universe! The White Snake and Black Lizard statues were only copies, created by Almira to bridge to our age. But Sesha is truly deathless — even the immortal Lords of Etan spoke of it with barely disguised awe."

"Then all missing understandings must be here!" exclaimed Arthur, already more than half seeing in Sesha the answers to the fundamental questions of his life. "I wonder how best to tap this record? Almost I feel as if I know. I can sense the unequalled authority of Sesha, its unlimited knowledge, its transcendental wisdom, but I can't... quite..." His words trailed off as he followed the thread inward he had just discovered. There was something in the closed place in his heart which knew Sesha perfectly! Something that led him into the locked passageways of his past. For although he remembered his lives as Mars and Naisan, he still knew nothing of Gana except by inference. But the power of Sesha was about to return him that memory.

David looked at Arthur to discover why he had stopped speaking. The adan was sitting stiffly erect, staring at the serpent with fervent intensity. But something about him reminded David of Emptiness! "Joab!" he cried, questioning his perception.

The Oathmaster understood Arthur's need instantly and fully. Lifting Sesha, he draped it over the adan's shoulders. The serpent slid once around him, then settled onto his left shoulder. Arthur's eyes drifted closed; within a moment a column of light shafted northeastward from his throat.

Joab followed it with his eyes, then exclaimed, "David! Do you not recognize this?"

"Should I? It is beautiful, a masterful expression of the One, but what — ?"

"No! That is Arthur's connection with his master form! Follow it with your senses — what do you see?"

"Yes, of course! Gana!" The shara was sitting motionless in an ice cave high in the Guardian Mountains, not far from Vashti. He had traveled there almost instantaneously: none of the Solar Race but Solon of the dawn ages could have matched his pace; certainly no human of these sunset days could make such a journey in so short a time. How long until Stevana could again find him?

Arthur's eyes suddenly flew open, he cried, "I remember!" Sesha slid around his neck and coiled on his right shoulder. Arthur stared at the beam of light and said quietly, as if to himself, "There is a question I must have answered. It lies somewhere in this region..."

Suddenly the seven rainbow wheels of fire were floating before them. The lower four were clear, magnificent jewels, but the upper three were changing rapidly. At one moment, they were bright with color, at the next, angry, dark.

"My staff, broken!" cried Joab.

"Yes, this must be the source of your vision," said Arthur slowly, concentrating on each word to be able to speak. "Yet, I don't feel it is exactly your staff. If you look where the Golden Thread is broken, there, just above the fourth wheel? Look as I magnify!"

Arthur's desire manipulated the vision: the seven centers expanded until each was the size of a human head. "Now. Look there, in the gap — see it? The finest thread passes through the break! If I magnify that, see?"

The fiber of light grew larger. In a moment, it appeared that Joab's diamond staff floated before them, borne by two hands: one, perfectly black; the other, perfectly white.

"The two hands of Almira!" exclaimed Joab with great excitement. "Only they have the power to change time! Thus Jonathan alone could wield the White Snake and Susan the Black Lizard."

"Yes!" agreed Arthur with mounting eagerness. These visions were infusing his mind with a clarity that was absolute: he felt as if he were standing on a lonely high mountain with the Universe spread as an open scroll before his feet. "You are correct. Watch as the black hand transforms to reveal Susan; the white, Jonathan. And look there! The fifth center contains Steven and the Five Hundred when bright, but when dark, it reflects the Salazian legions! The Empress' armies are the mind-created enemies of Gana's fifth center, whereas the Five Hundred form the structure when it functions properly, and — "

"Stop!" cried David. This was too intense; he was increasingly confused with each additional image. At one instant, he almost understood; at the next, he was thoroughly lost. "Explain this to me! `The staff is here, Susan is there, the Five Hundred are there.´ What do you mean? Why do these reflect inside Gana?"

The Oathmaster looked at him with surprise and answered, "Whence this problem? You know Gana is the incarnate consciousness of this Universe. Since this is so, we are all part of him; he of necessity embodies everyone and everything of our world. Gana *is* our Universe; he has descended onto this material plane to enliven the Seven here.

"Therefore, when his mind-created enemies are destroyed, his Golden Thread will be renewed. Said another way, our victory over the Salazian Empire will restore the connection of every living being to the One, without needing the medium of the diamond staff. Therefore the Universe will continue to evolve as before. But if we fail — "

"Gana and this Universe would be dead," finished Arthur. "Which is to say, we would have to rebegin from its first moments. David, I think I can show you we are all part of Gana. Watch."

The diamond staff distended and expanded before them; in a moment it was the perfect reproduction of the one flower of Vanas David had carried to Arthur. Each of the petals expanded further, gradually taking on a human form.

"The Ten Thousand!" exclaimed the Salazian. "All of them! And now, as they merge together again, a familiar visage forms: you, Arthur!"

Joab, laughing joyfully at the sweet taste of this draught, said, "Of course! Arthur and the Ten Thousand are Almira's power of Life, rising from the fourth center to the fifth! Thus they repair the Golden Thread!"

"Arthur!" David cried excitedly, suddenly understanding. "You imply that you can find anyone in Gana? Jacob, for example?"

Arthur saw that the Salazian had not asked his deepest question. Chuckling, he projected the fifth wheel. In it appeared the Oathmaster Atri — and Atri was the peasant.

David stared at the image of Jacob, seeking the one answer that still eluded him. Finding no solution in the peasant's eternal serenity, the Salazian tried again, this time plunging into the heart of his doubt, "Arthur, all my life I have wondered where I belonged. I found peace in Vashti, but could never rise to the perception that has now become the common experience of everyone of the Five Hundred: I have never seen Almira as the life-breath of everything as all the rest of you do. Is it possible I alone am from the outside? Could this be why Steven could never touch my mind, why I alone of the Five Hundred was never one with him? Arthur! Can you find me in Gana?"

Arthur smiled confidently as he let his desire fall back into the heart of the omniscient Serpent King. An image formed before them: someone was standing next to the break in Gana's Golden Thread, someone whose two hands, one perfectly white, the other perfectly black, were holding the diamond staff that contained the essence and future of our Universe. Someone...

The next instant, all three of them recoiled in horror: it was not the likeness of David floating before them: it was the Empress of the World!

The image vanished as soon as Arthur recognized Avera. Trembling, he reached out to touch David. The Salazian was gripping his head tightly by his hands; he was leaning forward, rocking and moaning. "I'm sorry," began Arthur, but stopped, finding no words adequate.

David, not looking up, groaned, "So. It is confirmed. I am not of your world. Who am I then? Will I never understand? All of the Lost Generation have remembered who they are! What have I not lost? Even Avera! Even that foully twisted incarnate demon has a role! For she must be the last mind-created limitation of the fourth wheel, the final Rakshasa in the Golden Thread, cast from Para when Gana and the Five Hundred fell. She at least has a position. What power she must have amassed to hold back the rising force of Almira!"

"Nearly infinite," agreed Arthur, staring at him with love and sorrow. "That is why this task is the hardest and most resembles annihilation."

"This terrifies me!" cried David, leaping up to pace his frustration. "Why only me? Joab! Why only me? My non-presence here proves what you and Arthur and Steven have hinted to me for years! I will be the Last Living One from Vashti! But why? Why me? Can't you tell me, even now?"

"Have you not always known it?" the Oathmaster answered softly, his ancient eyes wide with sympathy and strength.

"I suppose I may have," answered David, stopping pacing to stare at him. "No, it is true, I have always known, deep in the innermost recesses of my heart. I am not of your kind; I am an agent of a different Universe, here only as witness to the drama, or perhaps to pull the curtain closed at the end. But Joab! Why? Must your staff break? If so, of what use my life? These visions have proven again what the prophecies stated: all those of this world draw their life through the diamond staff! If it breaks, the Five Hundred, the Ten Thousand, Steven, Arthur, Deborah, Stevana, Jacobi, all life in the world will die! Yet you prophesied it would happen this way! Why! Don't you remember? Can't you tell me?" He looked at him with anguish.

The Oathmaster stared back at him with compassion. Leaving David in the grip of the ultimate unresolved mystery of the Universe was at once a potentially damnable error and a promise for great future glory. Which path would David choose? Joab replied, "What difference a life, even the life of a Universe? Sesha will hold everyone until the Seven are ready — " But before he finished, thirty of Avera's airships streaked overhead, heading with their explosives toward Vashti. Joab's logic ended with a shout, "It begins!"

<center>~~~</center>

Closer and closer Avera's bombers approached the valley, as the three wondered if Jonathan and Susan had fulfilled their quest. At the last moment, a nebulous *something,* not quite a white mist, not quite a human form, not quite a single hand, appeared above the mountains. As the airships entered the field of distorted space-time, they exploded, their component molecules unbound and scattered to the four winds as fine dust. Jonathan had adequately proven he had not been idle since Steven sent him from the society of the Five Hundred.

Only the last of the thirty turned in time: it raced back overhead, thrusting full speed toward its home in the west.

"David! This means Avera has mastered the staff! She now knows everything the Rakshasas know! You are betrayed!"

"This is long anticipated. Half a moment... There! How do I look?"

"Terrible! Golranel himself! But what of the Rakshasas?"

"This they do not know. I bind the Emptiness as closely to my heart when I wear this form as he ever did."

"And the original?"

"He remembered me from the day of Falon's death and found it curious I had grown no older in forty years. I have played him in Rhodos for nearly a decade. I should be all right. But Joab! For the last time, you still believe Avera must break the diamond staff?"

"There is no other way! Only then can Gana restore the Golden Thread. Until she acts, she cannot be destroyed: you know the staff has made her invulnerable. She must release her hold on it by destroying it. Let us trust in the old words, spoken when there were no shadows between me and the omniscience of the seventh wheel. All will be well. Only be perfect with this illusion! She is served now by the wisest of the Rakshasas. The smallest slip would be fatal for us all.

"Remember always, David: *A three-fold cord is not easily broken.*"

27
A Debt Repaid

At last At last I can sing again
Of life-loves' pearl streams of unending day!
Ah, come to me!
Break open the seven-sealed tomb!
Pass through each wheel of burning fire!
No longer breathes Emptiness
In night-time solitude!
Arise! Arise!
Sing of the Immutable One!
Resist not, scorn not, fly to me!
Para, Para! Re-awaken to your crying son!
Awake!
Awake!
Steal not one only silver-red cherry blossom
From the hidden-throned kingdom!
Open, my heart!
Sail to my sea-river border of crystal sands!
— Arthur

Almira approached Brihas in his mind-created world. The Ruler of the Seven was seated on his diamond throne, contemplating life, and seemed unaware of her approach through the multi-dimensional spheres. The seven suns that formed a rainbow arch over his head were dimmed, indicating his attention was inward; the seven majestic jewels that gave life to his central nervous system shone with brilliant light through his nearly translucent body, indicating his thought was of perfection; but the twenty-eight dancers before him were absolutely still, frozen in their last observed postures, indicating that Brihas did not think of the seven major or twenty-one minor perfections.

Realizing that only contemplating the One could so captivate him, Almira halted three paces below his throne and waited patiently.

A moment later, a mighty fountain of suns erupted from Brihas' forehead and formed a river of light around them as the dancers re-began their complicated weaving patterns, dancing to further his thought.

Brihas looked down at her with a strangely wistful expression and said, "You have finished, then." It was not exactly a question, but there was a faint lilt to his tone that told her his doubt.

Almira climbed up and knelt before him. Lowering her head onto his lap, she answered, "Father. We need one more year to complete our labor."

"Why should I not return that Universe to Sesha this instant?" he asked as he stroked her soft golden hair. "You must realize that if Valin grew powerful enough, he could corrupt other of Narain's perfect Spheres. The danger is too great, I must evoke the destructive force and collapse that Cosmos, let its entities rest in Sesha. Gana will of course return to his position among the Seven."

"Your will is my law, father. But consider this: because of the Grandfather's curse, Gana has traveled to the furthest reaches of the Emptiness that opposes us: he has allowed clay to course through his immortal veins. He has died, father, died! More times than I can remember! He has taken it all into his mind, all the weakness and false perceptions of humanity. And in the return to his true nature, he has grown mightier than we ever dared hope: the seven primary perfections are on the verge of being achievable by any human, due solely to his selfless dedication. If we are permitted to continue, I have not the faintest doubt all the Seven will be available throughout that Sphere, at any and every space-time moment. Is this not worth the potential expansion of Navril Hagar to greater mastery?"

"Perhaps... How many of those who failed to follow the Azure Star have remembered?"

"How many? Let me think: there are Steven's Five Hundred; Arthur's Ten Thousand; Swayam's Lords of Etan; the Vidyadharas; the celestials of my world and the Regions of Light — I suppose not quite one in twelve million, father. But the others grow closer daily."

"Only one in twelve million? Only *one* in twelve million? And you ask me for an extension? Your answer is an unqualified no. I have grown exceedingly tired of that troublesome Sphere, Almira."

~~~

Avera attempted one more aerial assault: three thousand bombers attacked Vashti from all directions and at different heights. It was a strong statement for the rigid training of her air corps that no one balked at such an insane flight pattern. Her officers flew it mindlessly, rank after rank diving in glittering symmetry toward their certain doom. Almost it seemed the sheer weight of their numbers might force at least some of them through Jonathan and Susan's immense distortions of space-time, but the will of the defenders held: with explosion after explosion, the war-machines of Avera's dominion vanished in the vapors of dis-creation that were almost human, almost hands, almost nothing at all.

Aided by legions of Rakshasas, one aircraft only managed to slip through. But Steven called upon the One in the wind: the bomber was caught in a violent down-draft that brought it to crashing ruin on a Guardian bordering Vashti.

~~~

"Now will you listen, your Excellency!" cried her Rakshasa counselor. "You must break that accursed staff! It is the life of those devils! You don't need it any longer! Destroy it, be free of it!

Its presence tortures me, prevents my seeing anything clearly around you. Trust me! The diamond staff is all that holds Valin prisoner! Break it and my master will again be free!"

Avera clutched the diamond staff tightly as she answered, "No. I can't. I won't. It's too filled with power, with glory. I need it to focus my mind." The Empress feared Joab's Seventh Staff Prophecy more than the destruction of her air corps.

"Excuse me, your Excellency?" asked David in the form of Golranel.

"Ah, I said, 'We must attack by land.' Transport the army there immediately."

It took eleven full days to amass the entirety of the Salazian forces. In all, one hundred and twenty-eight divisions mustered on the plain north of what had once been the great city Falon. There were just over eleven million soldiers — one for every century since Swayam had learned his will was being actively opposed.

~~~

Avera set her headquarters on a hill to the south of her armies. At dawn of the twelfth day, she ordered a continuous artillery barrage of Vashti. This was as ineffective as had been the air assault: the two shields of Jonathan's and Susan's will exploded the missiles harmlessly, far from the protected valley.

Thinking, *Why does the end so closely resemble the beginning?* Avera ordered the overland attack; the last and strangest battle of history began. The huge steel tanks rolled forward at dawn, followed by thousands upon thousands of infantry.

~~~

Arthur, garlanded still with Sesha, stood with Deborah and Joab at the foot of the Guardians on the plateau where fifty years before the Five Hundred had huddled in misery, witnessing the death of Falon.

Arthur was supremely confident. He and Joab had completed the training of the ten thousand children, begun so long ago in

Tala. They were as the reborn embodiments of Kanaan-dora's unsurpassed knowledge; they were as ten thousand rajanya Mordoms, fearless, unequalled in knowledge and power. Arthur had not the slightest doubt they would defeat the forces of Emptiness, those incarnate illusions of false belief. As he surveyed his legions of archers, concealed by a veil of invisibility created by Joab, he felt a powerful wave of pride.

Overhead, the celestials waited in brilliant golden symmetry: company after company, each after their own kind, stretching as far as he could see into the north, rainbow-tinted in the early colors of dawn. As the first light of the rising sun shone on them, Arthur laughed with unashamed joy to feel their concentrated majesty.

Deborah greeted the sun with innocent love, considering that brilliance much more wonderful than the army of children or even the celestials above. *May the divine radiance of the adorable Orah illumine my intellect,* she thought, remembering the innocent loveliness of Gurion on Martanda when she had been the Horse Elder Nediva and Arthur her beloved Aland, wisest of the Lion Lords.

She glanced at him to share this peaceful memory. He was still staring at the celestials above; she understood much of his thought without partaking of it. "My Lord!" she exclaimed softly.

Arthur looked at her with satisfaction and said with confidence, "Rejoice with me, Deborah! Our labor ends! As it is in the Shining World, even so it shall be here! Never shall Avera and her eleven million with all their technological prowess pass us! The Five Hundred and the Golden Thread shall be restored!"

His words were full of strength, but suddenly a moiling thunderstorm of Rakshasas raced to cover Orah's disk, marking the memory of his death as Mars. An awful fear clutched his heart with its icy fingers; he closed his eyes in pain, swaying slightly from the terrible internal pressure. The ancient warning, *Do not in pride rely solely on your own strength...* rang loudly in his ears. He shuddered, then said in a small voice, "Joab. Is that my own folly, about to ruin the world?"

Looking at Arthur with a complicated mixture of love, sadness and hope, the Oathmaster answered him, "Yours, my Lord Mars. And mine. And Deborah's. And any human's since this corrupt Sphere was first breathed forth by the Grandfather. We have all permitted the illusions of Emptiness a home in our hearts. Just now, at the conclusion of all things, the payment returns to haunt us with its hollow judgments of good and evil.

"Let us not hinder this labor by doubt, for that shall only increase our attachment to the Rakshasas and decrease our bond to the celestials. Be still in your heart, Naisan, and know that all things ultimately work to further Narain's Dreams of perfection. There can be no alternative to the One; sooner or later this will be proven to every entity throughout this Universe.

"For now, remember my prophecy about your role in this battle: *Death will be the fate of the world if Mars acts before Venus returns.*"

Avera, informed by her Rakshasa counselor, told her soldiers the evening before what to expect. At first hearing, most concluded her supreme authority had at last carried her the final step to lunacy. But the reality of the war was infinitely worse than she had been able to describe.

The Ten Thousand were young, not one was older than twenty, many were not yet even ten. But they had without exception returned to this world with complete knowledge of their past: they were the Ten Thousand of Kanaan-dora, here to reclaim their world; they possessed full knowledge of the earlier wars with Valin and his mind-created Rakshasas on Martanda.

The Ten Thousand fought with bows and arrows, but every arrow was a personally created marvel, an extension of its creator's mind. Each divided in the air fifty or one hundred or one thousand times as it flew with unerring accuracy to its targets. An archer could never loose more than one before a hail of bullets and grenades forced the celestials to weave their veils so tightly the archer disappeared. Occasionally, the Rakshasas prevented the veils from closing quickly enough: a child was hit. But never before Avera's infantry was decimated by arrows and their own strays.

~~~

Overhead, the towering black thunderclouds of the Rakshasas tore raging into the golden brilliance of the celestials. No more would they permit these weak beings of light to keep them from mastery of the world! For too long had they tolerated their puny insignificance! Valin must be freed now, today! The time for humanity to expand conquering through the Universe was at hand!

Their red eyes flashing terrible lightning, the vicious tools of Emptiness descended devouring: the radiant beauty of the celestials was swallowed by the vastly superior numbers of their insatiable enemy.

~~~

The battlefield alternated between nearly total darkness and the flashing lightning strokes of explosives below and celestial warfare above. Which fact at first only served to aid the children: most of Avera's soldiers panicked; within two hours, three million had been killed with but slight loss to the Ten Thousand. The archers were as the Masters of Time: there was almost nothing their human enemies could do to them.

But the children could not well both support the celestials against the Rakshasas and attack the humans — they were too few. And every death among the humans, every emotion of fear or hatred or despair among Avera's soldiers served to increase the already awesome might of the armies of Emptiness.

~~~

By noon, the celestials were all but defeated; most of the Rakshasas broke away and dove to the earth to attack the children.

With the descent of the Rakshasas, the archers' advantage was lost: their illusions were only partially effective against them; it was difficult to fight humans and Rakshasas at the same time. The Ten Thousand were forced into defense: they became as embattled ships in a sea of terrestrial and Rakshasa enemies. They were moving lights in a roiling chaos of utter nihility and dark despair; vastly outnumbered, almost without hope.

~~~

Arthur witnessed their plight and was filled with rage. "Joab! Free me to aid them!"

But Deborah held him and cried, "No, lalasa! You must obey the Oathmaster! If you act before Almira comes, all will be in vain! Hold your heart to calmness!"

He stared at her with anguish, fearing to act, fearing to not. What should he do?

David was experiencing a similar conflict. Avera and her Rakshasa counselor had grown ever more confident as they realized the fortunes of the world were turning in their favor. David was having difficulty in maintaining the veil of Emptiness next to his heart without it affecting him: he was increasingly tempted by the staff. If he could but wrest it from Avera, he could turn the battle for the celestials! He must act, and now! What difference what Joab had said?

His hands clenching and unclenching with impotent rage, David stood behind Avera, stared over the dark and brilliantly flashing battlefield, maintained the appearance of Golranel, and did nothing else except think over and over, *Why? Why me?*

~~~

The tension of Arthur and David intertwined, mounted in mindless desperation, finally forced its release. The power of their despair reached the only other one who had participated in the delivery of a not quite perfect golden flower. Susan suddenly realized she could as easily destroy Rakshasas as planes and missiles. Expanding her field of power twice as far as she was prepared to do, she covered the eastern half of the Guardian Mountains with a shimmering, golden film of celestial light that withered any Rakshasa that flew into it.

For a fleeting moment, there was a respite for the armies of the One. But what Susan did not foresee at once came to pass: her expansion revealed the location of her body to the enemy. As was Jonathan to the west, she was deep in a cave bordering Vashti; long ago she had closed her only entrance with the outside world.

The weight of the flow of time became too heavy for the triple thread Mirabeth, Malinda and Mirabel eternally weave to be sustained properly: a missile deflected by Jonathan's shield struck a fissure penetrating Susan's mountain. An ancient rift moved from the explosion; the ensuing earthquake crushed her instantly.

Not realizing she was lost and her shield now only a dissipating shadow, Jonathan did not move in time to check Avera's eastern barrage. Seventeen missiles slammed into Vashti.

The twin Rakshasas Destruction and Death for the first time raged devouring through that glorious memory of 'Ishtar's Isolde. Half the Five Hundred were killed outright; most of the rest were wounded.

Half the remaining celestials vanished from the skies; half of Vanas blackened and died; the left side of Steven's body was instantly paralyzed. The survivors looked at him with hope, but no one spoke: he had told them any deaths would be final — no power of this Universe could return to them what our world would forever lose.

On the plateau, Arthur felt the tearing agony of a massive heart attack as half his chest was devoured by Emptiness. Deborah poured the essence of her life into him, counting no loss too great if she might yet turn him wholly to the One. Sesha slid down his forearm and onto Joab.

In his cave near Vashti, Gana watched the Universe begin dissolving as half his body disintegrated. Inside him, a new shape began forming. It was not unlike his in appearance, but was composed wholly of Emptiness.

Stevana recognized the resurgence of the Asur Emperor Valin, but did not know how to halt his return. Exactly as was her mother that moment with Arthur, she flowed her life into Gana's heart, freely sacrificing everything of herself that he might yet prevail.

Of the forces of the One, David, Jonathan and Joab alone were physically unaffected by the loss of Susan. David looked with terrified eyes at the sudden diminution of life everywhere: of all the Universe, only the staff was still radiating as much energy as before. Because Avera had wound the Emptiness of her heart through it? Or because it had never been a part of Susan's energy flow?

Staring at it with longing, David questioned over and over, *Why must it break? Why am I the one? Why? Why me?*

~~~

Within two more hours, scarcely four hundred of the Ten Thousand lived; one million of the wisest veterans in the Empress' service were all that remained of her vast force. The celestials were utterly destroyed, but the Rakshasas had lost almost nothing of their ghastly power. Their entire host now opposed the final few archers.

The battlefield looked like midnight in hell: the sun, light, Truth, Beauty were but faint memories of an illusory past. The enormous black forms of the Rakshasas wandered about almost without opposition, devouring with their gaping mouths of infernal fire, descending in unending numbers on the last of the children.

~~~

Arthur had grown increasingly desperate as he watched his peoples killed. It had required all the strength of will of Joab and Deborah to restrain him.

Jacobi now fell, surrounded by hordes of Rakshasas. Dagora ran to aid his fallen sharan, but before he reached her, a Rakshasa arrow pierced his back. As his vibratory rate decreased, he became vulnerable to human weapons: a hail of bullets and shrapnel lacerated his flesh.

Arthur, witnessing both deaths, cried, "Curse you, Joab! I hold no longer!" Venus already stood beside him, embodied as Deborah! He did not need to await her! Joab was misinterpreting his own words!

Wild with anger, Arthur seized Sesha and forced the nearly infinite power of his mastery of the One through the serpent. One million identical cobras appeared in answer to his command: one beside every living soldier in Avera's army. In less than sixty seconds, Arthur's extraordinary but untimely act had slain them all.

~~~

The Rakshasas, recognizing the source of this expression of dominion, dove in one mass toward Arthur and Deborah. Joab defended them fiercely: drawing Nuriel, he spun it with a speed new even to himself, creating an impregnable hemisphere of protection.

It proved too late to intercept the evil of Arthur's wages: the adan's link with Emptiness had grown too mighty to withstand. Dragging Deborah with him into the realm of King Death, he fell dying at the Oathmaster's feet.

Joab knelt helplessly beside them as the final dregs of their lives evaporated into the Rakshasa-impregnated air.

~~~

The entire body of Gana now transmuted into Valin. The Asur Emperor looked up through Stevana and said with utter hate, "Never again shall you bind me, mother." Throwing her aside, he ran from the cave, calling to his servants, "To me!"

The Rakshasas raced to him from all sides, flowing their lives back into him. As their Emptiness re-united with him, he grew mightier, fuller with their infernal power. The winds of hurricanes raged howling about him as he stormed into Vashti for his long-awaited destruction of the world.

Forcing her terror into submission, Stevana gathered together the fragments of Gana's spirit and pursued Valin, not knowing what she could do when she reached him, but knowing she must somehow stop him: else the Universe was dead.

~~~

Steven, recognizing the Asur Emperor descending, united with the living of the Five Hundred and confronted him. Celestial fire flashed from him, dis-creating legions of Rakshasas. But the shara had been severely weakened by the losses of Susan, Arthur and Deborah, by the destruction of the celestials, by the deaths of most of the Ten Thousand and most of the Five Hundred. He could not prevent the raging descent of Valin to Vanas, could hardly even slow him!

~~~

Summoning larger and ever larger numbers of his Rakshasa hosts, Valin strode with wrath and increasing power toward the fulfillment of his desire. The fool Arthur-Mars was dead! Steven-Naisan was falling before his onslaught of Asur fire! Soon only the aged Joab would stand between him and the Golden Tree! And then the Universe would fall! He would be free from this cursed Golden Sphere!

The calling of the Rakshasas from the field of battle suddenly freed the last of the archers from any enemies. Even Avera's Rakshasa counselor answered his Lord's call. From her perspective, her army had been destroyed by magic, now even the Rakshasas were fleeing in fear! "Golranel! I am terrified! We are destroyed! What must I do?"

"There is nothing left to do, majesty," answered David with agony. "You alone must destroy those accursed devils, before you too succumb to their sorcery. You must fulfill Joab's prophecies! You must break the staff!"

"By Matrika! By Marzia! Is there no alternative? Is the tree of my folly grown so vast? Am I no more than a slave of that

Oathmaster's damnable vision? Golranel, Golranel, must I destroy this priceless tool?"

"See how quickly the last hundred of the enemy race toward us! If breaking your staff can stop them, as Joab's Fourth and Sixth Staff Prophecies foretold, what else can you do?" answered David's mouth. But he kept asking himself, *Why? Why? Why?*

"But the Seventh Staff Prophecy said the Last Living One would destroy me!"

"He said, `If the Last Living One can grasp my sundered staff,´ Avera! *If!* He foresaw you would discover the traitor among us! Why do you think he said all prophecies ended here? He couldn't see further! He couldn't bear the thought of your eternal reign! Break the accursed staff! There is no choice!" David's words were strong, clear, but his mind still hammered at him, *Why? Why? Why?* What was it about this that was so completely wrong? What was his error? What was he missing?

For an instant, David loosed his connection with the fiber of Emptiness that was keeping him invisible from the Rakshasas. Releasing his spirit from its created illusion caused a rebounding upward and outward of his awareness: for an instant, the Salazian glimpsed the full magnificence of the seventh wheel.

In that moment of unrestricted clarity, David saw Valin racing toward an embattled and weakened Steven with Joab too far away to assist him, saw that the world would be destroyed if the two embraced in the shadow of Vanas, saw that the source of this impending catastrophe was his own incompleteness and doubt!

In that instant of omniscience, David learned the one hope for the world lay in his mastery of the staff!

Avera had meanwhile slowly lifted it. She brought it down on the edge of the table. The staff shook violently, the world shook with it, but it did not break. She raised it again to strike harder.

Another vision suddenly burst into David's brain: it was Joab, screaming, "Stop her, David! Stop her! I remember! I was wrong! My staff is already broken! Gana broke it when he killed Almira!

You have only to take it from her and return to Vashti! Stop her! The diamond staff must not break!"

"No, Excellency, no!" shouted David, but too late: down came the staff, this time breaking in half.

"Why not?" she asked, turning toward him. But then she saw that not only the advancing archers but all her own aides were writhing in the sudden agony of unexpected death. All her own aides except Golranel who was actually David! and was running toward her with a drawn kris!

David leaped onto her to tear the shards from her. As they struggled, the world transformed around them: cut off from their source of life, virtually every living being in the Universe perished the instant the staff broke.

Avera had not gained her supreme position through any weakness, nor had the years of authority diminished her strength: she was a great warrior. Moving as swiftly and viciously as a panther, she knocked the dagger from his hand then clawed and fought him to the ground.

Holding him down with one hand, she grabbed for his dagger with her other. Clutching it tightly, she forced it into his back.

At the last instant, David broke her hold, rolled over and grasped both her hands. But still downward she forced the kris, using all the power she had wrested from Kaysta and Starbha, forcing the traitor to submit to her indomitable will.

The world was ruined; there was no life anywhere for David to call on to help master her. His desperate efforts were too few, too weak; relentlessly closer and ever closer came the questing point of his own dagger.

He could not slow its descent, not struggle longer against her all-powerful will: he felt the kris piercing his skin, sinking deeper and ever deeper toward his laboring heart.

~~~

At the final instant, a gale of dis-creation howled into Avera's command station. A vapor that was not quite a vapor wrapped its seething coils around Avera's neck; a man that was not quite a man pulled the kris from her hand; a giant hand that was not quite a hand lifted her as if she were no more than an insect and threw her down to her ruin.

"So, David!" came Jonathan's voice, rumbling from somewhere high above. "At last my life's debt is repaid. Though I must say, it appears a trifle late, judging from the state of things."

David scurried to locate the bottom of the staff. Finding it under the map table, he cried, "To Vashti!" Jonathan's projected form lifted David and Avera's corpse (still chained to the top of the staff) and carried them to Vanas.

~~~

The Five Hundred were all dead; they lay where they had fallen when the staff broke: tightly gathered around the Golden Tree to aid Steven in his struggle with Valin. The shara was dead, but still held his enemy by his throat. Valin was unconscious but breathing. Of all his generation, Gana alone had been deemed worthy of a self-luminous drop of Swayam's amrita: 'Ishtar and 'Sravasa felt him prepared for immortality. The thought of binding Valin inside him was a later idea: Gana's deathless body seemed the ideal prison. At the time.

Stevana's arms encircled Valin's chest: she had been attempting to pull him from Steven when she died.

Joab reached them now, thundering down the mountain on his stallion. As soon as he dismounted, the horse returned to his mind: Joab always enjoyed demonstrating the old adage that even Oathmasters are not without a certain flair for spectacle.

Sesha coiled lethargically on Joab's shoulder, seemingly unimpressed by the carnage everywhere throughout the Universe. It stared with its fiery eyes at David and almost yawned.

David looked at the Oathmaster with fervent anger and limitless sorrow and cried, "Joab! It is exactly as you foretold! But why? Of what use? Arthur and Deborah and the Ten Thousand,

Steven and the Five Hundred, even Susan and Vanas are dead! Why?"

"Why? Because of all beings in the Universe, only the five of us here and Susan and Avera did not draw our life through the staff, as you know perfectly well." He pulled Valin from Steven and Stevana. Sesha, still staring only at David, slid down his arm and onto the Asur Emperor's chest.

As soon as the serpent touched him, Valin's eyes burst open; he cried, "You have failed again, Rodavi! Look at your Universe now, fool! Your world is become a shadow, filled with the corpses of your puny intention! No closer are you to completion of the Seven. I shall yet be free of your damnable hell!"

"There can be no freedom for you, Navril," replied Joab calmly, "no escape from the One that underlies everything in Narain's infinite domain. Turn back and join us now — yes, even now! — and you can help remake this Sphere in perfection."

"With your time-withered hand holding the serpent to my neck? Thank you, but no. You see how meager your victory! Next time, or the time after — in some other space, some future or past age — I shall succeed! This Sphere has grown too weak to withstand me. I shall rule all!"

"You shall never rule anything except your illusions of nothingness, Valin. And your lordship of Emptiness will henceforth be only indirect once again.

"Gana! Return! Remember! Return!"

Valin's face distorted as Gana wrestled within him for control of the body.

"Jonathan!" cried the Oathmaster. "Your life! Return it to your master form!"

"Your will is my law," answered Jonathan in an inflectionless voice. Then he arrowed himself into the heart of Gana-Valin.

"Now I must follow," said Joab to David. "And after I am gone, you will be alone. Do you yet understand? There is nothing other than the One, you see." The Oathmaster did not wait for a reply, instead dissolved his life and dove his energy toward Gana-Valin's navel. The body writhed violently; Sesha calmly rode its twisting waves, staring still only at David.

~~~

The Salazian was mad with grief and loss: despair struggled within him, warring against a deep and silent knowing that everything was in fact *all right* — that even though Susan and then Arthur had erred and even though no one else in the entire Universe was now alive other than the serpent Sesha, one thoroughly demented immortal Etan and himself, that everything was still somehow not just all right but perfect and glorious.

David sat heavily and gazed with anguish at the bodies lying everywhere. Not one celestial, not one animal, not one blade of grass had been spared the final expression of the Downfall.

And yet — and yet, Gana still lived, did he not? And was Gana not the consciousness of everyone, everywhere at all times? And Sesha was still here. And what was the Serpent King? The repository of absolutely everything, Arthur or Joab had said. But what did that mean? Even if every being in the cosmos were still hiding in some strange alternate Universe inside Sesha, what could he do with them? And why was he still alive? Who was he, anyway? Why did he still exist when everyone else was dead? And how?

The world was becoming transparent. In the absence of living beings, its reality was being questioned. Being questioned, and failing to reply. How long until everything melted back into the undifferentiated light of the One? An hour? A day?

David stared at the lower half of the diamond staff he was rigidly holding in his left hand. But he found no answer there for these terrible mysteries.

Long the Salazian sat unmoving, trying to understand, growing not the slightest closer to any solution. He felt the answer must be before him, perfectly visible, but he could not stretch his mind enough to grasp it. How could he alone return Gana from his mind-created illusion of Valin? How could he alone restore the Universe? How alone could he amass such awesome energy? How?

David began seeking impulses of life. There were almost none anywhere. The Seven were working inside Gana-Valin, but their activity was becoming less and less independently conscious, more and more a simple division of Gana-Valin's mind. Sesha still lived, apparently would live forever, even if the material reality of the Universe ceased. David thought this must mean Sesha was the expression of Narain into his dreams of Universes, the foothold of Narain in the Spheres of space and time. Well and good. Quite logical. But so what?

And then there was himself. And who was he? He had absolutely no idea. And nowhere else, no matter how far he spread his groping awareness, could he find the slightest impulse of life, from the smallest microbe to the furthest reach of the most distant galaxy, from the earliest moment of time to the most distant future age. Nowhere in space, nowhere in time, was there the slightest hint of life. Nowhere.

No, he was wrong! He did feel the faintest glimmer of life, and not in some distant reach of intergalactic space or far-off time: right here! At the center of the heart of Avera's corpse, all but hidden beneath the massive illusory coverings of Emptiness she had drawn around herself, was the tiniest impulse of the One!

David bent over her, almost nauseated by the terrifying streams of Emptiness still radiating from her, and sought that fragment of life. His eyes drifted closed as he wrestled with the horror and hatred encircling her heart. He nearly despaired of reaching the One buried deep within her, yet onward and inward he relentlessly made his way. From love alone, he strove with death upon death to restore the Universe to itself.

~~~

Why me? thought David once more. And then, almost as if in answer, came the thought, *Why alone have I never beheld Almira?*

The two opposing yet similar questions drew him deeper and ever deeper into the prison of Emptiness that had enchained Avera's spirit.

~~~

No record states for how long the Salazian David attempted to reach the final expression of the One in Avera's heart. No one knows or will ever know whether hours, days, weeks, or a thousand million years passed as David moved inward, questing the final active impulse of life in an otherwise dead Universe.

There is no record, but there is also no question that the Salazian David at last succeeded: there before his questing mind lay a single refulgent and vibrantly alive manifestation of the One, absolutely isolated from space and time, changeless, perfect, pure.

~~~

David touched this active particle of the One with his mind; immediately the primal force responded, expanding upward and outward in a mighty rush of knowledge and power.

Avera's outer body disintegrated; in its place emerged the flawless form of Almira. She raised her hands toward heaven, as if joyfully awakening from an Eternal sleep; with her gesture, the One began racing with the speed of her mind throughout all of Creation, in an instant restoring the life of every particle of being.

~~~

Lifting the top of the staff from the ground, Almira embraced David, crying, "Open!"

The staff reformed in their hands as they fused into the hermaphrodite, who now cried, "Let the world rebegin!"

At once, the Five Hundred and Steven returned to life and with the hermaphrodite began rising upward.

When they were far above the planet, fire again flashed from the shara, but this time with the omnipotent power of the One, for the energy flowed not only through all the fully restored Five Hundred but also through the lower four centers of the universal nervous system. Many lands burned and sank; others rose from the seas for the first time in untold ages. The Empress' armies and the evil of the world were consumed by a rain like acid, but Vanas and the Ten Thousand and Stevana and Jacobi returned to life in a gentle golden shower of peace.

~~~

Stevana's first vision of her new world was of Gana, wearing his mind-created silver robes, garlanded with Sesha, bearing Kaystarbha. At his touch, Kaysta and Starbha had reformed, ending forever the equatorial fire. The jewel's brilliant opalescence rivaled the sun's splendor; its beams of light displayed constantly changing visions of Eternity.

Gana embraced her as his thoughts moved in her, *Dearest, Almira! Thus ends the most part of the Grandfather's curse.*

And the sixth year of our labor, my beloved Gana, her thoughts answered.

The slightest shade of confusion moved over his perfect face as he asked, "Then Brihas granted you your extension?"

"He did — the desire to manifest the One on the surface of the Universe tempted even him. We have one more of the Grandfather's years to complete our work: another three billion earthly years! Valin will remain bound in your heart until then. We are almost done!"

As the Crown of Emura floated from the sky into their hands, Jacobi materialized before them. The diamond staff of the Oathmasters leapt from the ground into her waiting hand. As she raised it toward heaven in salute to her adan and adaran, the staff began pulsing with a white healing light, ever after remembered as the symbol of her long custodianship.

~~~

Together the three walked throughout Vashti, recreating its glory by mere intention; they then crossed the Guardian Mountains of the Backbone Range and with the Ten Thousand began the labor of rebuilding the world.

*"As she raised the staff to heaven, it began pulsing
with white healing light."*

In time, their work surpassed even the wonder of 'Ishtar's Isolde.

The age known as Krita or Perfect, which later ages have remembered as Satya or Eternal, had begun. It lasted for the most part of the next two million years.

In their mind-created world, Arthur-Gana took the kris from Deborah-Almira's hand and thrust it deeply into her breast. The kris, an instrument of light, passed through her body of light and clattered onto the ground, doing no harm. Almira, bending to pick it up, laughed joyously, "How could you have ever believed otherwise?"

Simultaneously, Steven-Gana expanded with the speed of his mind to the sun, re-absorbing the energy of the last three mind-created Rakshasas in the Golden Thread as he overtook them.

Steven led Jonathan and Susan and the Five Hundred into the sun, Orah's paradise, their new home for the balance of Eternity.

And meanwhile David, the hermaphrodite, settled back comfortably in his cave in the Guardian Mountains. As he once more closed his eyes, he smiled with perfect contentment.

David was content because he had remembered he was the ruler of Gana's fourth center, Almira's World Para.

David was content because he had remembered he was Vaga the Emerald.

David was content because he had remembered he was Brihas' representative in our space-time matrix of Narain's uncorrupted Spheres.

But most of all, David was content because he had remembered that he lived forever in the heart not only of Gana but of everyone — he was the All, the One, the underlying essence of life and death. David was the Grandfather of all that ever was or ever would be.

David smiled, closed his eyes, and let Narain's Dream continue...

End of
Second Thunder
*in which is described
the growth of Gana through the first five centers
of the universal nervous system.*

Postcript

When Heramann ended his tale of Gana, the sun had long set. Solon had joined Adrian and Althea; the three of them had listened without question or pause for more than twelve hours.

In the sudden silence, the only sound was the surging pulse of the ocean breaking past the prow of the flagship. Finally Solon coughed once experimentally and said softly, "What of Gana's last two tasks, Airavata? What do you know of them?"

Heramann turned his lizard head toward him, rather surprised to find himself back in the present. "Solon!" he exclaimed. "How long have you been here?

"Did I explain that it was Stevana who sang me these histories? I returned to their world three centuries later, seeking the means to enter the past to re-create my race. What a wondrous civilization they had created by then! Even Etan could not equal it.

"I questioned Jacobi about Gana's final two tasks. Her answer confused me, for she said the whole of time must be purified before his sixth wheel could be clear.

"But I think now her sister led him into the past: Stevana eventually left their world and was reborn as Leor in Etan; Gana from love followed her and was reborn as Orah."

"And the seventh wheel?" asked the Lion Elder Adrian of Gurion. "Did she also mention his labor there?"

"She said only that the whole of Creation might not be a sufficient stage for that play," answered Heramann, turning a thoughtful emerald eye toward Martanda's desecrated firmament.

Gana's sixth task is chronicled in
Orah the Deathless Dancer:
Third Thunder - Book 1
a history of Orah on Martanda in the days of Etan.

Afterword
Resurrection

O fairest of creation, last and best
Of all God's works, creature in whom excelled
Whatever can to sight or thought be formed,
Holy, divine, good, amiable or sweet!
How art thou lost! how on a sudden lost,
Defaced, deflowered, and now to death devote!
—Milton

I awoke in my room in the Ishayas' monastery in the Himalayas. My first observation was that I was dressed in a black silk nightshirt, not my own. Why? I turned my head to look out my window; Edg was sitting on my one chair, staring at me intently.

"How was it?" he asked.

"How did I get here?" I asked in return.

"We carried you here four days ago. Some wondered if you'd awaken again. But I knew it, knew the day and the hour. Welcome back, wanderer."

"Thanks, I guess. It wasn't a dream then? Sharon's really dead?" There was no emotional charge. Later I knew there would be. But now the visions were still too strong in me.

"We buried her up in the grove where you two so often Ascended together."

"I guess I knew all along such sweetness could not endure for me. What an incredible woman. I doubt I'll ever again meet her like."

"She was. It makes her sacrifice seem all the more significant."

"Sacrifice? How do you mean?"

"You know — dying to save you and all."

"To save me? What are you talking about?"

"You really don't remember?"

"She was crawling toward me over the ice ledge; the arch broke; we fell together into the crevasse. That's all I know."

"That's not what I'm talking about at all, Gana." Edg stared at me with fire — the room faded as the memories of Para flooded back in full force. Edg transformed before me into Mordom, and Mordom was also Boanerge.

"The Black Ishayas are real," he said warmly. "Life is simpler than you yet believe, Naisan. Sleep now, awaken forgetful. You still have quite a long journey ahead of you, my son."

I awoke in my room in the Ishayas' monastery in the Himalayas. My first observation was that I was wearing my white cotton nightshirt. Then in a rush I remembered our fall. I turned toward my window and wept bitterly for the loss of my beloved.

They had rescued me from the crevasse and carried me down the mountain. I had been unconscious for one hundred and eight hours, dreaming fantastic dreams of other lives and worlds.

The Ishayas buried Sharon in our favorite grove up the stream from the monastery.

I walked up there the next day. The Novitiates had planted a circle of flowers around the mound of her grave. It all looked peaceful and lovely, as nice a place as could be desired for her body's final home.

I was numb, emotionally exhausted. None of this made even the slightest sense to me. I was alone again, as alone as I had ever been. Would life ever again be full of joy?

— MSI
Dedicated on Diwali, 1995

Ishayas are teaching and at the same time a wonderful story. First Thunder is the ideal book to introduce people to the experiential techniques taught by the Ishayas.

Orah the Deathless Dancer
Third Thunder
Book 1

This book expands upon the visionary theme begun in Second Thunder and continues with the tasks of Gana. In Orah, Gana travels back in time to meet up with Almira on the world of Martanda. Here he struggles to complete his sixth task and find his Beloved. This story is riveting, filled with many intense conflicts in the ongoing battle between forces of the One and those of the ego, represented by Valin, and his Asur armies.

Shamara the Oblation Bearer
Third Thunder
Book 2

In this companion volume to Third Thunder Book 1, we are introduced to the Pathway of Return. Here, Shamara is accompanied by two of Orah's brothers as she sets out to complete a task started many millenia ago. One that unveils a choice that ends separation and returns the ego to its rightful place as servant rather than master.

"In terms of visionary experience, re-centering occurs through the process of identifying the different internal characters, discarding those who do not serve the growth process, strengthening those who do, destroying that which is useless, creating that which is useful."

—MSI

From the Author

"In an instant of frozen time, no longer than the gap between two heartbeats, a being fully and permanently in contact with the Source Universe shared his vision with me. This was a free gift, a wordless joining of his infinite mind with mine.

In the years that have passed since that magical, suspended moment, I have only begun to appreciate what this means to my life, to remember that which I long ago knew fully well but then forgot. I am an Unbounded Being. Living in a human body, I experience the Ascendant continually, twenty-four hours a day. The Thunder books are an attempt to explain this state of consciousness, to describe the Reality of the wonder of this experience."

— from MSI's introduction to *Second Thunder*.

About the Author
Maharishi Sadasiva Isham –MSI
1949-1997

Happily married with three children, MSI's life transformed suddenly in 1988, when he lost his job, house, money, and family to divorce. Taking these changes as a sign that there was another purpose for his life, he set out to search for truth.

In the Himalayas he found the ancient order of monks known as the Ishayas; a journey he retells in his book, *First Thunder*. From them, he learned the techniques collectively known as "The Ishayas' Ascension". They instructed him to bring these techniques to the world in this time of great need.

Through his commitment and dedication to the Ishayas' Teaching, a group of qualified teachers is now established in the Tradition of the Ishaya Lineage.

Today, the Ishayas' Ascension is taught worldwide.
*This teaching is available only through personal instruction
from a qualified teacher.*

For more information about the Seven Spheres,
courses of instruction,
or in-residence Teacher Training, please write or call:

1-888-474-2921
contact@theishayafoundation.org
www.theishayafoundation.org

*Live each day in
Praise, Gratitude and Love
...the simple truth*

The entire collection of books written by MSI
may be ordered directly from
THE Ishaya FOUNDATION *Publishing Company*
or purchased through your local and online bookstores.